Geeks and Things

The Complete Series

S.E. Biglow

This book is a work of fiction. Names, characters, businesses, organizations, places, events and incidents either are the product of the author's imagination or are used fictitiously. Any resemblance to actual persons, living or dead, events, or locales is entirely coincidental.

If you enjoy this book, please consider leaving a review.

For information contact; www.sarah-biglow.com

Copyedited by: Ken Darrow, M.A.

Cover Design by: Deranged Doctor Design

Large Print Hardcover ISBN: 978-1-955988-99-5

10 9 8 7 6 5 4 3 2 1

Contents

Pains and Penalties

Forgive and Forget

Debts and Debtors

Have and Hold

Saints and Sinners

Pains and Penalties

Geeks and Things Book 1

A GEEKS AND THINGS COZY MYSTERY

Pains and Penalties

S.E. BIGLOW

PAINS AND PENALTIES (A GEEKS AND THINGS MYSTERY)

This book is a work of fiction. Names, characters, businesses, organizations, places, events and incidents either are the product of the author's imagination or are used fictitiously. Any resemblance to actual persons, living or dead, events, or locales is entirely coincidental.

If you enjoy this work, please consider leaving a review.

For information contact; www.sarah-biglow.com

Edited by Ken Marrow, M.A.

Cover Design by: Deranged Doctor Design

Published by Sarah Biglow: March 2016

2nd Edition Publish by S.E. Biglow: June 2021

10 9 8 7 6 5 4 3 2

 Created with Vellum

Chapter 1

Kalina Greystone stood behind the counter bent over a tablet double checking inventory when her nephew, AJ, appeared in the doorway to what used to be the stockroom. He toted a box of comics in his arms. She was converting it into a gaming space and mini theater. "This was all that was left, Aunt K."

Setting the tablet aside, she gave him a smile. "I'll take those."

He handed the box over and she settled it below the counter on the top shelf. It contained all of the unclaimed new arrivals for her customers. It still amazed her that she could call them *her* customers. Coming home to run the family's comic store hadn't been in her five-year plan after graduating business school, but life had a way of intervening when it seemed most inconvenient and guiding her to where she was needed most. AJ peered at the tablet and pointed to the paper file sitting next to it. "What are you doing?"

"Going digital. Your grandpa kept paper ledgers of everyone's orders and what we had in stock. I just finished transferring everything to the tablet so we can move some of the old files to your mom's basement." She motioned to the counter space that had until three months ago housed a clumsy, old-fashioned cash register. "And thanks to Square, we can do all of our business on the tablet, too. Send e-receipts, the whole thing."

"Damn, you really are going high tech. Guess that fancy MBA really paid off."

"Don't swear." She nudged his shoulder. "We still have a cash drawer, obviously, but it will be easier to reconcile at the end of the day."

AJ stepped behind the counter and pulled her into an unexpected hug. She returned the gesture if a little awkwardly. "What was that for?"

He shrugged one shoulder and didn't meet her gaze. "Nothing. Just missed you is all. Mom's glad you're back. Even if she doesn't say it."

"I missed you guys, too." Kalina often wondered if the relatively small age difference between her and AJ made him see her as more of a friend than an authority figure. She'd been eighteen when he was born fifteen years ago. Still, she couldn't deny she liked hanging out with him. "And I know she's happy she didn't have to take over the business. Now go make sure we have everything ready for the booth at the fair."

Before they could continue their conversation, the front door opened and the tiny bell tinkled to announce the customer's entrance. AJ disappeared back through the game room and Kalina turned to greet the first patron of the day. Usually Saturdays were busy, especially in the morning, but today was the exception. Everyone was heading down to the waterfront for the annual Solstice Fair to kick off the start of summer. People from neighboring towns came out to the little town of Ellesworth, Massachusetts to enjoy arguably the best homemade baked goods on the southern coast of the state and generally indulge in silly carnival games. A familiar face greeted her and warmth crept up her neck. Christian Harper.

"Hi." Her mouth went dry at the sight of him. They hadn't really spoken in the last fifteen years. Not since they'd ended their three-year relationship in high school. But he looked just the same with his bright blue eyes—the kind a girl could get lost in without trying—and slightly messy brown hair.

"Hey, Kal. How are you?"

Kalina coughed a time or two to find her voice. "Good. Busy... Well, I mean not at this particular moment with the fair today but..." She rambled when she was nervous. Taking a breath, she collected herself. "Can I help you with something, Officer?" Last she'd heard he had joined the police department out of college. Just because they hadn't spoken didn't mean she hadn't had ways of keeping up-to-date with his life. She'd also heard he was still single.

Chris smiled, his eyes crinkling around the corners. "Actually, it's Detective now." He tapped the top of his detective's shield. "And I was looking for some T-shirts for my nephews. They're big into superheroes these days."

"Nephews?" Kalina buried her face in her hands. How had she forgotten? "Of course. How old are they now?"

"Jackson is eight and Benji is ten."

She looked around the shop. The wall that normally housed the T-shirt selection was bare. "Well, we have some but we are taking them down to the fair. We have a booth."

"Well, if you don't mind the company, I'll go down with you. We can catch up."

"Sure. Let me just let AJ know he can head down and start setting up."

She was about to text him when AJ stuck his head in through the front door. "We're all set. Everything's in the car."

Kalina retrieved the locked cash box her father had kept for the fair from its spot on the back shelf. Holding it up, she gave it a shake. "You forgot this."

"I thought you said we were going digital?"

"Some things are tradition. Besides, you know all the proceeds from today go to the Wounded Warrior charity."

Her nephew rolled his eyes but grabbed the box and gestured for her to hand over the car keys. She arched a brow and nodded in Chris's direction. "I don't think so." She turned to Chris. "Want a ride?"

"Love one."

AJ led the small procession out of the shop. Kalina paused long enough to lock the front door—habits from her time living in the city—and climbed into the driver seat. Chris slid into the passenger and AJ settled in the back amidst the boxes of merchandise up for sale.

The trip down to the waterfront was brief and quiet. Apparently, 'catching up' didn't involve talking in front of a fifteen-year-old boy. Ten minutes later, Kalina's car was empty and the small booth with a "Geeks and Things" banner was laden with boxes. AJ wandered off in search of his friends, leaving the grown-ups to handle unpacking.

"I thought he was supposed to be helping you," Chris said as he laid out some new comics.

She waved dismissively in the direction he'd gone. "He'll be back. We're splitting our time so I figure he can get in on some rides before the lines get too long. What superheroes are the boys into?"

Chris scratched his chin. "Jack likes Hulk. And I'm pretty sure Benji mentioned something about Rocket Raccoon."

She rifled through a box of shirts. "So ... Detective, huh? Congrats."

"Thanks. I owe a lot to Captain Cahill. He trained me since I joined the force." That wasn't a name Kalina recognized, but there had been changes in leadership since she left to pursue her dreams of owning her own business.

"I bet." She nodded toward his badge. "You working today?" She found a couple of kids' smalls and held them up for his approval.

He gave her a thumbs up on both. "Sort of. But my shift doesn't start until later this afternoon." He smiled again and Kalina's legs went weak.

“You know, Kal, I was honestly surprised to hear you’d come back to town.”

She tugged at a few strands of loose, red curls. Could she admit to him she hadn’t entirely wanted to? Would that make her sound like an awful daughter? “Well, Dad left the place to me in the will. I couldn’t just leave it to wither away. He raised me on comics. It’s in my blood.”

“I’m sorry about your dad’s passing by the way.”

Her chest tightened for a moment at the thought of her father’s death. “Thanks. We knew he had heart trouble so the last heart attack wasn’t a huge surprise. But it means a lot that you care.”

More familiar faces passed by. Some waved or nodded in their direction. Kalina waved back. Despite not having wanted to come home, a part of her was happy to be back. She missed being a part of such a small community. She stowed the cash box behind a pile of old video games and leaned forward on the edge of the table. “So, you aren’t on duty for a while. You want to check out the judging for the pastries?”

"Absolutely. How much do I owe you for the shirts?"

Kalina started to say they were free but caught herself. "Five bucks each."

He handed over a twenty dollar bill but waved her off when she made a move to open the cash box. "Consider the rest a donation."

"Thanks."

AJ appeared from the crowd and ducked into the booth. His cheeks were flushed and he wore a dopey grin. The wrist band on his left hand signaled he'd been on the roller coaster and likely the Ferris wheel already. Kalina thought she spotted a smudge on his cheek that bore a strong resemblance to lipstick but she kept silent

"We'll be back. We're just going to check out the baking contest," Kalina said and patted her nephew on the shoulder. The contest had always been a favorite for her, especially since her great aunt Agatha and her friends had a habit of winning.

The fairgrounds bustled with people stopping by vendors on both sides of the promenade, buying everything from handmade picture frames to tote bags with hand-painted waterscapes. The pastry judging tent sat at the far end of the promenade. They always did the judging early on to encourage people to buy the winning sweets. It was never that much of a real competition. Mrs. Margaret Grant always won for her blueberry and raspberry scones. It had been that way since Kalina was a little girl. Usually, Kalina'a great aunt Agatha also won for her European sponge cake with lemon drizzle. Her mouth watered at the thought of the cake. She'd been away for the last few summers and had missed getting to share a slice while they chatted. Kalina walked with purpose towards the judging tent until she felt a hand squeeze lightly on her wrist.

"Sorry," she said when she saw Chris slowing her down. "I guess I still have some city habits to break."

"It's okay. You just don't need to be in such a hurry. You know they announce the winners over the loudspeaker."

She smiled sheepishly and fell into step beside him. The sun peeked out from behind a thin layer of cloud cover, highlighting thin veins of gold in Chris's hair. For a moment she remembered them as two high school kids who thought they were in love. But that time was past. They weren't kids anymore, maybe friends but nothing more. Not after she was sure she'd broken his heart when she went away to school. "So, did you ever settle down?"

"Nope. Still a bachelor. I guess I just never found the right girl. What about you?"

She shook her head. "There was a guy in college but ... it didn't end well."

They reached the judging tent and found both great aunt Agatha and Mrs. Grant sitting behind their respective entries. Kalina bent down to place an order for Mrs. Grant's scones and noticed another set of scones down the table manned by Andrea Nevins. She'd been a couple years ahead of Kalina and Chris in school.

"Nice to see you finally made it home, Kali," great aunt Agatha said with a smile. She reached out to pat Kalina on the wrist.

"Me, too, Auntie Agatha." She grabbed the pen in front of the sponge cake and jotted down an order as well. Agatha arched a silver brow.

"Well, this is new. You don't usually buy my cake."

Kalina smirked. "Well, maybe I felt a little guilty about missing the last few years. And honestly, it looks even better than usual."

"You're sweet, my girl." She gestured over Kalina's shoulder. "I see you two found your way back to each other."

Great aunt Agatha had always been fond of Chris. She was the first person Kalina had confided in when they'd started dating in school. "He just came by the shop to buy some shirts for his nephews. That's all."

"I told you that you two had something special. But I'm just an old lady, what do I know." She feigned annoyance but Kalina could see the sparkle in her eyes.

"You were never much of a match maker, Aggie," Mrs. Grant chided from her spot down the table.

"Oh hush, you," Agatha replied, waving her friend's comment away.

Kalina looked around, hoping to spot the third member of Aunt Agatha's trio, Cynthia Ellicott.

For as long as she could remember, the three women had been inseparable and they never missed the Solstice Fair. “Where’s Ms. Ellicott?”

Aunt Agatha and Mrs. Grant shared a look that Kalina couldn’t decipher. “She hasn’t been in the best health,” Mrs. Grant answered quickly.

“Oh, I’m sorry to hear that. Is there anything I can do?”

Aunt Agatha shook her head. “No, when she gets like this, it’s best to just give her space. But, it’s sweet of you to worry. You always had such a kind heart, Kali.”

Kalina darted around the side of the table and wrapped her aunt in a firm hug. “I’ll see you later.”

“I’ll save you a big slice of cake,” she replied with a wink.

“Well, good luck to both of you,” Kalina said and stepped back to allow other people to approach. At the far end of the table, a man in a police uniform stood beside someone Kalina didn’t recognize. “Who is that?” She addressed Chris and pointed at the pair.

"That's Captain Dan Cahill and the woman is his fiancée, Leslie Mayfield. She teaches at the elementary school. Benji is in her class."

They moved down the table and Chris placed an order for Leslie's apple tarts. "Good luck."

Leslie tucked a piece of hair behind her ear, not so subtly flashing her engagement ring, and smiled big. She turned to Kalina and offered her non-bejeweled hand. "Hi, I don't think we've met."

"I'm Kalina Greystone." They shook hands briefly. "My father used to own Geeks and Things up on Main Street. I moved back to run the store after he died."

"Oh, right, of course."

Dan leaned in and kissed Leslie on the cheek. "I think they're about to start the judging."

Kalina and Chris moved back into the crowd while the judges sampled the various sweets, concurring in low whispers and making notes on their clipboards. The town took the contest very seriously. Tension rose amongst the crowd as they awaited the announcement. At the far end of the table great aunt Agatha sat with her hands folded in her lap. Mrs. Grant shot Andrea annoyed looks as the judges handed the winning votes to the announcer, Theodore Maxwell. He cleared his throat and held the microphone too close to his mouth.

"We have the results of the baking contest. Remember, you can put an order in at any time to purchase the winning pastries. All proceeds go to the Wounded Warrior charity."

The feedback on the speakers squealed and Kalina covered her ears along with many of the people watching. Theo held the mic further from his mouth and studied the first scrap of paper. "The winner for best fruit tart goes to Ms. Leslie Mayfield."

Cheers went up from the crowd and Leslie grinned and waved. Captain Cahill let out a loud whistle, making his fiancée blush. He darted up to the stage and placed a huge bouquet in her arms. Theo waved his hand for quiet and the crowd settled down. "Best sponge cake, of course, goes to Mrs. Agatha Davies." The crowd's response was a little more subdued as Agatha stood up and took a little bow. Kalina noted the older woman's cheeks were a bit flushed when they hadn't been a few moments earlier. But she assumed it was just due to the excitement of yet another blue ribbon for her mantle. Beside Agatha, Mrs. Grant already had her hands on the armrest, poised to push herself up to accept the blue ribbon for her scones.

“And finally, the winner for the best scones is...” Theo stopped and turned to the judges. They nodded in unison and he faced the growing throng, clearing his throat as he did so. “The winner is Ms. Andrea Nevins.”

A hush fell over the crowd. Mrs. Grant jumped from her seat and marched toward the judges before Andrea could accept the ribbon. Chris stood beside Kalina, mouth agape as the older woman leaned in close enough to Theo’s microphone that her tirade carried across the fairgrounds.

“This is unacceptable. My scones were far better than hers.”

Andrea paled and dabbed her eyes before hurrying off the stage clutching the ribbon to her chest. A few members in the crowd patted her on the back and her older brother broke from the group to wrap an arm around her shoulders, leading her away.

“Mrs. Grant, please. This is just a friendly competition,” Theo said, trying to yank the microphone out of her reach.

She wasn’t having any of it. She waggled a finger at the judges, summoning them forward. “You three had better explain yourselves.”

From behind her, great aunt Agatha shuffled forward and tried to tug Mrs. Grant away but had no luck. “Margie, come on now.” Agatha’s words fell on deaf ears.

“It’s not that your scones weren’t good, Mrs. Grant. It’s just ... Andy’s were better this year,” one of the judges said.

People began to disperse, no longer interested in seeing Mrs. Grant lose her temper with the judges. Kalina nudged Chris in the ribs and nodded back towards the booth. “I should probably head back to make sure AJ is doing okay.” She looked at her watch. “Besides, he’s probably looking for an early lunch.”

“No problem.”

They walked side by side back down the promenade. Kalina made a mental note to stop by some of the booths near the end of the day to pick up some early Christmas presents for her sister and mother. The Geeks and Things booth came into view and she couldn't keep a smile from tugging at the corners of her lips. A small group of kids clamored around the table, picking up action figures and T-shirts. Money changed hands rapidly and AJ gave her a double thumbs up when he spotted her.

"Well, I'll leave you to hawking your wares," Chris said.

"Enjoy the rest of the fair." She waved and slid in behind the table next to her nephew.

He blew out a breath. "Thank God you're back. It's been super nuts. I'm starving."

Kalina chuckled. "Yes, yes. Go get food. Bring me back a fried dough. Extra cinnamon sugar."

He gave her a salute and raced out of the booth and toward the refreshment tent. Kalina settled into the metal chair behind the table and waited for people passing by to stop. She didn't have to wait long before Leslie appeared with her big smile plastered to her lips. She'd pinned the ribbon to her blouse. The bouquet was nowhere to be seen.

“Congrats again on your win,” Kalina said.

“Thanks. I’m sorry I didn’t recognize you before. I guess I’m not all that good with faces unless they are my students.”

“No worries. I left town for a while after high school. Big city dreams. Earned my business degree and worked in Boston for a few years. But I guess my heart was always back here in town.” Maybe if she told herself that enough time, it would make it sure. Kalina glanced around for Captain Cahill. “Where’s your fiancé?”

“Oh, getting some drinks from the refreshment tent. We’re going to celebrate. Did you want to buy some fruit tarts?”

“Sure. I’d love to.”

Their conversation died instantly when a high-pitched shriek went up from the direction of the food. Another scream followed it. Leaving cash box and merchandise untended, Kalina took off at a sprint. Thoughts of AJ spurred her forward. She didn’t bother to check to see if

Leslie was following or not. Kalina arrived at the tent to find people bunched together in a semi-circle around one of the tables. Kalina shoved her way to the front. AJ bent over a motionless great aunt Agatha. She lay on the ground, one hand pressed to her stomach, the other gripped around her throat. She'd already started to lose color in her cheeks. AJ looked up, his facial features contorted into a mask of helpless terror, and he said, "I think she's dead."

Chapter 2

Footsteps pounded on the hard-packed ground and Chris came into view. Kalina had no idea where he'd come from but he didn't look out of breath. On the other side of the table, Mrs. Grant pressed one hand to her chest, tears glistening in her eyes. She'd calmed down from her rant about the scones but now that same look of horror Kalina had seen in her nephew's eyes reflected in the old woman's.

"Dear Lord, this can't be happening."

It was barely audible above the crowd yelling for help, but Kalina heard it. The statement seemed an odd reaction and it piqued her curiosity. Kalina bent down and gently tugged AJ to his feet and away from Agatha's prone form. Chris took up AJ's spot and studied her. "Who saw what happened?"

AJ raised his hand. His fingers trembled and he quickly closed them into a fist to keep from shaking. A few other people inched forward, mumbling that they had seen what happened. From across the tent Captain Cahill approached, cell phone in hand. He pressed it to his ear and, amid the rumbling of the crowd, Kalina heard him request an ambulance. Ellesworth wasn't big enough to have its own morgue. She'd no doubt be taken west to Salem. Chris stood up and waved people back. "Everyone, I need you to back up. Do not touch anything on this table." He turned to AJ. "I'm going to need to talk to you. Why don't you come with me?"

"I'm coming with him," Kalina said.

"Did you see anything?"

"No. But you can't talk to him alone. He's only fifteen." She didn't think Chris thought AJ had done anything bad, but she also knew her nephew needed support and she wasn't going to let him go through witnessing a close relative just drop dead.

Chris looked unhappy about the intrusion but didn't object further. They headed over to an empty table at the back of the tent while Captain Cahill ushered the rest of the crowd out of the food tent. He disappeared as well, only to be heard moments later over the loudspeaker.

“Ladies and gentlemen, I'm sorry to announce we will be shutting down early this year. Due to a medical emergency, we ask that all vendors please conclude your transactions and pack up.”

This was not how Kalina had expected her first time running the booth in her own right would go. Turning her attention back to Chris and AJ, she reached over and squeezed her nephew's hand.

"Okay, AJ. Walk me through what you saw." Chris produced a notepad from his pocket. He came prepared for anything. His tone was gentle, supportive.

"I was in line for fried dough. Aunt K. wanted some, and auntie Agatha was sitting there having a cup of tea. She gave me a wave and I was going to stop by and see her before I headed back to the booth. Everything was fine and then she just started choking and bent over like she was going to throw up." He put his head in his hands. "I never saw anyone look like that."

Kalina took one of his hands in hers and gave it a firm squeeze. "It's okay. You did good."

He looked up at her through watery eyes. "But... I should have done something to help."

“Had you seen her before today? I know your family was close,” Chris probed.

“Uh, maybe a week ago she came by for dinner with me and my parents.”

“And how'd she seem then?”

“Fine. Why?”

“I'm just trying to get a sense of what might have made her start choking.” Chris glanced at the table she'd been sitting at. “You said she had tea. Was she eating anything?”

“No. Just the tea.”

Chris leaned over. "Did you see anyone tamper with her tea?"

"N-no. I don't think so. God, was she murdered?" His teenage falsetto shot his voice up an octave.

Chris shook his head. "I don't know. But something happened to make her stop breathing." Chris tucked his notepad in his pocket. " I'd like you to go down to the station and give a full statement."

"Does he have to do it right now? He's in shock," Kalina argued.

Chris's face softened. "No. Just make sure you get down there in the next day or so. If this turns out to be something more than accidental then we want to get people's recollections down as clearly as possible."

Kalina stared at him in confusion. He couldn't honestly believe someone would want to hurt aunt Agatha. She'd probably just choked on the tea and couldn't catch her breath. Sirens blared, sounding a prolonged wail from behind the food tent. Flashing red lights cast a bright glow over the faces of the few people still gathered to watch. Two uniformed paramedics climbed out of the ambulance and approached Captain Cahill who had returned to supervise. Chris had gone off to interview other potential witnesses.

Kalina wrapped a comforting arm around her nephew and said, "AJ, I want you to call your mom and have her pick you up. You don't need to be here right now."

"What are you going to do?" His eyes glistened with unshed tears. He was trying to put on a brave face and it broke her heart.

"I'm going to have a talk with Mrs. Grant. Something about this whole situation seems strange."

"Aunt K., don't get involved. Please."

"I'll be fine. Now go call your mom."

AJ wandered off. Kalina headed for the beverage table and picked up two bottles of water before retreating to Mrs. Grant. Chris reached out a hand to bar her path. “Not everyone needs a chaperone to talk to me.”

“I’m just bringing her some water. She looks like she could use it.”

She sidestepped his outstretched arm and proceeded to sit down beside Mrs. Grant. The woman hadn't torn her gaze away from the corpse, even as the paramedics loaded her onto a gurney and rolled her to the back of the ambulance. Kalina was certain she'd be hit with her own wave of grief at the loss of her great aunt but for the moment, focusing on other people was keeping that feeling at bay. She would break down in private if she had anything to say about it. Kalina pressed an opened bottle of water into the woman's free hand.

"Mrs. Grant, are you all right?"

Finally, Mrs. Grant blinked several times and turned her attention to Kalina. "I'm sorry. What?"

"I just wanted to see if you were all right."

"Well, of course I'm not all right! My friend just died." Almost instantly, her demeanor changed. Her body sagged and she took a swig of water. "Sorry. I didn't mean to snap at you."

"I understand. Believe me. Can I ask you something?" The woman nodded and Kalina continued. "You said something earlier, right after Auntie Agatha died. You said that this couldn't be happening. What made you think that?"

Mrs. Grant took several long gulps of water and fussed with the hem of her blouse. "I ... I don't know what you mean. I suppose I was just shocked. It all happened so quickly."

"Kalina, that's enough. Go back to your booth and pack up like the captain said. Please." Chris ushered Kalina out of the tent and back to the promenade. She expected him to return to questioning witnesses but he kept a solid grip on her elbow all the way back to her booth

She pulled her arm free. "You don't trust me?"

"You always had a thing for sticking your nose in other people's business."

"Agatha is my family, Chris. If something happened to her, you can't expect me to just sit on my hands."

"Unless you joined the police force without any of us knowing, the best thing you can do is make sure AJ gives his statement while his memory is still clear. Okay?"

"You know I will."

Chris retreated from view. There was no way she was backing off now. Being back home had reignited a sense of loyalty she'd missed while being away. And she owed it to Auntie Agatha to find the truth. Whatever it may be.

Chapter 3

Ten minutes later, Kalina stood by the car, loading the last box of merchandise into the back seat. AJ had disappeared again but she didn't have the heart to go find him. Settling the boxes so she could still see out the rear window gave Kalina a few private moments to let the reality sink in. The woman who'd been her confidante, her champion, was dead. Hot tears streamed down her cheeks and she barely kept a sob from passing her lips. She eased the back closed as her sister, Jillian, appeared from the gravel lot behind the refreshment tent. Her expression warned that she was not pleased. Jillian clearly hadn't heard the news. She stalked over to Kalina's car.

“What the hell is going on? You said you’d look after AJ for the day.”

“Aunt Agatha is dead, Jill.” Kalina dried her cheeks with the back of her hand.

“What? What happened?” Jillian demanded.

“I don’t know. She was sitting having tea and then she just fell over I guess. AJ saw it happen and he’s pretty freaked out about it. I figured you’d want him home with you guys. And the police have shut the fair down for the day.”

“The police are involved?”

“I don’t know that it’s more than just an accident but they’re looking into it. Chris wants AJ to give a statement down at the station.”

“Chris?” His name caught her sister off guard.

“Detective Christian Harper.”

Jillian let out a hiccup of laughter. “So you finally ran into the ex?”

“Yeah.”

The levity vanished as Jillian collapsed against the hood of Kalina’s car. “Aunt Agatha’s really dead? Oh God. And AJ didn't say ... just to come pick him up."

Kalina pulled her older sister into a firm hug. "He'll be okay. He has you to lean on."

Jillian rubbed at her eyes to dry them and composed herself. "We just saw her a few days ago. God, it's like Dad all over again."

"We got through that. We're going to get through this, too," Kalina reminded her. They hadn't been the type of sisters who did everything together when they were kids but in that moment, Kalina felt like she was closer to her big sister than they'd ever been.

"You've always been the strong one, Kal," Jillian whispered as they stepped apart.

Kalina wasn't sure she agreed with her sister's assessment. "You'll need to make sure he goes down to the police station to give a statement. I promised Chris he would."

"I can do that. God, someone has to let Mom know. We'll have to plan a funeral and someone needs to clean out her house."

Kalina could hear her sister spiraling and she cut it off. "We will have time to do all those things. You need to be with your son now. Go."

Out of the corner of her eye, Kalina spotted Mrs. Grant making her way to the parking lot alone. "I have to go."

Without another word to her sister, she raced off in the hopes of intercepting Mrs. Grant. She had to jog to catch the older woman. "Mrs. Grant, can I offer you a ride home?"

"No. Thank you. I just want to be alone."

"I don't mind. Really. I was hoping we could talk without so many people around."

Mrs. Grant glanced around as if she feared they were being watched. "Tomorrow. Come by for morning tea."

"Thank you. I'll see you then."

It wasn't the sit down she'd been hoping for but it would have to do. She couldn't explain why but she felt the need to go to aunt Agatha's house. Maybe it was because Jillian had mentioned it but maybe she just needed to feel close to her aunt one last time. The drive was short—less than twenty minutes and she pulled into the driveway. Agatha's car still sat there. She must have gotten a ride from Mrs. Grant to the fair.

Kalina may not have come to visit recently, but she knew her great aunt always left a spare key under the front mat. She bent down and flicked the top left corner down, finding the slender silver key where it had always been. She unlocked the front door and stepped into the front hall. She'd spent a lot of time in high school with her great aunt and she knew the layout like the back of her hand. She moved in the eerie silence to the bedroom first. It was empty, the bed made perfectly. Nothing felt off there and she retreated to the kitchen.

Everything looked in its place there, too. She had bowls from breakfast drying on the rack beside the sink. Her antique porcelain teapot sat on the stove ready for use. Kalina studied the pot and a memory flashed through her mind.

"You are going to do great things, Kali," Aunt Agatha said, pouring tea from the spout of the delicate pot.

"But, I've never been away from home this long before. And with Chris staying here, what if it

doesn't work out?" She was seventeen, about to go off to college.

"The universe has a way of working things out. Keeping that balance. Whatever is supposed to happen will happen, my dear."

Kalina doubted that the sudden death of her aunt was in the universe's game plan. But maybe Chris stumbling back into her life was a sign. She pushed that thought away as she made her way into the living room. It was cozy with overstuffed couches and a recliner. The low table that stood in the center of the room bore something crumpled. It wasn't like Agatha to leave trash around. She bent and caught sight of typed text. Her whole body began to shake and she took a step back, pulling out her phone.

She dialed the only number she had for Chris and waited.

"Hello?" His answer sounded distracted.

"Chris, thank God you still have your old number. I'm at Aunt Agatha's house and I think there's something you need to see."

She retreated to the front steps to wait for his arrival. When he pulled up, he looked all business, badge clipped to his belt and a pair of latex gloves sticking out of his pocket.

“What are you doing here, Kal?”

“I just felt drawn here. But it’s inside. Come on.”

She led him to the living room and the crumpled piece of paper. He arched a brow in disbelief. “You brought me out here for a piece of paper?”

“She doesn’t leave trash just sitting around.”

He donned his gloves and smoothed out the page, revealing a single line of bold, capitalized text: **LYING IS A MORTAL SIN**. She looked at Chris after a beat. “Okay, that’s cryptic.”

Chris carried the note out to his car and slid it into a clear plastic bag marked ‘Evidence’. Laying the bag on the passenger seat of his car, he turned and took her hands in his. Almost like he’d done the day he asked her to prom. “I know. But that’s why I need you to keep out of it, okay? Let me do my job. Please, Kal.”

The way he said her name, that small pleading note in it, tugged at her heart. They may have grown up and apart but he was still the sweet boy who'd been her first kiss. Her first many things.

"Okay," she answered softly. He relinquished his grip on her hands and she spun on her heel, retreating to her car before he could say more. As she pulled out of the driveway, she wondered if Mrs. Grant knew about the note.

Chapter 4

That night, Kalina couldn't sleep. The brief glimpse of Aunt Agatha's face—a twisted mask in death—invaded her dreams, waking her in cold sweats. She couldn't imagine how AJ was managing. Sure, she fancied herself a sleuth in theory, but maybe Chris was right. She wasn't equipped to handle dead bodies, especially when they were related to her.

"Don't focus on the dead," she mumbled to herself as the clock on her nightstand clicked over to two o'clock.

Kicking the sheets aside, she padded out to the kitchen to make a cup of coffee. If the day's events wouldn't let her sleep then she would embrace being the night owl. For a brief moment she wondered how superheroes like Daredevil managed to get any sleep with the nighttime crime fighting and a day job.

Settling in front of her laptop, steaming mug of coffee within reach, she logged on to the internet with the hopes of finding ... what exactly? For all of her progressive stances, Aunt Agatha had been a staunch opponent to social media. She'd insisted she didn't need everyone knowing all of her business. But she knew at least a few people who were frequent fair goers with accounts. And in a town as relatively small as Ellesworth, you were friends with everyone on Facebook. Small mercies. She logged on and scrolled through her news feed. Not surprisingly, lots of people had posted statuses from the Solstice Fair, often with accompanying photos. Photos were good. She scrolled through them all. Many were useless, images snapped at the top of the Ferris wheel or teetering over the first plunge on the roller coaster. But a few from folks her mother's age —yes, her mother had finally embraced the internet—had posted photos of some of the items they'd purchased and a few people had gotten shots of the pastry judging.

She let out a hiss between her front teeth at a not-so-flattering photo of Mrs. Grant laying into the judges. “Not a good look, Mrs. Grant.”

What she needed was a shot of Aunt Agatha before her untimely demise. The refreshment tent boasted photo-worthy dishes. There had to be someone who had caught her in the tent before she died.

She lifted her mug to her lips but found the contents gone. The clock on her screen noted it was almost four in the morning now. She'd been scrolling for nearly two hours and found nothing. Barely stifling a yawn, she retreated to the kitchen for a refill. She'd look for another half hour and then try to get some sleep. She had a breakfast date with Mrs. Grant to keep, after all. Kalina slunk back into her chair and continued scrolling, the infusion of caffeine jolting her nerves and synapses awake. Just as the clock ticked from 3:59 to 4:00 she had a breakthrough. One of AJ's friends—Devon Landry—had a thing for food and had meticulously photographed the tent's contents. He'd also dragged AJ into a selfie. It wasn't much but she could make out Aunt Agatha sitting at the table behind them in the right corner of the picture. She clicked to the next photo in the album and nearly spilled her coffee down her shirt. Agatha lay on the ground and her body contorted mid-spasm. He'd photographed her death. She still didn't know for sure that her great aunt had been targeted, no matter what that cryptic note said. The last picture in the album depicted Aunt Agatha just before the paramedics arrived. Captain Cahill—at least Kalina assumed it was him from the back of his head—stood over her, shooing people away. Something about the scene gnawed at her mind. There was something to it. She just couldn't see what. Maybe Mrs. Grant would feel a little more forthcoming when the shock had worn off a little. Kalina downed the rest of the coffee and flopped onto the couch, hoping to get at least a couple hours of sleep.

* * *

"Hello, Mrs. Grant? It's Kalina Greystone," she called through the screen door on Mrs. Grant's porch four hours later. She'd managed to sleep until seven.

No one answered. She waited before opening the screen door and knocking on the pale blue-painted wood behind it. Hand raised to knock a second time, Kalina stopped when the door eased open and Mrs. Grant appeared. Her eyes were red-rimmed and saucer-wide. The old woman hadn't gotten much sleep either.

"What are you doing here?" Mrs. Grant's gaze darted around as if she expected someone to jump out of the bushes.

"You invited me yesterday at the fair. And I didn't get my order of scones so I was hoping I could pick them up." Aunt Agatha would have insisted she keep her order.

Mrs. Grant peered around for another thirty seconds before she relaxed a little. Her shoulders rolled back and she stood up straighter. "Oh, yes. I nearly forgot. Please come in, my dear." She backed out of the doorway to let Kalina in. "And at least someone around here appreciates my baking."

Kalina didn't respond. She just followed the woman into her front foyer and took an immediate left into the living room. Mrs. Grant shuffled off to the kitchen without another word. Kalina took the time to check out the mantelpiece adorned with a simple silver urn at the center and a photo of a much younger Mr. and Mrs. Grant on their wedding day. She'd been to Mrs. Grant's house only a few times growing up, usually accompanied by Aunt Agatha. Kalina didn't have a very clear memory of Mr. Grant and in fact he'd rarely been around whenever she came by. But she didn't ever recall seeing an urn. A single framed photo of three women in their 30s sat on the other side of the urn. One of them was easily discernible as Mrs. Grant; the one in the middle bore a resemblance to Mrs. Davies and the third had to be Ms. Ellicott.

"Here we are. Do you take anything in your tea? I can never remember," Mrs. Grant reappeared with a tea tray.

"No, thanks." Kalina accepted the cup and saucer once Mrs. Grant had poured the tea. "When did your husband pass?"

"Alan? Oh, last year in a car accident."

"I'm so sorry."

Mrs. Grant glanced at the urn and gave a solemn nod. "It was a shock. But things like that always are."

Kalina took a sip of tea. "Like yesterday with Aunt Agatha."

Mrs. Grant fussed with her teacup, turning it one way and then the other atop the saucer. She wouldn't meet Kalina's gaze and, for longer than felt comfortable, she kept quiet. Kalina had time. She could be patient if that's what it took to make this woman open up about whatever she suspected.

"How are you and your family holding up?"

It was Kalina's turn to avert her gaze and contemplate the contents of her teacup. "I think we're all still in a bit of denial. I keep thinking we'll have to find her will, sort all of that out and then I shake my head because it just feels absurd. That she can't be gone."

"It's never easy when the loss is sudden," Mrs. Grant agreed softly.

Kalina took another sip of tea and cleared her throat. "I know you must still be processing what happened, too, but you didn't seem that surprised by what happened. If you think there's something else going on, you should tell someone. The police maybe."

“I don’t know about that. What do I know? I’m just an old lady.”

“But Aunt Agatha would want you to say something. You were best friends,” Kalina motioned to the framed photo on the mantle.

“Oh, we were. We’d grown up together, gone to school up through college and came back to Ellesworth after graduation. We met our husbands in the same circles. Goodness, that was a long while ago.”

“I’ve seen you two. You were practically inseparable when I was growing up,” Kalina pointed out. “That sort of friendship and loyalty runs deep. Please, if something did happen to her, I need to know. She was just as important to me as she was to you.”

Mrs. Grant finally took a sip of her own tea and tears sprang to her eyes. “It just feels so empty without her.”

Kalina nodded. “Believe me, I know. That’s why I’m asking if you can think of anything that might have seemed off about her or anyone else. Did you see anything out of the ordinary after you left the pastry judging?”

“What do you mean?”

“I don’t know. Was anyone paying more attention than usual to her?”

“Not that I recall. I mean she always had everyone swarming to place an order of her cake. It was just like every year.”

Kalina pursed her lips, trying to figure out how best to phrase her question. “Did you notice if anyone went near her tea before she fell?”

“I wasn’t paying attention. To be honest, I was just so upset about losing to that little...” Mrs. Grant took a long swallow of tea, cutting off the tirade.

“You’re sure you didn’t see anything at all? You didn’t happen to notice if she made her own tea?”

“I think someone brought it to her maybe.” Her brow furrowed. “Yes, I think someone brought it to her but I don’t know who. Do they know what actually happened?”

Kalina shook her head. “I don’t know.” It did get her brain whirring. Agatha had been fine before the pastry judging and she’d only interacted physically with the judges long enough to accept her ribbon. And if, like Mrs. Grant and AJ said, she'd only had tea, then that seemed to be the logical delivery system if someone was in fact targeting her.

Mrs. Grant set her teacup down, hands trembling. She still wouldn't look Kalina in the eye. "It was lovely of you to stop by but I'm afraid I don't have time to visit any longer. Things to do."

Kalina didn't want to accept defeat but Mrs. Grant wasn't opening up like she'd hoped. She took her time finishing the cup of tea before standing up. "I appreciate your time, Mrs. Grant. When should I pick up those scones?"

"They should still have them at the fair. You can get them there." Mrs. Grant shuffled toward her as if to shoo her out of the house.

What was she hiding? Should she bring up the note she'd found in Aunt Agatha's house? It was a detail no one besides the police had right now "The police found a threatening note in Aunt Agatha's house. You wouldn't know anything about that would you?"

"N-no. I'm afraid not. I wish I could point you

or the police to who would have wanted to hurt my friend, but I'm useless."

Kalina tried to give a sympathetic smile and offered the older woman a brief hug. "Thanks again for having me over."

Mrs. Grant shut the door behind Kalina, shoving her unceremoniously into the screen door. She let out a little grunt as the scratchy mesh snagged on her shirt and a loose wire scraped along her forearm. There was definitely something going on with Mrs. Grant. Just as she eased the screen door shut behind her, her phone beeped with a text message from AJ: "Can we talk?"

She sent back a quick note letting him know he could stop by the shop. In the meantime, she had some research to do and the shop was as good a place to do it as any.

Chapter 5

It was a short trip from Mrs. Grant's house to Geeks and Things. Kalina pulled into the back lot and headed in through the game room, pausing to take in the new look of the space. It may not have been her first choice of dream job, but she knew she was far surpassing what her father would have expected of her. The shop was quiet as she settled behind the counter and pulled up a browser on her tablet. She stared at the search page that popped up, momentarily at a loss for what to do. If she was working off the theory that someone had intentionally targeted Aunt Agatha, then she just needed to figure out how they could have done it. The tea seemed the most efficient method. So, poison maybe? She typed in 'symptoms of poisoning' into the search bar and waited. The search engine helpfully populated the phone number for Poison Control as the very first entry. She scrolled through the thousands of results and was about to click on one just as the bell sounded above the door and AJ walked in. Dark smudges under his eyes and pale skin signaled he hadn't slept much the night before either.

"Hey. How you holding up?" She knew it was a redundant question given what had happened and his physical state but she couldn't help herself.

Her nephew hiccuped a breath and burst into tears. She laid the tablet aside and rounded the counter to fold him into a hug. "Shh. It's okay. You're going to be fine."

"I just feel so guilty. I should have done something. CPR or I don't know. I shouldn't have just stood and watched."

"It happened so fast I don't think there was anything you could have done."

He sniffled and scrubbed at his tear-stained face with the backs of his hands. In that moment he was the little boy she'd babysat for on summers home from college, so young and vulnerable.

"Have you had your follow-up conversation with he police?"

"No. They called this morning and said that I needed to come down. They talked to Mom but it sounded serious. Can you come with me? Mom offered but I'd feel better if it was you. Besides, she's been super clingy since yesterday It's like she's afraid I'm going to kick it next."

"Sure. Let me just grab a few things."

She retrieved the tablet and keys, killed the lights and followed her nephew outside. The police station was only a five minute walk from the shop and so they headed down the sidewalk side by side. Normally the fair would be rolling into day two but she assumed that given Aunt Agatha's death, it was cancelled. Aunt Agatha had been a fixture in the community. There would no doubt be an article in addition to the obituary for her but with so little to go on, even the hungriest of journalists wouldn't print anything just yet.

"Do you think the police think something might have happened to her? Like on purpose," AJ shoved his hands into the pockets of his shorts.

Kalina hesitated. She didn't want to speak for the police. There was every chance Chris had looked into the threatening note and discarded it. And she wasn't really supposed to have that information in the first place. "I don't know. Maybe. I'm sure if something did happen on purpose, they'll figure it out."

"Mrs. Grant seemed pretty upset yesterday," he offered.

"I went by this morning to see her. She's shaken up." She leaned in closer and whispered, "I think she might think someone was out to get Aunt Agatha. But she wouldn't say anything more. I'll figure out a way to get her to open up."

"Did you offer to buy her scones?"

"I did but that didn't work either," she said with a little laugh before sobering up. "I did find something at Aunt Agatha's house that might be fueling the police interest in her death."

"What?" Her nephew prompted.

"I really shouldn't be involving you," she said, trying to wave away his interest.

"What'd it say? Come on, Aunt K., don't hold out on me."

"Your mom wouldn't want me getting you involved in this."

"I'm already involved."

"Okay, fine. But this stays between us."

He gave a small fist pump in the air as the station came into view. "So, what did you find?"

"It was a note. It seemed out of place and it definitely was creepy. It said, 'Lying is a mortal sin.'"

They'd arrived at the station and Kalina held the door open for AJ to go first. The conversation died as soon as they crossed the threshold. Ellesworth PD was a small unit with about twenty uniformed officers, seven or eight detectives, one lieutenant, one sergeant and the captain. The precinct seemed strangely empty, especially if the fair had been called off for the second day, too. Chris sat at a desk studying a report. Kalina nudged AJ forward.

“Uh, Detective Harper, I’m here to give my statement,” AJ said, inching closer to Chris’s desk.

Chris jumped in his chair and gaped at AJ for thirty seconds before regaining his composure. Kalina settled in a seat at a vacant desk nearby. “I told you I’d bring him by today. I keep my word.”

“I appreciate it.” He sounded tired. Chris pushed the file aside and opened a document on his computer to start taking down AJ’s recollection.

Kalina turned her attention to her tablet. Luckily, the department was cheap enough not to password protect their Wi-Fi and she logged on to continue her internet search on poisons. She wasn’t sure it would yield anything helpful but it was worth a shot. By the descriptions she found after clicking through a couple of sources, she was more convinced that this could be Aunt Agatha’s cause of death. They all seemed to reference respiratory failure but the type of poison was less obvious. The coroner's office had probably done a toxicology report but those took weeks to come back, didn't they? And even though she was family, she wouldn't be privy to that information.

She was so lost in her thoughts she didn't notice the interview was finished until AJ snapped his fingers in front of her face. She blinked until he came into focus. He seemed relieved to have given his official statement. Kalina licked her lips and swallowed to dispel the cotton ball feeling in her throat.

"I'm all done. Do you want any help back at the shop? Maybe figuring out what inventory to order?"

"Uh, yeah. Sure, that would be great."

She turned to thank Chris for his time but he'd disappeared. She fixed her nephew with a quizzical look but he just shrugged. The file Chris had been reading was still sitting on his desk. If he'd really wanted to keep her from snooping he would have put it in a drawer or somewhere less obvious and open. AJ said nothing as she crossed the short distance to Chris's desk and bent over the file.

Kalina was wrong. Apparently, Chris had specifically asked the lab to rush the toxicology report. Initially, she wasn't sure what she was looking at. The graph with thin spikes of different items in Aunt Agatha's blood was like reading a foreign language when you didn't know one word. She flipped through to a different page but it only listed a myriad of technical jargon.

"Uh, Aunt K., you might want to hurry. He's coming back."

Kalina glanced around but Chris was nowhere to be seen. Still, she trusted AJ not to let her down. She turned to the last page with the summary paragraph. Bingo! According to the test done, it showed that Aunt Agatha had high levels of inorganic arsenic in her blood at the time of her death. She had definitely been poisoned.

"Aunt K., come on," AJ hissed and made a move to tug her away from the desk.

She flipped the file closed and set it back on the desk where she'd found it. Exhaling a breath she hadn't realized she'd been holding, she and AJ headed for the front of the building.

"Hey, Kal," Chris said, appearing with a coffee cup in hand.

"Yes? Did you need me to give a statement, too?"

"No. I was just wondering, did I hear right that you're planning on running a game of Cards against Humanity at the shop?"

That was an awfully personal question for someone she hadn't spoken to in years. And he'd never exactly been the gamer type. Her cheeks flushed. "That's the plan, yeah."

"Well, count me in."

Either he'd developed a fondness for slightly inappropriate games or he was looking for a reason to see her. She couldn't deny that either option interested her. She nodded to show she

D heard his statement and turned around, wrapping a shaking arm around AJ's shoulders. She bit the inside of her cheek to keep from embarrassing herself. She hadn't ever thought she would be reconnecting with an old flame. They made it through the front door before her cell phone rang. The call ID said it was from the shop, which meant it was call forwarding.

“Hello, this is Kalina Greystone.”

“This is Margaret Grant. I needed to tell you... Agatha wasn’t the only one who got that note. I got one too.”

Chapter 6

Kalina stopped mid-step. Had she heard that right? Did she just get a break in this whole thing? It sure sounded like it. She forced her voice to work. “Oh. I can come right over.”

“No, not here. The church down on Shore Drive.”

“All right. I’ll be there as soon as I can.”

She ended the call and turned to AJ. “That was Mrs. Grant. She wants to talk.”

“About what?”

“She said she got the same note I found at Aunt Agatha’s house. This sounds like someone is targeting them. I just don’t know why.”

AJ turned back to the front doors of the police station. "Shouldn't you tell Detective Harper about this?"

"Not yet. I don't know what she knows. I don't want to waste his time if it's nothing."

"But she said she got one of those creepy notes."

"Saying it and meaning it are two different things. I'll let him know if anything solid comes out of this."

"Okay. What should I do now?"

"Go to the shop. I'll see you back there when I'm done."

They parted ways and, just as Kalina headed down Main Street toward the beach, she caught Chris watching her from a window. He just stared at her. She hoped he didn't try to follow her. She needed to find out if Mrs. Grant was telling the truth on her own. She needed to know she could do this.

The walk to Shore Drive was calming. It allowed Kalina to gather her thoughts and prepare for what she needed to ask Mrs. Grant. The Ferris wheel at the fairground rose up in the distance off to the right. She could imagine the workers starting to dismantle the machinery. Aunt Agatha's death had cast a pall over the festivities. She turned her attention to the simple, stone church up to her left. According to town history, it had stood since the 1700s. The interior had undergone renovation in the last few decades but the exterior stonework still held. She hadn't been inside since she was a teenager at AJ's christening. She didn't have anything against churches or organized religion but, as an adult, she didn't find faith particularly comforting or necessary to her life. But it was the perfect place for a confession.

Kalina blew out a breath as she eased open the doors to the narthex. She hadn't spotted Mrs. Grant's car but it wasn't that far of a walk, even for a woman in her 60s. The church was eerily silent. Despite being Sunday, services had been cancelled in order to help support the fair and the charity. She moved deeper into the sanctuary and spotted Mrs. Grant seated in the second pew from the front. Time to find out her secret.

"Mrs. Grant?" she called, not wanting to surprise the woman.

“Here, dear.”

Kalina strode up to the front of the church and took a seat next to the older woman. They stayed quiet for a few moments, each taking in the image of Christ on the cross adorning the front of the pulpit. A powerful image for sure. The silence started to press on Kalina like a weight.

“You said you got a note too.”

“Yes.”

Kalina turned to sit sideways in the pew. “Did you bring it? Can I see it?”

Mrs. Grant opened her oversized purse and pulled out a folded piece of white paper. She started to hand it over but Kalina held up her hands. “I don’t think I should touch it.”

The older woman unfolded the page and held it up so that Kalina got a good look at it. **LYING IS A MORTAL SIN** was typed in bold caps just like the one she’d found. Whoever had killed Aunt Agatha appeared to be targeting Mrs. Grant as well.

“When did you get it?”

"Last week. It just appeared under my front door, folded like that. I thought it was a flyer from one of the children or a reminder about the fair. I nearly had a heart attack when I saw what it was."

"Do you know who sent it to you?"

She folded the paper and shoved it back in her bag. "No. I don't. But the message seems pretty clear. And it scared me."

"Did Aunt Agatha get hers at the same time?"

"Maybe. She didn't say anything to me about it."

"Are you sure? Because it seems to me that whoever killed her might be coming after you too."

"She didn't say anything. And I mean what I said that I don't know who might have sent it. But... I might know what this is all about."

"Okay. Why don't you fill me in on what's going on?"

"There were three of us. A long time ago, thirty years or so, we did something"—she looked up at the crucifix—"unforgivable. There was a crime and someone went to jail. But ... it wasn't the right person."

"How do you know they weren't the right person?"

"Because we lied. We said we saw what happened but we didn't. Not as clearly as we thought we had when it happened anyway."

"So you filed a false police report."

Mrs. Grant shook her head and her eyes glistened with unshed tears. "We did more than that. We lied during the trial."

Kalina let that revelation sink in. Mrs. Grant, Aunt Agatha and someone else had committed perjury and sentenced an innocent person to prison. She didn't want to believe that the women were capable of such a thing. Aunt Agatha had been one of the most honest and trustworthy people Kalina had ever known.

"Are you absolutely sure you got it wrong? I don't believe that you'd do something like that. And neither would aunt Agatha," Kalina protested.

Mrs. Grant dabbed at the corners of her eyes.

"Times were different. This town was different," she answered. It didn't explain anything.

As Kalina sat there beside the woman, she realized that whoever was targeting them had to know about the trial and the false testimony. But that could be anyone. And maybe this had nothing to do with the trial.

"Is there anything else that the note could be referring to?"

A single tear slid down Mrs. Grant's cheek. "No. I don't think so."

Kalina turned back to the front of the church. A chill slithered down her spine as she considered her next question. "Who was the third person?"

"Cynthia Ellicott." Mrs. Grant's shoulders sagged but Kalina couldn't determine if it was relief or resigning her friend to the fear of being next on the killer's hit list. "But she won't talk to you. We had a bit of a falling out about a month ago. She got so mad at Aggie, I can't imagine she'd be happy to see her great niece show up on her doorstep."

Kalina couldn't imagine the trio falling out. They'd always been close and it didn't fit with what Mrs. Grant had told her the day before. Unless she was trying to avoid an argument from Aunt Agatha. Ms. Ellicott had babysat for she and Jillian when they were younger but her relationship to the woman hadn't gone much beyond seeing her at the fair in later years. "Thank you for telling me all of this. You should take that note to the police. They can keep you safe."

Mrs. Grant didn't respond to Kalina's suggestion. That was all right. She'd tip Chris off as soon as she got back to the shop. She needed an internet connection so she could do a little research on the trial. That was the key to finding the killer.

Chapter 7

Kalina made great time getting back to the shop. She pushed through the front door and stopped dead in the doorway. Chris stood at the counter, chatting with AJ about what looked like a video game. Both looked up when she entered.

“Hi, Kal.” Chris waved.

“Hi. What’s going on? I thought AJ gave you everything you needed and I didn’t need to give a statement.”

“This isn’t official police business. This is a social call.”

From behind the counter AJ gave her a wink and a quick thumbs up. *Brat!* Kalina was lost for words. One day back in each other's orbits and he was already making social calls. The high schooler buried deep inside her jumped at the potential for rekindling their romance. But they were such different people now; it couldn't be that easy to just fall back into each other's arms. *Could it?*

"I wanted to see what kind of games you had. See if any of them were appropriate for Jack and Benji."

"Um, okay."

It wasn't the way she wanted to break the news about what she'd discovered but it would have to do. There was the risk he'd berate her more in person as she couldn't just hang up, but it was one she had no choice but to take.

"Have fun," AJ said with a small wave.

Kalina led Chris back to the game room. She planned on getting more games as people requested them but she had a few staples that she'd picked up at a couple small conventions she'd attended. This wasn't exactly the venue she'd intended to share what she'd learned from Mrs. Grant but it would have to do. He browsed the table of games and picked up a small canister.

“Zombie Dice?” she said with a smile.

“Want to play?”

“This must be new. Like an uncle thing because you never used to like these kinds of games,” she said but gestured to the table in the center of the room.

“They've grown on me,' he admitted with a sheepish grin.

“I have something to tell you,” she broached, pulling out a chair.

“We can talk and play.”

They settled across the table from each other and Chris went first. She wasn't paying attention to the dice as they skittered out across the table but she spotted the red shotgun blast. She was working herself up to telling him the truth.

“So I saw Mrs. Grant today.”

“Oh?” He fished three more dice from the container and rolled them. She would have thought he would need an introduction to the game but he seemed quite competent.

“Well, she seemed so upset yesterday I wanted to make sure she was doing okay. She and Aunt Agatha were always so close. She was kind of like a de facto aunt, too.”

“I guess you didn’t forget your hometown manners being away in the big city.”

“She told me something. She got a note just like the one I found at Aunt Agatha’s house.”

The dice slipped from his fingers and rolled both a green and yellow shotgun. His turn ended. “You shouldn’t be digging into things. We’ve got it under control.”

“She volunteered the information. What was I supposed to do, just ignore her?” Kalina took her turn but didn’t pay much attention to the outcome.

“So, are you sure she got one?”

“She showed it to me.” She picked three more dice and rolled them. One shotgun and two brains. “I didn’t touch it. I made sure not to.”

"Where is she?"

"I left her at the church. You should send someone there and to her house to make sure she doesn't destroy it. Not that she would but ... just to be sure."

He pulled out his cell phone and sent a text. "Did she tell you anything else?"

"She said there might be a third person who got a note. Cynthia Ellicott. But I'm not sure. I guess she and Aunt Agatha had a falling out a few months back. So she might not be in the mood to talk."

"Did she say what the falling out was about?'

She picked up on his tone. He was slipping into interrogation mode. "No, she didn't. You don't think that Ms. Ellicott would hurt Aunt Agatha over an argument? I mean, she wasn't even at the fair. How could she possibly have done anything to..." She stopped short of saying 'poison her'. She wasn't supposed to know that information.

He held up his hands in surrender. "No, you're right. That doesn't make sense. But what makes Mrs. Grant think Ms. Ellicott might be a target, too?"

Kalina licked her lips. "She said they committed perjury thirty years ago."

"I should still speak to her, to confirm if she is indeed a target."

"I'd like to come with you."

"How many times do I have to tell you—"

"She might be willing to talk to both of us. If you just show up, it might spook her. Even if she wasn't on the best terms with Aunt Agatha, maybe she'll see me as a friendly face."

"You saying I'm not friendly?"

"No. But she used to babysit my sister and me when we were little."

"Fine. But you do exactly as I say, got it?"

"You have my word."

They left the table with dice spread across it and headed out through the front of the shop. AJ leaned on the counter, his nose mere inches from his phone.

“Hold the fort,” she called. A sense of unease settled on her as she followed Chris to his car. She hoped that Ms. Ellicott could shed some more light on this mystery.

Chapter 8

Ms. Ellicott's house stood on the edge of the town away from everyone else. The more Kalina though about the woman the more she remembered her being kind of opinionated and irritable even as a younger woman. It was probably a good thing to be going as a pair to talk to her; Chris flashing his badge would only annoy her. Despite the summer warmth, the shutters were all closed on the front windows and the front door was shut. Stepping up onto the front porch, Kalina felt the tiny hairs on the back of her neck stand on end. Chris didn't appear to have the same reaction, or at least he hid it well. He yanked open the screen door and knocked sharply.

“Ms. Ellicott, this is Detective Harper with Ellesworth PD. I’d like to ask you a few questions.”

No response. Kalina paced the length of the porch and noted the windows on both sides of the house were also closed up tight. “Maybe she decided to go on vacation.”

Chris knocked again. “I don’t think so.” He pivoted and pointed to the car parked in the driveway. “Stay here. I’m going to check around back.”

“Okay.”

He jogged around the back of the house and Kalina tried the front door but found it locked. Standing there alone made her nervous. Something about this was wrong. Even people who didn’t want to be around other people didn’t shut themselves up like this. Not in this town. She abandoned the front of the house and made her way around the back, taking the same path Chris had to avoid spooking him. She hadn’t seen a gun on his belt but that didn’t mean he didn’t have one concealed somewhere else.

"Chris?" she called out, hoping to give him even more warning that she was coming.

He didn't answer her and she picked up the pace. She rounded the back of the house and found him leaning against the side of the house bent double. The back door, which led to the kitchen, was open and a putrid smell wafted from the house.

"Oh God, what is that?" She gagged.

"We're too late."

Holding her breath, Kalina peered inside. Just within view, Ms. Ellicott lay on the floor with something silver protruding from her chest. There didn't appear to be much blood. She hoped the poor woman had gone quickly. For a split second, Cynthia's face vanished, replaced by Aunt Agatha and Mrs. Grant's. This could have been either of them. Her stomach churned and she backed away from the house, trying not to throw up.

"Do ... do you know how long she's been dead?"

Chris shook his head and coughed a couple times. "No. And being shut in the house like that is going to make it harder to figure out. I need to get a forensic unit down here."

"What should I do?"

His eyes watered, likely from the smell, and he pointed to the front of the house. "Go wait out front. Direct the EMTs when they get here."

"I can do that."

Chris pulled his phone from his pocket and hit a speed dial. "This is Detective Harper from Ellesworth PD. I need an ambulance to 1849 Spring Road. And I'm going to need a forensic team too. We've got another one."

Kalina retraced her steps back to the front of the house and took a seat on the front steps to wait. Someone was definitely targeting the women who'd lied at the trial thirty years ago. And they were succeeding in doling out punishment. She really needed to figure out who was after them. If she did, maybe she could prevent Mrs. Grant from being the last victim. A short time later, sirens wailed and an ambulance pulled to a stop in front of the house.

"Where are we going?" a male paramedic asked as he climbed out of the driver side.

"Straight back. She's in the kitchen."

She rubbed the back of her neck and waited for the forensic team to show up. She stared out at the trees and grass lining the street, anything to keep her from closing her eyes and seeing the dead woman inside the house. It was far worse than Aunt Agatha. At least her aunt had gone quickly. She had questions she wanted to ask but knew they couldn't be answered yet. Finally, a forensic van showed up and, just as the team disappeared toward the back of the house, Chris appeared.

"How are you holding up?"

"I don't know. I mean do you think if I'd told you sooner we could have stopped it?"

He sat beside her and wrapped his arm around her shoulder. "I don't think so. Even without the heat of the house she's probably been dead at least a day."

Now she knew exactly how AJ felt witnessing Aunt Agatha's take her last breath. They sat together in silence and she leaned into his solid presence. She almost expected him to kiss her cheek reassuringly. But that was the thought of an enamored schoolgirl. She pushed down those feelings and squeezed her eyes shut to ward off tears. She needed to stay strong to solve this case. She owed it to Agatha and her friends, even if they had lied in the past. That didn't justify murder in the present.

"I know I'm not a cop but ... I feel like I'm a part of this case, Chris. Please don't keep me in the dark. I need to know what happened to them."

"I can't make that promise, Kal."

"You don't have to let me sit in on any interviews or anything, but what was it that killed her?"

"It looked like a letter opener."

"Did you find a note like the others got?"

"I don't know. Forensics is still working."

"Was it her letter opener?"

"I didn't get a good look at it."

"This has to be connected to that trial."

“Maybe. But forensics will do what they do and let me know what they find. As much as we want answers right now, we have to be patient. We want to make sure we have all the evidence to put whoever is doing this away.”

“I know. I ... this is just scaring me a little. I come home and all of a sudden people are being murdered left and right.”

“I’m pretty sure it wasn’t you.”

She smiled at him. “Thanks.”

One of the forensic techs approached with two evidence bags in hand. One bore a white, printed piece of paper and even from this distance Kalina spotted the identical message. The second bag contained the letter opener. The silver handle bore what looked like a monogram etched into it.

“We found the note in the bedroom,” the tech said.

“Okay. Let me see the weapon.”

The tech handed over the letter opener and, for his part, Chris didn’t stop Kalina from bending over to examine it with him. It was slender and the point was dulled with use. She tried not to look at the rust-colored stains marring the tip and half of the shaft. She'd been right about the top being monogramed. On closer inspection, she spotted an ornate "MG" embossed in flowery script underneath black fingerprint powder. She noted the swirls and whorls of an exposed print. She thought she spotted some blood on the sharp left point of the M but she didn't say anything. Pointing out evidence wasn't her job.

"I'm going to go out on a limb and say this wasn't hers," she said.

"I'm inclined to agree with you. Hopefully, the lab can identify whoever's fingerprint and blood that is."

She didn't want to say it but it looked like the letter opener belonged to Mrs. Grant. It would explain why she'd been so reluctant to open up about the letter and the trial. Seeds of doubt took root in Kalina's mind. After all, with both Aunt Agatha and Ms. Ellicott dead, there was no one to confirm they'd in fact had a falling out. But she couldn't leap to conclusions just because the evidence was pointing in her direction. She would wait for proof before sharing her theory. Chris's phone beeped with a text message. He set the letter opener on the stair to his left and checked the screen. He frowned and rubbed at his temple.

"What's wrong?"

"I sent an officer to the church but Mrs. Grant wasn't there. She wasn't at her house either."

"Maybe she went back to the fairgrounds to help clean up."

"Yeah, maybe. I think I need to talk to her myself."

"If you don't mind, I think I'm going to head back to the shop and check on AJ."

"Good idea."

The paramedics rolled by with Ms. Ellicott on a gurney. The smell of death followed them and up close Kalina saw the fear etched into the woman's features. She didn't deserve to die. Not this way. Neither of them did. She pushed herself to her feet and raked a hand through her hair while she waited for the ambulance to pull away. Maybe they were lucky no one else lived close by. They didn't need people gossiping and spreading rumors. The ambulance eased back down the street without fanfare or sirens. They weren't keen to announce another death either.

"I guess we'll have to finish our game another time," Chris said as he placed a hand on her arm. "I've got to head back to the station and fill Captain Cahill in."

"Okay." Time for her to actually do that research she'd planned on.

Chapter 9

"Where'd you go?" AJ asked as soon as Kalina walked through the front door of the shop. She'd made a stop at home to pick up her laptop. She needed the extra processing power.

"You can't tell anyone but … we found another body."

"Oh, crap. Who?"

"I can't tell you. Not if I want Chris to trust me enough not to leave me out of the loop going forward." She shut the door and flipped the sign to "Closed".

"Come on. You told me everything else. Maybe I can help."

“I appreciate it but this is more serious than we thought. I need you to go home.”

“Please, Aunt K., let me help.”

“I need to do this on my own, kid. Please just go home. I’m sure everything will come out when this is all over. But right now I don’t need a sidekick.”

“You know, the hero kicking the sidekick out never ends well,” he muttered but took the back exit.

She felt a little guilty about booting him out of her research but she knew Jillian would never forgive her if he got mixed up with a killer—well, any more mixed up than he already was. But she would be the good aunt and do everything she could to protect her family. It seemed the killer had a specific target but she couldn’t discount the possibility that he or she might lash out if the police closed in. She pushed those worries aside while she waited for her laptop to boot up and connect to the store’s Wi-Fi. She navigated to the town’s library webpage and searched for links to old newspaper articles. Unfortunately, it didn’t look like they’d scanned all of the editions yet.

They'd gone as far back as 1990 but she needed the 1980s. At the bottom of the list of available editions she saw a disclaimer that editions from the 1980s and earlier could be found at the library itself and the website offered a list of article titles from those editions. At least they were trying to be helpful.

Kalina typed in the search terms "trial" and "Cynthia Ellicott". She was the easiest to use because she'd never married so Kalina didn't have to worry about a name change after marriage. The page populated a list of results. There were a couple of articles in which Ms. Ellicott's name came up in connection with a trial. They were from the spring editions in March and April 1986. There was also an article from June 1987 linked to those from the year before. That was what she needed to find. She copied the article titles and editions and emailed them to herself, pulling the email up on her phone's email app before heading out to the library. She could feel a break in the case coming. Answers were almost within her reach.

A short time later, she sat in the newspaper archive section of the library in the basement. It was quiet and she was grateful for the solitude. She didn't need people asking questions she wasn't ready to answer. She started with the March editions, combing through the aged, brittle paper until she found what she was looking for. The article was buried within the third page and was shorter than she would have expected.

Local Man Charged with Murder to Stand Trial

By: Adam Jenkins, Staff Reporter

It was a quiet night on February 18, 1986 when the authorities were called upon to investigate the body of a young girl found down near the waterfront. The victim, later identified as 16-year-old Alice Beech, appeared to have sustained injuries consistent with a physical assault, according to police who were on scene. The case developed no leads as Alice's family begged the townspeople for someone to come forward. They offered a reward for any information leading to the capture of their daughter's killer.

> A break in the case came as blustery February turned into March. Three witnesses, including Ms. Cynthia Ellicott, came forward stating that they had been out for a walk on the beach when they observed a car speeding away toward the center of town. According to their statements, the vehicle passed by street lights illuminating the face of the driver. The suspect, identified as Samuel Gordon, 31, was arrested at his home on March 9, 1986 and he has been indicted on charges of murder. A trial is expected to commence on March 24th in the Salem County Courthouse. Gordon remains in custody as bail has been denied. According to sources, Gordon has relatives out of state and the judge believes him to be a flight risk. At this time it is unclear whether Ms. Ellicott and the other witnesses will testify at trial.

Kalina leaned back and let out a breath. She'd been a toddler when Alice Beech died. No one in town liked to talk about it. In fact, she couldn't even recall the case ever coming up after church on Sundays when she was young. And those ladies always liked to gossip. She checked the list on her phone again for the next article. It came from the April 10th edition. This time Mr. Jenkins made the front page with a faded color photo of the defendant sitting in court. He looked vaguely familiar, which was ridiculous. She'd never met the man. This article was also short on detail. Apparently Mr. Jenkins and his editor believed in brevity.

Gordon Trial Drags On, Public Restless for Result

By: Adam Jenkins, Staff Reporter

Trial is still underway at the Salem County Courthouse. The prosecution's case closed on Friday. Defendant Samuel Gordon has yet to take the stand and reports indicate he may not testify in his own defense. While he is not required to do so, there is no doubt the jury will consider it a strike against him.

Perhaps the highlight of the prosecution's case came when Ms. Cynthia Ellicott, 30 and two other witnesses testified as to their recollections of the night in question. Ms. Ellicott testified that she, "saw a man driving away very fast from where poor Alice was found." Ms. Agatha Hammersmith testified that, "Yes, I'm sure it was the defendant who killed that poor girl," and when asked how she knew this, replied, "I saw his eyes. I could never forget the look of madness in them." Finally, Ms. Margaret Cook testified that she, "recalled the license plate of the car and it matched the car driven by the defendant."

Public sentiment is clear. They want a conviction sooner rather than later. Alice's parents asked the defendant to simply confess to the crime so they could let their daughter rest in peace.

It definitely seemed like Mrs. Grant, Aunt Agatha and Ms. Ellicott had been sure of what they'd seen. It also appeared that Mr. Jenkins was very pro prosecution. He'd barely afforded Mr. Gordon any humanity. Even if he was guilty of the crime, he was still a person who' was supposed to be innocent until proven guilty. Kalina had no way of knowing which details were fabricated but she was beginning to suspect most of them had been made up. Perhaps someone in the police force had pressured them to make statements against Sam Gordon. Or perhaps the real killer had threatened them for their perjured testimony. There were two more articles on the list. She had to retrieve a new set of editions from the shelves to find the one from April 18th. Again, Mr. Jenkins made the front page. This time the photo depicted Sam Gordon, face in his hands. The article was a short paragraph.

Gordon Sentenced to Life

By: Adam Jenkins, Staff Reporter

After an abbreviated defense, in which counsel for the defendant, Alan Grant, did not question anyone but Gordon's wife, Catherine, to attest to his character, the jury retired for the shortest deliberation in the history of Ellesworth. Only ninety minutes after being issued jury instructions, they returned with a verdict: guilty. Gordon was sentenced to life in prison for Alice

> Beech's murder. He was seen crying as the bailiff removed him from the courtroom. He was not permitted to say goodbye to his wife or son.

Kalina let out a gasp and a single tear ran down her cheek. She was beginning to understand why someone would want revenge on the people who led to the wrongful conviction and imprisonment of this man. As she dried her eyes and returned the newspaper to its protective folder, she had to wonder. Why had Gordon's lawyer not let him testify? Surely he had an alibi? Why did the attorney not cross-examine the witnesses? Had the attorney had something to do with setting Gordon up? She scanned the article one last time before she put it back.

"Oh damn!" She bit her tongue for swearing but there was no one around to hear her.

The pieces were starting to come together. She had to check one piece of information but she had an idea why the three women were involved. She still had one final article, from June 1987, to review and it didn't make sense to abandon the newspaper archives until she'd done so. The final article was even shorter than the one about the verdict.

> **Murderer Samuel Gordon Takes Own Life**
>
> By: Adam Jenkins, Staff Reporter
>
> In what can only be deemed a further admission of guilt, one year and two months after he was sentenced to life in prison for the brutal murder of Alice Beech, Samuel Gordon was found dead in his cell. Reports confirm he hung himself. Gordon is survived by his wife Catherine and their son, Danny. Unable to take the shame, Catherine and her son moved out of the area. It is rumored she now goes by her maiden name.

"Well, that's as clear a motive as you're likely to get," she said to no one in particular.

She needed to go check marriage records. If she could figure out what the former Mrs. Gordon changed her name to, she might have a better shot at pointing Chris in the right direction. Her phone buzzed with an incoming call. There was no Caller ID.

"Hello?"

"Kal, it's Chris Harper."

"Hi. Is something wrong?" She almost felt guilty for using her phone in the confines of the library. Almost.

"I wanted to let you know that the lab put a rush on that fingerprint on the letter opener."

Kalina's heart started to race at the unexpected news. He was keeping his word about looping her in on the investigation. Maybe she could point out that she had discovered the motive for the killings. "Who does it belong to?"

"You aren't going to like it. It matched Margaret Grant."

She let out a groan. "No, that can't be right."

"Well, I'm afraid it is. I mean, come on. It was monogramed with her initials."

"But you don't know that it was hers. Plenty of people in town have those initials."

"Name one."

"I... I can't think of anyone off the top of my

head. But, Chris, I think I found something. Have you looked into the trial angle?"

Muffled sounds came over the line. "Believe me, we're following all the leads. I have to go. Officers just brought Mrs. Grant in. They found her at the cemetery visiting her husband. I just wanted you to know."

He hung up before she could share the news that, even if the evidence pointed to Mrs. Grant, the poor old woman was being framed. Just like Sam Gordon. She rose halfway out of her chair and stopped. Should she finish up here or go and try to observe the interrogation? Was that even possible? She didn't have time to debate. If she didn't move fast, the wrong person would be arrested for a crime they didn't commit—again.

Chapter 10

Kalina hastily put the newspapers back in their respective bins and took the stairs to the main level of the library two at a time. Pushing the front door open in a hurry, she staggered as the summer heat smacked her in the face. Sweat prickled along her hairline and her upper lip. She hadn't noticed how cool the basement had been. The sudden change in temperature only spurred her on to get to the police station.

By the time she arrived, she felt as if she'd been dunked in salt water. A quick glance in the mirror in the women's bathroom dispelled the idea that she was drenched in sweat. The central hub of the station was still sparsely populated, save for the two uniformed officers.

They looked like they were right out of the academy, maybe only a few years older than AJ. They were both staring at a TV monitor that looked like it belonged in the early 1990s. At least it was in color and the audio seemed to be working. Mrs. Grant sat on the far side of a rickety-looking, faux wooden table. Chris sat across from her with a bulging folder. Kalina inched closer to better hear the conversation.

“Mrs. Grant, are you sure you don’t want a lawyer present?”

“If I really needed one, you would have told me that you’re charging me with something.”

“Ma’am, I need you to affirmatively state that you are waiving your right to have counsel present during this interview.”

Mrs. Grant pressed her lips together and squared her shoulders. “I do not want a lawyer. Is that clear enough for you?”

Chris coughed. “Yes, thank you. Now, I’d like to talk to you about Cynthia Ellicott.”

“What about her?”

“You two are friends?”

"I suppose."

"In fact, you were friends with both Cynthia and Agatha weren't you?"

"Yes. What does that matter?"

"You know that Agatha died at the fair. We discovered Cynthia Ellicott's body earlier today in her home. She'd been stabbed—" he retrieved the bloodstained letter opener, still safely sealed in its evidence bag "—with this."

Kalina waited for Mrs. Grant to react. The older woman studied the letter opener through the clear plastic in silence for what seemed like hours. Finally, she let out a shudder and dabbed at her eyes.

"That's terrible."

"Have you seen this letter opener before?"

"I don't know. Why should I have?"

"We lifted a fingerprint from the handle." He pointed to the swirls of fingerprint powder still clinging to the metal. "It was a match to you. So would you like to rethink your answer?"

Mrs. Grant kneaded her hands together in a nervous tic. She glanced around the small interview room, anywhere but at Chris. “I leant that to Cynthia ages ago. She never returned it. She was always forgetting to give things back even when we were girls in school.”

“When was the last time you saw her?”

“Last week. I cooked for her a few times a week. Those awful frozen meals were no good for her health.”

“When was the last time Agatha saw her?”

“A month or two ago. They had a falling out.”

“Over what?” Chris prodded.

“Neither of them wanted to tell me.”

“But you knew them both well. Couldn’t you guess?”

“You’re right, I knew them well. Which means I knew not to press when they didn’t want to talk about it.” She rubbed at her upper lip, her gaze darting to the letter opener again. “You can’t honestly believe I would murder my friends. That’s lunacy!”

Chris didn’t respond. Instead, he reached into the folder again and produced one of the notes. Kalina couldn’t tell which one it was. They’d all looked identical. Chris pushed the evidence across the table to Mrs. Grant. “Do you recognize this?”

“Someone slipped it under my door.”

“When?”

“I don’t remember. Last week maybe.”

“Last week or you don’t remember, which is it, Mrs. Grant?”

She fidgeted and kneaded her hands again. “Last week.”

“When you went over to Ms. Ellicott’s house, did you talk about the note?”

“No, it didn’t come up.”

Kalina chewed her lower lip. She didn’t like where this was going. Sure, the evidence looked bad but she knew the reason. Someone was framing Mrs. Grant. She needed to get that information to Chris before he made a huge mistake.

“Okay, let’s talk about Samuel Gordon,” Chris said, her words freezing Kalina in place.

“I don’t want to talk about him,” Mrs. Grant said.

“I’m aware that all three of you testified in his trial thirty years ago.”

“Well it wasn’t a secret,” she murmured.

“No, but you didn’t tell the truth back then, did you?”

He really had looked into the trial like Kalina had suggested. She was rooted to the spot, waiting to hear what Mrs. Grant said. “You talked to Aggie’s niece I take it.”

“It’s my job to look into every possibility and trust me, she’s a smart woman.”

Kalina smiled in spite of the situation. Still, she needed to share the pieces that were coming into focus. She cleared her throat and caught the attention of the rookies watching the interrogation.

“Can we help you?” One of them asked.

She gestured to the monitor. “I need to talk to Detective Harper about the murders of Cynthia Ellicott and Agatha Davies. Tell him it’s Kalina.”

The one who'd spoken to her scurried off and moments later appeared on the screen. He bent down to whisper in Chris's ear. Chris stood and addressed Mrs. Grant. "Excuse me. I'll be right back."

he appeared in the bull pen and gestured for her to follow him back to his desk. The other officers eyed them but didn't intervene.

"What are you doing here, Kal?"

"You called me, remember?" She noted. he fixed her with an irritated look. "I have a theory about what's going on and I thought you should know."

"I thought we agreed you'd leave the police work to me."

"You're going to get it wrong if you just follow what the evidence says."

He grabbed her by the elbow and ushered her into Captain Cahill's empty office. "Tell me why I shouldn't follow the evidence, then."

"You already know about Sam Gordon's trial. I read the news articles from back then. They weren't very favorable to him. The coverage of the trial was sparse, which seems kind of weird.

And Mrs. Grant admitted to me that she and the others lied during the trial. I think someone involved in the case somehow is coming back to get revenge."

"Targeting the witnesses," Chris murmured.

"Not just the witnesses. Mrs. Grant's husband was Sam's lawyer. He did a shoddy job defending him. And Mrs. Grant told me he died a year ago in a car accident."

"That's right. Pretty nasty scene from what I heard. Slammed into a tree," Chris explained.

"When last year?"

"I don't know. Summertime."

"June?"

"I would have to double check but that sounds about right."

"What about the reporter, Adam Jenkins?"

Chris' brow furrowed. "Hang on." He stepped out of the room and spoke quietly with one of the rookies. Kalina watched him move to a computer and begin typing. Minutes later a sheet of paper spat out at a nearby printer and Chris retrieved it. He returned back to the captains' office and held out for Kalina to see. Adam Jenkins had suffered a heart attack back in April.

"Whoever this is is smart. They're making it look like accidents and they're framing the rest of the people involved," she said.

"I promise, we're going to do everything we can find out who is behind this."

She headed for the front door and caught sight of one of the new officers coming out of the interview room looking shell shocked. He approached Chris and said, "She wants a lawyer."

"Go home, Kal. There's nothing more you can do here. I promise as soon as we crack this case and have the killer in custody, I will personally let you know," Chris said. The way he pressed his hand to her arm and leaned forward suggested he wanted to do more than just usher her out the door.

If she could figure out one final piece of information she could finally solve this puzzle.

Chapter 11

Kalina's nerves tingled as she jogged back to the shop. She could do her last bit of research there. The records she needed were electronic, even that far back. She hoped it would take a little while for Mrs. Grant to get her lawyer. It would give Kalina the time she needed to figure out who the real killer was and, hopefully, allow Chris to catch them before any more lives could be ruined

"We're closed," AJ called when Kalina tried the front door.

"AJ, it's me! Let me in."

The lock released and her nephew appeared in the doorway. "Sorry."

"I thought I sent you home," she chided and pushed past him.

"You did. I didn't listen. What did you find out?"

"I'm not sure I should tell you."

"I'm not a little kid anymore. I can handle it."

"No. I'm not going to be responsible for putting you in therapy. You can stay but only if you go clean up the game room."

He rolled his eyes. "I wasn't even the one who made the mess."

"And yet I'm the boss and I say go clean it up."

"Fine."

She swatted his arm as he walked by. Now alone in the front of the shop, she grabbed her tablet and fired up the library website. The town was small enough that the library housed most of the town hall records regarding marriages, births and deaths. She found the listing for marriage licenses and typed in Samuel Gordon. With any luck he'd be the only one in town. It seemed luck was on her side. There was a single entry for a Samuel Gordon dated February 9, 1975. There was a scanned-in version of the actual license and she opened it up in a new tab. She had to enlarge the picture to get the image clear enough to read.

The tablet fell out of her hands and clattered on the counter. It couldn't be right. Taking two deep breaths, she picked up the tablet again and looked. She'd been right the first time. Samuel Gordon had married one Catherine Cahill. Her stomach sloshed, suddenly uneasy, as she navigated to birth records and typed in Daniel Gordon. Sure enough, a record appeared from April of 1976. Daniel Michael Gordon had been born a healthy little boy to Samuel Gordon and Catherine Gordon.

Kalina slumped against the countertop, her ears ringing with the realization of what it all meant. How could she have missed it? The last article had practically screamed the information at her! But she needed to be sure. The phrase the three women had been sent was very specific. Something deep down in her mind insisted she had to be absolutely sure of the killer's identity before she started accusing people. Chris wouldn't believe her unless he had actual proof.

Swallowing several times so she could speak, she dialed Chris' number and waited. It rang three times. Four. Five. Finally, just before it flipped to voicemail, he picked up.

"Hey, we're still waiting for her lawyer."

"I uh..." Her voice shook.

"Is everything okay?"

She should tell him what she'd found but she couldn't get the words out. "Yeah, fine. I just... I needed to know something. Where did you say the officers found Mrs. Grant?"

"The cemetery. Why?"

"No reason. I was just wondering. I have to go."

She hung up before he could question her further. Did Mrs. Grant have it figured out too? Or did she just want to pay her respects and voice her apology to the man she and her friends had pushed to an early grave? Either way, she needed to find that gravesite. With a quick glance toward the back room, she rushed out through the front door. AJ could handle himself.

The cemetery was on the other side of the church. Mrs. Grant probably hadn't left the area after they'd spoken. By the time she reached the main gate, Kalina's calves had cramped from running and her chest burned from the stress of the run. She wasn't out of shape by any means but the whole situation was taking a toll. As she eased through the gate and began searching the stone markers, she wondered how it could have only been two days since Aunt Agatha died. It was clear that Ms. Ellicott had, in fact, been the first victim. An involuntary shiver danced down her spine. Nothing like this was supposed to happen in Ellesworth. It was just a sleepy, little coastal town with nice people.

The headstones varied in color, some brand new, others beaten down and almost illegible with age. She longed for a helpful "You Are Here" map but was left to wander aimlessly through the rows of the dead. She had nearly reached the back fence when she spotted what looked like fresh flowers leaning up against a slightly weathered headstone. They looked familiar somehow. Kalina's heart sank when she reached the stone to find it belonged to none other than Samuel Gordon. He'd been buried at home after all. The epitaph read, “Lying is a mortal sin and you never did.” She had all the proof she needed now. She snapped a photo of the grave and sent it off to Chris with a message that she had found the proof that Mrs. Grant was being framed. And the flowers finally clicked in her addled brain. Captain Cahill had given the same flowers to Leslie when she won at the fair the day before. Now she just needed to get to the station and warn Chris about Captain Cahill before it was too late.

Chapter 12

This time, Kalina really was drenched in sweat as she staggered through the front door of the police station. Chris hadn't responded to her text but she hadn't really expected him to. The station was eerily empty and quiet. Where was everyone? She moved slowly, afraid something or someone might jump out at her at any second. The tiny hairs on her arms stood on end, another warning sign. She finally reached the monitor linked to the interview room. Mrs. Grant still sat there, alone, a plastic bottle of water cupped between her hands. Where was her lawyer? She'd asked for one nearly an hour ago. And where was Chris?

"Hello?" she called out.

No response. This wasn't right. She studied the video feed and noted that the folder of evidence was no longer strewn across the table. It didn't explain why Mrs. Grant had been left alone. Kalina's stomach churned again and she swallowed back the rising acid. She fished her phone from her pocket and dialed Chris's cell phone. This time it rang five times before clicking over to voicemail.

"Chris, this is Kalina. I don't know where you are but I figured it out. Please call me back."

Her palms turned slick with sweat as she ended the call and the phone slid from her fingers, clattering to the floor. She bent to pick it up and stopped with her fingertips brushing the screen. The front door squeaked open. The irrational part of her brain told her it was Cahill and he had come to finish what he'd started. Her heart began hammering in her chest and the blood rushed in her ears, drowning out all other sound. Balancing with one hand on the floor, she swore she felt vibrations as someone walked into the room. The vibration intensified and then stopped.

"Kalina? What are you doing?" Chris offered his hand.

Forgetting her phone for the moment, relief washed over her. She allowed him to pull her up and she collapsed into his arms. He staggered back a step under her weight before he eased her into a chair and retrieved her phone for her.

“You look pretty freaked out,” he said.

“Why is Mrs. Grant in there alone?”

“It’s taking her lawyer longer to get here than we thought.”

“I texted you, why didn’t you answer?”

“I was chasing down some other evidence. I think you might be right and Mrs. Grant is being framed. There are some inconstancies in the evidence that don’t fit.”

“So why is she still sitting here? You should let her go.”

“I still have to follow protocol.”

“I know who the real killer is. We need to get Mrs. Grant somewhere safe.”

“I don’t know how many more times I have to say it. I’m on this.”

“You aren’t listening to me. The killer is—” she began but he held up a hand.

“I don’t need your speculation. Come on, I’m taking you home. No more digging into things.”

He didn’t give her a choice as he dragged her out of the station and into his car. She caught movement out of the corner of her eye but Chris pulled out of the small lot and onto Main Street before she could get a good look.

Chapter 13

“Who did you send to watch Mrs. Grant?” Kalina’s throat felt raw.

“Everything will be fine. The captain is on it. He won’t let anyone near her.”

Kalina’s whole body went numb. In a foolish move she reached for the steering wheel, anything to get Chris to stop the car. Panic flushed his face and he slammed on the breaks. The car narrowly avoided plowing into a mailbox. She was going to regret that action.

“What the hell are you doing? You could have killed us!” His voice echoed in the confines of the car.

“I’m sorry but you can’t leave her with him. She won’t be safe.”

“Why not?”

“Because he’s the killer!”

Her declaration hung in the air between them for far too long. She tugged on the seatbelt release but it wouldn’t unlatch. Chris stared at her, mouth hanging open in obvious disbelief. She could tell he was trying to find words but they wouldn’t come. Finally, the seatbelt unhooked and slid with a sharp ‘zip’ back to its original position.

“What… I don’t understand.”

“Sam Gordon, the man who killed himself, had a son named Daniel. After Gordon killed himself, his wife and son left town and started going by her maiden name, Cahill. It’s all in the town records. I don’t think that Alan Grant’s accident was an accident. Or that Adam Jenkins really had a heart attack. And I bet you Cahill was on the scene for both. We have to go back before he finishes what he started.”

Chris continued to stare at her, taking the information in. She needed to act, to turn the car around and get back to the station. She snapped her fingers in front of his face; it did nothing to rouse him from his trance. Finally, the blare of a nearby emergency vehicle snapped him out of his shock. An ambulance flew past them in the direction of the police station.

“Put your seatbelt back on,” Chris ordered before he gunned the engine and the tires squealed on the pavement as he turned the car to follow the path of the flashing lights.

Kalina didn’t have time to bother with the seatbelt. She gripped the edge of the passenger seat and braced herself against the door as Chris employed driving skills better suited to a race-car driver than a mild-mannered police detective. They rolled into the station’s parking lot maybe two minutes after the ambulance. Two paramedics—not the ones who had been on scene for Aunt Agatha or Ms. Ellicott—jumped out of the rig and raced through the front door with medical bags slung over their shoulders.

“I need you to stay out of the way,” Chris said and shoulder-checked his door open.

“Yeah, okay,” she replied and followed suit.

She could stay out of the way and still see what was going on. She flashed to all kinds of horrible scenarios in the thirty seconds it took them to get inside. She imagined Mrs. Grant lying on the ground stabbed to death like Ms. Ellicott. The reality was worse. The camera feed to the interview room was still active. A man who looked to be in his forties sat on the floor cradling Mrs. Grant's head in his lap. The paramedics ordered him to stay out of the way as they checked for a pulse and an airway.

"Just like Aunt Agatha," Kalina whispered just loud enough for Chris to hear.

"You don't know that."

"Chris, the water. You have to tell them it was arsenic."

"How do you know about that?"

"I saw the report on your desk. Look, yell at me later. She's going to die!"

Chris waved a hand at her to shut her up and took three long strides to the open doorway to the interview room. "She may have been poisoned with arsenic."

One of the paramedics nodded and started to do chest compressions. His partner held Mrs. Grant's limp wrist lightly between his fingers. "I've got a pulse. We need to move."

Kalina and Chris backed out of the way as the medics loaded Mrs. Grant onto a gurney and raced with her out the front doors of the building. Sirens wailed as the ambulance took off. Kalina had no idea if time was on Mrs. Grant's side or not. She hoped they wouldn't have to bury three people at the end of this. The man who had been in the interview room—she assumed he was Mrs. Grant's attorney—dragged himself to a standing position and looked around dumbfounded. Chris closed the distance and leaned in close.

"What did you see? What happened?"

"I don't know. I got a call that Margaret needed an attorney. I was with my son and daughter. I had to find someone to watch them. I came as soon as I could. When I got here she was slumped over in the chair. So I called 9-1-1."

Chris ran a hand through his hair and let out a frustrated breath. "You didn't see who brought her the water?"

"No. I'm sorry. I should go to the hospital."

Chris dismissed him with a wave of his hand and the lawyer moved with brisk steps until he disappeared from view. Kalina studied the empty station in shock. What were they supposed to do now? They knew that they needed to find Captain Cahill but where to look? A single 'beep' punctured the silence between them. Chris glanced at his phone and tapped the screen a couple times.

"Damn it!"

"What is it?"

"DNA came back. There were minute traces of blood on the letter opener that didn't belong to Cynthia. You were right. It belongs to Captain Cahill. And the only prints on the teacup belonged to Agatha and the captain."

"Chris, I'm so sorry." She wasn't sure why she said it but it felt like the right thing to say.

His facial features hardened into a mask of determination. "You don't have anything to be sorry for. If it weren't for you pushing me, I'd be slapping cuffs on the wrong person."

Before she could respond, one of the fresh-faced officers wandered in. “Sir, what’s going on?” His voice shook with nerves.

Kalina stepped out of Chris’s orbit. The officer was in for an interrogation of his own. Chris launched himself at the kid and grabbed the front of the officer’s uniform in his fists. “Who gave Mrs. Grant that bottle of water?”

“I ... don’t know what you’re talking about.”

Chris dragged the officer into the interview room and shoved the man’s face to within a few inches of the bottle. “This one. Who gave it to her?”

“I did. She said she was thirsty.”

“Where did you get it?”

“The fridge. What’s going on? Where’s the witness?”

“You poisoned her,” Kalina said in a soft tone.

The officer blanched. “What? No I didn’t. I just ... gave her water.”

“She’s on her way to the hospital. She didn’t look good when he left here,” Chris said, his tone sharp.

"Chris, I don't think he had anything to do with this. We should be focusing on finding the captain." She walked into the room and placed a hand on Chris's bicep, trying to exude calm.

Chris's entire body tensed under her touch. Slowly, second by second, he relaxed and released his grip on the officer. The officer leaned against the table, clearly afraid of another outburst. Without realizing it or intending to, Kalina slid her hand down Chris's arm and took him by the hand, leading him back into the open space of the station.

"We have to find him," Chris said.

"I know. Can you ... I don't know, track his phone or something?"

"You're brilliant." Chris pulled her into a one-armed hug and planted a kiss on her cheek as he dialed a number on his phone. "This is Detective Chris Harper out of Ellesworth PD. I need a trace on a phone."

Kalina didn't hear him rattle off the captain's number. She was too focused on the kiss. Maybe there was something left between them. Two minutes later, Chris ended the call and rounded on the officer who had slowly inched his way out of the interview room. "You need to get your partner and follow me. No lights or sirens. We are going in quiet."

"Where are we going?" Kalina asked.

His phone beeped twice at him and he opened a map app. A tiny red dot blinked from the middle of the screen. "The cemetery. Let's go."

Chapter 14

Kalina sat in the passenger seat of Chris's car in silence. She stared ahead at the road in front of them, leading to the cemetery and the church. They could have walked it from the station but Chris insisted on driving. Maybe he needed to feel in control of the situation. She didn't argue. She was just grateful he was letting her come along. It had to be violating who knew how many rules to have a civilian involved in an arrest like this. She was also surprised that Chris only had the two new officers for back up. He pulled the car into a spot near the front gate and cut the engine. The car clicked and rattled as the engine block cooled. He turned to her but she held up a hand to silence him.

“I know. Stay out of the way. I got it. I’m not stupid or a hero. This is your show.”

“Thank you. I mean it.”

“Thank me when this is all over.”

He quirked a half-smile at her before easing the driver side door open and shutting it as quietly as possible. The two uniformed officers climbed out of the cruiser beside them. Chris removed his gun from its hip holster and the other officers followed suit. Chris consulted his phone before stepping through the open gate.

“The grave is near the back fence on the far right,” Kalina offered in a whisper.

Chris pointed at each officer and then to the left and the right of the cemetery. They were going to surround Captain Cahill. He might try to jump the fence but it was wrought iron and spiked at the top. There wasn’t much chance he would make it over before Chris or the other officers got to him. Chris let them go first before he started forward, gun gripped in his right hand but down by his thigh. Kalina stayed behind him a few paces, just as she'd promised.

The cemetery felt strange as they moved through it. It hadn't held any special meaning for Kalina before, but now—even with all the other people around—she felt the quiet awe and respect for the dead one should have upon entering this place. And she could swear she felt a touch of sadness for Sam Gordon's fate. She thought she might feel a little sliver of empathy for Captain Cahill but she didn't. He may have been acting out of a place of love for his father but his actions were inexcusable.

They reached the back fence and found the captain kneeling in front of his father's grave, rearranging the bouquet of flowers. The uniformed officers hung back just out of sight, weapons at their sides. Chris motioned for Kalina to stay where she was as he took a few steps closer to the headstone. He still held his gun against his thigh. He made sure to step on some loose twigs.

"Captain," he called.

Captain Cahill turned to face them. He didn't look surprised. Had he really expected they would catch him? He stayed crouched down but pulled his hands away from the flowers. He held them out, fingers splayed in a gesture that Kalina assumed meant he was unarmed.

"Sir, I'm going to need you to pull the weapon out of your ankle holster and toss it to me," Chris instructed.

With slow movements, Captain Cahill complied. Chris bent down, scooped up the gun and tucked it into his waistband. Dead air filled the space between the two cops; neither seemed to know what to say. Kalina longed to speak, to say she understood why Cahill felt betrayed, but that wasn't her job. She was here to be a silent observer.

"We found your prints on the teacup and your blood on the weapon that killed Cynthia Ellicott."

Captain Cahill sighed and rotated to face Chris head on. "I didn't realize the thing had cut me until later."

"And the teacup? Seems pretty sloppy."

The captain shrugged. “Someone would have noticed if I was wearing gloves.”

“That’s why you went back and touched the cup after Aunt Agatha died.” Kalina couldn’t help herself.

Both Chris and the captain looked at her. “I saw it in a picture on Facebook.”

“I guess I should have been more careful.”

“You had to know you wouldn’t get away with it,” Chris said.

“I nearly did. You had Margaret Grant in for questioning. If you hadn’t noticed that damn little speck of blood you would have charged her with at least one murder. Probably both.”

“Would it have been worth it?”

Captain Cahill let out a bitter bark of laughter. “They killed my father. They lied and put him in jail. He couldn’t handle it in there and so he took the easy way out.” His eyes shone with unshed tears. “My mother thought by moving away we could escape the shame but it never left me. Oh, I wasn’t ashamed of my father. I knew he hadn’t hurt that girl. But the injustice stuck with me.”

Chris loosened his grip on his gun. “So you came back as a cop, hoping people wouldn’t remember you.”

“I left here as a child. People change a lot in thirty years. I made sure when my predecessor retired, I was in the right place at the right time to assume his position. I knew people wouldn’t think I could be behind it.”

“The car accident with Alan Grant. That was you too,” Kalina said. She just couldn’t keep her mouth shut.

“Clever aren’t you? Yes, that was me too. He had my father’s case forced on him. And can you believe he went on to marry one of the witnesses who put my father away? They had to pay for their crime.”

“What about Adam Jenkins?” Chris posed.

Cahill shook his head. “That was a lucky coincidence.”

Chris holstered his gun and pulled a pair of handcuffs from his belt. “I need you stand up.”

Captain Cahill again complied without argument. He got to his feet and turned around, hands behind his back. The officers who had been on the periphery approached, weapons aimed at the ground. Chris snapped the cuffs in place. "Daniel Cahill, you are under arrest for the murders of Alan Grant, Cynthia Ellicott and Agatha Davies and the attempted murder of Margaret Grant. You have the right to remain silent. Anything you say can and will be used against you in a court of law. You have a right to an attorney to be present during questioning. If you cannot afford an attorney, one will be provided for you. Do you understand these rights as I have read them to you?"

"Yes. I am waiving my right to counsel and I would like to give a written confession."

Kalina hadn't been expecting that response. If it shocked Chris, he didn't show it. He just led Captain Cahill through the maze of headstones and back to the car. He situated the man in the back seat before turning to address Kalina. "Thank you again. We can take it from here."

"Sure. I'm just glad I could help."

She watched both cars pull out of the parking lot and head down Main Street toward the station. She wasn't sure what to do so just started walking. With the killer caught, there wasn't much left to do but wait for the trial, if there even was one. If Captain Cahill was refusing a lawyer and willing to sign a confession, something told her a trial might not be in the cards.

Chapter 15

Monday morning came as a shock to the system for Kalina. She hadn't heard anything else from Chris but she wasn't expecting to. At ten minutes to nine, she flipped the front door sign to "OPEN" and settled behind the counter, ready for an influx of teenagers and older patrons. After all, she had a host of new arrivals waiting to be distributed. She'd given AJ the day off from helping out, given everything he had gone through. He seemed grateful to just be a kid for a little while. He had plenty of time to grow up. The stillness of the shop wrapped itself around her, seeping into her thoughts, and calmed her.

The bell sounded above the front door and jarred her out of her trance. Chris stood in the doorway, framed by morning light. He was dressed in jeans and a t-shirt. He looked exhausted. Kalina stood up and approached him.

“Hi.”

“Uh, hey. I hope this isn’t a bad time.”

She made a show of looking around the shop. “Perfect time. How are you?”

“Honestly, I’m still trying to process everything. Dan, he wrote out a confession yesterday. He’s meeting with the prosecutor to discuss a plea. Avoid trial. He’s going to do time and a lot of it.”

“I know you looked up to him.”

“I thought he was a good guy. Good police officer. I guess I never realized just how much darkness he was carrying around with him. I can’t imagine going through what he went through. And it kills me that I even feel sorry for him.”

“Vigilante justice isn’t right but sometimes the system is broken and making things right gets messy." She motioned to the stacks of comics. "Isn't that what most of these are about?"

"I guess you're right."

"Has there been any word on Mrs. Grant?"

"It sounds like they got her stabilized. She's going to make it but they said she's probably going to have some nerve damage from the arsenic."

"How awful."

"I was going to head over and let her know that we caught Dan. Would you like to come with me?"

"Are you sure that's appropriate?"

"If it wasn't for you, Kal, she'd probably be dead and the case would still be open. I couldn't have done this without you."

"If you can wait a few hours I'll close up for lunch and we can go over."

"Yeah, of course. I don't know why I expected you to just drop everything. You have a business to run."

"I'll see you over at the hospital at noon, okay?"

He didn't say anything, just pulled her into a tight hug. She held on tight too. She hadn't been imagining the way they were falling back into each other's orbits. Maybe there was something there to rekindle.

She let that thought buoy her through the morning. By noon she was ready to get out of the shop. She hung up the lunch sign and locked the front door. Chris waited for her just outside the shop. The hospital was at the other end of town from the waterfront. It afforded easier access in case of accidents on the highway. They checked in at the front desk and were escorted to the ICU. Mrs. Grant lay in bed, her skin ashen and her eyes half-closed. But she was most definitely alive.

"Mrs. Grant? It's Kalina. I wanted to see how you were doing," Kalina said and took a seat at the woman's bedside.

Mrs. Grant roused herself and turned to face her. "You told him, didn't you?"

"I had to. But we know you didn't do anything to Cynthia or Agatha. We caught the person responsible. He's going to jail for a very long time."

"Who?" She coughed. "Who was it?"

"Daniel Cahill. He was Samuel Gordon's son."

Silent tears streamed down Mrs. Grant's sunken cheeks. "I should have known." She looked directly at Chris. "We were going to come forward and admit what we did. We talked about it. I'm sorry I wasn't truthful with you before."

"Do you know who really killed Alice Beech?"

Mrs. Grant's eyes suddenly shown with tears. "Yes. There was a car speeding away that night and we did see his face. But it wasn't Samuel Gordon. It was the Police Captain's son, Andrew Paxton. The officers on the scene knew it , too, but I guess Sam had been pulled over for speeding that night and they just decided to make him the scapegoat. I'm assuming it was Captain Paxton's orders. Alan was good friends with him and agreed to take the case to keep Andrew out of jail." Tears trickled down her pale cheeks.

"Why did you lie?" Chris asked from the foot of the bed.

"The captain threatened us. At first, anyway. Then he tried to bribe us. In the end Alan convinced me that we were well liked enough in town to be believable. It was the biggest regret of my life."

"Did you marry him to keep the secret?"

"He'd already proposed. After a while it just sort of faded into the past."

Chris just nodded. "Good luck with your recovery, Mrs. Grant."

The admission about coming forward seemed to tire Mrs. Grant out and Kalina and Chris soon left her to rest. As they wound their way back to the front of the hospital, neither of them spoke.

"Are you going to charge her with perjury?"

"I think she's been through enough hell. She's going to be living with a permanent reminder of what she did and what it cost her. That's enough."

"That's really kind of you."

"I wouldn't call it that. But I don't see the point in putting an old woman behind bars at this point." He pulled out his phone. "I am going to have Andrew Paxton and his father arrested. Alice Beech is going to get the justice she deserved."

"I'm glad Sam's death won't have been for nothing." She checked her phone. "Hey, I'm still on lunch for another half hour. You want to come back and finish that game of Zombie Dice?"

"You're on."

They lazily made their way back to the shop, sequestered themselves in the back room with lunch and started the game over. Kalina even let him go first. As the dice clattered around the table in a bid to escape, a sense of normalcy settled over the shop and its two inhabitants. While darkness and death had touched the town, it would soon be pushed to the back of the townspeople's collective memory. Ellesworth would resume being a nice, waterfront, Massachusetts town. There was little chance Kalina would get wrapped up in another case of wrongful convictions and vigilante justice. She was just a comic book shop owner, after all.

Forgive and Forget

Geeks and Things Book 2

A GEEKS AND THINGS COZY MYSTERY

Forgive and Forget

S.E. BIGLOW

FORGIVE AND FORGET (A GEEKS AND THINGS MYSTERY)

If you enjoy this work, please consider leaving a review.

For information contact; www.sarah-biglow.com

Edited by Ken Marrow, M.A.

Cover Design by: Deranged Doctor Design

Published by Sarah Biglow: April 2016

10 9 8 7 6 5 4 3 2 1

 Created with Vellum

Chapter 1

An unusually oppressive early morning summer heat shimmered on the pavement as Kalina Greystone took off at a steady jog from the front of her shop, Geeks and Things. She had barely taken enough steps to get to the next block on Main Street when her phone beeped at her, displaying the temperature: 81 degrees. At seven in the morning.

"Wonderful," she groaned before settling on a playlist and picking up the pace. Heat or no heat, she needed to get her run in before she had to open up for the day.

The end of summer was a big money maker for the shop, especially with kids getting ready for school. There was little doubt in her mind that most of the teenagers in town would be turning in summer reading lists crammed with comics and graphic novels. She only felt a little guilty that the next generation wasn't reading actual books.

The notion that this was *her* shop, *her* livelihood, had finally settled in. People in town had stopped comparing the way she ran the business to her father—at least to her face—and it made the decision to come back home to Ellesworth feel like the right call. The little seaside town moved at a slower pace to the city, where she'd spent most of her adult life, but it had some perks, too. She'd managed to reconnect and rekindle a spark with her high school sweetheart, Christian Harper.

Kalina took a sharp left and sucked in a deep breath as she took the hill leading in the direction of the cemetery and the town's one church. As her heart pounded in her ears from the exertion, she flashed back to three months ago when she and Chris had stood in the cemetery and solved a pair of murders. The frenzy surrounding Aunt Agatha and Ms. Ellicott's passing had finally died down and the town was back to being quaint and normal. Kalina's phone buzzed in her pocket and she pulled it out to see a text from Chris asking her if they were still on for dinner. She smiled and slowed to a walk before responding that they were definitely on for dinner. They were lucky that their first break-up had been amicable. They were on different life tracks and they had been mature enough to get that. When he held her hand or kissed her goodnight she still felt like a giddy schoolgirl. Of course, she'd dated in college and grad school but being with Chris now was different. They were finally in a place where they could be together as adults and make it work.

Phone stowed back in her pocket, Kalina took off at a sprint to make it up and over the hill and settle back into a comfortable pace. As she ran she spotted Theo Maxwell in his boxers and undershirt scooping up the morning paper. He blushed bright red and waved before darting back inside. She chuckled to herself and took the next right, heading past the church. The door eased open and a lone figure stepped out looking subdued and tired. Leslie Mayfair, the former almost-Mrs. Cahill. A pang of sadness tightened Kalina's chest as she watched the usually bubbly school teacher hunch her shoulders on her way to her car. She hadn't known her fiancé had been killing little old ladies for sending his innocent father to prison. They made eye contact for a brief, uncomfortable moment and Kalina opened her mouth to say 'Good morning' but held her tongue. Leslie yanked her car door open and climbed into the driver seat.

Kalina waited until the car was out of sight before continuing her morning circuit. Sweat glistened on her bare arms and matted her short, auburn curls to her forehead as she veered away from the church and out towards the coast. Only a handful of people lived out by the water these days thanks to beach erosion. The salty air was a few degrees cooler and she sucked in a big gulp. Trying to shake the unease from seeing Leslie, Kalina put on another burst of speed and took the rolling slope of Ocean Front Lane at a decent clip. Her phone vibrated again and, in her earbuds, an automated voice announced that AJ was calling.

"Answer call," she said and slowed to a walk. "Hey, AJ, what are you doing up this early?"

"Hey, Aunt K. I was just checking in. I wanted to see if you needed help at the store today," her nephew answered.

He had done a lot of 'checking in' in the last couple months. Not that she minded. It put her mind at ease that he was doing okay after watching Aunt Agatha die. "If you want to stop by this afternoon you can. I don't know that I'll have too much for you to do, though."

"Great. Are you okay?"

Kalina continued along Ocean Front at a slow pace, getting her heart rate back down to normal. "Yeah, I'm just out for a run."

"Oh. You've been doing that a lot since..."

He didn't have to finish the thought for her know what he meant. "We all cope in different ways. And I could use the exercise."

Kalina rounded a bend in the street and a three-story house came into view. It belonged to the Larrabees. She'd been friends with their daughter, Nadine, in high school. Normally it wouldn't have drawn her attention in the cookie-cutter section of town. Today, she stopped and stood with her mouth hanging open. A man's body lay prone in the middle of the house's small driveway and a woman about Kalina's age sat on the front steps, rocking back and forth.

"Aunt K., are you there?" AJ's voice sounded tinny in her earbuds.

"I have to call you back," she said and yanked the buds from her ears. She moved into view slowly so as not to startle the woman. "Nadine?"

The woman looked up and Kalina saw her eyes shine with fresh tears. At this distance she could see Nadine's hands covered in what Kalina assumed was blood. A dark stain had spread under the man's head on the asphalt. "Oh, God. What did I do?" Nadine whimpered.

Kalina pulled the cord out of the headphone jack of her phone and dialed 911. She waited for the operator to give the standard response before speaking. "I need an ambulance at 1609 Ocean Front Lane. Send the police, too. A man is dead."

Chapter 2

Ignoring the operator's order to stay on the line, Kalina shoved her phone in her back pocket and slowly approached Nadine, hands held out in front of her in a placating gesture. Nadine continued to rock back and forth, her gaze glued to the dead man in the driveway. Kalina moved to the left to block the view in the hopes it would snap her old friend out of her trance. Nadine finally blinked and a tear trickled down her nose and landed precariously on her upper lip. Careful not to interfere with what might be considered the crime scene, Kalina bent down in front of her friend and placed a hand on the woman's shoulder.

"Nadine. It's Kalina Greystone. I've called the police." Her tone was barely above a whisper.

Nadine blinked again and her shoulders relaxed the slightest bit at Kalina's words. It had been a good fifteen years since they'd really seen each other and Nadine looked like she'd been through some tough times—the dead body notwithstanding. The last time they'd seen each other—a week before they both headed off to college—Nadine had been all wild curls and caramel complexion. Now her hair hung limply around her face in a tangled, stringy mess and her cheeks were sunken.

"Kal? What ... what are you doing here?" Nadine asked in a scratchy voice.

"I was on a run and I found you." Kalina glanced over her shoulder as sirens wailed in the distance. Emergency personnel would arrive soon and she would be shunned aside so Nadine could be questioned officially. She would make good use of the limited time she had left. "Nadine, honey, what happened?"

"I... I don't know." She scrubbed at her face, smearing blood from her fingertips onto her cheeks. "I think ... maybe I did it. I can't remember." She erupted into a fresh onslaught of tears. "I'm not crazy. I swear I'm not."

Kalina made soft, shushing noises and patted her friend's shoulder. "It's okay. Everything will be fine. Just try to calm down."

The siren wails grew more insistent and Kalina did her best to comfort Nadine while getting a look at the dead man on the pavement. It had been a while but it looked like Nadine's father. She couldn't be sure, though, and she wasn't about to go rifle through a dead man's pockets to be sure. That wasn't her job.

"Damn," she groaned. She'd promised herself she wouldn't get dragged into something like this again. But Nadine had been a good friend and she needed Kalina.

Tires squealed and a familiar car pulled up to the curb. An ambulance rolled up and two paramedics jumped out of the rig. Kalina stood up and turned just as Chris let out an exasperated sigh. "Hi," she said.

"I should have known."

Kalina arched a brow and closed the gap

between them. "What's that supposed to mean?"

"When people die from mysterious causes you seem to always be around."

"That was one time. And I wasn't the only person there."

He nodded and peered over her shoulder at Nadine. "Want to tell me what you're doing here with a woman covered in blood and a dead man in the driveway?"

"I was out for a run before opening up and I saw Nadine sitting there and the body. I called you guys as soon as I saw it. I didn't touch anything."

Chris pointed to the front door, which sat wide open. "That was like that when you got here?"

"Yes. And Nadine hasn't moved."

One of the paramedics tended to Nadine, checking her over for any injuries, while the other checked Mr. Larrabee. "He's been dead maybe a few hours. We'll have to get him to the morgue for a better time of death."

"Don't move. We aren't done," Chris said and turned his back, pulling his phone from his shirt pocket. He dialed and then said, "This is Detective Christian Harper, Ellesworth PD. We are going to need an ME assist and a second ambulance." He ended the call and hit what Kalina assumed was a saved number. "Jimmy, it's Chris. I need you to get to my current location to secure the scene."

Suddenly chilled, Kalina wrapped her arms around her torso and watched the paramedic help Nadine to her feet. Without the distraction of Nadine sobbing on the front steps, Kalina studied the rest of the scene. How had Mr. Larrabee ended up on the driveway? She noted an open window on the second floor. Was the fall enough to kill him? Chris hung up and pivoted back to face her. "Did Nadine say anything to you?"

Kalina shivered again. "She was pretty incoherent. I think she was mostly in shock. I mean her father's dead right in front of her."

"Detective," the medic who had been tending to Nadine called, "she doesn't have any visible signs of injury. I'd guess the blood is his."

Kalina watched as they shared a look. She didn't need to be law enforcement to interpret the slight downturn of his mouth or the way his shoulders tensed. She may not have mentioned that Nadine claimed to be guilty, but he would find out sooner or later.

"I'd like to go to the hospital with you. She might feel more comfortable opening up if I'm there," Kalina blurted.

"Fine. But you are there for moral support. Nothing else. And you're riding with me," Chris said.

"Okay."

They waited until Jimmy and the second ambulance arrived. The paramedic who climbed out of the back sported a digital camera. Apparently, they weren't waiting for the crime scene technicians from Salem to show up to take Mr. Larrabee's body for autopsy. They headed off to the hospital as the paramedic snapped a few shots and his partner laid a sheet over the corpse. Kalina buckled into the passenger seat and looked at Chris. "I guess we won't be doing dinner tonight, after all."

Chapter 3

The car ride was silent as Kalina and Chris made the short journey to the hospital. Chris had the air blasting and, despite the heat outside, her arms broke in goose bumps. She tried to read his expression in the rearview mirror but he wouldn't meet her gaze.

"Chris, don't be mad at me. I swear I didn't mean to stumble on a dead man on my morning run. And I promise I'll stay out of the way."

He didn't respond at first. His hands tightened around the steering wheel and his knuckles turned pale. "I'm not mad at you, Kal. I just... After what happened with Dan Cahill I thought... I thought things would go back to normal. We don't have people getting murdered in this town."

She reached over and pressed her hand reassuringly against his shoulder. "I know."

Chris had taken Captain Cahill's vendetta harder than most. She couldn't really blame him. His mentor had fallen hard from grace. It was a tiny consolation that Chris had managed to broker a plea deal for the real culprits behind Alice Beech's murder and Samuel Gordon's false conviction. Andrew Paxton and his father would be spending the next decade behind bars. Before either of them could say anything more, her phone buzzed and the store's number flashed on the screen.

"Sorry, I need to take this," she said and hit 'Accept'. "Hello, this is Kalina, how can I help you?"

"Aunt K., it's me," AJ said on the other end of the line. "I came by the shop but you aren't here. And you hung up earlier."

Kalina bit the inside of her lip. She'd forgotten she'd given him a key in case of emergencies. She should have expected his end-of-summer restlessness to result in an earlier-than-promised visit. “I know. Something came up. I’m not sure when I’ll be back to the shop.”

“I can handle things if you want.”

“That’s sweet, but no. You aren’t old enough and you don’t actually work at the shop. Just close up and lock the front door for now, okay? People can deal with waiting for their comics a little longer today.”

“Okay. Oh, there’s some sort of delivery scheduled for this afternoon. I checked the calendar. What should I do about that?”

Kalina opened her Calendar app and saw she was expecting a delivery of new Valiant Comics. “Damn. I’ll handle it.”

“What’s going on? You sounded kind of freaked out earlier.”

The hospital loomed ahead of them. “I’ll fill you in later. I have to go.”

Chris eased into the parking lot and pulled into a spot near the doors to the emergency room without another word. Kalina shoved her phone back into her pocket and climbed out of the passenger seat. She didn’t see the ambulance that had transported Nadine but she assumed it had beaten them there. Chris turned to look at her and his expression softened for a moment.

“I’ll make dinner up to you,” he said and kissed her cheek.

“Don’t even worry about it. Just focus on your job. We have plenty of time for dinner dates.”

She resisted the urge to take his hand as they walked into the hospital side by side. True to her word, she stayed quiet as he asked the young man at the registration desk where to find Nadine. Chris finally ushered Kalina out of the waiting room and back to a small, curtained-off area. Nadine lay on a bed with an IV already hooked up at the crook of her elbow. She looked less frantic, her eyelids drooping heavily. The paramedics had at least tried to clean the blood off her hands.

“Miss Larrabee, I’m Detective Harper. I’m with the police. Do you remember meeting me at your house?”

Nadine nodded her head but didn’t speak. Kalina moved to sit beside her old friend and pressed her hand gently against Nadine’s blanket-covered knee. Just enough to let the woman know she wasn't alone.

"Do you mind if I ask you a few questions about what happened?"

Nadine's gaze flickered in Kalina's direction and tears glistened. Kalina gave the woman a smile. "I'll be right here. Detective Harper just wants to help."

Nadine wet her lips and sat up a little straighter. "Okay." Her voice cracked on the last syllable.

Chris retrieved a small pad and pen from his pocket and sat on a stool on the other side of the bed. Kalina felt Nadine tense up beneath the blanket. She had to fight to keep from interfering. She knew Chris was only doing his job by questioning Nadine.

"Can you tell me what happened to your father?"

"I... I found him on the driveway this morning."

"So the blood on your hands was from checking on him?"

"Y-yes."

"Can you think of anyone who might have wanted to hurt your father?"

"No. I hadn't been in his life until recently. We had a falling out after my mother..."

Kalina bit her tongue—wincing at the pain—to keep from interjecting to ask about Mrs. Larrabee. Fresh tears rolled down Nadine's cheeks as Chris simply nodded in understanding.

"So you didn't hear anything at all last night?"

"I don't remember... It's all kind of a blur. Please, I'm tired. I'd like to rest now."

On cue, a nurse clad in pale purple scrubs appeared, chart and a plastic container of pills in hand. "I'm afraid you're going to have to come back later if you have more questions. The doctor has ordered that Ms. Larrabee be sedated."

Nadine's eyes grew to the size of quarters and she tried to wiggle away from the nurse as she approached. "No. I don't want them. Get away from me!"

Chris had already moved to get out of the way of the medical staff and he grabbed Kalina by the wrist, pulling her free as more staff in scrubs flooded the tiny area. They held Nadine down until someone got the medication into her. Kalina's pulse quickened as she watched how the girl she'd known for years was manhandled into submission. There were missing puzzle pieces in all of this and she was going to find out exactly what had happened.

Chapter 4

With Nadine safely unconscious—at least for now—Kalina and Chris headed back to the parking lot. The day continued to heat up and Kalina wiped the sweat from her neck before slipping back into the passenger seat.

“Can you drop me at the shop?” she asked.

“Yeah, sure. I need to head back to the scene to make sure it’s being processed.”

“You don’t trust Jimmy?”

Chris shrugged. “He’s still pretty green and I think it would make him feel better if I was there.”

The engine hummed to life and silence fell between them. Kalina wanted to ask Chris what he knew about Nadine's past and her mother but she kept quiet. He would no doubt tell her to stay out of it and that this was a police matter. She still refused to believe that Nadine was capable of harming anyone, let alone her father. Chris took a sharp left onto Main Street and pulled up in front of Geeks and Things, the car still idling.

"I'll call you if I can get away later." He kissed her cheek again.

She returned the gesture, holding it a little longer than necessary. "Bye."

Kalina shivered in the heat and watched Chris pull away and disappear down the street. She fished her keys from her pocket and jammed them into the lock on the shop's front door. The sign read 'Closed' so at least AJ had done as she'd asked. She could do a little archive browsing from the comfort of the shop and be there for the new shipment before trying to find out what she could about the crime scene. She flipped the light switch by the front door and waited for the energy-efficient bulbs to brighten the storefront. Turning the sign to

'Open', Kalina headed for the small bathroom and a waiting change of clothes. She would have loved a shower but there was too much to do.

Slicking her damp hair back into a tiny, messy bun, she took up residence behind the front counter and sent AJ a text letting him know the shop was back open. Almost immediately, her phone flashed with a request to FaceTime. She tapped the 'Accept' button and waited for AJ's face to fill the screen.

"Hi, Aunt K.," he said.

"Hey. Is there something specific we need to talk about?"

"Not really. I just wanted to check in."

"Things are fine here. I should be around for the next few hours anyway."

"I mean about whatever happened this morning."

Kalina massaged the bridge of her nose. She loved her nephew and his sense of curiosity but she didn't want him to go running off with wild theories about what happened, especially when she wasn't even sure anyone else in town knew

Mr. Larrabee was dead. “I know I said I’d fill you in but there aren’t enough pieces for me to make sense of it right now. When I know more for certain, I’ll tell you.”

“It happened again, didn’t it? Someone’s dead and there’s something weird about it.” AJ’s face lit up as he spoke. She thought she saw a hint of fear beneath the curious expression.

“I need you to keep this to yourself. The police are still investigating and we don’t need to panic people if there’s no reason. I’m sure everything will turn out fine.”

AJ bit his lip and looked away from the camera. “If you say so.”

“Look, you can still come by later if you want but I need to take care of things around here, okay?”

“Yeah. Okay.”

The screen went dark and the connection died. Kalina set the phone down on the counter and massaged the cramp out of her hand from holding the phone steady. She hated that she couldn’t give her nephew more reassurance that everything would be fine but that couldn't be helped right now. Blowing out a breath, she booted up the tablet and connected to the internet. Her first stop, logically, was Facebook. She scanned through her list of friends but Nadine didn't come up. Either she didn't have an account—unlikely even for their generation—or Kalina had never gotten around to adding her as a friend. Even if she could find a friend in common, there was only so much information she could glean from the other woman's profile and what she was searching for wasn't likely to be available to casual viewers.

Closing down the app on her tablet, she brought up a browser window and logged into the library website, quickly navigating to the periodicals and the newspaper archives. If something happened right after high school, it would have made the paper. Ellesworth was small enough that most big events—good or bad—made the front page. Unlike the last time she'd needed to do a newspaper search, the editions she needed were all digital. Biting her lip in concentration, she selected '2000-2001' editions and typed 'Larrabee' into the keyword search.

A front page article from July 2000 appeared at the top on the results page.

Local Family Rocked by Tragedy

By: Angeline Reagan, Contributing Writer

Independence Day is meant to be a celebration of our country's birth as a democracy, but for one local family, the holiday will forever be remembered as a day of loss. Coming home from a late night celebration, Edwin and Michelle Larrabee were involved in a collision that left Edwin with several lacerations and a broken arm. Unfortunately, his wife is reported to have suffered severe head trauma and is presently in the intensive care unit at Ellesworth Hospital.

The couple's nineteen-year-old daughter, Nadine, was reportedly asleep in the backseat and suffered only minor cuts and bruises. Officers on scene refused to release any information about whether Mr. Larrabee was intoxicated, however eyewitness reports note that he swerved to avoid an

> oncoming truck, which was driving in the wrong lane.

Kalina set her tablet down on the counter and sighed. How could she have missed something so huge? Her parents would have told her the news, right? She tried to remember if they'd let her know that Nadine's mom had been in a serious accident but she came up blank. She hit the back button and found a second reference in the last edition for July. Her chest tightened and she fought back tears as she picked up the tablet again.

> **Obituaries**
>
> *Michelle (Marcus) Larrabee*
>
> Michelle Larrabee of Ellesworth, Massachusetts passed away on July 28, 2000 from complications after a car accident left her in a critical condition. Michelle is survived by her husband, Edwin, and their nineteen-year-old daughter, Nadine.
>
> Michelle was an active member in the town's annual Solstice Fair committee and served on several church boards.

> She had a passion for poetry and spearheaded open mic nights at the local high school. Services celebrating Michelle's life will be held at the local church on July 31, 2000.

"Oh, Nadine. I'm so sorry," Kalina whispered to the empty store.

She felt like the worst friend in the world. She'd gone off to Boston to pursue her dreams in the big city and left her best friend behind. Nadine must have felt so alone losing her mother like that. Did she blame her father even if it wasn't his fault? Could there actually be some motive Kalina hadn't considered before?

No matter how much she didn't want to admit that the girl she'd once known was capable of such a horrific act, she had to admit she didn't really know the woman she'd found sitting on the front steps. She chewed on her lower lip, debating what to do next. There was probably very little chance that Chris had already obtained useful information but that didn't mean she couldn't snoop around a little later on.

The bell above the front door rang, signaling a customer, and Kalina quickly dried her eyes and closed down the browser. The tall, burly form of Andrew Chambers loomed on the other side of the counter. He slammed down a handful of comics.

“Good morning, Mr. Chambers.” She fixed him with a smile. “Can I help you with something?”

“You can stop selling this crap to my kid.”

Kalina glanced down at the pile of Daredevil comics and back to Mr. Chambers. “I’m sorry you don’t approve of your son’s reading habits but parenting him isn’t my job.”

“He’s supposed to be reading books. Not this ... stuff.”

Kalina cleared her throat and leaned forward on her elbows. “Maybe you should be happy he’s reading anything at all rather than spending his time stuck online. You may not think he’s learning but he is. And if what he’s buying makes you uncomfortable, talk to him. But as long as he’s not buying issues that are too highly rated for his age group, I’m going to keep selling them.”

She spun around on her stool and straightened the hem of her blouse. “If that’s all, I have some inventory I need to get to. Have a nice day.”

Mr. Chambers grabbed the comics and with a scowl he stalked out, slamming the front door behind him. Kalina shook her head and let out a slow breath. “Jerk.”

Chapter 5

Morning quickly turned to late afternoon and Kalina found herself organizing the game room for the third time in as many hours. Even on slow days she could usually occupy herself with more success. Out front the bell rang again and she straightened.

“It’s just me, Aunt K.,” AJ called.

She met him halfway between the front counter and the game room. “It’s pretty dead right now, kid. There’s not much for you to do.”

“Yeah, I know. I just wanted to ask you something. Before you say no, I’ve already cleared it with Mom.”

"Okay. What is it?"

"How would you feel about hiring me for like after school and weekends? Once I'm sixteen I mean. I could help with inventory or supervise the game room."

"I don't know, AJ."

"Please. This was always supposed to be a family business, right? And I've helped out before over the summer."

She nodded. "Yes." She raked her fingers through her hair. "I'll think about it."

AJ pulled her into a hug and she returned the gesture. "You're the best aunt ever."

She laughed a little. "Thanks. You know, we could test it out right now if you want. I don't expect anyone to come in but I have to run an errand."

"I do know how to operate a cash register. I promise I won't burn the place down."

"Okay. Fine. Text me if there are any problems." Kalina grabbed her keys from below the counter and headed for her car. She could easily walk to her destination but the heat was still too oppressive.

Twenty minutes later, she pulled into the parking lot at the police precinct, a bag of take-out Chinese in the passenger seat. She'd called the hospital while waiting for her order but the nurse on duty had said Nadine was still sedated. That worried her. Sure, Nadine had been upset at the scene but anyone would be. She tried to shake the feeling as she headed inside.

"Evening, Kal." Jimmy greeted her from his post at the front desk.

She stopped and rested the bag on the desk. "Hey. So you're back from the scene?"

The precinct was fairly deserted but he still leaned in close. "Yeah. Man I'm glad they covered the body before I got there. Just seeing what was left made me almost lose my breakfast. I never saw a dead body before." He paled and swallowed loudly. "I mean I know we're trained to deal with these things but it's different thinking about it and doing it, you know?"

Kalina nodded. “I bet. Did you find anything … interesting?”

He smiled. He was young—maybe 25—and eager to please. She felt only a tiny twinge of guilt at playing on his insecurity. “Well, I’m just writing up my report now.” He looked down at the screen in front of him. “Oh, yeah the weird thing was the way he landed.”

“Really?”

“I think the medical examiner is going to do a test to see if he was pushed.”

Interesting, indeed.

She scanned the rest of the bull pen and spotted Chris bent over a file. “Well, good luck with the report, Jimmy.” She made a show of picking up the take-out. “I’d better get this over to Detective Harper.”

Jimmy beamed back at her. “You have a good night.”

Kalina waved goodbye and crossed the bull pen to Chris’s desk. He rubbed at the nape of his neck as he studied a file in front of him. Plopping down in the empty chair across from him she cleared her throat. “Hey.”

He jumped a little at her greeting but he smiled back at her. “I didn’t know you were coming down.”

“I thought I’d surprise you. And—” Kalina opened the bag and pulled out a container of pork fried rice “—I wanted to make sure you didn’t forget to eat.”

Chris chuckled and closed the file. “Thanks. That’s really sweet of you. I’ll go see if I can find some plates.”

While he disappeared into the small kitchen, Kalina unpacked the rest of the containers and plastic utensils. Casting a furtive glance around the rest of the bull pen, she reached over and opened the file he’d been reading: Nadine’s medical history. She’d been institutionalized for six months about five years ago. First thing in the morning she was making a trip back to the hospital to have a chat with her old friend.

“Found them!” Chris called.

Kalina quickly replaced the file and took a steadying breath as he returned. She dished out some Kung Pao Chicken onto her plate along with a teriyaki beef strip and some rice.

Chris loaded his plate down and leaned back in his chair.

"So, how was the rest of your day?" he asked around a mouthful of food.

"Pretty slow. Andrew Chambers came by to try to chew me out about his son reading comics."

"I hope he wasn't rude."

"Oh, he was but I told him he should actually parent the kid and talk to him if he didn't like what his son was reading."

"Good for you."

"And I'm thinking of hiring AJ on to help out around the shop after school once he's sixteen. He seems really excited."

"I think he just likes hanging out with his cool aunt in nerd heaven."

"Probably." She briefly turned her attention back to the food on her plate. "Can I ask you something?"

"Sure."

"Nadine's mom... I had no idea she'd died."

"Yeah. From what I heard it was pretty rough. Her dad was pretty broken up about it after she passed."

"I can imagine. Did they ever figure out what happened? With the accident I mean."

Chris's brow furrowed. "I don't know what you mean."

"Well, I read an article that said it might have been another driver's fault. Or Mr. Larrabee might have been drunk."

"I'm not really sure."

"Don't you think it might be important?"

"Maybe. But, Kal, that's my job to figure out."

"I know... Sorry. I was just trying to help."

"Even if it means implicating a good friend in a murder?"

Kalina sniffled. "Yes."

The conversation fizzled out and Kalina was grateful. She wanted to just enjoy her boyfriend's company and pretend for a short while that everything was fine and the lives of the people around them weren't falling apart at the seams. She was so absorbed in the moment that she didn't hear the footsteps until Jimmy peered over Chris's shoulder at the leftovers.

"They always give you an extra fortune cookie," he said and snapped up a plastic-wrapped cookie without asking permission. "Oh, boss, here's my report from earlier."

Chris took the report and slid it on top of Nadine's medical history without looking at it. He turned to the officer and gave him an expectant look. Jimmy blissfully ignored him as he fussed with opening the plastic and cracking open the cookie.

"Hmm—" Jimmy studied the fortune "—that's not really a fortune. I mean everyone could have good luck this week, right?"

"Uh, Jimmy, you need to get back to the desk now," Chris said.

"Oh right. Sorry! You guys are on a date. I'm such an idiot I should have realized."

Kalina tried to give him an understanding smile but devolved into a fit of giggles as soon as he was out of earshot. “He’s like a lost puppy sometimes,” she said.

“I hate to admit it but you’re right. He means well, he’s just a little clueless sometimes.”

The tension over Nadine’s situation lifted for a moment and Kalina picked up one of the remaining fortune cookies. She popped the plastic and cracked the cookie. She studied the tiny slip of paper with mild amusement that quickly turned sour. ‘An old friend will come into your life in an unexpected way’.

“Get something good?” Chris leaned over to take the paper from her.

“Just hitting a little close to home. I’m sure it’s just a coincidence.” She cleared her throat. “I should get going. I’m sure you have lots to get done before the end of your shift, too.”

She gathered up the empty food containers and tossed them in the trash nearby. Before Chris could say anything she was halfway to the front door. She gave Jimmy a hasty wave before she braved the evening heat. Footsteps pounded on the pavement behind her and she slowed down.

“Kal, wait a minute,” Chris said and spun her around to face him. “It’s just a fortune cookie. It’s not meant to be serious.”

She let out a huff of annoyance. “I know that. It’s just been a long day. That’s all.”

He tucked a few strands of hair behind her ear and leaned in for a kiss. “Good night.”

Chapter 6

Kalina headed to the hospital just after eight the next morning. The shop remained closed with a sign indicating that the closure was due to inventory. It was an outright lie but she could handle a little lost business. Nadine was more important. As she waited to check in at the nurse's station she wondered why, after all these years, she felt so compelled to be there for Nadine. As she headed down the east wing to a private room, she realized she felt guilty. She needed to apologize for letting them drift so far apart during college. Sure, Nadine could have reached out, too, but given her current situation, Kalina was more than willing to heap the extra blame on herself.

Taking a left turn at the next junction, Kalina finally found Nadine's room. It was a single occupant room with a view of the distant shoreline. Nadine sat on the bed, staring out the window. She looked calmer than she'd been the day before and Kalina breathed a sigh of relief that her friend was awake and alert. She knocked on the doorframe and Nadine turned with a ghost of a smile on her lips.

"Can I come in?" Kalina asked, standing in the doorway.

"Sure." Her voice was stronger than it had been the day before, too.

Kalina crossed the room in two big strides and she settled in a chair under the flat-screen TV mounted to the wall. Nadine tugged at a few curls and kept her gaze on the floor. Awkward silence filled the room. Kalina wasn't sure what to say.

"How are you?"

Nadine shrugged one shoulder. "They are letting me leave today. I guess that's good."

"Yeah, definitely."

"I can't go home. Not after... I just keep seeing him on driveway."

Kalina reached out and took Nadine's hand in hers. "You can stay with me if you want. I have a free futon."

"You don't have to do that. This isn't your mess."

"You're my friend. At least I hope you still are and I want to help. And once the house isn't a crime scene anymore I can go pick up some clothes and stuff for you."

"You'd do that?"

"Of course."

Nadine squeezed Kalina's hand. "Thanks, Kal." She glanced over her shoulder towards the empty doorway. "The nurse said she'd be back with discharge papers but that was like twenty minutes ago."

"I'm sure you'll be out of here before you know it." Footsteps echoed down the hallway, growing louder. "See, I bet that's the nurse now."

Her shoulders fell a little bit when Chris appeared in the doorway. He raised an eyebrow at her but said nothing. Nadine pulled her knees up to her chest in a protective posture and didn't let go of Kalina's hand.

"How are you feeling, Miss Larrabee?" he asked.

"You can call me Nadine. We all know each other," Nadine said.

Chris cleared his throat. "All right, how are you doing, Nadine?"

"I'm okay. They're discharging me now."

"That's good to hear." He turned to Kalina. "I trust you're here just as a friend."

Kalina nodded. "Nothing more, I swear."

"I need to ask you some questions about your father's death, Nadine. I'd like you to come down to the station this afternoon."

"Do I need a lawyer or something?"

"That's up to you. But right now you are the only witness to what happened and we need to get your statement."

“I’ll make sure she gets there.” Kalina released Nadine’s hand and stood up. “Can I talk to you for a minute, Detective?”

He gestured towards the hallway and they stepped out of the room. “What’s wrong, Kal?”

“So she’s a *witness* now?”

“She’s always been a witness. She might be a suspect, too, but right now there’s nothing to support charging her.”

Kalina studied his face for any sign that he was bluffing but she couldn’t find any. Maybe he really didn’t have anything. But Jimmy seemed certain the forensic team had been to the house so they had to have discovered something. Chris lifted her chin so they were eye to eye.

“I’m doing everything I can to figure this out. I just need you to be a little patient. Can you do that?”

“Yes.” She fought the urge to lean in for a kiss. “What time do you want her there for the interview?”

“Bring her by around three.”

Before she could reply, a nurse in pale pink scrubs approached with a clipboard and some paperwork. They moved out of her way and waited while Nadine signed the forms. The sound of a heart monitor went dead and Nadine appeared with the forms in hand.

“Can we get out of here?”

The three of them walked back to the main entrance of the hospital and out to the parking lot. Kalina and Nadine parted ways with Chris as he climbed into a marked police cruiser and pulled away. Kalina unlocked her car and they settled in.

“So, is there something going on with you and Chris?” Nadine asked as Kalina started the engine.

“We’ve been seeing each other since June.”

“I guess first loves do come back to you if you let them free.”

Kalina smiled a toothy grin. “I guess so.”

“Thanks again for doing this,” Nadine said, rubbing at her forehead.

Kalina reached over to pat the woman on the shoulder. They would get through this together. She did her best to squash her doubts about Nadine's innocence in the whole mess. Nadine needed her support right now, not judgment.

"Do you mind if we stop by the shop for a bit?" Kalina asked as she eased to a stop at a stop sign. Geeks and Things sat half a block up on Main Street.

"Shop?"

"I took over my dad's comic book shop after he died a few months back."

"Oh, I didn't realize. Sorry about your dad."

"That's okay. I didn't know your mom had died, either. I'm sorry I wasn't around for you back then."

"It would have been nice to have my best friend there but ... people drift apart after high school. And I could have made more of an effort."

Kalina smiled at her friend. Kids had it so much easier these days with Facebook keeping everyone connected. The whole phenomenon had been just a little behind their college experience. “I want you to know I’m here for you now.” She accelerated through the intersection and pulled in behind the store. She’d spotted a few people on the sidewalk, lounging by the front door. The late opening wasn’t hurting business after all.

“So did you want to take over the store after your dad passed?” Nadine asked as they climbed out and Kalina pulled her keys out of her pocket.

“Yeah. I ended up going to grad school for business. It’s kind of a dream come true, honestly. I was always more into all the nerdy stuff than Jillian and I didn’t realize it until recently, but I love being able to keep the family business alive. It kind of feels like my dad’s still around a little bit.”

Nadine nodded wordlessly and waited while Kalina unlocked the back door. They made their way to the front of the store through the game room. Kalina moved with quick steps to the front door, unlocking it and pulling it open. “Come on in.”

Customers lined up in front of the counter and Nadine stood off to the side, watching intently.

Kalina darted to the back to retrieve their waiting orders. Thank goodness none of them were waiting on Valiant Comics. She hadn't had a chance to sort through the new inventory yet. She'd gotten through the first customer when the bell above the door rang and Andrew Chambers walked in. Kalina suppressed a groan and motioned Nadine to join her from where she was lurking in the back.

"Can you run a register?"

"Yeah. Why?"

She nodded toward Mr. Chambers. "I need to take care of something. Everything is written on the folders. Thanks so much."

Kalina blew out a breath and motioned for Mr. Chambers to follow her into the game room. She braced herself for another confrontation but it seemed it might not come. He shuffled into the room behind her, hands in his pockets and his gaze cast downward.

He cleared his throat and said, "I wanted to apologize for my behavior yesterday."

"Oh." She hadn't been expecting an apology.

"It's just"—he looked around the room—"Kevin's grades weren't that great this past school year and I thought maybe it was because of the comics. But I did like you said and talked to him. It wasn't a fun talk, believe me. But he's been having issues since his mom left."

Kalina's expression softened. "I'm so sorry to hear that."

He shrugged off her concern. "It was a long time coming. I guess I'm not so good at all the emotional stuff. Look, do you think maybe when school starts he could hang out here after school and do his homework? He's promised he'll do it."

"He's welcome to come by."

Mr. Chambers smiled. "Thanks. And, again, I'm sorry I lost it on you."

"I'm used to it."

"Hey, Kal. I need some help," Nadine called.

"I'll let you get back to work."

Kalina offered her hand to Mr. Chambers. He shook it and headed out of the shop. Kalina rejoined Nadine at the counter and helped her sort out a glitch with Square. Finally, the shop was quiet again. Kalina fiddled with the tablet for a few minutes before she set it aside and leaned on her elbows. "Can I ask you something?"

"Yeah."

"Do you remember the accident? I read what was in the paper yesterday but it seemed kind of vague."

Nadine's cheeks paled and she slumped onto the stool. She took several deep breaths. "We were at a Fourth of July party. I didn't want to go but my mom made me. I don't think she wanted to be alone with my dad. He'd been drinking but refused to give Mom the keys."

"So he was drunk. There was no truck in the wrong lane."

"There might have been. It was late and I was half-asleep when it happened." She closed her eyes tight as if trying to remember that night. "I can still hear the tires and brakes squealing and the sound of the airbags deploying. The rest is kind of a blur though."

"Did they test your dad's blood alcohol level? I mean even if there was a truck he shouldn't have been driving when he was drunk."

"They probably did but I don't know what happened. All I know is no one wanted to charge him with anything. He was buddies with the chief of police at the time and he just looked the other way."

"Police corruption at its best."

"Yeah. I heard about what happened with Dan Cahill. That's crazy."

"Yeah, it was. I was there when he was arrested."

Nadine let out a nervous hiccup of laughter. "You were? Why?"

"I was sort of unofficially helping Chris out with the case. Not that he'd ever admit to that."

"Do you think you could come with me to the police station?"

"Yeah, of course. I don't think he'll let me sit in with you on the interview but I could probably wait outside."

"I need to call Adam."

Kalina cocked her head in curiosity. “Who is Adam?”

“My boyfriend. He’s a lawyer. I think I need one.”

“Chris just wants your statement about what happened.”

“I think I might have done something, Kal. It wouldn’t be the first time.”

“What do you mean?”

“Not many people know but I was locked up in a psych ward for about six months. My father had them convinced I was bipolar. I’m not. I know I’m not but even without a law degree I know that looks suspicious. I don’t speak to my father for years after I’m committed and then we reconnect and he ends up dead. That doesn’t look good for me, Kal.”

“I’m sure you didn’t do anything.”

“The night’s kind of fuzzy to be honest. But what if I did do something?”

“But you said you aren’t bipolar.”

“No, but he drugged me before. What if he did it again and I blacked or something?”

"Could you really have pushed him out a window, even if you were drugged?"

"Maybe—" she dug the heels of her hands into her eyes "—I need to call Adam and let him know what's happening."

"You can borrow my phone if you want." Kalina unlocked her phone and slid it across the counter.

Nadine picked it up and entered a number before hitting 'Call' and disappearing to the game room for some privacy. Kalina's stomach lurched at Nadine's revelation. She hadn't wanted to believe her friend could be responsible for killing a man but Nadine was right. There was definitely some motive. And if they were the only two people in the house then she had no alibi and she'd been sedated with enough drugs at the hospital it could have messed up any toxicology test the doctors ran. Maybe eavesdropping on Chris's interview would shed some more light on things.

Chapter 7

At ten minutes until three, Kalina and Nadine pulled into the parking lot of the police station. A car Kalina didn't recognize pulled in behind them and a tall man climbed out. Nadine lunged out of the passenger seat and threw herself into his arms. He held her tight and kissed her forehead. From her spot by the driver side door, Kalina could make out that he had a few strands of gray in his otherwise full head of dark brown hair. He could have been their age or a little older. She tried to not intrude on their private moment. After Nadine finally relinquished her grip around his torso, he closed the distance between the two cars and extended his hand to Kalina.

“Adam Shepard, Nadine’s boyfriend.”

“Kalina Greystone. Friend. I also hear you’re an attorney.”

“Yeah. One of the partners in my firm helped Nadine out a few years ago. That’s how we met.”

Nadine stayed close to Adam’s side as they headed into the precinct. Jimmy was no longer at the reception desk. He was bent over something at Chris’s desk.

“Hey, Jimmy, is Chris here?” Kalina called.

The young officer jumped and turned to face them. “Oh, uh… Hi, Kal. Yeah he’s around here somewhere.”

“Can you let him know that Nadine Larrabee is here for her interview?”

“Right. I’ll let him know right now.” He hurried off toward the chief’s office.

The department was even more short-staffed since they hadn’t gotten around to replacing Captain Cahill. No one seemed to want the job. She suspected they would eventually have to bring in someone else from outside of the town to oversee things. Behind her, she could hear Adam and Nadine speaking in hushed voices but they stopped the moment Chris appeared.

"Thank you for coming in. If you'll follow me." He pointed to the only interrogation room the department had.

Kalina stayed where she was, dutifully not butting in on her boyfriend's job. She smiled politely as Jimmy walked past her and sat down at the front desk. She gave Chris a thumbs up when he gestured for her to stay put. With a quick glance over her shoulder to make sure Jimmy was distracted, she settled in at Chris's desk and watched the interview on the small monitor nearby.

"Miss Larrabee, can you tell me what you remember from two nights ago? What were you doing at your father's house?"

Nadine crossed her arms over her chest. "We were having dinner. I'd brought Adam over to meet him. I thought maybe it was time we tried to put our differences behind us. He'd been sober for a year."

"Adam Shepard, your attorney?"

"I'm here in my official capacity as Nadine's counsel," Adam said.

Chris scribbled something on his notepad. "So you had dinner."

"Yes. It ... wasn't the greatest meal. I don't think he really liked that I had a boyfriend."

Chris nodded. "Then what happened?"

Nadine shrugged. "We were going to leave but my father insisted I stay. Adam left. He had to prepare for a trial the next day. I thought things were going to be okay but then my father poured himself a drink. I didn't have anywhere else to go so I made some tea and went to bed."

"So you didn't argue with your father about him breaking his sobriety?"

"No. I don't think so. It's kind of hazy after I went to bed. I thought I heard arguing but I must have been dreaming. Then I woke up and found him the next morning, lying in the driveway."

"But no one else was in the house at the time. Just the two of you?"

Nadine glanced over at Adam who said nothing. "Yes. Just the two of us."

Chris flipped open a file—likely Nadine's medical history—and paged through it. "I see you were hospitalized for psychiatric concerns a few years ago."

"I'm not crazy. We proved it. He was drugging me to make me look like I was bipolar."

"Why would he do that to his own daughter?"

"Because he's a cruel man. He knew his side of the family had a history so it would look credible."

"I still don't understand why he would want to fake a mental illness. What reason would he have?"

"Detective, I don't see how this is relevant," Adam chimed in.

"Just getting all the facts on the table, Counselor. Your client's relationship with her father, both presently and in the past, may speak to any potential motive."

"Motive? So now she's a suspect?"

Kalina knew where this was going and, as much as she wanted to know what happened between Nadine and her father, it wasn't going to come out now that Adam was on the defense. Instead, she turned her attention to the files littering Chris's desk. His normally clean and organized workspace had been overtaken by the case at hand. She flipped open the top folder and almost wished she hadn't. A close-up photo of Mr. Larrabee's face, bruised and bloody, greeted her. Once the shock wore off, she took a closer look. In all of the commotion of finding Nadine two days ago, she hadn't really noticed that he'd landed face down on the pavement. No wonder Jimmy said the medical examiner thought he'd been pushed.

She closed the folder and spun around in the chair. Jimmy drummed his fingers on the keyboard at the front desk, clearly bored. Hoping she could get lucky twice in two days, she ambled over to him and put on her best flirty smile. "Hey there. Can I ask you something?"

Jimmy sighed and looked toward the interrogation. "Man, I wish I could be in there.

I want to make detective someday. I could be learning so much from Chris."

"I'm sure you'll get there. Hell, you'll probably end up running this place one day."

Jimmy blushed and finger-combed his hair nervously. "Thanks. Did you need something?"

"Yeah, actually I was hoping you could help me out. I'm sure Chris doesn't want Nadine going back to the house. But I promised I'd pick up her stuff for her. Overnight bag. That sort of thing. Do you know if forensics has cleared the scene?"

"Oh, yeah they did that yesterday. Wasn't much there."

"Do you think you could go with me? I don't feel comfortable going alone."

"Sure thing, Kal."

A sound from the monitor nearby drew Kalina's attention back to the interrogation. Chris pushed an evidence photo of what looked like rope across the table. "Have you seen this before, Miss Larrabee?"

Nadine shook her head. "No. Why?"

“We found it in your father’s study. The lab is running it for fingerprints right now. What do you think we’ll find?”

“That’s enough, Detective. If you have something to charge my client with, do it; otherwise, we’re leaving.” Adam stood up and took Nadine by the elbow, guiding her away from the table and towards the door.

“I know you aren’t local anymore, Nadine, but don’t leave town,” Chris said and gathered up his materials.

Kalina darted from Chris’s desk and raced to stand near Jimmy. He didn’t react to her sudden presence, which was a blessing. Nadine and Adam appeared and made a bee line for the door, not bothering to stop. But as they passed, Kalina overheard Adam tell Nadine she could stay with him at the only hotel in town. So at least she knew where they were going. Chris appeared next, making his way to his desk and tossing the files on top of the ever-growing pile. He rubbed at the back of his neck—a clear sign of stress—and headed for the front of the building as well.

"I need some air," he announced to no one in particular and disappeared from view.

Jimmy rounded the front desk and held up the keys to the squad car parked in the front lot. "Ready to go?"

Chapter 8

The trip to the Larrabee house was surprisingly short. There was little need for conversation until Jimmy cut the engine at the end of the driveway. He pulled the keys from the ignition and nearly dropped them between his feet. Kalina pretended not to notice his nerves.

"You okay, Jimmy?"

"Yeah. Just ... being back here kind of freaks me out a little. Don't tell Detective Harper."

Kalina mimed locking her lips and throwing away the key. "Your secret is safe with me. Besides, being here kind of freaks me out, too."

Together they exited the squad car and marched up to the front door. It was still unlocked. Jimmy nudged it open with his forearm and stepped inside first. The house didn't feel any different than any other house. Somehow she'd expected it to be marked by death with a draft or scent of blood. It was a normal house that brought back memories of spending afternoons with Nadine doing homework in high school.

"I think the bedroom is on the second floor," Jimmy announced but stayed at the foot of the stairs.

"I remember," Kalina murmured and started up the staircase.

She stopped on the second floor landing and just took in the décor. It hadn't changed in fifteen years, except for a picture of Nadine at their high school graduation. She looked so happy and full of potential. So much had happened to dampen her spirit. It wasn't fair. With a soft sigh, Kalina crept up to the third floor to take a look around. From what she remembered of the layout and the position of Mr. Larrabee's body, she ignored the master bedroom and half bathroom and headed straight for the study. It was a mess with papers strewn across the desk. There were scuff marks on the hardwood floor and the desk chair had been turned over. It certainly appeared as though there had been a struggle. Bending down to right the chair, Kalina noticed what looked like bloodstains on the tan leather armrests.

“What happened in here?”

Sidestepping the chair, she approached the window and peered down at the driveway below. From this angle she had no doubt a fall from this height could kill a person. Had the police done their test yet? Surely that would give Chris an idea of whether Nadine was involved or not. She longed to know more about what happened between father and daughter that could lead to something like this. A floorboard creaked behind her and she spun, her right hand pressed to her chest in surprise. Jimmy stood in the doorway.

“I thought the bedroom was on the second floor?”

Kalina caught her breath and nodded. “It is... I just got curious. I know it sounds awful but I wanted to see it for myself. Don't tell anyone, please?"

Jimmy nodded and she followed him back down to the second floor landing. He waited patiently outside Nadine's room as she gathered up the clothes strewn on the floor, tossing them in the overnight duffle bag laid beneath the window. Nadine really hadn't been planning on staying long. The bed had not been touched; the covers still haphazardly kicked to one side. A half-empty teacup sat on the nightstand on the left side of the bed. Curiosity got the best of her and she picked it up.

"Find something?" Jimmy called.

"Maybe. Did anyone examine this tea?"

Jimmy scratched at the stubble on his chin. "Um... I don't think so. Why would they do that? Mr. Larrabee wasn't killed in here."

Kalina bit her lip, unsure how much to divulge about her earlier conversation with her friend. "Nadine said she thought her father might have drugged her the night he died. Maybe some of whatever he used is still in the tea."

Jimmy's cheeks burned bright red in embarrassment. "Oh ... right. Like with Mrs. Davies."

"Exactly."

Jimmy pulled out his phone and disappeared back down to the first floor. Kalina took one last cursory look around the room before joining him. Neither of them had touched the tea and so she assumed chain of evidence hadn't been ruined. He hung up just as she got to the bottom of the stairs.

"They said I should bag it myself and bring it to the station. They'll have someone pick it up there to run some tests."

"Can you do that?"

He puffed out his chest. "Yeah. Detective Harper always makes us keep extra gloves and evidence bags in the squad car just in case. Us being such a small department and all."

"I'll wait here while you do that," Kalina said.

Jimmy hurried out to the car and returned moments later with blue gloves and a clear baggie marked 'EVIDENCE- ELLESWORTH PD' on it. True to her word, she waited outside while he headed upstairs to retrieve the teacup and its potentially-drugged contents. As she waited, the third story window drew her attention. Nadine didn't have time to wait for a lengthy police procedure to determine her guilt or innocence. Kalina would find a way to test the theory of whether Mr. Larrabee was pushed or not.

"What's going on out here?" An older man's voice pulled her from her thoughts.

She turned her attention to the man standing just over the property line to the next house over. Mr. Martin Beech had lived there for as long as Kalina had been alive and friends with Nadine. He was a bit odd but harmless enough.

"Oh, hi, Mr. Beech. You probably saw all the emergency personnel here the other day for Mr. Larrabee." Two days seemed more than enough time for the news to begin spreading. She was quite impressed that people weren't spreading rumors already.

"Course I did. With all the racket they were making, how could I not?"

Kalina set down the duffle bag on the front steps and closed the distance between them.

"Did you see anything strange the night before?"

Mr. Beech waved his hand dismissively. "I don't like to pry."

"Oh, of course not. I didn't mean to imply you were prying. But you are pretty observant from what I remember. Nadine and I couldn't sneak anything past you when we were kids."

Mr. Beech grinned, his dentures gleaming. "You girls were always a handful. But I do like to keep an eye on the neighborhood."

Flattery at its best. "I'm sure Nadine would be really grateful if you did happen to see something the other night. She's really torn up about her father's death."

"Oh, sure. Poor thing. You know, it was kind of a surprise to see her around. It'd been maybe five or six years since I'd seen her at the house. She seemed subdued when I said hello. Like she had something else on her mind. But whatever it was, she must have gotten over it because she stayed the night."

Kalina leaned in conspiratorially. "You don't

think she had anything to do with his death, do you?"

"Little Nadine? That girl couldn't hurt a fly. You know, now that you mention it, I did notice something odd."

"What?"

"Well, I've had trouble sleeping the last few nights. The heat just doesn't agree with me. So I was up around two in the morning." He paused, seeming to collect his thoughts. "Yes, it was two. I went downstairs to get a glass of warm milk when I saw a car."

"A car? Did you recognize it or the person driving?"

"Well, it looked like the car Nadine showed up in earlier. I guess the fellow she was with had left but it looked like he came back. Now, I don't mean to be nosy but that fellow went inside and then maybe ten minutes later came back out and left the door wide open!"

"So there was someone else in the house besides Nadine and her father."

"Saw him clear as day."

"Did Nadine introduce him to you earlier?"

Mr. Beech shook his head. "I'm afraid not." His face lit up. "But I did write down the license plate. I thought it was rather suspicious it being so late at night and all. I'll go get it."

Before Kalina could ask any more questions, Mr. Beech tottered off towards his front door and Jimmy appeared, carefully cradling the cup in both hands.

"Sorry I took so long. Wanted to make sure it didn't spill."

"That's okay. I was just having a nice conversation with Edwin Beech. I think he might have seen something."

"Seen what?"

"A car coming and leaving the house between two o'clock and two fifteen the morning Mr. Larrabee died."

Jimmy did a little hop of excitement at the news and tiny droplets of tea sloshed against the clear plastic. His cheeks reddened again and he walked, stiff-legged, down to the squad car to secure the bag. Mr. Beech reappeared and waved a slip of paper in Kalina's face.

"Here it is."

She plucked it from his outstretched fingers. "Thanks. You've been a huge help."

"You tell Nadine I'm thinking of her."

"I will." Kalina retrieved the overnight bag and walked down the driveway to join Jimmy. She handed him the paper with the license plate number and they both climbed in.

"Boy did we get lucky you happened to strike up a conversation with him," Jimmy said and nestled the teacup into one of the cup holders. He punched the license plate number into the minicomputer synced to the DMV database and let out a long whistle as the computer went 'ping' with a result.

"What is it?" Kalina tried to read the result but Jimmy blocked the screen.

He hit speed dial on his cell phone. Whoever he was calling picked up after the first ring. "Detective Harper, it's Jimmy. I think you might want to bring Adam Shepard back in for some questioning."

Chapter 9

Kalina stared open-mouthed as Jimmy repeated the information. She had no problem letting Chris think it was all Jimmy's doing. After all, she'd said she would keep out of the investigation, not do their job for them.

"I understand. I'll see you back at the station, Sir." Jimmy ended the call and looked at Kalina. "Nadine's lawyer boyfriend came back that night. Wonder why she didn't say anything before?"

Kalina shrugged. "Maybe she didn't know. If she really was drugged then she wouldn't remember him coming in or out."

Jimmy ran a hand over his hair. “Detective Harper wants me back at the station. Can I drop you somewhere?”

“The shop would be fine.” She really wanted him to take her to the motel but that would have looked suspicious. If Chris didn’t want Jimmy to pick up Adam from the motel for questioning, then Chris was likely getting the lawyer to the station under false pretenses. She might have some time to get to the motel first.

Five minutes later, Jimmy pulled up to the shop. AJ stood outside, arms crossed over his chest. He did not look happy. Kalina climbed out of the passenger side with the overnight bag in hand and waited for the squad car to pull away.

“Do you have any idea what time it is?” her nephew asked with mock annoyance.

“Yeah, yeah. Come on. You wanted to know what’s been going on; well, it’s time I filled you in. I’m going to need your help anyway.”

They headed inside and AJ flipped the front sign to ‘Closed’. He pointed to the bag but Kalina tossed it aside.

“An old friend of mine’s father died two days ago. It looks like it was murder and Nadine is the prime suspect. There was some bad blood between her and her father but I’m not sure about the whole story. We just found out someone else was there the night her father died. Chris is investigating.”

“What do you need from me?”

“I need you to look up how to test if a person was pushed or fell from a high altitude.”

“You mean the ‘Push Jump Fall’ test.”

Kalina furrowed her brow. “Where’d you learn that?”

AJ grinned. “Heroes.”

Kalina let out a soft laugh. “Of course. Now, I need you to look up how to test it and see if you can find a dummy we can use.”

“I know just where to look.”

“You can’t tell anyone what you need it for. Chris can’t find out we’re doing this.”

AJ nodded. “So while I’m doing this, what are you doing?”

'I'm going to the motel and, hopefully, I can get Nadine to fill in some of the blanks about her past. It might be the only way we can figure out what really happened to her father."

"You can count on me, Aunt K."

She pulled her nephew into a brief, one-armed hug. "I knew I could. Now, call me when you've got everything. And remember—"

"I know. Don't tell anyone what we're doing."

Kalina picked up the overnight bag and headed out across town. She supposed she was lucky that Ellesworth was small enough to only have one motel. If anyone came to stay in the area, they usually stayed in Salem and drove down to the beaches here. She reached the parking lot some ten minutes later to find only one car there bearing a familiar license plate. Adam hadn't left yet. What was Chris waiting for? She paid the front desk a quick visit to get the right room number and walked down three doors and stopped. She could hear voices coming from inside the room.

"I don't understand why he wants to talk to you alone," Nadine said.

“Don’t worry about it. Everything is going to be fine. I promise.”

“You’re hiding something. I can tell. What is it?”

“Nadine, just let me worry about it. I’m looking out for you.”

Kalina raised her hand to knock when the door flew inward and she nearly collided with Adam.

“Sorry!” she said and stepped out of his way.

“I didn’t see you there,” he said and headed for his car.

Nadine sat on one of the small twin beds with her knees drawn up to her chest. She looked paler than she had two days before when her father’s death was fresh in her mind. Her hair was damp and hung around her face in stringy clumps. Adam had probably gotten the call when she was still in the shower. Kalina stayed in the doorway for a moment longer to be sure Nadine registered her presence. Then she crossed the threshold and set the bag on the floor.

“Hey, how are you holding up?”

Nadine scrubbed at her face and let out a long sigh. "Honestly, I don't know what to think anymore. Detective Harper just called Adam down to the station for some questions but he didn't want me there. He wouldn't say anything else."

Kalina just nodded. She didn't want to admit she'd overheard part of their conversation. Instead, she sat on the other bed and said, "I'm sure if either of them have anything to tell you, they will." Should she say anything about Adam returning in the middle of the night?

"I wish I could remember something ... anything."

"Was there anything you didn't tell Detective Harper in your interview?"

"Like what?"

"I don't know. The reason your father drugged you all those years ago."

"God, you think I did it! You think I had a motive." Nadine jumped from the bed and took a defensive posture.

"No, of course I don't." Kalina held her hands up in front of her. "I am just trying to understand how the family I knew growing up could be torn apart so violently. What happened?"

Nadine turned to face Kalina, resting her chin in her hand. "I guess it started after I turned eighteen. My parents needed to redo their wills to get rid of the need for a guardian or something. They ended up waiting an extra year. I'm not sure why. I didn't know the details but my dad got really upset that my mother was keeping the house only in her name and she was passing it to me when I turned 25. It was supposed to be held by the estate lawyer until then."

"What's so special about the house?"

She shrugged. "It's been in the family for a long time. I think my mom wanted to keep it in her side of the family. They had a pretty big knockdown, drag out fight over it right after I got home from school for the semester in June. He insisted on going to the party on the fourth of July. My mother didn't want to go. She didn't tell me but I could tell he'd been drinking more often. He wasn't the same. Always on edge and angry." Tears shone in her eyes and she tried to blink them away. "I wish she'd just given him the damn house. Maybe then he wouldn't have insisted on going to the stupid party."

"So you blamed him for what happened to your mom." It came out as more of a statement than a question.

"Maybe. I think I resented him for being so obsessed with the house. You know, that's why he drugged me and had me committed."

Kalina scratched her head, trying to follow the logic. "To get the house?"

"Yes. There was some legal loophole that said he could get control of the deed if I was declared legally incompetent. But he waited until after I turned 25 so it was legally in my name so he could force feed me whatever drugs he thought would help make his case." Her tone turned bitter. "He gave me downers so that I spiraled into a massive depression and then he gave me psychotropic pills to make me look manic. He kept giving them to me until one day I just lost it and started hitting him. He called the police and they dragged me off to the psych ward at Salem Hospital. I rotted there for six months before

Adam and one of his partners figured out what was going on and got me released."

"You were able to prove it all?"

"I even tried to sue him but the judge wanted it settled out of court. He never came out and said it, but I think he felt it was just too messy. I got some restitution financially and a restraining order."

"If you had a restraining order, why did you go to see him and have dinner?"

"I let it lapse about a year ago. Adam thought it might be good to reconcile, or at least try to put the past behind us. He said there was no point in letting it eat away at our happiness."

Kalina did her best to stifle a bitter laugh of her own. "You know, I think maybe you were drugged this time, too."

"So you believe me?"

"I found the teacup and the lab is running it. And there was someone else there in the house that night."

"Someone else? How do you know that?"

It was time to spill the beans. “When I went to get your stuff from the house I ran into your neighbor, Mr. Beech. He was rather chatty. He said that that night, around two, he saw someone show up to the house and then leave a little while later.”

“Who?”

“Adam.”

“No, that can’t be.”

“Mr. Beech wrote down the license plate and Jimmy ran it. It belonged to Adam’s car. I think that’s why Chris wanted to talk to him alone.”

Nadine scooped up the room key and headed for the door. “We have to get there now. I need to know what’s happening!”

“Slow down, Nadine. We can’t do anything.”

“If he tells Detective Harper anything I deserve to know about it. I knew he was keeping something from me. I just didn’t know it was this.”

Chapter 10

Nadine was out the door before Kalina could say anything else. They didn't have a car so it was going to be a brisk walk to the station. On the way, Kalina checked her phone for any missed calls or texts from AJ. She couldn't share that particular theory with her friend yet. She needed to process the fact that her boyfriend had been there and might have had something to do with her father's death. Was he confessing to the crime as they raced to the station? He could have certainly had enough strength and force to push a grown man out a window.

"Come on," Nadine urged as the station came into view up the street.

Kalina stowed her phone back in her pocket and trailed Nadine through the front doors. Neither of them bothered to acknowledge the officer at the front desk. Jimmy was nowhere in sight and the bull pen was empty. Chris's desk was still a mess of files and paperwork. Speaking of Chris, she spotted him on the interrogation room monitor sitting across from Adam.

"Your vehicle was seen arriving at the Larrabee residence at two in the morning and leaving at two fifteen. Want to tell me what you were doing back there in the middle of the night?"

"What evidence do you have?"

"An eye witness who recorded your license plate. Now, I'll ask you again. What were you doing back there?"

Adam let out a breath and unfolded his arms. "I didn't like how we left things with Nadine's father. I had a trial the next day but I should have insisted she come stay with me. The stories she told me were unsettling. The last time he was alone with her in that house, he purposely drugged her to get the deed to the house."

Chris opened one of the files on the table and flipped through what appeared to be court documents. “And you know all of this because of the civil suit Nadine filed against her father.”

“Yes. I was part of the team that worked on her case and got her released from the hospital when it was determined she was not mentally impaired due to a disease.”

“So you went back to give Mr. Larrabee a piece of your mind then?”

“No. I went back to get Nadine to go with me. When I got there she was asleep. I tried to wake her up but she wouldn’t. I assumed he’d drugged her again.”

“So you left her there?”

“I went to confront Edwin.”

Kalina stood transfixed by the conversation. She hadn’t anticipated Adam admitting he’d confronted Mr. Larrabee about what had happened with Nadine. She hadn’t wanted the possibility that he was the killer to be true any more than she wanted that status to fall to her friend.

“He came back for me,” Nadine whispered. “I thought I dreamed that.”

“You remember him showing up?”

“A little, maybe. It honestly felt like a dream. That means the rest wasn’t a dream either.”

Kalina turned to look at her friend. “The rest of what?”

“I thought it was a dream. I went upstairs because I heard voices and loud noises. My father was tied to his office chair. He looked so scared. I think he told me to run but I had to untie him. Whatever else he’d done to me, he didn’t deserve to be tied down. I know what that’s like. Then I stumbled back down to my room. I guess Adam did wake me up.”

“Did you happen to see a clock at any point during that whole thing?”

“No. Why?”

“Well, if you went and untied your father after Adam left then that doesn’t make him a suspect anymore.”

“But it still doesn’t clear me. And why would Adam tie up my father? It was the middle of the night. I know he was drinking again but I don't think he would have done anything to really hurt me."

"I don't know but Chris needs to know what you just told me."

Nadine worried her lower lip and looked between the door to the interrogation room and the monitor. The conversation had died down. The station was eerily silent when Kalina's phone sang out the opening bars to "Hooked on Feeling"—AJ's ringtone.

"Sorry. I need to take this." She stepped away and watched as Nadine headed for the interrogation room, her shoulders squared and her head held high. "Hey, kiddo. Tell me you got what we need."

"Took longer than I thought it would but, yeah, I got it. So what's next?"

Kalina pulled her phone away from her ear to check the time. It was already well after six. "Go wait for me at the shop, around back. I'll pick you up and I'll throw in pizza when we're done."

"Sweet. Did you find out anything else?"

"I'll fill you in when I get there."

"I'll let Mom know I won't be home for dinner."

"I'll see you soon," she said and ended the call.

Nadine appeared on the monitor and took a seat beside Adam. Kalina couldn't see Chris's facial expression but, by Adam's body language, at least one of them wasn't pleased to see Nadine waltz right in and start talking. She couldn't really blame them. If anything, it was usually the attorney barging in on the interrogation. She wanted to stay and hear what else was going on in the interrogation room but figuring out if Mr. Larrabee had been pushed or not was of more importance. She was so close to finding out what had really happened and, hopefully, clearing her friend's name. The deeper she got into the fact, the more convinced she was becoming that Nadine just didn't have it in her to kill her father, no matter what had transpired between them in the last decade. With one last glance back toward the monitor, she made the trek back to Geeks and Things.

Chapter 11

“What took you so long?” AJ exclaimed as she rounded the back of the shop.

She let out a huff and bent over to catch her breath. Sweat glistened on her arms and she could feel beads threatening to spill from her forehead.

“Give me a break, kid. I had to walk from the other side of town. I got here as fast as I could.”

He pointed to a large CPR dummy. “That will work, right?”

“It’s perfect.” She fanned herself with her shirt

as she caught her breath. "Where'd you find it?"

"A friend was doing CPR training and lent it to me. I told them I wanted to practice in case I wanted to take the class."

"You know, should I be worried about this criminal mastermind thing you've got going?"

He laughed and grinned from ear to ear. "Just don't tell Mom."

Together, they managed to fit the dummy in the backseat of Kalina's car without it looking suspicious. The sun had begun its descent toward the horizon as she pulled out of the back lot and made her way toward Ocean Front Lane.

"So, what friend is this? Have I met them?" AJ was trying to fill the dead air between them.

"I don't think so. We hadn't spoken in a long time. Since high school really. But the minute I saw her and realized she was in trouble, I had to help her."

"That's nuts that you would have that connection again after so long."

"It sounds cliché but it's true. Your true friends are the ones you don't see for years and you pick up right where you left off when you see them again. Of course, it doesn't usually involve murder."

"So do you think she did it?"

Kalina shook her head as she eased to a stop at stop sign. "I don't think so. I understand her relationship with her father better now but ... even with all of that behind her, she was trying to reconcile with him."

"What about the other person in the house?'

"Maybe. I am hoping this test will tell us one way or the other if Mr. Larrabee was pushed."

"Detective Harper is going to be pissed when he finds out."

"That's why we aren't telling him until we've done it. Besides, I'm sure he's got someone doing the same thing in a lab somewhere. We're just confirming results, really."

A few minutes later, she pulled up in front of the Larrabee house. She hoped Mr. Beech wasn't around. She didn't need him interfering or ratting them out to the police. Despite it being the end of the work day, the streets were mostly empty. That would work in their favor.

"Are you sure we can get in?" AJ asked as he struggled to drag the dummy out the passenger side of the backseat.

"Yes. The front door isn't locked."

"And you know this how?"

"I was here earlier with Jimmy and we didn't lock the front door when we left."

"Oh. Right."

Kalina locked the car and helped AJ carry the dummy up the driveway to the front porch. She kept moving, forcing her nephew to keep up so he wouldn't have time to gawk at the dark stain still on the pavement. She was a little surprised no one had come to clean it up. They paused long enough for AJ to throw the front door open and duck inside. With one last glance over her shoulder to make sure no one was watching, Kalina eased the door shut.

"Up to the third floor," she instructed.

It was a clumsy affair dragging the dummy up

the two flights to the study but they managed it.

“This is a nice house,” AJ said as they stopped outside the study so he could work a kink out of his wrist.

“Yeah. I spent a lot of time here when I was your age.”

AJ wrinkled his nose. “Don’t say it like that. It makes you sound old.”

She swatted his arm. “I am old.”

He rolled his eyes but resumed his grasp around the dummy’s torso so they could maneuver it into the room. The window had been closed. Maybe Jimmy did it when he went back to collect the teacup.

“Put it against the chair,” she said and went to unlatch the window.

“Man this place is kind of a mess,” AJ responded.

“I’m sure people would say the same thing about your room.” She turned back to face him. “So ... what’s next?”

He retrieved his phone and fiddled with it for a minute. “Ok, so we just have to simulate someone being pushed, jumping or falling. Seems easy enough.”

“Right. I think I should be the one to do the pushing. Nadine and I are about the same height and build. If I can get the dummy to land the right way then we will know if he was pushed.”

“Got it. I’ll head back downstairs.”

She waited for him to reappear outside before she hefted the dummy over to the window. She turned it so that the dummy was facing her before she gave it a solid shove. It tipped over the windowsill and fell head over feet to the pavement below.

“Uh, Aunt K. I’m guessing the head is supposed to be over this dark spot,” AJ called up.

Kalina leaned out the window to check the final position. The feet were where Mr. Larrabee’s head should be and the dummy had landed face up. “Yeah. That clearly didn’t work. Bring it back up.”

AJ lugged the dummy back up the front porch and appeared in the hallway a few minutes later. She motioned for him to head back out and he groaned before doing as he was told. She waited until he was in position again and turned the dummy to face away from her before giving it a hard shove. It fell straight down but, again, wasn't in the right position.

"It's closer," AJ said.

"But not quite right. It's still too close to the house. Bring it up again."

He picked up the dummy roughly by one arm and started dragging it behind him. Kalina leaned farther out the window.

"Be careful with that!"

As she leaned back into the room, a thought occurred to her. If her theory were true then Nadine and Adam would be off the hook for Mr. Larrabee's death. AJ finally appeared and slumped into the office chair, not taking note of the blood specks on the leather. He set the dummy on the floor and wiped visible beads of sweat from his forehead.

"For a teenage boy you aren't in very good shape," Kalina scolded.

"I'm a nerd. Exercise is my kryptonite." He took several deep breaths before hoisting himself back to his feet. "I'll head back down."

"No, stick around up here. I think might have figured it out. And I think I need your help."

"What do you need me to do?"

"Help me lift the dummy so it's standing on the ledge."

"Seriously?"

"Just do it."

They lifted up the dummy and positioned it on the ledge of the window. Kalina looked at her nephew. "On the count of three, let go. One. Two. Three."

The both let go. Gravity took over and the dummy fell face first onto the pavement in the general spot where Mr. Larrabee had been discovered. AJ let out a low whistle.

"So he jumped."

"It certainly looks like it. I need to let Chris know."

"Remember, he's gonna be pissed at you."

Kalina smirked. "I'll make it up to him."

AJ gagged. "Gross. I didn't need to know that." He wandered over to the desk and started rifling through papers while Kalina pulled out her phone. "Hey, Aunt K. I think you should look at this."

"Don't touch it. It could be evidence."

He pulled his hands away and took a big step away from the desk. "Sorry."

"Just point to what you found," she said and walked over to stand beside him.

He indicated a pile of official looking documents with a notary seal at the bottom. She bent down to study the text more closely. "He was giving it back."

"Giving what back?"

She waved her nephew's question away. She walked to the other side of where he stood and nudged pages with the side of her phone. A handwritten page fluttered to the floor. She bent down to read it but didn't touch it.

"Oh, God."

AJ bent down to read it too and Kalina backed away, hitting 'Call' on her phone. It rang twice before someone answered.

"Ellesworth Police Department."

"Hi, I need to speak with Detective Harper right away."

There was a pause and then, "He's in an interrogation right now."

"I know. But I need to talk to him right away."

"Who should I say is calling?"

"Kalina. His girlfriend. It's about the case he's working. Please, just put him on the line."

She started to pace as the line went quiet. She could hear vague footsteps echoing on the other end of the line. Hopefully, her pleading had been enough to get the desk officer to summon Chris. Finally, the line clicked as someone picked up.

"Kal? What's going on?"

"I know what happened in Nadine's case."

"What are you talking about?"

"I know you're going to be angry with me but just hear me out. It would be better if you came to the Larrabees' house. Bring Nadine and Adam, too. They need to know what happened."

"We are definitely going to talk about this later." Chris's voice had taken on a hard edge of annoyance.

"Just get here, please."

Chapter 12

Kalina and AJ waited on the front porch for everyone to arrive. AJ had turned pale after reading the note from Mr. Larrabee. She could understand his anxiety. It broke her heart a little to think that Mr. Larrabee had taken his own life. She only hoped it would somehow bring Nadine some comfort knowing that she hadn't blacked out and killed her father. Tires squealed in the distance and the squad car rolled up moments later. Chris climbed out, his face clouded with emotion. Nadine and Adam climbed out of the back. Neither said a word. Nadine was visibly shaking at the sight of her family home. Adam tried to place a hand on her shoulder but she shrugged it off. Kalina wondered what else had been revealed during that interview after she'd left.

“Why is there a CPR dummy in the driveway?” Adam asked.

“We were testing a theory,” Kalina answered.

“What theory?” Nadine's voice was barely above a whisper.

“We were trying to figure out how your father landed the way he did. Whether he was pushed or fell.”

“And?”

“He jumped. It looks like he climbed onto the windowsill and just let gravity take him.”

Nadine's eyes welled with tears and she didn't try to stop them. They stained her cheeks in seconds. “Why would he do that?”

“It's better if you see what else we found.”

“And what exactly did you find?” Chris kept his shoulders back and gaze straight ahead. All business.

"It's better if you see it for yourselves."

Chris briefly returned to the car to grab an evidence bag and some gloves before they all headed up to the study in a silent, single-file line. Kalina had made sure AJ hadn't moved the note from where it had landed on the floor. She would let Chris handle that. Immediately, Chris spotted the note and snapped on his gloves. After taking a cursory look he faced Kalina.

"Neither of you touched this?"

"No. I mean it fell when I was moving some other papers but I used my phone. We didn't touch anything."

"What is that?" Nadine asked.

Chris slid the note into the evidence bag and handed it over. "A suicide note."

Nadine's hands trembled as she took the bag and sunk into the leather chair in the middle of the room.

Nadine,

I have spent so much time being angry about your mother's passing when I realize now it was my fault. I let my desire of material things get in the way of loving my only daughter and for that I am sorry.

The horrors I put you through are not something I can ever atone for. I do not seek your forgiveness. I only hope you are able to move forward with your life and be happy. Don't let the troubles of the past haunt you anymore.

Please don't see this as your fault. I have been struggling with this decision for some time. It is the only out I can see. I am truly sorry for everything.

Dad

The note fell to the floor as Nadine crumbled. A loud wail escaped her and filled the room. Adam picked up the fallen evidence and handed it back to Chris. Kalina went to wrap Nadine in a comforting hug, all the while wondering why Adam didn't seem surprised by the discovery.

"I missed something," Kalina said.

Chris tucked the evidence bag under his arm and blew out a breath. His shoulders relaxed a little. He was relenting. "Adam was here the night Mr. Larrabee killed himself." He looked to Adam. "You might as well explain."

Adam cleared his throat. "I was worried about Nadine. I came back to get her but, when I got here, she was out cold, or at least I thought she was. I came up here to confront Edwin about drugging his daughter again and I found him standing on the chair with a rope around his neck. I managed to get him down and... I tied him to the chair. I know it was stupid. I should have called the police but, to be honest, I was just in shock and a bit of a panic. I tied him up and I left. I knew it would look bad but at least he would be alive."

"So he was definitely alive when you left?" AJ interjected.

"Yes. He was. I didn't realize Nadine had woken up and untied him."

"I... I let him go so he could jump," she sobbed into Kalina's shoulder.

"It isn't your fault. None of it. He was sick for a while and he thought this was the only way he could make things right," Kalina whispered.

"He didn't have to kill himself."

“Grief makes people do unthinkable things,” Chris said.

“That’s a long time to hold on to grief,” Kalina said.

“So, this is over then? The investigation is done? We aren’t suspects anymore?” Nadine had stopped crying.

Chris’s phone beeped, putting a halt to the conversation. He scrolled through whatever message he’d received. “The lab just came back with results on the rope we found as well as the tea. There were traces of both of your DNA on the rope along with Mr. Larrabee’s. There were traces of NyQuil in the tea. So it sounds like you were drugged and the rest of the evidence lines up with the version of events you’ve shared. So, yes, it’s over.”

“There’s one more thing”—Kalina pointed to the desk—“it looks like he changed his will.”

Chris—still wearing gloves—picked up the paper from the top of the pile. “You’re right. It looks like he deeded the house back to Nadine.”

"After everything he went through to get the damn place and now he just gives it back?" Bitterness colored every word.

Adam bent down in front of her and took both of her hands in his. She didn't pull away this time. Apparently, knowing neither of them had been directly responsible was enough to thaw her emotions towards him. "You don't have to worry about it now. I think, as long as Detective Harper says it's okay, we should go back to the motel to get our stuff and leave town for a little while. We should put some distance between us and this place."

"Tomorrow. I just want to sleep. I haven't had a good night's sleep in a long time."

Adam pulled Nadine to her feet and with an affirmative nod from Chris they headed downstairs, no doubt in for a long walk back to the motel. Kalina looked at AJ and nodded her head towards the hallway but her nephew seemed oblivious to the hint.

"AJ, can you wait for me outside, please? Get the dummy back in the car, too."

He mouthed 'Good luck' on his way out, leaving Kalina and Chris alone. He set the evidence bag down on top of the will and crossed his arms over his chest.

“Go ahead and yell at me. I deserve it.”

“You are too nosy for your own good sometimes. We would have solved the case eventually but what you did helped.”

Kalina stared, open-mouthed. “That’s it? No rant about getting involved in police business or threatening the chain of evidence?”

“You didn’t threaten the chain of evidence. You’re smart enough not to touch things you aren’t supposed to. Technically, this wasn’t a crime scene anymore so you being here wasn’t disturbing anything and thanks to you I got information out of Nadine sooner than I would have if you hadn’t been around. I have a feeling Adam would have ended up stonewalling me in an effort to protect her. Hell, he might have even taken the fall for her if it came to that.”

Kalina thought about mentioning Jimmy’s role in her snooping but decided it wouldn’t be very nice to throw the poor kid under the bus with Chris. She liked to think maybe she was giving Jimmy some on-the-job training in critical thinking along the way.

“You know what we need to get our minds off of this?” she said.

He shook his head. “No. What?”

“A game of Cards against Humanity. I’ve got a deck at home,” she said with a smirk. After all, she’d told AJ she would find a way to make things up to Chris.

Chapter 13

The next morning, Kalina rolled over in bed to find the space where Chris had been empty, the body heat dwindling. She sat up and rubbed at her eyes with one hand, searching for her phone with the other. After groping along the edge of her nightstand, she finally found her phone and checked the time: 7:02. She kicked the sheets aside and staggered out of the room. She found Chris standing by the coffee maker with two cups in hand.

“Hey, I didn’t want to wake you,” he said and handed her a mug.

“That’s okay. I was planning on going for a run this morning anyway.”

He spooned several generous helpings of sugar into his own mug and stirred before taking a sip. “Do you think you’re going to stay in touch with Nadine?”

Kalina slid into a chair by the kitchen table and tugged at her hair. “Yeah. This whole time I felt like such a terrible friend. If I hadn’t gone off to the city and been so lost in my own world and drama things might have been different.”

“What do you mean? You couldn’t have stopped any of this.”

“Maybe not. But she wouldn’t have felt so alone after her mother died. Maybe I would have noticed a change when her father was drugging her and could have gotten her help.”

“Don’t think about it like that. You were there for her now. As I said yesterday, you probably helped her keep it together through everything.”

“I still can’t believe you aren’t mad at me for getting involved.”

“Annoyed maybe but not mad.”

“I swear I don’t mean to get dragged into

things. But I get curious and then I have to know what happened."

"I know. And it's why I love you. You are so concerned with the people of this town."

Kalina took another swig of coffee and laughed. "I was telling Nadine the other day that I was really glad to move back home because I didn't realize how much I missed the people. This is where I belong."

"Are you sure you want to go for a run? I could just drop you off at the shop on my way to the station."

"That's all right. I think I need the time to myself."

Chris downed the rest of his coffee in two big gulps and set the mug in the sink. He kissed her forehead before he disappeared to get dressed. She waited until he left before she went back to her room to pull on her workout clothes. Barring any unforeseen disasters, she fully intended to come home and shower before heading into work.

With ear buds in her ears, she took off at a steady jog. The weather was far more cooperative than it had been a few days ago and she settled into a comfortable rhythm. She took a different route, going up past the high school and fire department. She waved to a few of the firefighters heading on to their shifts as she went by. Veering off to the right at the next intersection, she found herself once again running along Ocean Front Drive. She hadn't intended go there but her subconscious must have been driving her. She stopped when she spotted a car in the driveway at 1609. She tugged the headphones out of her ears and approached it. The sound of running water caught her attention.

"Hello?" she called.

Water snaked down around the car's tires and she stepped out of its path. Kalina rounded the front of the car to find Adam holding a hose, washing away the last remnants of what had happened.

"Oh, hi," she said.

He shut off the water and tossed the hose aside. "Hi. If you're looking for Nadine, she's in the kitchen."

"Thanks."

She hadn't been looking for her friend but maybe they did need to talk. She wanted Nadine to know that she wanted them to remain close. Wiping her feet on the front mat, she headed straight back to the kitchen. Nadine sat at the table, staring at nothing in particular.

"Hey, I hope it's okay that I stopped by," Kalina said, snapping Nadine out of her fog.

"Yeah, of course."

Kalina took the seat across from her friend. "I'm a little surprised you're back here. I thought you and Adam were heading out of town today."

"We will but we needed to get this place cleaned up. I wanted to take a few pictures of my mom, too."

"What are you going to do with it now that it's yours again?"

"Sell it. There is too much sorrow and sadness in this place for me to stay here. I don't need the reminder of all the horrible things I suffered because of these four walls. It tore our family apart and if I'm going to move forward and heal from this, I need to not be here. I need to make a clean break."

"That's understandable. I'm sure you'll find a buyer quick."

"Honestly, I don't even care about the money. I'll list it for whatever it's worth and take whatever I can get. I already called a broker, Thomas Chase. He's coming over this afternoon to do an appraisal."

"That is pretty quick."

"Like I said, I need a clean break." She twisted a few strands of hair together and looked down at her lap. "I have to write an obituary for my father. But I don't think I can do it yet. Adam said he talked to the coroner out in Salem and they are ready to release my father's body."

"You have time. And you don't have to do it alone. Adam and I are here for you."

"I just don't want people to ask questions. Knowing he took his life out of guilt is hard enough for me to deal with. I don't think I could handle everyone else knowing because then they would wonder what he felt guilty about. They'd assume it was my mother."

“You don’t have to write that he took his life. You can say that he passed away suddenly while you were home visiting him. Keep it really vague. No one has to know the truth. It’s your life and your family. You’re in control of what happens now.”

“What about a funeral? I can’t pay for that. I don’t even know if he wanted one. And I don’t know what to do with his body. My mother was cremated but I have no idea if that’s what he wanted, too. And do I put him with her or with his own family?”

“Have you looked at his will?”

“Adam did. I couldn’t bring myself to look this morning.”

“Then let him help you figure all of that out. That’s what boyfriends are for, especially ones who are lawyers. He’ll know what to do or he’ll know the person to talk to. Lean on the people who care about you, Nadine.”

“Thanks. It’s just so overwhelming and I just want it to be over.” Tears shone in her eyes but they didn’t fall.

Kalina reached across the table to give her friend's hand a firm, reassuring squeeze. She looked around the kitchen at the familiar, pale yellow wallpaper and cream colored drapes. A tiny part of her would be sad to see it come into new ownership but she understood Nadine's desire to move on. It had been a harrowing few days for both of them but somehow they'd made it through. Maybe it was because they'd had each other for support.

"The reason I stopped by was because I wanted you to know that I don't want us to lose touch again, even if you're moving somewhere else with Adam."

"I'm glad you said that. I think it will be easier now. Besides, I know where to find you, Ms. Business Owner."

Kalina smiled. "It is pretty amazing that I actually got to become what I'd dreamed of and run the very store I'd always wanted."

"Not everyone is so lucky," Nadine said with a note of sadness in her voice.

"Things are going to work out for you. You've got a great guy in your life and you can put all of this behind you. We're still young. You have plenty of time to find what makes you happy. And if a nerdy mood strikes, you get the friends and family discount."

Nadine laughed a deep belly laugh. Her eyes crinkled at the corners and it had to be the happiest she'd been in a long time. It warmed Kalina's heart to see that, even with just kind words, she was helping her friend piece her life back together. Sure, tragedy had struck this family but the town was still at peace and unscathed.

Debts and Debtors

Geeks and Things Book 3

A GEEKS AND THINGS COZY MYSTERY

Debts and Debtors

S.E. BIGLOW

If you enjoy this work, please consider leaving a review.

For information contact; www.sarah-biglow.com

Edited by Ken Marrow, M.A.

Cover Design by: Deranged Doctor Design

Published by Sarah Biglow: May 2016

10 9 8 7 6 5 4 3 2 1

 Created with Vellum

Chapter 1

Raindrops pelted the kitchen window in Kalina Greystone's small apartment. Heat from the kitchen fogged the interior of the glass, obscuring the view outside. Kalina wiped sweat from her forehead with the back of her arm. The weather—in addition to being wet—had turned cold in early November and she'd turned up the heat to compensate. She was up to her elbows in dessert. This was the first Thanksgiving she'd been home with her family in a few years—and the first since her father and Aunt Agatha's passing—and she didn't want to disappoint. Checking the recipe for the spice applesauce cake frosting one more time, she moved the saucepan of brown sugar, cream and butter to the burner set on high. It reached a boil in only a few minutes and she feverishly stirred it to make sure it didn't burn. Master cook she was not. Her phone buzzed with an incoming call, slowly vibrating toward the edge of the table.

"Not now!" she moaned, hastily pulling the concoction from the stove and scooping up her phone.

Luckily, it was just an alarm to remind her she needed to leave for Jillian's house in a half hour. Chris was supposed to be coming over so they could drive together. The thought of having her very serious romantic partner joining her for a family holiday made butterflies swarm in her stomach. Things between them had been better than ever the last few months. In fact, they were in the process of moving in together. The process had been put on hold due to the holidays but before long she wouldn't have to live alone. Her front room was already strewn with partially packed boxes. Her landlord was being generous and letting her leave most of the furniture in the place. Easier to rent a fully furnished place in a town like this. She couldn't believe how lucky she'd been, moving home, taking over the family business and falling back in love with her high school sweetheart. Some days she had to pinch herself to make sure she wasn't dreaming.

Setting her phone aside, she added the remaining ingredients to the frosting mixture, gave it a good stir and carefully poured it over the cake. It still needed to cool a little bit but that's what her sister's fridge was for. Making sure the stovetop was off, she headed to her room to clean up. Ten minutes later she reappeared in a nice, pale blue blouse and black slacks. She slipped into rain boots and tossed a pair of flats into her purse.

She checked her phone, expecting a text from Chris letting her know he was waiting out front. No new messages. "Come on, where are you?"

Kalina busied herself packing up the cake and pulling on her jacket but still no word from Chris. Finally, she sent him a text. 'Are you on your way? We're going to be late.'

Still no response.

This was not the way she wanted to spend her Thanksgiving but she couldn't help feeling a little annoyed that he was suddenly ignoring her. Finally, she pulled on her coat and stowed her phone in her pocket for safekeeping. Time to brave the storm.

Torrents of water buffeted her all the way to her car. She practically dove into the driver seat; the cake container almost landed sideways on the passenger seat. She let out a breath—air condensing in front of her—and started the engine. She set the wipers on high and waited for the heat to kick in before she pulled out of the driveway and turned left down her street.

Her phone began to ring loudly halfway to Jillian's house. "Great."

Her mood already on edge, she pulled over to the side of the road and yanked the phone free. Chris's number flashed on the Caller ID. She hit 'Accept' and put the phone on speaker so she could keep driving. "Hey." She did her best to keep her tone neutral.

"I am so sorry, Kal."

"You can meet me there. That's fine."

"I don't think I can make it."

"You promised." It came out as more of a whine than she'd intended.

“I know. I wish I could be there, believe me. But I got called out to the beach for a case. I swear I will find a way to make it up to you.”

She took several breaths before she responded. “Fine. I get it. You have to work. You can’t choose when dead bodies turn up.”

“Please don’t be mad at me. I told the guys I was off today but Jimmy called last minute and said he needed my help on this one.”

Kalina’s anger softened a touch at the young officer’s name. He was a good kid but eager to impress. She also wasn’t above gently grilling him for information when she needed something. But that hadn’t happened in months. She was trying to stay out of police matters. She was a comic book shop owner, after all. “Okay. I’ll pass on your regrets to everyone.”

“Thanks. I love you.”

She smiled. “I love you too.”

Easing to a stop at a crosswalk, she hit ‘End’ and set her phone aside. Her sister’s house loomed up ahead on the side of town farthest from the beach. Jillian had insisted on staying local but when AJ had come along she'd wanted a yard too. Somehow, Kalina's older sister got exactly what she wanted. She was lucky that way. Even getting pregnant right out of college, Jillian managed to make it all work.

Through the downpour she spotted her mom's car in the driveway. She pulled up beside it and braced herself for the short trek to the front door. Pulling the hood of her coat up over her face, she grabbed the cake container and darted from the car. Thirty seconds later, she was safely inside the front hall being greeted by her nephew, AJ.

"It's really coming down out there," he said and took the container so she could peel her soaked jacket from her shoulders.

"It's insane. I wouldn't be surprised if it turned to snow later tonight." She leaned against the door to kick off her rain boots and put on her flats.

AJ lifted the lid of the container and took a sniff. "Where's Chris?"

"Working. He got called away on an urgent case."

"Lame."

"Behave yourself," she chided and quickly finger-combed her hair so she looked presentable before her sister appeared.

"AJ, put that in the kitchen," Jillian ordered. She stood a good four inches taller than Kalina and she'd inherited their mother's wavy curls and light brown hair.

No one would have ever accused them of being siblings, and yet they'd shared a bedroom until Jillian had gone off to college. They weren't especially close these days but Jillian seemed pleased that Kalina was keeping AJ out of trouble.

"Sorry I'm late ... and dateless," Kalina muttered.

"It's a hell of a storm out there. I'm just glad you made it over safely." Jillian's facial features softened and she pulled her sister into an impromptu hug.

"How many glasses of wine have you had?" Kalina whispered.

"Shut up." Jillian pulled away but smiled. "Do you want red or white?"

“Whatever’s open,” Kalina said with a dismissive wave.

“Red it is.”

Kalina followed her sister into the kitchen. Her brother-in-law, Daniel, stood by the stove dutifully stirring their mother’s homemade gravy. He was a decent guy. He’d stuck with Jillian and married her after he’d gotten her pregnant. They seemed to have a solid marriage now. She had to give them both credit for sticking it out and really building something in the years since AJ came along.

“Hey, where’s Mom?” Kalina asked, accepting the glass of wine Jillian hastily shoved into her hand.

“Living room. She’s … not handling things well today.”

Kalina excused herself with a nod towards the living room and disappeared. Her mother sat on the couch, staring out at the storm. She settled in beside her and leaned over to give her a kiss on the cheek.

“Hi, Mom. How are you?”

"Fine, sweetheart." She didn't look away from the window.

"Mom, come on, it's me. I know you miss him and Aunt Agatha. We all do."

Her mother turned to face Kalina with tears already staining her cheeks. "I thought I would be okay, having you girls with me. I'm so sorry."

Kalina set her glass down on the table and wrapped her mother in a hug. "You don't have anything to be sorry about, Mom. You have a good cry."

They sat together for a few minutes in silence, the only sound the occasional murmurs from the kitchen and the hammering of the rain outside. Kalina briefly wondered where her nephew had disappeared to but her curiosity died when a loud knock echoed from the front of the house. She didn't move, unsure whether it was a knock on the front door or if it was just the weather raging. When the sound came again—this time a more distinct knocking—she extricated herself from her mother's embrace and went to answer the door. A woman—maybe in her early forties—stood on the front porch, purse clutched to her chest. Her hair was matted to her scalp from the rain.

“Can I help you?”

“I’m looking for Jillian.”

Kalina turned toward the kitchen and called, “Jillian, there’s someone here for you.”

Her sister appeared in view and immediately raced forward. “Come in, come in.”

Kalina stepped out of the way, letting Jillian dote on their surprise guest. She waited to be introduced but in all of her fussing Jillian seemed to have forgotten the rest of the family. Even AJ had appeared—from his room it turned out—to survey the commotion.

“You want to introduce us, Jill?” Kalina asked.

Jillian blushed. “Sorry. This is Savannah Hennessey. We went to college together.”

Savannah stood shivering and dripping on the welcome mat. “It’s actually Chase now. Thomas and I got married a couple years ago.” The mention of her marriage brought tears to Savannah’s eyes and her lower lip quivered. “I think something awful has happened to my husband."

Chapter 2

Awkward silence filled the front hall as everyone present processed Savannah's declaration. Kalina bit the inside of her lip at the realization that she'd been secretly itching for a new mystery to solve. She caught AJ's eye and he looked as eager as she felt. They were, of course, premature in their excitement. There was every possibility that there was no mystery in need of a solution.

"Why don't we get you out of those wet clothes and you can tell us what's going on?" she said, taking charge of the situation. She turned to Jillian. "I'm sure you've got something she can borrow."

"Of course. You're right."

Jillian helped Savannah out of her coat and they disappeared upstairs to the master bedroom in search of dry clothes. Kalina shut the door and looked pointedly at her nephew. "Don't get ahead of yourself."

He held up his hands in a defensive posture. "I didn't say anything."

Daniel poked his head out of the kitchen. "I take it we'll be setting another place for dinner?"

"No. Well, just use Chris's place setting. He can't make it."

Her brother-in-law nodded and ducked back into the kitchen to tend to the meal. Kalina ushered AJ into the living room where her mother still sat on the couch. She looked a little perkier at least. They waited in silence for Jillian and her friend to come back downstairs. After what seemed like an hour but was likely only fifteen minutes, they reappeared. Savannah had blow-dried her hair and wore a sweater and jeans. They fit remarkably well. She'd clearly dried her eyes, too. Jillian carried a box of tissues as a precaution.

"So, what makes you think something's happened to your husband?" Kalina asked.

"I haven't seen him since yesterday morning. He always comes home, even if he's late. I started to get worried when he didn't come home at all. If he's going to be late at the office he always calls me. He knows I worry."

"Did you go to the police?"

Savannah shook her head. "No. I thought I had to wait forty-eight hours before I could report him missing."

"Actually, you can report after twenty-four," AJ piped up.

Jillian gave him a cross look and he closed his mouth. "Well, either way, you should report it as soon as you can."

Savannah tugged at the ends of her hair. "They aren't working today."

Kalina couldn't help but feel a little bitter. "They're always working."

Outside the wind picked up to a vicious howl and rain slammed against the siding and windows. Lightning split the sky in vibrant arcs and thunder boomed not long after. The storm was far from over.

“I think you may have to wait until tomorrow. It isn’t safe to be out in this weather,” Kalina said.

Savannah sniffled and wrapped her arms around her torso. “He could be out there all alone. Why didn’t he come home last night?” Fresh tears trickled down her cheeks.

Jillian disappeared into the kitchen and returned with a glass of wine, which she shoved into her friend’s quivering grasp. She took several large swallows before setting it on the coffee table in front of her.

Daniel stuck his head out from the kitchen doorway. “Dinner is ready.”

Jillian cleared her throat and ushered their mother and Savannah into the dining room. She motioned for Kalina to follow her back into the kitchen. AJ busied himself helping direct people to their seats.

“I meant to tell you that AJ can’t work this weekend,” Jillian said and handed Kalina a serving dish of mashed potatoes.

“And why’s that?”

"He just needs some time at home, that's all."

"Well, that's not how a job works, Jill. You know that. You were the one who wanted him to take on more responsibility, get some actual job experience for his college applications, and that's what he's doing. If he needs the time off for school work then fine. But that request comes from him, not you. Mommy can't call him out sick in the real world."

"Kalina, that's not fair."

Kalina took a deep breath to calm her nerves. They didn't need to fight, especially not in front of their mother. She was emotionally fragile as it was given the nature of the holiday. Kalina carried the dish to the table and set it between the green beans and stuffing. Making one last trip to the kitchen, she poured herself another glass of wine and settled in at the table between her mother and AJ. She tried to put on a happy face but felt the edges of her mouth turn down into a scowl when she caught her sister's gaze.

"Thank you for letting me stay and share dinner with your family," Savannah said once everyone was seated.

“You were like family in college. Of course you’re staying. And don’t even think about going home tonight. We’ll make up the spare bedroom for you,” Jillian said.

They didn’t bother with grace. They were never an overly religious family as it was. Daniel worked skillfully at carving up the turkey. Working in a butcher shop as a teenager had been a blessing, at least for Thanksgiving and Christmas dinner. With plates piled high, everyone fell silent, focusing on the food in front of them.

Several hours later, Kalina’s mother retired to one of the third-floor rooms. The nice part about having a three-story house was all the extra rooms. Kalina flaked out on the couch in the living room in a bit of a haze. Her head throbbed from too much wine and she knew she should probably lie down in bed but she was too comfortable to move. She was vaguely aware of someone pulling a blanket over her and footsteps on the stairs but didn’t register specific people. The storm continued to rage outside, lulling her to sleep. Sometime later, she woke with start at the sound of something rumbling. Disoriented and still half-asleep, she looked around for the source of the noise but couldn't find it. A bright light passed through the front window, making shadows on the living room floor, but it was gone almost as quickly as it came. With a sigh, she curled up beneath the blanket and drifted back to sleep.

Chapter 3

Sunlight streamed through the front window of the living room, rousing Kalina from her half-asleep state. She sat up, rubbed her eyes and looked around the living room, remembering she'd fallen asleep on the couch. She untangled her legs from the blanket and headed upstairs to brush her teeth and wash her face. She hadn't intended to spend the night and had no other clothes to change into. She wasn't about to borrow something from her sister's closet. After doing what she could to make herself presentable, she headed back downstairs and made a beeline for the coffee pot. Her brother-in-law stood in front of it.

"Mind pouring me a cup?" she asked.

Daniel jumped and a plate clattered to the counter, revealing the remnants of some of her applesauce cake. He blushed bright red and she couldn't help but giggle.

"I won't tell Jillian," she said and brushed some crumbs from the front of his shirt.

"Thanks." The color receded a little as he reached for a mug and delivered the requested beverage.

Kalina savored the coffee, letting the caffeine wake up her senses. She peered out the kitchen window into the backyard. To her surprise the few trees in the yard hadn't lost any branches. "That was one crazy storm yesterday," she said.

"Yeah. It was." He set his plate in the sink and ran water over it, getting rid of the evidence of his non-traditional breakfast. "You know, I heard what you said to Jillian last night about AJ working at the shop."

Kalina choked on the sip of coffee she'd just taken. "Oh."

"I agree with you. She can't just pull him away from work whenever she feels like it. But what she probably wouldn't tell you is that she's been having a hard time letting him go and grow up. I mean he's got his learner's permit now and he's becoming more independent. I think she's just scared about him being out in the real world on his own in a couple of years."

"I get that but when I'm at work I have to treat him like an employee, not my nephew."

"Believe me, I understand."

Kalina caught sight of the clock on the microwave and nearly spit in her mug. "Is that the time?"

Daniel glanced over his shoulder. "It's not even eight yet."

"It's Black Friday."

"Oh, big comic buying day, is it?"

"Big retail day period."

Daniel laughed, lips spreading wide to reveal a straight, white smile. "I'm only kidding. If you need to head out, go for it. I'll give your best to Jill and AJ and Mom."

"I could actually use AJ's help."

Her brother-in-law looked toward the staircase. “If you can drag his butt out of bed, be my guest.”

“Oh, and tell Jill I’ll meet her at the station when I can get a break. I want to be there when Savannah reports her husband missing.”

“Any particular reason?”

She pursed her lips. “I just want to make sure she gets all the important information to whoever takes the report.”

“In other words, in case it isn’t Chris, you want to make sure the boys in blue don’t screw up.”

Kalina held a finger to her lips. “Something like that.”

Draining the coffee mug, she set it in the sink and headed upstairs to rouse her nephew. She knocked twice on his bedroom door before sticking her head in. The person-shaped lump beneath the covers signaled he was still in dreamland.

“Hey, you need to get up. I need you down at the shop.”

He moaned and poked his head out from beneath the blankets. “Do you know what time it is?”

“I do. Now get moving, kiddo. You’re on the clock in a half hour. Don’t be late.”

AJ pulled the blankets back over his head. Kalina turned to head back down to find her car keys and nearly knocked Savannah down the stairs. “So sorry!” she apologized.

Savannah managed to regain her footing and rubbed at her eyes. They were red-rimmed as if she’d been crying again. “So you really think I should go to the police?”

“Yes. I’d like to go with you. I know the lead detective in the department and I can make sure he takes the case.”

“That’s so nice of you. You really don’t have to help me.”

“Don’t be ridiculous. My sister treats you like family, so you are family. I’ll meet you two down at the station around eleven.”

“Thank you.” Savannah pulled Kalina into an awkward one-armed hug.

Kalina wiggled out of the hug as best she could and took the stairs two at a time. Daniel stood at the bottom of the stairs, holding her coat out for her.

“What a gentleman,” she said and slipped it on.

“I’ll make sure AJ’s at work on time,” he said as she fished her keys out of her coat pocket.

She was halfway out the door when Daniel caught her wrist and shoved her phone into her outstretched hand. She flashed him a smile before heading out. She needed to stop by her apartment and clean up before she headed into work. It would also give her time to give Chris a call and see how he was. She didn’t want to be angry with him and she figured it was a good idea to give him a heads up that they were coming in so someone would be around to take the missing person report. Once she’d maneuvered her car around the others parked in the driveway and was on the road, she gave Chris a call, making sure to put it on speaker phone. It rang three times before he picked up.

“Hello?” He sounded exhausted.

“Hey, I just wanted to check in and see how you were,” she said.

“It was a long night. I just got in a couple hours ago.”

“Jeez. It was that bad?”

“Getting techs out in the storm was tough. Look, I’ll make it up to you about last night.”

“Don’t worry about it. You didn’t miss much.”

“But you made my favorite dessert.”

She grinned at herself in the rearview mirror. “I’ll make some for you.”

“You’re the best.” He yawned on the other end of the line.

“Look, I just wanted to ask who is working at the precinct today.”

“Should I be worried?”

“No, not really. I just had to refer someone to the police to file a report and I wanted to make sure there were actually bodies at the station today given all the craziness yesterday.”

“Yeah. Someone will be there.”

“Great. Look, go back to sleep. I’ll see you later. I love you.”

"Love you too."

The line went dead and her phone hung up the call on its own. She pulled into the driveway of her building and raced inside to grab a quick shower. Feeling refreshed and ready to face the day, she climbed back behind the steering wheel and made the short journey to Geeks and Things. There was already a line of beleaguered adults accompanying young kids all eager to pick up their Black Friday swag. She unlocked the back door just as her nephew rolled up on his bike. He still looked half-asleep.

"Perk up, kiddo. You play your cards right and you'll get a bonus out of this," she said with a smirk.

"Black Friday is evil," he mumbled and followed her inside.

Kalina flipped on the lights in the game room and the front of the store and booted up the tablet so it was ready for transactions. AJ unlocked the cash drawer for the likely onslaught of cash purchases—kids saved up all of their allowance for days like today—and did a quick cash count.

"I think we're ready," he said, appearing to wake up a little more as the silhouettes of eager customers shifted outside the front door.

Kalina put on a big smile and said, "Let's do this thing!"

The next three hours were a blur of giddy yelps of excitement as kids bought her wares for the first time with their own, carefully saved up, money. She had some usual customers come in for their weekly orders and some new, curious faces drop by thanks to the holiday weekend. Some of the adults shooed the children accompanying them into the game room while they attempted to do some covert Christmas shopping outside the view of prying eyes.

"Thanks so much for shopping at Geeks and Things. We hope to see you again for all your nerdy needs," Kalina called as the last customer walked out.

She collapsed against the counter and glanced at AJ. He looked wide awake and a bit shell shocked. He eased the cash drawer shut and slumped on to the stool behind the counter. "That was insane, Aunt K."

"There might still be more. And I need you to hold things down for me for a little while."

He let out a whine. "Where are you going?"

"I promised your mom and Savannah I'd go with them to the precinct so Savannah can file a missing person report."

"Oh, right. Do you think he is really missing?"

"No idea. People don't come home for lots of reasons. Not all of them are the worst case scenario."

"Don't worry about the shop. I got it covered."

She reached over and ruffled his hair before she went in search of her coat and keys. Just as she climbed in behind the wheel, her phone buzzed with an incoming call from Jillian. "Hey, I'm heading over to the precinct now."

"Oh, good. I guess we'll see you there. Now, you're sure someone will be there?"

"Yes. See you in a few minutes."

Tossing the phone onto the passenger seat, Kalina started the car and made a U-turn out of the parking lot. As she got situated back on Main Street, she saw a few more people wandering in the direction of the shop. She sent off a silent ‘good luck’ to her nephew. He was a smart kid and could handle the shop for a little while. She assumed she would be back by lunchtime and she could take over so he could eat. A couple minutes later, she found a spot in the parking lot outside the precinct and spotted her sister’s car two spots over.

“Ready?” she asked Savannah once they all stood at the front door.

“No, but I don’t have a choice.”

Chapter 4

Kalina trailed the other two women as they walked in and stopped at the reception desk. Jimmy sat there with a distant look in his eyes. Kalina knew he'd been on the scene with Chris most of the night. What was he doing there now?

“Hey, Jimmy. I'm surprised to see you here,” Kalina said, taking control of the situation.

He yawned, barely stifling it. “When the boss says to pull a double, you do it.”

They still didn't have a new Chief of Police and Chris seemed adamant about not taking the position. Kalina didn't entirely get why, since he was a good cop and everyone looked to him for guidance anyway. If they wanted to keep things in-house after the debacle of Captain Cahill, he was the logical choice.

"I heard yesterday was rough." She gave him a sympathetic smile. "The reason we're here though is a friend of ours needs to file a missing person report. You can help her with that, right?"

Jimmy looked to Savannah who gave him a plaintive look and tugged at her hair. Oh, yeah, he was definitely paying attention now. He scrambled from behind the desk and ushered them toward the bull pen and an empty desk. He dutifully pulled out a chair for Savannah to sit in before he booted up the computer. Jillian pulled over a chair from a nearby desk and settled in beside her friend. Kalina remained standing over Savannah's right shoulder and looked around. Chris was probably still sleeping. Or maybe he was down at the crime scene. Speaking of which, she spotted some photos of a man taped to a whiteboard with 'John Doe' scrawled across the top. It was bloated and waterlogged but she could swear he looked familiar.

“Okay, now Miss... ” Jimmy trailed off, waiting for Savannah to fill in the rest.

“Mrs. Chase. I... I would like to report someone missing.”

“And who would that be?”

“My husband. Thomas Chase.”

Jimmy hastily jotted down notes on a pad in front of him. Kalina tuned out of the conversation for a minute, focusing on the board across the room. She’d met Mr. Chase only once—when her friend Nadine sold her family home—but she remembered him well, with thinning, grey-brown hair and sincere, green eyes. She couldn’t verify eye color but the hair on John Doe looked right.

She leaned over to whisper in Jillian’s ear. “Take a look at that photo on the board over there. Does he look familiar to you?”

Savannah stopped mid-sentence—having heard Kalina’s question—and turned to look at her. She got up from her seat and inched closer, studying the picture. Her body language changed almost instantly. Kalina raced forward when Savannah started to sway and guided her back to the chair. Jillian had turned pale.

"Is something wrong, Mrs. Chase?" Jimmy asked. Poor guy wasn't exactly the world's most perceptive investigator.

"Why ... why is there a photo of my husband on that board?"

Jimmy cleared his throat, opened his mouth and closed it again. "Um ... you're sure that's your husband?"

"Yes. We've been married for three years. I think I'd know the man I share a bed with."

Jimmy looked to Kalina as if she held the answers to his questions but she shook her head and gestured to her phone. She mouthed 'Chris' and his cheeks flushed. He took a deep breath and picked up the receiver. "I'm going to call Detective Harper. He should really talk to you about this."

Chapter 5

Jillian went in search of tissues for Savannah while Jimmy made the call to Chris. Kalina stayed standing, observing the whole situation with a growing sense of unease. A million questions flooded her thoughts. Namely, how had Thomas Chase ended up dead in the last day? At least his death explained why he hadn't gone home the day before Thanksgiving. Jimmy tapped his fingers nervously against the desk while he waited for Chris to answer the call.

"Detective Harper, it's Jimmy. I need you to get down to the station right away. We've got an ID on the"—he glanced over at Kalina—"case from yesterday." He paused. "His wife came in to report him missing."

He nodded his head as Chris said something on the other end of the line. Jillian returned and handed a wad of crumpled napkins from the kitchen area to Savannah. She wiped at her eyes and sniffled loudly while Jimmy wrapped up the call. Finally, he set the receiver back in the cradle and cleared his throat again.

"Detective Harper will be down shortly to speak with you about your husband. I'm sorry for your loss, ma'am."

Kalina felt bad for Jimmy. He'd no doubt never had to notify anyone about the death of a loved one before. The only other big cases he'd been involved with had victims who didn't have any living relatives or were already aware of the crime. Thinking back on those cases, Kalina wondered how Nadine was faring. They'd talked and emailed around Halloween and she'd been settling in but the family holidays were probably still rough for her.

"Can I ask ... where he was found? And what happened?" Savannah asked between sniffles.

"It's probably better if you just wait for the detective. I'm not really handling the case."

An awkward silence fell over the station. Jimmy stood up and hurried back to the front desk, leaving the grieving widow in the care of Jillian and Kalina. For her part, Jillian made soft shushing noises and wrapped her friend in a wordless hug. Kalina moved away, wanting to give them privacy, and she approached the front desk.

"You okay? You look a little freaked out."

"I've never had to tell someone their husband was dead."

"It's part of the job, right? They train you for it."

"I know. I just feel so bad for her. This is supposed to be a time that's all about family and being thankful and now she's got to bury the man she loves."

"I'm sure you could help ease her mind if you shared just a couple details. Nothing gruesome. But maybe if he was alone when it happened?" Sure, she wanted the details herself but she wanted Jimmy to be able to handle things on his own as a cop. Chris wouldn't always be around to steer him.

He stood up straighter and pivoted to head back to the desk where Savannah and Jillian sat huddled together. He'd only a few steps before the front doors opened and Chris rushed in looking disheveled. His shirt wasn't tucked in and his hair was more bed-head than naturally tussled. Kalina motioned for Jimmy to continue his task and she spun to stop Chris before he got too far.

"You want to fill me in?" he asked as she smoothed down his hair and straightened his shirt.

"Savannah Chase. Wife of Thomas Chase. He's a real estate broker I think. She ended up at my sister's house yesterday because she hadn't seen her husband in a day and she was worried."

"Why'd she go to your sister?"

"They're college friends. I convinced her to come in and report him missing. Looks like there's a reason he didn't come home."

"Thanks." He gave her a quick kiss before stepping around her and sidling up to the group.

Suspecting the conversation would be longer than the previous one, Kalina grabbed an empty chair and pulled it up. Chris didn't even comment on her and Jillian's continued presence during the interview. He retrieved a notepad and pen from his own desk and settled in.

"Mrs. Chase, I'm very sorry to have to inform you that your husband was found last night."

"Where was he? What happened?"

"He was in an abandoned property down by the beach. He'd been shot."

Savannah devolved into another fit of hysterics and rocked back and forth. Jimmy visibly recoiled at the emotional outburst. Chris sat patiently, pen at the ready to jot down notes. Kalina had to admit she liked watching him work.

"I'm sorry," Savannah mumbled into the wad of damp napkins. "I don't understand who would want to hurt him."

“Remind me what your husband did for a living.”

“He was a real estate broker in town. Everyone liked him. He’d never hurt a fly. Please, do you have any suspects?”

“We’re still investigating. It would help us establish a better timeline if you could give us some information about the last time you saw him.”

“It was the day before Thanksgiving. He went into work like he always does. He didn’t come home at the normal time but that’s not unusual. He’ll always call me and tell me if he’s running late so I don’t worry.”

“Did your husband call you that night?”

“No. Which is why I started to get concerned. He always called.”

Chris scribbled something on the pad and looked up. “How often would your husband work late?”

“What?”

“Out of a month, how many nights do you think he worked late?”

"A few. I don't really remember."

"Can you try to think a little harder?"

"I guess maybe five or six times a month. It didn't seem that frequent. Why? Is that important?"

Chris cleared his throat and pursed his lips. Kalina could tell he was choosing his next words carefully. "Is it possible your husband wasn't working late those nights?"

The color in Savannah's cheeks drained. "Are you accusing my husband of cheating on me?"

"I can't imagine there was much reason for a real estate broker to work late that often."

"He'd never cheat on me." Savannah's cheeks burned bright red and her shoulders stiffened. Chris had clearly hit a nerve.

"I don't mean to sound insensitive but you aren't Mr. Chase's first wife," Chris said.

Kalina shot Jillian a confused look. There'd been another Mrs. Chase? Clearly, being away from town during college and afterwards had done her more of a disservice in being in the know on town gossip than she'd realized.

“That isn’t fair, Detective,” Jillian interrupted.

“His first wife died of breast cancer six years ago. It took him a really long time to get over her,” Savannah said, her tone much quieter now.

Kalina tried to hide the shock on her face but quickly realized no one was really paying her any attention. Chris looked down at the notes he’d taken and then back up at Savannah.

“I wasn’t implying anything negative about his first wife. But … it is a little suspicious that a woman such as yourself would be interested in a man like Thomas.”

“What’s that supposed to mean?”

“You’re quite a bit younger than he was.”

Savannah leapt from her chair, her hands balled into fists, and shouted, “Are you calling me a gold digger?”

Chris didn’t appear fazed. “No. I’m merely stating that it might seem strange to some people that there was such a big age difference.”

"We were in love."

Jillian tugged on Savannah's arm until the blonde woman sat back down. Her facial features stormed with anger and insult. If Chris had struck a nerve with the implication that Thomas had cheated on her, she was livid with the accusation that she'd only married him for his money.

"I don't appreciate you dragging me or my husband through the mud like this, Detective. I want to know what you're doing to find out who did this to him!"

"I apologize, Mrs. Chase. I didn't mean to upset you. I can assure you we are looking into every lead we can. Was your husband selling any beach-front property that you knew of? Maybe he was meeting a client later in the day out there?"

"He didn't talk about his work much."

"So you didn't know which properties he was currently trying to sell?"

"No. I'm sorry. Not that I can think of anyway."

Chris tapped his pen against his notepad and stared intently at it. Kalina could tell he was weighing the best option on how to move forward. By the way his shoulders tightened and he leaned forward, she guessed he wanted to continue to question Savannah. But she appeared to be closing herself off.

“Mrs. Chase, I’m going to need you to go to the morgue and make an identification just so we can be absolutely sure it’s your husband. Do you think you can do that?”

Savannah let out a couple more sniffles and dabbed at her eyes. “I think so. Can Jillian go with me?”

“Sure. I’ll have Jimmy go with you.” He waved to get Jimmy’s attention.

Jimmy pulled on his jacket and waited for Jillian and Savannah to stand up and gather themselves. Kalina stayed seated, as did Chris. He scribbled down a few more notes before spinning around his chair.

“Mrs. Chase, just one last question.”

She stopped and looked over her shoulder. “Yes?”

“What company did your husband work for?”

"Eastern Seaboard Realty."

"Thanks."

Chapter 6

Chris blew out a breath as soon as they were alone. Kalina scooted her chair over and took his hand in hers, hoping it would help alleviate some of the stress keeping his jaw and shoulders tight.

"That went ... sort of well," she offered with a one-shouldered shrug.

"If it really is her husband, I feel sorry for her."

"Do you really think someone would want to kill him? A client or something?"

"I don't know. Maybe. I mean real estate can be rather competitive."

"I met him once. A couple months ago when Nadine was selling her place. He seemed nice enough and she was happy with the money she got from working with him."

"What's your take on Mrs. Chase?"

Kalina arched a brow. "What do you mean?"

"Do you find her credible?"

"If you mean do I think she's really upset that her husband is dead then yeah. I'd say she's credible. Other than that, I only met her last night. All we talked about was her husband being missing. Dinner wasn't exactly full of conversation."

"Everything all right?"

Kalina let out a sigh. "It was just an argument with Jill about AJ working at the shop this weekend. It will get sorted out."

"Speaking of which, isn't today a big sales day for you guys?"

"Yeah. I left AJ in charge." She glanced at the time. "I should get back. I promised him I'd only be gone an hour."

"I might bring my nephews by a little later."

"I'll look forward to it. And I hope things work out with this case and you get a lead." She kissed him for longer than strictly necessary. He didn't seem to mind in the least.

She retrieved her phone and sent off a text to her nephew, assuring him she'd be there in a few minutes so he could take lunch. She hoped the lunch rush wouldn't be too bad because she had a little research she wanted to do on Eastern Seaboard Realty.

Five minutes later, she pulled in behind the shop. There weren't hordes of people beating down the doors so maybe she'd get lucky and have some peace and quiet. AJ greeted her at the back door—another sign things weren't too busy—and grinned at her.

"Things went awesome while you were gone. We made a bunch of sales. I even convinced some people to get more than they came in for."

"Good job. I'll take over for a while."

"I could stay if you want. Just in case."

She pushed past him into the game room and

headed to the front of the store. He trailed behind her like an eager puppy.

“I think you should take a little time off,” she said without looking at him.

“Why? I thought I was doing well?”

“You are. You’re been a great help.”

“So what’s the problem?”

She turned to face him. “This isn’t a punishment, okay? Your mom and dad told me last night that your mom’s been having a hard time with you being away from the house so much.”

“So she put you up to this?”

Kalina kneaded her temples. “You are growing up so fast and before you know it you’ll be out in the world at college and living your own life as an adult. Your mom isn’t ready to let you go just yet. I think she just wants to spend a little time with you. That’s all this is. I promise.”

Her nephew pouted and his shoulders fell as if he’d been scolded. He looked so much younger than his sixteen years in that moment and she had to resist the urge to wrap him in a tight, comforting embrace. Here, she was his boss not his aunt. Hugging an employee would be totally inappropriate.

“It’s only for a couple days,” she said and tried to give him a reassuring smile.

He rolled his eyes and made his way back through the game room. The back door slammed shut and Kalina let out a sigh of frustration. Why did teenage boys have to be so moody? She settled in behind the front counter and checked the transaction log on the tablet and did a quick cash count just to be sure everything looked right. She had to admit she was impressed with the number of sales. She made a mental note to compare next year to see if the holiday weekend was consistent.

Satisfied that the books were temporarily settled, Kalina pulled up the browser on the tablet and easily found the contact information for the realty company. According to the contact page, the company’s main office was not far from the waterfront where Thomas had been found. After deciding to play the part of a prospective client, she entered the number into her phone and hit ‘Call’.

After four rings, a bored sounding woman's voice answered, "Eastern Seaboard Realty. How can I help you?"

Kalina put on her bubbliest voice possible. "Oh, hi, I was hoping to speak with one of your realtors about listing my house for sale."

"Hold for a moment."

The line turned to static as Kalina was put on hold. She pulled the phone from her ear to check that the connection was still good. The timer on the call continued to tick off the seconds. She started kicking her heel against the bottom of the stool while she waited for the woman to come back on the line.

"I'm sorry, all of our realtors have full client lists."

"Are you sure? A friend of mine referred me. She said the realtor she had was great. Thomas Chase was his name."

"He doesn't work here anymore." Her tone shifted, taking on an edge.

"Are you sure? She only worked with him a couple months ago."

“Yes. I’m sorry but we can’t help you.” The line went dead and this time the timer stopped and ended the call.

Kalina stared at her phone in confused silence. Her little experiment had only yielded more questions. Did Savannah know her husband was no longer working for the real estate company? When did he stop working there and where had he been going all this time? More importantly, why couldn’t the firm help her even if Thomas was no longer an employee? There was definitely something off about the whole situation. Before she could decide what to do next, her phone screen lit up with a call from her sister.

“Hey, I wanted to let you know that I gave AJ the weekend off.”

“Oh, thanks.” She was clearly distracted.

“How did it go at the morgue?”

“It’s him. It was so awful seeing him lying there like that.”

“Tell Savannah I’m so sorry.”

“Yeah. Look, I need Detective Harper’s direct number. Can you send it to me?”

"Sure. Why, what's going on?"

"Someone vandalized the Chases' house. Broke and smashed up a bunch of stuff."

"Oh, God, is everyone okay?"

"We think it happened while Savannah's been with us."

"I'll get you Chris's number right now."

"Thanks."

Chapter 7

Kalina let the phone fall from her fingers and clatter to the countertop. What would make someone want to vandalize the Chases' house? Maybe whoever shot Thomas had been watching the house and did it after Savannah left the night before. Something about the timing piqued her curiosity and she flipped the front door sign to 'Closed' and headed out again. If Chris asked why she was at the new crime scene, she could reasonably say she was there to support her sister and friend. She also wanted to tell him about Thomas no longer being employed at the real estate firm.

She had to look at the address online before she headed out. It turned out that the Chases lived in a not-so-modest, three-story, sprawling house near the beach. It was set far enough back that high tides wouldn't cause trouble but close enough that they could still claim they had beach-front property. The flashing lights of the police cruiser nearly blinded her as she pulled up and parked one house over. Crime scene technicians were already flitting in and out of the house with evidence bags and fingerprint powder. Savannah huddled with Jillian off to the side, talking to Chris. Kalina climbed out of her car and got within earshot long enough to hear the gist. According to Savannah, the house had been fine when she left on Thanksgiving and she hadn't been back until then so that had to be the window of opportunity.

"Once the techs are done, I'd like to do a walk through with you, just so we can have an accurate inventory of anything that might be missing," Chris said and Savannah nodded.

There was something off about the front door. Trying not to look too obvious, Kalina made her way over so she had a clear view. Someone had spray painted the word 'Traitor' on the front door. Traitor of what? To whom? This only made things more complicated. She really needed to share with Chris what she'd found about Thomas's employment situation but she wouldn't just horn in on his conversation with a grieving widow. In her peripheral vision, she spotted a man dressed in a dark suit and tie standing at the end of the road, observing the scene. Immediately, the tiny hairs on the back of her neck stood on end, signaling he didn't belong. Abruptly, the man turned and strode off, hands in his pockets. Kalina discreetly followed him until he stopped halfway up the beach at a sign for Carlisle Premiere Developments.

"Excuse me, sir!" The words were out of her mouth before she realized she'd spoken.

The man stopped and waited for her to catch up and spun on his heel to face her. Up close he was imposing with a sharp jaw and linebacker shoulders. He pressed his lips into a thin line of displeasure at his day being interrupted by a silly comic shop owner playing detective.

"Yes?" His voice was high and nasally, not at all what Kalina expected to come out of such a large man.

“You don’t happen to work for the development company do you?”

Instead of answering, he reached into his breast pocket and produced a business card. She took it and glanced over the text. The mystery man was Victor Mackland, Asset Protection Manager. Mr. Mackland did indeed work for the development company.

“I saw you down the street and I wanted to ask what you could tell me about what’s happening here on the waterfront. I’m relatively new to town.” She prayed he hadn’t seen her on Main Street any time recently.

“The company is building a new hotel and some high end waterfront condos.”

“Oh, wow. That sounds great. I mean it will just boost tourism to town and increase revenue. But ... what about the people who live here?”

“I’m sorry, Miss. If you have more questions, you’ll need to speak to one of our girls in sales. Good day.”

Before she could say more, Mr. Mackland did an about face and strode off out of sight. Kalina stayed put for a minute trying to process the new information. She needed to do a little fact checking to see if there really was a new development project happening and how Thomas Chase was involved. Shaking her head, she made her way back up the beach and the street to the Chase house. The technicians were loading up the last of their gear and Chris and Savannah had disappeared. Jillian stood alone by the front steps.

“This is getting pretty crazy,” Kalina said and sidled up to her sister.

“Savannah is going to stay with us until this is all over. It clearly isn’t safe for her to be here alone.”

“That makes sense. Hey, do you know anything about a new hotel and condos going up on the beach?”

“Yeah, a lot of people weren’t too happy when that contract came through.”

“Why not?”

Jillian rolled her eyes. “Honestly, Kal. Read a newspaper sometime. Building the new hotel and condos means the people who live there now will have to give up their houses. And a lot of the older population of town live out there. They don't have anywhere to go. But the town agreed to the project so there's not much they can do."

"Thanks. I need to get back to the shop. Let me know if you need anything."

Her sister gave a weary smile and nodded. Time to do some more digging.

Chapter 8

The trip back to the shop was short and she found AJ flipping through the Cards against Humanity deck at the front counter. She set her phone down on the counter beside him and scooted him out of the way.

“Things seem to have slowed down,” he said.

“That’s how it usually is.”

“Sorry I got mad at you before, Aunt K.”

“Don’t worry about it.”

“So what’s the latest news on our dead guy?”

“Well, he hasn’t worked for the real estate firm in at least two months and there was a man from Carlisle Premiere Developments lurking around the Chase house after it had been vandalized. That was kind of suspicious."

"Oh, they're the guys who are building the luxury hotel on the waterfront."

"So I'm told. But something seems off. I can't really explain it."

"You know who you remind me of?" her nephew said.

"Who?"

"Jessica Jones."

She smacked his arm. "I am not."

"You help people without being asked and you are pretty awesome. Plus you own your own business."

"I'm also not a super powered drunk."

"She's got charm."

"Yeah, OK. Look, I need to see what I can find out about this company so I'm going to be in the back if you want to hang out here."

"Absolutely."

Kalina grabbed the tablet from beside the register and headed to one of the big, comfy chairs in the corner. She could still keep an eye on the store and dig up some dirt on the development company. Needing to concentrate, she put in her earbuds and turned on some instrumental music. With the world effectively drowned out, she did a quick search for Carlisle Premiere Developments. Her search brought up a minimalist website with a contact number and some flashy photos of upscale developments. So at least the company was real. Navigating through the menu at the top of the page, she found a list of affiliate companies. She didn't have to look far to spot Eastern Seaboard Realty. Had Thomas Chase jumped ship from brokering real estate deals to developing high-end luxury hotels and condos? The change didn't make much sense to her but her gut told her there was something to this connection.

"Hey, AJ," she called, tugging one earbud from her ear.

Her nephew materialized in the doorway between the front of the store and the game room. "Yeah, Aunt K., what's up?"

“How did you hear about the hotel development going up on the waterfront again?”

“It was in the paper and, as I said, a lot of people weren’t too happy about it going up.”

“When did all this start? I mean I know I was away for a while but the fact they are moving forward feels kind of sudden.”

“Uh, maybe over the summer. Well, I know Mom and Dad went to some town meetings back in January or February—before Grandpa died—about using the land for the new development. I think they only finalized the deal in like September. Why?”

“It might be relevant to the case. Apparently, Mr. Chase doesn’t work for the real estate firm anymore. I know he did in late September or early October because he helped Nadine sell her house but I called earlier and they said he doesn’t work there anymore.”

“So?”

She handed over the tablet. “His firm is an affiliate company with the developer. I’m thinking maybe he went to go work for them. I’d imagine it paid better I just don’t know what a real estate broker would be doing at a development firm."

"Maybe call and ask them? It can't hurt, right?"

"I'm not so sure about that. Remember, the development firm had some Asset Protection manager lurking around while the police were investigating the break-in. When I tried to ask him questions, he blew me off and walked away."

"Weird. Does Detective Harper know that Mr. Chase left the company?"

"I don't know. I haven't told him yet but I know he was going to check into it."

"As I said, it can't hurt to call and see if they'll admit Mr. Chase worked for them. You can borrow my phone if you want."

Kalina gave her nephew a grateful smile but shook her head. "Your mother would kill me. I'll use mine."

She pulled the earbuds from the headphone jack and dialed the company's main number. It rang twice before a chipper-sounding woman answered.

"Carlisle Premiere Developments, how may I help you today?"

Kalina let out a breath. "Hi. I might have the wrong number but I'm trying to reach Thomas Chase."

"One moment please." Static filled the other end of the line. "I'm sorry, he's not in today and I'm not sure when he'll be back in. I can leave a message for you if you'd like."

"No, that's all right but thanks so much. You have a good day now."

Kalina stared dumbstruck at her nephew as she ended the call. "Remind me to give you a raise. You are a smart kid. He definitely worked there before ... he died." She managed to catch herself before she said murdered. Sure, it was accurate but it sounded overly gruesome.

"If only we could talk to his boss at the old place, maybe find out why he left."

"There's no 'we' here. But I might be able to drop a hint or two. Thanks kiddo."

"I'm here all week. And by the way, you are *totally* Jessica Jones."

The bell above the door jingled, signaling a new customer, and Kalina shooed AJ back to front desk duty. She had plenty of reasons to drop into the police station without Chris becoming suspicious of her motives. Besides, he owed her for missing Thanksgiving with her family.

Chapter 9

Kalina waited until after 6:30 to grab some pizza and head over to the station. She'd picked up a couple extra slices in case Jimmy was around. He tended to horn in on their office dinners, even if he didn't mean to. She found Chris hunched over his computer staring at some file or other.

"Hey, I brought food," she announced.

He looked up and smiled. The bags under his eyes were more pronounced than they'd been that morning and he looked paler. "Thanks."

She settled in beside him and handed over a big slice of Hawaiian and a napkin. It was half gone with two bites. She nibbled on a slice of sausage and green pepper. They ate in companionable silence for a few minutes before she set her food down and looked at him.

“I know you can’t say much but how is Savannah doing?”

“She seems to be holding up. She’s going through hell though. First her husband is killed and then her house is ripped apart.”

“Did she know what they were looking for?”

“She claims to have no idea.”

“But you don’t believe her?”

“It just seems odd that a real estate broker would be the target of these kinds of crimes. Especially in this town. Despite the few incidents recently, we aren’t a high crime area.”

“He isn’t working for the firm anymore.”

Chris propped his elbow on the arm of the chair and stared at her. “And you know this how?”

Kalina studied her hands. “I called and asked

for him and they said he didn't work there anymore."

"I guess I would have found that out anyhow tonight."

"Oh?"

"Mr. Chase's ... former boss is coming in for questioning in about an hour."

"That's late isn't it?" She took a bite of pizza.

"It fit with his schedule."

Kalina nodded. "There's more."

"Of course there is."

"There was a guy from the development company looking around and when I called and asked for Mr. Chase, the secretary told me he was out. That all but confirms he worked there. And the real estate firm is an affiliate of the developer. It says so right on their website."

"That's definitely strange." A new message bubble popped up on Chris's computer screen. He turned to study it, his brow knitting together in concern. "That's not good."

Kalina leaned forward to try to read over his shoulder. “What is it?”

“I just got information back on the gun we found at the scene. It was registered to Mr. Chase.”

“And I’m betting Mrs. Chase doesn’t know he had a gun.”

“I’m thinking not.” He rubbed the back of his neck—a telltale sign of stress and frustration—and blew out a breath. “Honestly, none of this makes sense.”

She rubbed his back gently to help ease some of the tension. “I’m sure it will.”

Two sets of footsteps echoed on the linoleum behind them, drawing Kalina’s attention. Jimmy—her go to for inside information—walked by the front desk, accompanied by a man in a navy suit. He was balding with sparse hair left on the sides. It could have been brown at one point but it was grey now.

“Sorry to interrupt, boss, but Mr. Linden is here to see you,” Jimmy announced. He eyed the extra slice of Hawaiian pizza on Chris’s desk.

Chris spun around and took in the realtor before him. Without a word, Kalina grabbed an extra napkin to go with the pizza and offered Mr. Linden her chair. She and Jimmy retreated a safe distance—still within earshot—before she handed over the pizza.

“You didn’t have to,” he said before taking a big bite.

“You guys work too hard,” she said.

Mr. Linden settled into the chair Kalina had vacated while Chris hastily cleared away the pizza remains and retrieved his pen and notepad. Kalina couldn’t keep from smiling at how he clung to old school traditions. It only made her love him more.

“Thanks for coming down, Mr. Linden. I appreciate it.”

Mr. Linden shrugged one shoulder. “Not sure what I can tell you. Thomas Chase is no longer an employee with our firm.”

“So I hear. Can you describe what happened?”

“Nothing to say really. Decided he wasn’t interested in selling homes anymore and quit.”

“So you didn’t have any concerns about his performance?”

“None. He was a good worker. One of our best in fact. It was a shame to see him leave.”

“Were you aware of anything going on in his home life that might have prompted a change?”

“Like what?”

“Anything. I know that Savannah Chase is his second wife.”

“As far as I know, things were fine between them. He didn’t talk about her much. Just between us, I thought it was a little strange he married again. They just don’t seem compatible.”

Chris tapped the capped end of the pen against his lower lip. “Did you know Mr. Chase was employed by Carlisle Premiere Developments?”

“No I didn’t know that.”

“Does that surprise you?”

“A little.” Mr. Linden’s cheeks paled.

Even from where Kalina stood, she could see sweat break out on his temple. Chris clearly noted the change too.

“Do you have any idea what sort of work Mr. Chase would be doing for a development company?”

Mr. Linden coughed and averted his gaze. “Can’t say that I do. You’d be better off asking them.”

“Oh, I will be. Is there anything else you can tell me about Mr. Chase? Can you think of anyone who would have wanted to hurt him?”

“No idea. I’m sorry. If that’s all, I need to be going.”

Chris offered his hand and Mr. Linden shook it. “Thank you again for coming down.”

Mr. Linden stood, straightened his suit jacket and strode out of the station without a word to anyone else. The interview had been somewhat illuminating but Kalina realized it was time to talk to Savannah again. She couldn’t believe she hadn’t noticed her husband change careers. And she couldn’t get the image of the developer goon out of her head.

"Hey, Jimmy, can you tell Chris I'll see him tomorrow? I need to go check in with my sister to make sure everything is going all right at her house."

"Sure thing, Kal."

Chapter 10

Kalina texted AJ to let him know he should close up the shop for the night. She'd swing by afterwards to double check the register and handle the books for the day. The lights were on in the living room of her sister's house when she pulled into the driveway. She pulled in behind Daniel's car and took the front steps two at a time. She didn't bother knocking, instead choosing to make a bold entrance. She found her sister and Savannah sharing a bottle of wine in the living room.

"You know doors are meant for knocking, right?" Jillian said before proffering a third glass.

Kalina waved dismissively at the offered glass. “I just figured you’d want to hear what I have to say.”

“Is it about Thomas?” Savannah’s cheeks were flushed from the alcohol.

“Yes. I was having dinner with Chris and he told me that Thomas left the real estate firm a few months ago and was working for the developers who are putting up the hotel and condos on the waterfront.”

“That’s ridiculous,” Jillian scoffed.

Savannah’s cheeks flushed more and her eyes grew bright with unshed tears. “I feel awful.”

“Why?” Kalina sat down on the couch beside the woman.

“I just remembered that he had left the firm. I didn’t realize he didn’t work for the same type of company anymore. Oh God, am I going to get into trouble with the police?”

“Of course not,” Jillian interjected, shooting Kalina a look that clearly said ‘she better not get in trouble’.

"I think if you just sit down with Detective Harper and tell him whatever you've remembered, he'll understand. After all, you've had quite a shock the last couple days."

Savannah nodded and rubbed at her nose with her free hand. The tension in the room eased a little but Kalina was still on edge. She needed to probe a little more about some of the other information she'd gathered.

"There's something else that Detective Harper found."

"What now?"

"The gun that was found with Thomas's body ... the one used to shoot him was registered to him."

"That isn't possible. He didn't keep weapons in the house. Thomas hated guns."

Kalina leaned in a little closer. "Did you have a gun?"

"God, no!" The wine glass slipped through her fingers and smashed against the coffee table, spraying the carpet with red wine and glass shards.

Jillian jumped into action, rushing out of the room and returning moments later with a dustpan and brush to sweep up the shards. She glared at Kalina but Kalina stayed put. Savannah curled into herself on the couch and dabbed at her eyes.

“You could help,” Jillian snapped.

Just as Kalina opened her mouth to fire back at her sister, her phone buzzed with an incoming call from AJ. He must still have been at the shop. Without excusing herself, she stood up and left the living room.

“Hey, you should be home soon, right?”

“Yeah I’m on the way but I wanted to tell you something.”

“OK. What is it?”

“I did what you’d do and did some newspaper digging. There was an article back in the summer about the fear that the property would displace people in the area. And I have a friend, Adrien Parker and his family are moving because the bank foreclosed on their house. And get this ... when I mentioned Mr. Chase,

Adrien got all pissed off. Said that was the guy who showed up and forced them to accept the foreclosure."

"Where do they live?"

"Um, not far from the waterfront."

"Thanks, AJ. You did great. Now get your butt home before your mother has a heart attack."

Her nephew hung up and Kalina studied the blank screen for a moment. Things were starting to make sense. She didn't know much about foreclosures and the like but she did know someone who did and she was going to pick their brain as soon as she could make an excuse to get out of the house. But first she needed one final answer from Savannah.

"Who was that?" Savannah asked as soon as Kalina walked back into the room.

"Oh, that was nothing. Just someone calling the shop's main number. It forwards to my cell. I actually need to get back but I wanted to ask you one last thing. Did you notice if any of your neighbors had been moving away or getting foreclosed on recently?"

"No. Why would you ask that?"

"Well, I was just wondering why someone would spray paint 'Traitor' on your front door, that's all. Sorry about the wine, Jill."

Chapter 11

Kalina climbed back into her car and let out a sigh. If Thomas Chase was working for the developer and forcing people out of their homes so the hotel and condos could be built that would definitely brand him a traitor, especially to families living on the waterfront. And it might give someone a motive to want him dead. She didn't quite believe that Savannah didn't know that her husband had changed careers and had gone from selling people homes to ripping them away from families. She pulled out her phone and dialed the switchboard number for the police station.

"Ellesworth Police Department," Jimmy said on the other end of the line.

"Hey Jimmy, it's Kalina. I need a favor from you."

"Sure, what's up?"

"Do you know anything about debt collection and foreclosures?"

"Some. My brother Alex knows more."

His brother worked as a firefighter in town. A family of public servants. "Is he off shift today?"

"I think so. Why, what's going on?"

"I'm just curious about some things. With the big development going in on the waterfront I want to be more informed about how it's happening. Can you guys swing by Geeks and Things in say an hour?"

"I'll give him a call. Should I let Detective Harper know?"

"That's not necessary."

"If you're sure. I'll hopefully see you in an hour."

"Great, I appreciate it."

Tossing the phone on the passenger seat, Kalina headed back to the shop to make sure she was ready for her late-night visitors. A part of her felt bad leaving Chris out of this investigative mission but he had other things to worry about. Besides, he needed to get some sleep.

Waiting for their arrival gave Kalina time to settle the day's bookkeeping. The shop had done well in profits. Black Friday was officially a success. The bell above the front door jangled and she looked up to see Jimmy and Alex stride in side by side. Alex was older than Jimmy by at least six years and had a broader build.

“Thanks for coming over, guys. Why don't we grab a seat in the back?”

They settled around one of the tables strewn with pieces of Settlers of Catan. Jimmy fiddled with a few pieces while Alex sat with his arms crossed over his chest.

“So what do you want to know about debt collection?”

“How it works. Why someone might get

involved in it." She pulled out a pen and notebook Chris had given her to take notes.

Alex rubbed his chin. "Well, you get into it for the money. See when the bank or a credit card company has a client who isn't paying their debts off, they sell the debt to a collector on the cheap. A five thousand dollar loan might get sold for one thousand. Then the collector goes to the debtor and offers to wipe the debt clean if they pay twenty-five hundred. The collector nets fifteen hundred of that for himself."

"And the bank or the credit card company doesn't get anything for it?"

He shook his head. "No. They get the money on the front end when they sell the debt package."

"So someone would have to actually have the money to buy the debt in the first place and then they make it back with collecting on the debts. Pretty lucrative if you don't mind ruining people's lives."

Kalina nodded as she scribbled down the example he'd given. It still didn't seem like a career a mild-mannered guy in his 60s would suddenly take on. It was also suspicious that

Savannah wouldn't have known if her husband made a huge purchase.

"You know ... we found a receipt for a money transfer in the study at the Chase house. Something like thirty thousand dollars," Jimmy said.

Kalina leaned forward, pen poised to write. "Who was it to?"

"Didn't say. Just had bank information on it."

Alex cleared his throat and eyed his younger brother. "I don't think you should be sharing details about an ongoing case, Jim."

"Right, of course. Just forget I mentioned that."

Kalina gave Jimmy a smile. "Don't worry about it. I appreciate you guys explaining the debt collection stuff though."

"That kind of life can be dangerous too. You try to collect from the wrong person and things could go sideways fast," Alex said and stood up.

"That's what I'm afraid of," Kalina muttered.

"I need to get home. I'm on shift tomorrow,"

Alex announced and Jimmy followed his brother out.

Kalina barely stifled a yawn as they left. It had been a busy day and she'd been running on adrenaline more than she'd realized. She rubbed at her eyes and yawned again. Time to go home and sleep on the information she'd gathered. Maybe things would make more sense in the morning. Before she turned out the lights and headed home she set a reminder in her phone to check city planning records in the morning.

Chapter 12

The next morning Kalina woke with a headache. It had taken far too long to fall asleep the night before and her dreams were filled with disparate pieces of the Thomas Chase puzzle. She dragged herself out of bed and into the kitchen for a much needed cup of coffee. Her phone beeped at her to remind her of the task she'd set. Thankfully, the town made all building plans digital when they were approved; it made fact checking as easy as a couple mouse clicks. She downed her first cup of caffeine in record time, pouring herself a second cup before she settled in front of her laptop in the living room. She had to move some boxes off the couch so she had a place to sit.

"OK, let's see what we've got," she muttered to herself and found the listing of most recently filed plans.

She didn't have to look very long before she found the plans for the condo and hotel layout. It loaded in a new tab and she had to blow it up to read any of it. She wasn't an expert with building plans but it was pretty obvious that the layout of the building stretched over a large section of the waterfront, including the Chase residence. In fact, it was right in the middle of the whole thing.

"Damn."

The little pieces of information she'd been gathering were all starting to fall into place now. The developer had likely hired Thomas because they needed his land to build the hotel and they thought getting him to collect on debts would get them what they wanted. Whether they expected his neighbors to turn on him and run him out of town or some other scenario, they likely counted on him handing things over to them before long. She doubted they'd intended to kill him. The guilty party could have been one of his neighbors but it didn't explain the gun registered in his name. Perhaps a trip to the only pawn shop in town was a good idea. She also wanted to head back out to the waterfront and see if she could talk to anyone whom Thomas might have tried to collect from.

Kalina forced herself to eat something before racing off for her day of investigation. Her curiosity was so overpowering at times that she forgot to eat. But fainting in the middle of things wasn't going to do anyone any good—least of all her—so she hastily downed a banana and some soggy oatmeal before heading out to her first stop. The pawn shop sat on the edge of town closest to the highway. In fact, it wasn't that far from her sister's place now that she thought about it. The parking lot was small—only three poorly marked spaces in front of the dimly lit front window. It gave her the creeps but she squared her shoulders and strode in.

"Well, I never thought I'd see you set foot in

here," a deep baritone said from behind the front counter.

Blake Jansen had been a few years ahead of her in school and, much like her, had inherited the family business. He was big but in a non-threatening way. It was all belly fat and smile lines.

"Hey, Blake. How's it going?"

"It's going. I hear your place is hopping."

"People love their comics and nerdy stuff."

"What can I do for you today?"

"You may not be able to tell me but I was wondering if you know Thomas Chase."

"Real estate guy? Yeah, he helped my parents sell their place before they moved down south."

"His wife asked me to check if he'd been in to buy or sell anything recently. They came into some money recently and she's just worried he might be trying to sell off some antiques."

"Nope. Can't say that I've ever seen him in here."

"Really? Because she said she also found a gun case in his closet."

"Well, if he bought a gun, it wasn't through me. That I'd remember. There isn't anyone less likely to come into this place than him."

"Does anyone else work at the shop besides you? Maybe he came in when they were working?"

"I was out a few days last month with the flu. Had my cousin's kid cover for me. I'll check the receipts for you."

Kalina leaned on the countertop. "Thanks. I know his wife will really appreciate it. I'm just hoping to put her mind at ease."

"How do you know the current Mrs. Chase?" Blake asked as he pulled a rolodex of cards from beneath the counter.

"She was friends with my sister in college."

"That so?" He flipped through some cards.

"Why? Is there something I should know about her?"

Blake shrugged and continued to sort through the cards. "I heard she majored in theater.

Fancied herself something of an actress. If she's worried her husband's been pawning stuff, I wouldn't necessarily believe her."

"I didn't know that."

"Yep. I was honestly surprised she married Mr. Chase. I never thought he quite got over his first wife and I can't say I see what he does in her." He stopped flipping. "Well, I'll be damned."

Kalina tried to lean over to read the card he now held in his hand. The handwriting was too tiny and slanted for her to get a good look upside down.

"What is it?"

"Says he bought a handgun last month." Blake handed over the card for her to look at.

She pointed to the bottom of the card. "Is this his signature?"

"Looks like it. I guess I was wrong about them both. Sorry to say."

"Thanks. You've been really helpful. Do you mind if I take a picture of this just so I have proof for Savannah?"

"Normally I don't go handing things like this out unless there's a warrant involved but it can't hurt just this once."

Kalina whipped out her phone and snapped a picture, making sure to get a good image of the signature. She had been with Nadine when she'd signed the final documents with Thomas on the Larrabees' family home and this signature looked slightly off. After her next stop she'd definitely share what she'd learned with Chris. As much as she hated to admit how cliché it sounded, she was beginning to suspect that Savannah had a hand in Thomas's death.

"Thanks again for your help," she said before heading back to her car and the fresh air.

Armed with this new knowledge, she made the short trip to the waterfront and started browsing for houses with foreclosure and for sale signs until she spotted Leslie Mayfair sitting on her front porch with a for sale sign stuck into the small front lawn. Kalina would have preferred someone else to question but this was what had presented itself. It wasn't Kalina's fault that Leslie's former fiancé had turned out to be a vengeful murderer.

"Hi, Leslie," Kalina greeted as she left the driver side door open.

"Oh hi."

Kalina gestured toward the sign. "I didn't know you were moving."

"I was. The bank was going to foreclose but..."

"What happened?"

"The man they sent to collect on my debts offered to forgive them completely. He said he respected me and the value I add to this town too much to force me out."

"He just forgave them," she snapped, "just like that?"

"Yes."

"That wasn't Thomas Chase was it?"

Leslie nodded. "How'd you know?"

"I'd heard he'd gone into debt collection."

"Well, he said it sickened him what the town was doing with the development company. He said I wasn't the only person he had forgiven. Since the bank doesn't have any claim on this place anymore I don't have to move."

"And I'm guessing they can't build the hotel and condos if you're still here."

"Nope."

"I never said I'm sorry about what happened over the summer."

Leslie's eyes shone with unshed tears but she smiled. "I don't blame you, you know. I should have seen what was going on right in front of my face. The man I loved wasn't real. Just a façade."

"Still, it wasn't fair that he ruined your life too."

"I appreciate that." Leslie stood up and smoothed out the creases in her pants. "Can I ask why you were asking about Mr. Chase?"

"I realized I've been so busy getting my life sorted out I didn't know what was happening in town and I felt I should take more of an interest. This is home, after all."

Leslie glanced around the property and sighed. "Yeah, it is." With a grin she crossed the short distance to the sign and yanked it free, tossing it aside.

Kalina turned to get back into her car when she caught a hulking figure in the distance. She had an idea who would be lurking around this area and it sent shivers up and down her spine.

Chapter 13

Kalina slid back behind the wheel and closed the driver side door. Time to tell Chris everything. Just as she reached for her phone, it began to buzz along the passenger seat with an incoming call: Jillian.

"Hey, look, I'm sorry I butted in earlier," she said after hitting 'Accept'.

"Forget that. Your boyfriend's little shadow, Jimmy, just showed up and arrested Savannah."

"What? Why?"

"I don't know. They won't tell me anything. This is insanity. She couldn't have killed her husband."

"Get her to call a lawyer. I'm going to the station to try to find out what's going on. I promise."

"A lawyer. God, this can't be happening."

"Jillian, stay calm. We're going to sort this out. You just need to stay level headed and don't get in their way."

"Fine. Just hurry and get there. Please," her sister pleaded.

Kalina revved the engine and did a quick U-turn at the end of the street, tires squealing as they tried to catch traction on the road. She raced up the street and caught sight of Mr. Mackland still lurking. Her heart thumped painfully against her ribs until he was out of sight in her rearview mirror.

Her thoughts raced as she made her way to the station. What could they have arrested Savannah for? Had they found incriminating evidence in the $30,000 or some fingerprint on the gun? She pulled into the station parking lot and killed the engine. Before she could unbuckle her seatbelt, a second car came screaming into the lot and pulled in beside her, far too close for her to get out of her car without scratching the paint. She grabbed her phone and, as covertly as possible, hit Chris's number on speed dial. He might already be in with Savannah but maybe she'd get lucky and they were waiting for a lawyer to show up. She tried to ease the driver side door open but the driver of the other car stepped out and loomed large: Mr. Mackland. She glanced at her phone to see that it had connected and then placed it in her pocket. She eased her door shut and rolled down the window despite the chill that was settling over the day.

"Excuse me, I need to get out," she said as politely as possible. She thought she heard Chris's muffled voice from her pocket.

"What were you doing talking to Ms. Mayfair?"

"That's none of your business."

"It is my business if it affects my employer's business plan."

"Well, that's not my fault. Leslie and I are friendly. You may not have heard but she had a bit of a rough time over the summer. Her fiancé was arrested for murder. I wanted to check on her and see how she was doing."

Mr. Mackland shrugged one beefy shoulder and slid his hand into his pocket, pushing the edge of his suit jacket back far enough to show her the gun holstered underneath his armpit. Her mouth went dry.

“You’ve been nosing around things that don’t concern you.” His tone implied the threat of the weapon he carried.

She pulled her phone out of her pocket as if it had just started to ring with a call. “Hi, Detective Harper.”

“Kal, what’s going on? I’m about to go into an interrogation, here.”

“I needed to stop by and see you but a Mr. Victor Mackland from Carlisle Premiere Developments won’t let me get out of my car.”

Mr. Mackland stayed where he was, not even flinching at the mention of Chris’s title. Kalina tried to stare him down without showing fear but she doubted it was very effective.

“I’ll be right out.”

“Great. Thanks.”

She hung up but kept the phone in view. She tried to keep her breathing even for the thirty seconds it took Chris to make his way out to the parking lot. Her pulse slowed a little at the sight of him. At least now she didn't have to worry about the thug pulling his gun on her. He couldn't be that reckless.

"Are you Mr. Mackland?" Chris asked and stopped mere inches from the man.

"I am."

"You need to move your vehicle and let Ms. Greystone get out of her car. I'd hate to have her file a harassment complaint against you."

"She's been snooping around where she doesn't belong."

"That still doesn't give you the right to intimidate her. Now move your car or I'll move it for you. Do I make myself clear?"

Mr. Mackland glanced between the two of them before he let out a grunt and stormed around to the driver side of his car and backed up enough for Kalina to get out. She rolled the window up and climbed out, throwing her arms around Chris without thinking.

“Thank you. He has a gun,” she whispered in his ear.

“Go inside. I’ll handle this.”

She pulled away a little before saying, “I have to show you something about the case. It’s important.”

“When I’m done here you can show me.”

“Please be careful.” She gave him a quick kiss on the cheek before heading inside.

Chapter 14

Jillian sat at Chris's desk and Savannah was nowhere in sight. Kalina assumed she'd already been taken to the interrogation room. For once, the monitor showing the room was turned off. Kalina pulled a chair next to her sister and let out an anxious breath.

"They haven't questioned her yet. She asked for a lawyer," Jillian said, her tone flat.

"Good. I just had a run-in with a security guy from the developer."

"What do you mean?"

"I took a drive to the waterfront to see what's been going on and I talked to Leslie Mayfair.

This security guy, Victor Mackland, followed me back here. I met him the day after Thanksgiving while Savannah was giving her statement about the break-in. He threatened me just now. Chris is handling it."

"Threatened you?" Jillian took Kalina's hand, going into protective older sister mode. "Did he touch you? Are you OK?"

"I'm fine. It was more an implied threat. He made sure I could see he had a gun. But I'd called Chris so he knew what was going on. I think I've figured some things out about Thomas's death. I just need Chris to get back in here so I can tell him. It might help Savannah."

"You know sometimes I don't know why he lets you poke around in his cases."

"Because I'm helpful? And I don't really mean to poke around, I just get curious and have to know what happened. He appreciates it, even if he doesn't say so."

On cue, Chris reappeared through the front door of the station. He held a business card by the tips of his fingers. "Jimmy! Get the fingerprint kit," he called before approaching his desk.

Kalina cleared a spot for him to work and noted Victor Mackland's name on the card. "What happened?"

"I told him politely if he ever went near you with a loaded firearm again I'd arrest him."

"Thanks. What's with the fingerprint kit?"

"I have a hunch."

"Can I tell you what I found out?"

Chris glanced at Jillian who promptly stood up and made herself scarce. Kalina took the spot her sister vacated and pulled up the photo of the paperwork from the pawn shop on her phone.

"So, after you mentioned that Mr. Chase had a gun registered to him, I paid Blake Jansen a visit. He said someone came in and bought a gun under Mr. Chase's name." She enlarged the photo of the signature. "I'm no expert but I've seen Thomas Chase sign his name once or twice and this looks off."

"You think someone bought it using his name."

"Yes."

Chris brushed excess fingerprint powder into the trash and held up the card with a fresh print on it. "We found prints on the gun and the spray can that don't match Mr. or Mrs. Chase."

"And you think it was Mackland."

"I'm beginning to." He stuck the card in an evidence bag and scribbled information onto the label. "Jimmy, get this to the lab and tell them to rush it."

Jimmy grabbed the bag and disappeared. She could tell they both wished they had equipment to check the print themselves but the department was still strapped.

"There's more," Kalina said and set down her phone. "I think I might know why someone would want Mr. Chase dead and why Mr. Mackland would be involved."

Chris leaned back in his chair and steepled his fingers beneath his chin. "I'm listening."

"He was working for the developer as a debt collector. They needed to force people out of their houses so they could seize the property to build their new project. Basically, he offered to wipe people's debts clean if they paid part of their debt and he pocketed the difference between what they paid and what he bought the debt for."

"I understand how debt collection works, Kal."

She felt color warm her cheeks. "Well, it sounds like Thomas got fed up with the debt collecting life because he was forgiving loans for people who have property in strategic locations that really mess with building plans."

"That certainly establishes a motive and would also explain why Mr. Mackland was looming around the scene the other day."

"And why he came after me," she added.

"Right."

The conversation died when a middle-aged man in a faded blue suit appeared in their peripheral vision carrying a briefcase. He stopped momentarily at the front desk before approaching Chris's desk.

"I'm here for Savannah Chase," he said.

"She's in the interrogation room. I'll be with you in a moment."

Kalina craned her neck to follow the attorney's path into the room. "Why'd you arrest Savannah?"

"Mr. Mackland isn't the only one with a motive."

He disappeared without another word. She waited until he closed the door to the interrogation room before she flipped the switch on the monitor. She tuned out the pleasantries and turned to the computer in front of her. She didn't know why she hadn't thought to check property records before but it would be easy enough to see who held the title to the Chase home. A quick search revealed what Chris likely already knew—Savannah owned the home and had been transferred the deed about six months after she married Thomas. The dead man's name drew Kalina's attention back to the interview.

"We found a receipt in your home for thirty thousand dollars. You said before that Thomas didn't have that kind of money."

Savannah glanced at her attorney and then said, "No. I mean we weren't poor by any means but that kind of lump sum would have been noticed in our joint account. Believe me; I keep an eye on it."

"I'm sure you do."

"You come from a fairly wealthy background yourself, don't you, Mrs. Chase?"

"I don't know what you mean."

"Your relatives were well off and you received a pretty hefty inheritance a few years ago."

"So?"

"We traced the money transfer that was sent to Carlisle Premiere Developments. The money originated in your account."

"Then maybe Thomas accessed it without me knowing."

"You are the only name on the account and we called the bank. You are the only person who could have authorized a transfer out of the account. Why did you want Thomas to take the debt collection job?"

"I didn't."

"Mrs. Chase, you need to stop lying now. You authorized the payment so Thomas could buy the debt collection package. He didn't seem the type to get into the business of shaking people down. So the pressure had to come from somewhere else. Like you."

Kalina pulled herself away from the questioning when she felt a presence behind her. She turned slowly to find Jimmy standing off to one side.

"Did you know their house was in the middle of the building zone?" Kalina asked.

"It's all making sense now. Huh."

"I'm assuming Chris knows that. And that she owns the house outright."

The color drained from Jimmy's cheeks and he started for the interrogation room.

"Uh, Jimmy, you might want to pick up that stuff on the printer first," Kalina said after hitting print on the land records and the building plans.

He gave her a nervous smile and headed into the room, appearing on the monitor moments later.

“Sir, I thought you should see these,” Jimmy said and handed over the information.

Chris took the printouts and flipped through them. Kalina waited with baited breath for him to act. It wasn’t that she wanted Savannah to be guilty but everything was pointing that way. Then again, maybe Blake was right and she’d gone into her marriage to Thomas with ulterior motives. Chris set the papers down in front of him and turned to Jimmy before standing up.

“Detective, what are you doing?” Jimmy’s face failed to mask his confusion.

“This is your information, Jimmy. I think you should question our witness about what you found.”

Kalina smiled as Chris stepped back and let Jimmy sit down. Jimmy would become a good cop one way or another and it made her a little proud to know she had a hand in it. Jimmy licked his lips and clasped his hands in front of him on the table.

“Well … Mrs. Chase we’ve found records that show your home is in the middle of the development zone.”

“What information is that?” her attorney asked.

Jimmy slid the printout of the zoning plan across the table and waited while the lawyer looked it over.

“And we also found out that you own the home outright. We have the land records that show Mr. Chase transferred the deed to you two years ago.” He slid the second page across the table.

“Is there a question, Officer?”

“Well, it just seems suspicious that your husband would work for the people who are trying to buy out the rest of that area and then end up dead. I mean I suppose with him gone, there’s no one to protest when you sell the house. I mean, if it were me, that’s what I’d do.”

“I didn’t kill anyone,” Savannah said quietly.

“But you know who did. And we think you had knowledge of it beforehand. If you tell us everything you know, we’ll talk to the prosecutor about being lenient,” Chris said from his spot by the door.

Even over a monitor, Kalina could see the color drain from Savannah's cheeks. Her shoulders hunched and she suddenly looked very frail. Her attorney looked between Jimmy and Chris and then loudly cleared his throat.

"I'd like a minute to speak with my client."

"Of course," Chris said.

He and Jimmy left the room and shut the door behind them. Kalina tried to look as if she hadn't been eavesdropping but Chris fixed her with a half-smile.

"Thank you for that information," he said.

"That was all Jimmy."

Jimmy opened his mouth to contradict her but stopped and blushed. "Just trying to do my job."

"Either way, I think she's going to confess."

"You think she'll identify Mackland as being involved? I wouldn't put it past him to kill Thomas if he was really going against the company's orders," Kalina said.

"I'm pretty sure whatever she tells us will be enough to get a warrant for his arrest."

She nodded and silence settled between the three of them. Kalina caught glimpses of Savannah huddled in with her attorney. She glanced around the station, suddenly wondering what had become of her sister.

“I think your sister went outside,” Jimmy offered, as if reading her thoughts.

“Thanks. I should go check on her. I think she’s been taking this whole thing personally. She did always have a flair for the dramatic.”

The door to the interrogation room opened behind them and Savannah’s attorney appeared, motioning for them to come back in. Kalina bit her lip, torn between hearing Savannah’s confession and checking on Jillian. If she was quick she might be able to do both. On a hunch, she headed out the front of the building. Jillian sat on a bench to the right of the entrance.

“Hey,” Kalina said and sat down beside her.

“What’s going on?”

“It looks like Savannah was involved in what happened to Thomas. I think she might be confessing.”

"But she's not a killer."

"They think someone else killed him but she might have details about who that is. I'm sorry that you got dragged into all this."

Jillian let out a bitter laugh. "Don't apologize. She was my friend. She came to me and I let her into my home, offered her support."

"People change. And they do things for all kinds of reasons. Neither of us knows what was going on in her life or her marriage to prompt her agreeing to let someone murder her husband."

"I want to know why she did it."

Kalina offered a hand to her sister. "Come on. We can watch from the bull pen. I think you need some closure as much as Thomas."

Chapter 15

The sisters walked back inside hand in hand. It appeared they hadn't missed much at all. Jimmy was just settling into another chair beside Chris. Savannah's cheeks were flushed and she kneaded her hands together nervously.

Chris leaned back in his chair. "So what has your client decided?"

"I'll tell you what I know." She sat up a little straighter and licked her lips. "A couple months back, the head of the development company came around our neighborhood and offered to buy a bunch of people out so they could build the condos. Thomas said no like most everyone else. I wasn't home when they came by the first time so I didn't know how much was being offered."

"I'm guessing it was a pretty nice sum."

"More than the house was worth. Thomas got it appraised every couple of years. He says it's out of habit. It was in his family for three generations. His grandfather built it maybe seventy years ago. He took full ownership around the time he married his first wife. When we married he put the deed in my name."

"Why did he do that?" Chris asked.

"He said that, since life is so short, he didn't want me to be without a place to live if something were to happen to him." Tears spilled down Savannah's cheeks. She let them fall, hands still clasped in front of her.

"What happened next?" Chris prompted.

Savannah took a shaky breath. "The developer sent a man to try to convince us to sell."

"This man?" Chris held his phone out.

Kalina couldn't see what he was showing her but she had to assume he'd managed to snap a picture of Victor Mackland.

"Yes, that's him." She dabbed at her eyes. "I don't know ... I guess they thought if we went along with it, other people might follow suit. But Thomas was still against selling. When the man came by again, he offered Thomas the opportunity to work for them and in exchange they'd pay him anything he wanted for the house. I told him he should take the job, work for a little while and then we'd cash out. They wanted thirty thousand dollars for the debt package. We didn't have that kind of money."

"Not jointly. You had it in your inheritance."

"I told Thomas we could use my money but it meant he had to take the job and do what they said."

"Did you know he was going to die?" Jimmy interrupted.

Savannah shook her head. "No, I swear. Last week Thomas came home and told me that he was done working for them and he'd been forgiving loans. I don't know how but maybe Mr. Mackland was following him because they found out. Mr. Mackland contacted me and said we needed to keep Thomas in line. He said he'd handle it. He was just supposed to talk to Thomas. Scare him a little bit."

"And instead he ends up dead."

"I swear I really was going to report him missing when I came in. I lied about when I'd seen him last but I really was worried."

"What did you get out of this, besides being able to sell the property without him objecting?"

"They were going to pay me three times what the house was worth. I could go anywhere; do anything I wanted with that money. I'm not proud of it but it's the truth."

Chris drummed his fingers on the metal table for a beat and then leaned back again. "We didn't find any prints in the house when we searched after the break-in. Were you involved?"

Back in the bull pen Jillian shook her head, tears of her own shining in her eyes. Kalina kept a firm grip on her sister's hand the whole time but she could still feel Jillian's hand trembling in her own.

"I just don't understand. She had money."

"Sometimes people get greedy, Jill. And maybe she felt she had no other choice. I've met Mr. Mackland, remember."

Back in the interrogation room, Savannah let out a slow breath. "On Thanksgiving night I got a text from Mr. Mackland telling me to meet him at my house. He said we needed to make it look like someone broke in. I don't know why since I thought that would lead the police to look into what Thomas was doing but I didn't argue. I trashed the place myself. I thought I'd gotten rid of the bank transfer receipt but obviously not."

"So Mr. Mackland orchestrated everything."

"Yes. That's right."

"Would you be willing to sign an affidavit to that effect so we can arrest him?"

"She'll do whatever you need," her attorney said before Savannah could protest.

"Thank you, Counselor. Sit tight and we'll be back."

Chris stood up and Jimmy followed him out of the room, leaving the door ajar. Kalina let go of her sister's hand and closed the distance between her and Chris.

"So what happens now?"

"We draft the affidavit, she signs it and we get a warrant for this guy's arrest."

"That's it?"

"Right now, yeah, that's it."

"What will happen to Savannah?" Jillian asked.

"That's up to the prosecutor. She's a cooperating witness so that helps her. She may not face any jail time but I can't say for sure."

Kalina put a hand on Jillian's arm in the hopes of getting her sister out of Chris's way. He didn't have the time to waste talking to them. Not when a killer was still on the loose.

"Come on, Jill. Let's go home and let them do their jobs. There's nothing else we can do here."

Jillian nodded mutely and started for the front of the building. Before Kalina got two steps, Chris's hand wrapped around her wrist, arresting her momentum.

"Can you come by tonight? There's something I need to talk to you about."

"Sure."

"Good. I'll see you later." He kissed her on the lips.

The gesture made her cheeks warm—not just because it was a sudden moment of passion—and she had to pull away to catch her breath.

"Get this guy."

"I promise."

Chapter 16

The parking lot seemed oddly empty as they walked out into the afternoon air. Kalina started for her car—intent on following her sister home to make sure she didn't have a nervous breakdown at the revelation that her close friend was capable of selling out her spouse for money—but stopped when she noted her back tires were slashed.

"You've got to be kidding me," she groaned.

"Do you think that Mr. Mackland did this?" Jillian said from behind her.

"Who else would try to keep me from leaving?" She pulled out her phone and hit Chris's name on speed dial.

It rang once before he answered. “Forget something?”

“No, someone slashed my tires.”

“And by someone you mean our murder suspect?”

“Yes.”

“Come back in and we’ll file a report.

“No, I’ll catch a ride home with Jillian. You need to focus on catching this guy for the bigger crime. My car will survive.”

“I’d feel better if you filed a report.”

“I promise I’ll do that as soon as you have the guy in custody.”

“Fine.”

“Oh, it’s just a hunch but you should try looking for this creep at the developer’s main office. It’s the address on the business card he gave me the other day.”

“Will do.”

She ended the call. Jillian shifted from foot to foot, waiting for something else to happen. Kalina flashed her sister a smile. “Come on, you should go home. Spend some time with Dan and AJ. After all, I gave him the weekend off so you could hang out as a family."

"You talked to Dan didn't you?" her sister said as they walked side by side to her car.

"Maybe."

Together they checked to ensure that her car was intact before climbing in and making the short journey to Jillian's place. Jillian put the car in park and cut the engine but didn't move from her spot behind the wheel.

"You're going to be okay," Kalina said and patted her sister's hand.

"I know. It's really selfish of me to even feel betrayed or hurt. I'm worried about what's going to happen to Savannah.'

"You heard Chris. The prosecutor will likely give her a deal. She might not even see any jail time."

"She's ruined here though. She can't stay. Everyone is going to know what happened."

"I sort of got the feeling she didn't want to stay here anyway."

"I suppose you're right."

"Jill, I'm sorry this happened. It's never easy finding out the people we thought we knew and could trust aren't the people we thought they were."

"I guess we're all learning that the hard way."

"Yeah. Come on, let's go inside. I think we could both use a drink."

"It's the middle of the day."

"It's a weekend and it's been one hell of a couple days. We deserve it."

They both climbed out and headed up the front steps. Jillian dug her key out of her purse. "I'll get the glasses."

Kalina kicked off her shoes upon entering the house and headed straight for the living room. Daniel and AJ were nowhere to be seen. Just as Jillian returned with a bottle of white and two glasses, footsteps thundered down the stairs and AJ appeared.

"Hey, what's going on? I thought we were supposed to be doing this whole family time thing this weekend."

“Your aunt solved the case,” Jillian said, growing misty eyed.

“Not really. Well, maybe I helped a little.”

“Stop being modest, Aunt K. You probably cracked the case wide open.” He settled on the couch between them—taking up far more space than a teenage boy should be able to—and fiddled with the cork from the wine bottle. “So what happened?”

“I don’t really think—” Jillian began.

“He’s going to find out when it hits the news,” Kalina interrupted.

“I guess you’re right. Savannah was involved. She didn’t kill her husband but she knew a very dangerous man was trying to threaten him.”

“Why?”

“For money. She was promised a lot of it if she cooperated with getting people to leave so the development could be built.”

Kalina let out a bitter laugh. “I have a feeling the project won’t be going forward any time soon.”

“Good. Then people won’t have to move.”

“Exactly.” Kalina took a long sip of wine and let it burn down her throat. She’d needed it more than Jillian to calm her nerves. She hadn’t wanted to admit it but she was scared of Victor Mackland. She had no doubt he’d be out of their lives soon but until he was in handcuffs and carted away she couldn’t relax.

She was so lost in her thoughts she didn’t hear her phone ring. AJ nudged her in the thigh, causing her phone to dig into her leg. She yanked it out and saw a missed call from Chris’s cell phone.

“Excuse me.”

She extricated herself from the couch, set her wineglass down on the table and retreated to the kitchen for some privacy. She hit redial and waited while the line connected.

“Hi, sorry I missed you,” she said when he picked up.

“I wanted to let you know we have Mackland and his boss in custody. It looks like he’s going to be fairly cooperative with us. His boss was already starting to talk on the ride back to the precinct.”

"That's great. You have no idea how much better I feel right now."

"We still need you to file a report about your tires."

"You know what; it's not even worth it. I'll get new tires. It's not a big deal. Focus on making the murder charges stick to this guy."

"If things go well I should be able to get away in a couple hours."

"Why don't I come by the house around seven?" Kalina offered.

"That sounds perfect. I'll see you then. I love you, Kal."

"I love you too."

Kalina couldn't keep a smile from spreading across her lips. The danger was past. If he was willing to confess easily, it made Chris's job much easier. She returned to the living room and Jillian's face brightened instantly.

"Good news I take it?"

"They have him in custody and it sounds like he's going to confess. This whole mess is going to be over."

“Oh, thank God!” Jillian tipped the bottle over her glass until it was almost overflowing.

Kalina grabbed the bottle before it spilled and drained the rest of it into her own glass. The raised them in a toast and she took a long drink. This time it didn’t burn on the way down. A few minutes later they both set down empty glasses and Jillian pulled Kalina into a hug.

“I’m so glad you were on this one, Kal. I couldn’t have handled all of this without you. I’m sorry I was so bitchy before. I love you.”

“You’re forgiven, Jill. And I love you too.”

Normally, this much show of affection from her older sister would have made Kalina uncomfortable but the relief that washed over Jillian’s face made it bearable. Now she could look forward to whatever Chris needed to tell her tonight.

Chapter 17

Seven o'clock came far faster than Kalina expected. She'd gotten AJ to give her a ride home so she could change with enough time to walk to what would soon be her house. On the way over, her phone buzzed with a call from her mother. Guilt twisted Kalina's gut at the realization that neither she nor Jillian had been keeping their mother apprised of what was happening.

"Hi, Mom," she said and slowed her pace to a stroll.

"Hi sweetheart. How are you?"

"I'm OK. I'm sorry I didn't check in after

Thanksgiving. Friday was really busy at the shop."

"It always was for your father too."

"I'm sorry we didn't keep you in the loop on what happened with Thomas Chase."

"Your sister filled me in just now. How horrible. A part of me feels bad for that young woman but the rest me is just disgusted that she'd agree to coerce a man she claims to love into doing something against his principles."

"Yeah. You think you know someone and then this happens. I think Jill is taking it harder than she's letting on. But we can be there for her."

"Yes, of course. Honey, you sound a little winded. Are you sure you are all right?"

"Yes, Mom, I'm fine. I'm just walking to Chris's."

She could almost hear the smile in her mother's voice. "You're going to have to stop calling it his house soon."

"I know." The squat, two-story house came into view and it sent excited shivers down her spine. "I'm here. I should go."

"I love you."

"Love you too."

Kalina ended the call and stowed her phone in her purse. Checking her hair in the glass inlaid in the front door, she rang the bell and waited. She spotted Chris through the glass and beamed at him when he opened the door.

"Right on time," he said and pulled her in for a kiss.

He was certainly being more affectionate than normal. He must have really felt guilty for missing Thanksgiving. He finally pulled away, leaving her breathless.

"Can I get you something to drink? A glass of wine or coffee?"

"I think that depends on what you need to talk to me about. Should I be sober for this conversation?"

Chris's brow furrowed for a moment as the overhead light caught the strands of gold laced through his hair. "Coffee's better."

"Then, sure, I'll have some coffee."

He smiled at her and disappeared into the kitchen. She made herself comfortable on the couch and studied the room. They'd brought over some smaller items like pictures already. Even these little touches made the place feel like home already.

"Here you go," he said, handing her a mug.

She gripped it between both hands and inhaled the aroma. "So did everything go well at the station?"

"He confessed to everything including slashing your tires."

"Guilty conscience?"

"He doesn't strike me as the guilty feeling type. I think he realized there was nowhere to go and no one to protect him. The head of the company also confessed to his part in everything. The project is going to be shut down."

"Good. I'm glad everything worked out."

"Yeah." He took a slow sip from his mug and set it on the table. He turned to face her and pulled one of her hands from her mug to cradle between both of his. "I really am sorry I missed

Thanksgiving."

"It's fine. You had work, I understand that. Besides, there will be other Thanksgivings and Christmases to spend with my family."

He gave her hand a squeeze but stayed silent.

"Chris, what is it?"

He relinquished his grip with his right hand; it dipped into his pants pocket, producing a small box. "I'd planned to do this on Thanksgiving. Your mom and sister were in on the whole thing too." He opened the box. "Kalina Greystone, will you marry me?"

Sound fell away and all she could see was the delicate diamond ring nestled in the jewelry box. Of all the things he could have said, she wasn't expecting a proposal. They'd been together less than six months. But even though their time together again was short, her heart told her she was ready. Their history had led them to this very moment.

"Kalina? Did you hear me?"

She blinked and the world came rushing back. Clumsily, she set down the coffee mug and threw her arms around him, kissing whatever part of him she could reach. “Yes. Of course the answer’s yes!”

“It is?”

She leaned back to give him a proper kiss on the lips. The kiss bubbled over into a fit of laughing when she caught the surprise on his face. “Of course. We’re moving in together. Why would I say no?”

“I don’t know … maybe you thought it was too fast?”

“We’ve been working towards this since high school, Chris. I think we’re ready. Besides, I think we both know there’s no one else out there for us.”

His shoulders relaxed and he slid the ring—a perfect fit—onto her finger. The diamond caught the light from the table lamps and sparkled merrily from its new perch. She curled up in his arms and sighed with contentment. This was the perfect way to end a crazy, hectic few days. Sure, a chapter of a man’s life had come to an end but this one in hers was just being written.

"I can't believe my mom and Jillian kept this a secret." She laughed. "No, scratch that. I'm surprised AJ didn't find out and spill the beans ahead of time."

"I only wish I could have asked for your father's blessing."

A twinge of sadness pulled at her heart but it passed after a moment. Her father would have been proud of her for everything she'd accomplished in the last few months.

Have and Hold

Geeks and Things Book 4

A GEEKS AND THINGS COZY MYSTERY

Have and Hold

S.E. BIGLOW

HAVE AND HOLD (A GEEKS AND THINGS MYSTERY)

If you enjoy this work, please consider leaving a review.

For information contact; www.sarah-biglow.com

Edited by Ken Marrow, M.A.

Cover Design by: Deranged Doctor Design

Published by Sarah Biglow: June 2016

10 9 8 7 6 5 4 3 2 1

 Created with Vellum

Chapter 1

A crisp blanket of snow covered the front yard as Kalina stared out the second-story bedroom window. They didn't get a lot of snow on the coast. It usually turned to rain by the time it reached the small town of Ellesworth but today, in late January, the storm was raging and heavy. It buffeted the windows and the wind howled in the distance. Her attention diverted to the slender stick in her fingers: a positive pregnancy test. She'd had her suspicions but this confirmed it. She supposed she was lucky that she and Chris were already getting married. Still, she wanted to wait until after the wedding to share the news. She didn't want him to feel pressured into tying the knot just because of a baby. She also needed to get used to the idea of a child. She hadn't been against the idea of being a mother, but it hadn't really been in her life plan. Still, it brought a certain sense of excitement and she knew her mother would be thrilled. She hid the test in a wad of tissues and tossed them in the trash just as the bedroom door opened and Chris appeared in his dress uniform. Since he'd made detective he hadn't needed to be in uniform. But today was a special day. After almost nine months without a captain, Chris had finally accepted the appointment.

"Well, don't you look handsome," she said and pulled him in for a kiss.

"You're going to be there right beside me," he said when she'd pulled away.

"You earned this. I'm so proud of you."

"I don't know about that. A man that I respected turned out to be a killer. I got this job because someone else murdered little old ladies."

"Chris, come on. You know you earned this. You put in a lot of hard work to keep this town and its people safe."

"I wouldn't be half as good at it without you."

"I don't know what you're talking about." She'd only been involved in a few cases but Chris had always been the one to get the credit.

"Yes, you do. I know I can't stop you from being curious."

"I'm just a lowly shop owner," she said with a sly smile.

"I just worry one day it will get too dangerous."

"I'll be fine. I promise."

He settled on the bed to lace up his shoes and Kalina took the break in conversation to put on earrings and tame her short curls into submission. She studied her reflection in the mirror, scrutinizing her waistline to see if she was showing yet. She couldn't spot any noticeable difference so her secret seemed safe.

"So have you talked to your mom about coming down for the wedding?" she asked.

"Yeah. I called her the other day. She's going to be here for everything. She said she was sending over a present early. Her instructions were very clear to open it before the wedding."

"That's kind of strange."

His reflection shrugged. "She's a little weird sometimes. But I figure I'm the last kid to get married so I'll humor her."

"I get that." She was the second of two siblings getting married in her family too.

"I have to admit I'm happy you didn't want a big ceremony," he said and moved to stand behind her, wrapping his arms around her waist.

Breath caught in her chest for a split second before she exhaled and leaned into him. "A big, flashy affair just isn't us. Besides, we're paying for everything and a cop's salary and what I make from the shop isn't the big bucks. So we do what we can."

"Exactly." He kissed her cheek and released his grip.

She checked herself in the mirror one last time before following him downstairs. She paused before going down to consider how far they'd come. They'd been engaged since

Thanksgiving and had only been living together since then as well so they'd taken a few months to figure out what they wanted and who was on the guest list. She'd settled on a dress around Christmas but had to pay for it in installments. People liked their comics and other nerdy paraphernalia but the dress was still more than she felt comfortable paying for in a lump sum.

"Come on, we don't want to be late," Chris called, holding out her coat.

"Right, sorry."

She hurried down the stairs and let him help her into her coat. She wrapped a thick scarf over her face and pulled on gloves before they braved the snow. Chris opened the front door to find a package perched on the front steps, covered in a thin layer of snow. He picked it up and heard something move inside. He stepped back inside.

"We're going to be late if we open your mom's gift now," Kalina said.

"I don't know that this is from her. No return address."

It was addressed only to Detective Christian Harper. Kalina peered at the postage. “It’s from the right zip code though.”

“They aren’t going to start without the guy getting the promotion. We can be a couple minutes late,” he said and fished in his pocket for his keys. He kept a pocket knife attached and slid the blade along the tape on the top of the box. He folded back the flaps to find a small jar with clear liquid inside. The jar held a human finger with a sparkly engagement ring. Kalina tried not to scream but the sound still came out as a strangled moan. She’d seen dead bodies before but somehow the severed finger was worse. It ignited too many questions that she didn’t want to contemplate: chiefly whether the finger’s owner was still alive. Chris moved with quick steps to the kitchen—ignoring the snow he tracked across the floor—and flipped on the light.

“Why would someone send you a finger?” Kalina rasped.

“I have no idea,” he answered and pulled out his phone. “But I don’t think this is a coincidence.”

Chapter 2

Kalina kicked off her boots and went in search of a towel to clean up the mess Chris had tracked in while he stood by the sink, phone pressed to his ear. Her own phone buzzed in her pocket, reminding her that they were already late for the ceremony. She bent down to wipe away the mess just as Chris's call connected.

"Jimmy, it's Chris. I need you to send someone over to my house immediately. You know what, why don't you just come yourself?" A pause and then, "Someone's sent me a finger in a jar."

Kalina tossed the sopping paper towel in the trash as Chris hung up and rubbed his forehead with the back of his hand. She watched him exhale a slow breath and toyed with the diamond on her left ring finger. The ring on the severed finger had to mean something. She bit her lower lip, mentally chastising herself for jumping into the investigation. Chris didn't need her help.

"What do you think?" he asked after such a long pause that she jumped.

"I think they'd better reschedule the ceremony because someone sent the acting captain of the department a human finger."

He smiled and shoved his phone in his pocket. "I meant about the finger."

"I have no idea. I didn't really take a good look. It isn't something you expect to come in the mail."

"Yeah. Jimmy and some lab techs are coming over to look at it."

"Can't we just bring it to the station since we were heading there already?"

"No. I don't want to expose it to the elements more than necessary. It's better if they examine it here."

"OK."

She steeled herself to head back into the living room. Her stomach churned at the thought of having to examine the finger before the police had their chance and she didn't think it had anything to do with the new life growing inside her. She took shallow breaths as she bent down to examine the jar that held the finger. It looked as normal as a finger cut off its hand could. Its owner was dark-skinned, Hispanic or Black perhaps. The nail was trimmed and French manicured. She wasn't a science expert but she could guess it was suspended in formaldehyde. The clear liquid distorted the cut of the ornate diamond just above the second knuckle. Still, the ring looked oddly familiar. She tried to remember where she'd seen it before but two sharp knocks at the front door broke her concentration. Before she answered the door, she snapped a quick picture of the ring on her phone, being sure to zoom in as close as possible on the ring.

"Hey, Kal," Jimmy said as she opened the door.

Jimmy was one of the youngest officers on the force but something about being in his dress blues made him look very grown up. He pulled latex gloves from his coat pocket and slipped them on, all business. A tall, female lab technician in a hat and knee-length puffy jacket ducked in behind Jimmy with a field kit. Chris emerged from the kitchen and immediately pointed to the box sitting on the living room table.

“Any idea when it arrived, Captain?” Jimmy asked, addressing Chris by the title he had not yet received.

“It had to have been in the last hour or so. I didn’t see anything earlier.” He turned to Kalina. “Did you see anything?”

“No. The windows upstairs usually give a good view of the front yard and the porch. I don’t remember seeing anyone drop off the package. Besides, our mail doesn’t usually get delivered until the late afternoon.”

The lab tech opened her kit and pulled out fingerprint powder and a brush. She leaned over and started first with the jar. “Did either of you touch this?”

“No,” Kalina and Chris answered in unison.

She turned back to the purple powder and let the bristles glide over the glass jar. Nothing appeared. "Whoever sent this was careful enough not to leave prints."

She moved next to the exterior box and found a plethora of prints. Most likely the majority belonged to Chris and Kalina. His prints were already on file but hers weren't.

"Jimmy, why don't you get a fingerprint card and get Kal's prints to speed things up?"

"Sure thing, boss."

Kalina led Jimmy into the kitchen so they were out of the way and settled at the table and studied her fingernails. She'd had a manicure herself less than a week ago. The wedding was in two weeks and she'd had gel put on just to make sure they lasted long enough. Jimmy fumbled to take off the gloves and opened the ink pad.

"Just roll your finger right to left," he instructed.

Carefully, she allowed him to guide her fingers —left hand and then right—along the pad and paper until ten crisp prints lay on the page. She left him to fill out her identifying information while she scrubbed the ink from her fingers, trying not to mess up her nails. She could hear lowered whispers from the other room but her attempts to eavesdrop from beside the sink failed. For his part, Jimmy kept glancing furtively through the open doorway too.

“I don’t think Chris would mind you going back in there. He called you after all. Asked for you specifically,” Kalina said.

“I know. I’m just trying to figure out why someone would send him a body part. And at his house, not the station.”

“Why would that matter?” She slid into the chair beside him.

“I don’t know ... it just seems like if you want to taunt the police, send it to the police station. This seems like it could be personal to the captain.”

“The finger has an engagement ring on it,” she supplied. He would find out sooner rather than later just by looking at the jar.

Jimmy fiddled with the limp latex gloves on the table in front of him. Kalina could tell he wanted to say something but she stayed quiet until he was ready. She had an inkling of the question he wanted to ask her. But she'd let him ask the question rather than assume.

"He was almost married once," Jimmy stated.

"I know."

They'd shared all of their pasts since getting back together. It had been an amicable break after high school, allowing them both to find themselves as adults. She got her degrees in business and he became a decorated cop. She'd dated a few guys in college and graduate school but none of them had gotten to the engagement stage. Chris, on the other hand, had gotten to the point of wedding planning but shortly before they were to walk down the aisle he'd found out that she'd been cheating on him and he'd broken things off. Kalina's mother had been upset that the ring was the same one he'd given to the cheater. She saw it as Chris holding out hope that the ring would wind up on the right person's finger. She was quite proud that the ring was now nestled between her left pinkie and middle fingers. It had quickly become a fixture on her hand so that she often forgot she was wearing it but could always tell when it was absent at night or in the shower.

“I know you tried to keep things quiet with your engagement and everything but do you think someone from his past could have found out?”

Kalina shook her head. “Even if they did, I don’t see why she’d send him a severed finger. For one thing, it looks as though whoever it belongs to is Hispanic or of color and she was the one who ruined the engagement, not Chris.”

“Fair enough. And I hate to ask but is there anyone who might have wanted to send something like this to you?”

“No. I had boyfriends but none that got serious enough for a proposal. I’m not sure this is personal other than to freak us out.”

“All right. Well, I’m going to see what’s going on out there.”

“Sure.”

Jimmy gathered the kit and fingerprint card and headed for the doorway leading to the living room. “You look really nice, by the way.”

She smiled at him. “Thanks.”

Kalina pulled her phone from her purse as soon as Jimmy was out of view and studied the photo she’d taken. There wasn’t much she could do about the identity of the finger—although she secretly hoped whomever it belonged to was still alive—but she could look into the ring. It looked strangely familiar but she couldn’t figure out where she’d seen it before. They’d gone ring shopping in the city, and according to Chris her engagement ring had been bought elsewhere too. But she was sure she’d seen the ring somewhere before. Its silver band, unadorned except for the large diamond, was a fairly standard design. Chewing her bottom lip, she went in search of her tablet. Chris and their guests were busy studying the jar and the package so didn’t take notice as she darted upstairs in stocking feet and found what she was looking for in the study. She’d turned it into a home office. It was nice to have someone to come home to now and so she tended to do the books for the comic shop at home. The tablet sat docked to its charger on the desk and she settled in front of it.

“Where did I see this before?” she muttered to herself as she waited for the browser to load.

While she let the thought percolate, her phone issued a loud ‘ding’, signaling an incoming text message from her sister, Jillian. She checked it. “Mom wants to know if you wanted the emerald earrings for the wedding. Sorry for late notice.”

Kalina had completely forgotten that her mother had wanted them to have matching jewelry for the wedding. It was something small she could do and it would have made their father extremely happy. The thought that her father wouldn’t be walking her down the aisle brought tears to her eyes. She wiped them away and responded to the text.

“That sounds great. What jeweler is she getting them from?”

In her heart, she hoped her sister’s response would give her an early clue to where the engagement ring in the jar had been purchased. If the shop was local, she could visit it on the pretense of picking out the earrings for her mother. She didn’t want to drag her mother into a police investigation—about the only family she'd willingly let tag along was her nephew, AJ—but it would give her the perfect excuse if Chris asked about it.

Her sister's response took a good two minutes to come through. "Carmichael Jewelers."

"Thank you, Jill," Kalina said even though her sister couldn't hear her. She fired off a short text saying that she would check what they had and turned her attention to looking up the jeweler.

After a brief Google search, she discovered that Carmichael Jewelers was the only jewelry store in town. How she hadn't known that was a little baffling. Her embarrassment was assuaged a little when she saw that they'd only been established in town since the mid-2000s. She'd been off to college then so it made sense that she didn't know. Maybe being an unknown to the owner would be helpful in her search. Either way, she intended to pay them a visit the following morning. The snowstorm outside didn't seem to be letting up and she'd already closed down the shop for the day so the excuse of going to the shop wasn't believable.

Footsteps echoed on the stairs and she hastily shut down the search window as Chris filled the doorway to the study. He gave her an apologetic smile. “I’m so sorry about all this.”

She waved his apology away. “You have nothing to be sorry for. Do they still want to do the ceremony today?”

“Yeah. We should head out in about a half hour. There isn’t much we can do with the evidence until we get an ID on who the finger belongs to. Might as well carry on with our lives. It’s the best way not to let the bad guys win.”

She pushed herself out of the chair and wrapped him in a hug. Going out to the ceremony would give her an excuse to check out the jeweler without being too obvious.

Chapter 3

The storm had let up a little by the time Kalina and Chris headed out for the rescheduled ceremony. She was working up the nerve to tell him she needed to stop by the jewelry store afterwards. She didn't want to get him involved. After all, in his dress blues, he more than screamed police. As Chris pulled into the parking lot of the station—there weren't that many people coming—he glanced over at her.

"Are you OK?"

"Huh, yeah. Just thinking. My mom wanted me to pick out some earrings for the wedding and I realized I forgot to do it."

"I could come with you if you want."

She shook her head. “No that’s OK. I don’t really know what I’m looking for and you have so much other stuff going on with work right now. I’ll be fine.”

“If you’re sure.”

“I am. Come on, let’s get you all sworn in as captain.”

They walked arm in arm through the front of the station. The small police force was assembled and in their dress uniforms as well. The mayor stood chatting with Jimmy in low tones, Kalina hoped it wasn’t about the finger but they pointed in Chris’s direction and her heart fell.

“I’ll be right back,” he said with a quick kiss to her cheek.

It turned out not to be about the finger, just logistics for the ceremony itself. She thought it was sweet that Jimmy would get to give Chris his captain’s stripes. She settled in the front row and got her phone ready for some good photos. A hush fell over the bullpen and all eyes turned to the mayor, Chris and Jimmy. It was a brief exchange when all was said and done. The mayor gave a short welcome and thanked Chris for his dedicated service to keeping the town safe. Jimmy stepped up and tried to hide his excited grin as he adorned Chris's uniform. They saluted each other and then the applause from the rest of the force erupted. Kalina snapped a few quick pictures before Chris pulled her to her feet and into a bear hug.

"Thanks for being by my side for all of this," he whispered.

"There's nowhere else I'd rather be."

She could feel her phone buzzing in her purse and stepped away to see what was going on. Chris was immediately swallowed up by other people congratulating him. Her sister's number flashed across the screen.

"Hey, Jill. I'm looking into the earrings," she said automatically.

"What earrings?" AJ asked.

"Sorry, kiddo. I thought you were your mom. Grandma wants me to pick out earrings for us to wear for the wedding. Your mom reminded me this morning."

"Oh. Cool. You excited for that?"

"Of course I am." She switched the phone to her other ear. "What's up?"

"I just wanted to know how the ceremony went."

"It was fine. You could have come, Chris wouldn't have minded."

"I've kind of been on lockdown for break. Mom wants me studying for the stupid SATs."

"She's got a point. Getting good SAT scores will help you get into college."

"I know. It's just boring as hell. And I miss work."

Her nephew had been working for her during the school year on weekends and nights and she had to admit she was glad for the company. It made the small, family-owned comic shop feel homier having him around. And their shared love of all things nerdy was a bonus. Jillian had insisted he take a few months off to focus on studying for the SATs and she had agreed. She opened her mouth to tell him about the mystery package from that morning but stopped short. He would want to get involved and if someone was sending pieces of people to the police, that wasn't something she wanted her sixteen-year-old nephew caught up in.

"You still there, Aunt K.?"

"Yes, sorry. I need to go. If you want to swing by the shop tonight I can probably convince your mom you need some air and we have some inventory to sort through."

"You're the best."

Kalina laughed a little and ended the call. She felt a hand on her shoulder and spun around, coming face to face with the mayor. He was a doughy man in his forties with a thick head of blond hair and sharp, brown eyes.

"Didn't mean to scare you," he said with a smile.

"That's OK. The ceremony was really nice. Thanks for convincing him to accept the position."

"It wasn't just me. I have a feeling his beautiful fiancée had something to do with it too."

Heat warmed her cheeks and the back of her neck. "Not really. He knew he was right for the job. Would you excuse me? I have an errand I need to run for the wedding."

He nodded and she went in search of her coat at the front of the building. Jimmy lounged by the reception desk, keeping an eye on the phones.

"Hey, can you let Chris know I'm heading out?"

"Sure. Everything OK, Kal?"

"Everything's fine. I just need to run an errand. Let him know I'm taking the car."

"If you need to talk about what happened this morning, I'm here," Jimmy said in a sudden, somber tone.

"Thanks, Jimmy. I really appreciate that."

Kalina pulled on her coat and scarf and headed out to the car. She could still picture the ring in her head, sitting primly on the severed finger. Holding on to the small hope that its owner was alive—losing a single finger wasn't usually fatal—she headed to Carmichael Jewelers. It was a small shop with a clean exterior. Sets of earrings and watches adorned the front windows on display. She could see a single counter inside as she parked in one of the few spaces in the lot. Whoever owned the place had taken care to shovel the sidewalk in front of the door for ease of access. An electronic sound tolled as she pushed the door open. Gentle lighting reflected off the display cases on the center counter. It was definitely a small operation but the owner clearly had good taste in fine jewelry.

“Hello? Is anyone here?” Kalina called out.

Silence answered her at first. She took a quick look around the small space until she spotted the single section of delicate diamond rings with a small sign announcing there was a discount for “wedding season”. Finally, footsteps echoed from beyond the counter and a man in his forties appeared. He wore a sweater vest over a white dress shirt with navy blue slacks. His jet black hair lay in a natural swirl off his forehead, drawing attention away from beady grey eyes.

“Sorry, I must not have heard the bell,” he said and set a ledger down on the counter.

“That’s all right. I’m guessing with this storm you weren’t expecting anyone to come in anyway.” She unwound her scarf and undid her jacket. Her engagement ring caught the light and twinkled on her finger. His gaze zeroed in on the ring.

"How can I help you? Wedding bands perhaps?"

His directness made the little hairs on her neck stand on edge. "I'm sorry?"

He pointed to her ring. "Well, I'm assuming you're already engaged. I have some lovely bands. Is your fiancé joining us?"

"Oh, no. We have our bands picked out. We're getting married in a couple weeks and I was wondering if you had any emerald earrings I could look at for myself and my matron of honor."

"Earrings?"

"Yes. To be honest, my mother is insisting and you know it is important to keep the mother of the bride happy."

He smiled briefly and coughed. Clearing his throat, he waved her over to a case of delicate studs. He pulled out a tray and pointed to a few of them. "How about these?"

"Um, I was thinking something that dangled. We're wearing our hair up so it would be a nice contrast."

"I'll have to see what I have in the back."

He started to move away and her gaze darted to the ledger book sitting on the other end of the counter. An idea was forming but she needed one more piece of information before she could implement it.

"Oh, actually, before you do that, there's one other thing I wanted to look at."

He gave an exasperated sigh at being interrupted but turned back to face her. "Yes?"

"A friend of mine is thinking of proposing to his girlfriend and it would be really nice if he knew what was out there. I noticed your collection. Could I take a look?"

"You're quite the busy bride, aren't you? Wedding on the horizon and checking out what's out there for other people?"

"He's still working up the nerve to buy the ring but it would go a long way if I told him there was a great jeweler with reasonable prices right here in town."

The compliment seemed to bolster the jeweler's mood and he pulled out the tray of engagement rings. She bent low to study them, looking at the tiny tags and their ID numbers. It was exactly what she'd needed. She even spotted one that looked remarkably like the one from the mystery finger. She pointed to that one and he handed it over. She committed the ID to memory before handing it back. She also noted that there appeared to be three empty spots that used to hold rings that had been sold.

"I could put it on lay away for your friend, if you'd like?"

"I'll ask him." She licked her lips and turned back toward the other display. "So, about those earrings?"

"Yes. Of course. I'll see what I can find. Just wait here a moment."

He disappeared back the way he'd come and she seized the opportunity to pour over the ledger. It was open to a page conveniently marked "Engagement Rings". Despite the three empty slots, she found only two people had come in within the last month to purchase diamonds for their sweethearts. Instead of jotting down the names and addresses, Kalina retrieved her phone from her purse and snapped a shot, making sure to zoom in close for the names of the buyers. The fact that this particular entry had been left open was a little strange but she tried to brush it off. Maybe he was just cataloging his inventory. She understood how that went.

She replaced the ledger and retreated to the other side of the counter. He returned a moment later and presented two pairs of silver earrings with simple emerald stones. They were definitely beautiful and exactly what she'd imagined wearing. She checked the price and tried not to look stunned. They were not cheap. But she only got married once and if she left without a purchase more than just her fiancé would be suspicious.

"I'll take both pairs."

"Very good. I'll just need to get your information."

"Thanks for making this so simple, Mr. Carmichael," she said.

"Oh, my name's Bruce Hempstead. Carmichael's is a franchise."

"I just assumed. I'm so sorry."

He gave her a toothy grin and boxed up the two pairs of earrings. Ten minutes later she piled back into the car and shoved the key in the ignition. She needed to share what she'd found with Chris. She was about to hit speed dial when a call came through from his number.

"Well, this is good timing. I've got something to show you," she said.

"That's good because we have an ID on the finger."

"I'll come to the station right away."

Chapter 4

Kalina's heart hammered against her ribs as she made her way back across town to the station. She had a bad feeling that one of the men in the ledger was going to have a fiancée with one less finger. The parking lot was emptier as she pulled into a spot and cut the engine. The rest of the officers had returned to their patrol duties and the few townspeople who were in attendance likely had gone back to their day jobs. Kalina stowed the earrings in the glove box just to be safe before heading inside. Jimmy and Chris stood side by side at Chris's desk.

"You said you found out who the finger belongs

to?" she said without waiting for them to look up from the file between them.

"Her name is Gabriella Baez," Chris answered.

The name didn't sound familiar. He showed her a photo from a missing person's report but Kalina still didn't recognize her. She did, however, recognize the name of the person who filed the report. She pulled up the photo of the ledger she'd taken and toyed with her phone.

"What'd you find, Kal?"

"So, um, don't get mad at me. This was in plain view the whole time. I didn't even touch the pages. But it looks like a couple of guys bought engagement rings similar to the one we found from Carmichael Jewelers recently and one of them"—she zoomed into the first name—"might be connected to Ms. Baez."

Chris and Jimmy both bent forward and examined the neatly handwritten ledger for a Mr. Duncan Westford. Jimmy flipped through the pages of the missing person report and let out a sound of understanding.

"I think you're right. Mr. Duncan filed the report. Ms. Baez is his fiancée and she didn't return home after their engagement party."

"When was that?" Kalina returned the photo to its original size while Jimmy skimmed the report.

"Looks like at least three days ago."

"I doubt she cut off her own finger. If she didn't want to marry the guy she would have just returned the ring," Chris remarked and rubbed at his chin.

"But why would he report her missing if he hurt her?" Jimmy asked.

Kalina and Chris both started to speak but stopped. As they both knew, many things—money, or the promise of it, included—could be powerful motivators to falsely report a person as missing. After all, Jillian's college best friend had attempted to do just that when she knew her husband was dead and she'd had a hand in it.

"We need to contact Mr. Westford, have him confirm the ring belonged to his fiancée," Chris said.

“You aren’t going to show him the finger are you?”

“No, we’ve had one of the lab techs remove and photograph it separately. We got lucky that her prints were in the system.”

“How? She doesn’t look familiar.”

“She’s a teacher in the state. They have to get fingerprinted before they start teaching and we have access to the database.”

“Oh. So when is he coming in?”

“Not until tomorrow morning most likely. We have officers making the notification right now.”

“So what do you do now?”

Chris let out a sigh. “Now I got home and celebrate my promotion with my beautiful fiancée.”

Kalina smiled. “Oh, I don’t know if it helps or matters but you should probably take down the name of the other person who bought a ring like Gabriella’s. If it isn’t her fiancé, there might be someone else out there who is at risk.”

Jimmy took her phone to copy down the information before he gathered up the missing person report and his notes and headed for the reception desk. Chris tugged on his coat and hat and offered her his arm.

“Shall we?”

“Actually, I promised AJ I’d let him come by the shop and help me do some inventory.”

“I thought he was taking some time off.”

“He is, but he’s going a little stir crazy doing constant SAT prep. Jill’s going a bit overboard.”

“Well, I would like to spend some time with you later.”

“I won’t work too late. I promise.”

Chapter 5

After stopping to grab a sandwich and bottled water, Kalina settled in the game room with the inventory boxes spread around her. She heard the back door swing open and she looked up only briefly to see her nephew kick snow off his shoes and unwind the scarf around his face.

“Thanks for doing this, Aunt K.,” he said and settled into a chair beside her.

“Hey, I can use the help.” *Especially when the baby comes*. She caught herself before she could voice that particular concern. Not before she’d shared the news with Chris.

“So anything new and exciting going on?” AJ probed.

“What makes you think there’s anything exciting going on?”

“You sort of have that look.”

Her brow furrowed. “What look?”

“The ‘there’s a case I’m not supposed to be looking into but I’m doing it anyway’ look.”

“I don’t have ... fine. But if you breathe a word of this to your mother, you’re fired.”

He mimed locking his lips and throwing away the key. “I promise.”

“We got a severed finger in the mail.”

“We?”

“It was sent to the house. It belongs to a woman who was reported missing a few days ago. Chris is looking into it.”

“Why would someone send you a finger?”

“I have no idea. And it was addressed to Chris. I’m guessing because he’s the new police captain.” She raked her fingers through her hair. “But it had an engagement ring and the person who reported her missing had just bought one. Chris is supposed to talk to him tomorrow."

"Did they find her?"

"Not yet." She wanted to tell him that the woman was fine but she couldn't force the lie past her lips. "But that was my day."

"Do you think the guy hurt her ... the one who bought her the ring?"

"I'd like to think not. If he cared enough to ask her to marry him, I can't imagine he'd want to cut off her finger after she'd accepted his proposal."

"You know, I don't remember anything this weird happening before you moved back to town," AJ said with a half-smile.

"Are you saying I've bad mojo or something?"

He shrugged a shoulder. "Maybe. All I know is in the last year we've had more crazy stuff happen in town than ever before."

"Great, my nephew thinks I'm cursed and to blame for people getting killed in town."

"Not what I'm saying at all! If you weren't

around to help out, they wouldn't figure out what was really going on most of the time."

"Give Chris and the rest of the force some credit. They get there eventually. And I think at this point they've kind of accepted I can be useful."

"Well they'd be dumb not to."

"I just worry that, if it isn't the fiancé, there are other people out there who could be in danger."

"Why?"

"Just a feeling." She couldn't tell him any more about the case or her hunch. Especially since she hadn't shared her worry with Chris yet and if she was going to tell anyone, it should be him.

They fell into silence as they turned their attention to the task at hand. Together, they managed to get the inventory entered into the system and organized for the usual customers to pick up their new issues. Kalina's phone gave a loud double beep at 6:30. She glanced at the screen to see a text from Chris. "See you at home."

“Hey, Aunt K. I should probably get home. Thanks for the break in monotony.”

“That’s a good SAT word,” she teased and ruffled his hair.

He gave her an annoyed look but said nothing as he pulled on his scarf and jacket. She checked the front door to ensure it was locked before she followed him out to the small back lot. He started to trudge through the snow.

“I’ll give you a ride,” she called.

Her nephew’s face lit up at the offer and he scrambled into the passenger seat as Kalina climbed behind the wheel and started the car.

“I hope you find the lady with the missing finger and that she’s okay,” he said ten minutes later, after navigating the snow piles in the center of town.

“Me too.”

As soon as AJ was out of the car, she did a U-turn and headed home. She found Chris waiting for her with a glass of wine and a roasted chicken cooling on the sideboard. She hesitated as she took the glass, tipping it to her lips but not drinking any.

His gaze narrowed. “What’s wrong?”

Kalina set the glass down and shook her head. “Nothing.”

“Come on, after the day we had, you have to want a drink.”

“I’m just not in the mood for it, I guess. Thinking about what happened makes me kind of queasy.”

“Oh. Can I get you something else?”

“I’m fine.”

The scent of the cooling chicken simultaneously made her mouth water and her stomach churn. She wasn’t going to be able to hide things for much longer. Maybe now was the best time to spill the beans. They were only two weeks away from the wedding anyway. There was little chance he’d abruptly change his mind about marrying her.

“Actually, I need to tell you something,” she said and motioned for him to sit down.

“OK. What is it?” In one fluid motion he pulled out the chair and slid onto the seat.

She settled into the seat across from him and smoothed out the winkles in the hem of her dress. She opened her mouth to speak—hoping just blurting it out would quash the fear bubbling up in her chest—when Chris's phone rang.

"It's the station. Just give me one second." He answered the call and swiveled to face the sink. "Captain Harper."

She couldn't see his facial expression and the call was turned down low enough she couldn't overhear who was on the other end of the line. Chris let out a sigh. "You're absolutely sure?" A pause. ""And there was a finger missing? The same one?"

Chris turned back to face Kalina and she knew she wasn't going to be able to share her news with him. His cheeks were suddenly drawn. "They found a body out on the beach by the water."

"Oh God. Is it Gabriella Baez?"

"No. It's a different woman. This one's white. She had ID on her. Her name is Margaret Fink. She was twenty-six."

“You think she had her finger cut off with an engagement ring on it?”

“It would be my guess.” He pinched the bridge of his nose. “If Gabriella isn’t dead yet, I suspect she will be soon. We might have a serial killer on our hands.”

“You’ll figure this out,” Kalina said and twisted the still-full glass of wine in front of her by the stem. “Who do you think killed this other woman?”

“I don’t know. We are still bringing Gabriella’s fiancé in for questioning in the morning. All the officers told him is that we had some information on his fiancée’s whereabouts and we needed to talk to him. And we’ll have to look into Margaret’s life to see if she also had a fiancé.”

“Do you think either of the fiancés could have killed them?”

“I don’t know. Honestly, if he’d just proposed to her and she’d said yes, it doesn’t make sense. But then again, people have plenty of reasons to end engagements.”

Like cheating partners.

He scrubbed at his face with the heels of his hands. “This is not how I hoped this would go.”

She reached across the table to give his hand an affectionate and supportive squeeze. “I know. But you’ll find out what happened.”

“Sorry, what did you need to tell me?”

“Don’t worry about it. It can wait. The case is more important. I understand if you want to go back to the station to wait for the field reports.”

“No, I think right now I’m right where I need to be.” He kissed the top of her hand. “With you.”

Chapter 6

Kalina barely slept that night. Her mind refused to quiet, instead spinning wild theories about some maniac chopping off unsuspecting women's ring fingers. She had held off telling Chris about the pregnancy too. He needed to be laser focused on the case. News of the baby would only distract him. When the clock read 6:07 a.m., she snuck out of bed and headed down to the kitchen to make some tea. The sun was barely above the horizon as she stared out the window above the sink waiting for the water to boil. As she stood there in the silence of the early morning, the tiny hairs on the back of her neck twitched, signaling danger.

“You’re just imagining it,” she mumbled to herself but it didn’t stop her from checking the front step. No soggy box with a human finger waited for them this morning.

A tiny sigh of relief escaped her lips as the tea kettle whistled loudly. Several minutes later she sat on the couch in the living room, tea mug in one hand and her laptop propped on her knees. Chris had been using it the night before when she’d gone to bed. His work email sat open on the screen with a new message and attachment from Jimmy. The field report from Margaret’s crime scene. Without hesitating, she opened the email and read the report.

“The victim was found near the low tide marker on the beach. She was buried under snow and appears to have suffered blunt force trauma to the head. The left ring finger was likely severed prior to death based on clotting. Coroner estimates the victim has been dead for at least seventy-two hours; however, recent weather conditions may make proper determination difficult. A more accurate time of death will follow with the autopsy.”

Kalina scrolled down and stopped at the photos. The winter storm had preserved Margaret's face in a mask of terror. She'd seen an elderly woman look that way when she and Chris had solved the revenge killings perpetrated by the police department's former captain. It was not a sight she'd ever wanted to see again. The tea that had warmed her now roiled in her gut and she hastily set both computer and mug down to race to the downstairs bathroom. She would have liked to blame it on the morning sickness but she was nearly through the first trimester.

"Kal, are you OK?" Chris's voice came through the closed door of the bathroom a few minutes later.

She rinsed out her mouth and opened the door. "Fine."

"You're pale"—he pressed his hand to her forehead—"and clammy. I think you might be coming down with something."

"I'm not. I swear."

His gazed narrowed and he crossed his arms over his chest. "Something is going on with you. And I think it has something to do with what you wanted to tell me last night."

"I told you, it can wait. You need to focus on this case and find whoever's doing this before anyone else gets hurt."

"Right now, I need my fiancée to tell me the truth."

She relented and pushed past him out of the bathroom. "I was going to wait to tell you until after the wedding. I didn't want it to affect why we are getting married. But I'm pregnant. Almost twelve weeks."

She'd pictured his reaction in her head a million times. Stunned, slack-jawed silence. Maybe some sputtering as he tried to find words. Instead, he beamed from ear to ear and pulled her into a gentle hug. "We're having a baby!"

"Yeah. We are." She returned the hug and let all the stress of not telling him melt away.

"That explains the wine last night," he said in her ear.

"I honestly wasn't expecting this reaction," she said and leaned back to study his expression.

“We’ve talked about wanting kids.”

“I know. Just, after the wedding.”

“Technically it will be after the wedding,” he said with a smirk.

She laughed a hearty belly laugh. This was why she loved him and why she wanted to spend the rest of her life with him. They stood there, wrapped in each other’s arms, until Chris’s phone once again interrupted their domestic bliss. Chris let out a groan and fished it out of his back pocket.

“I’ll call Jimmy back later.”

“No. Take it. It’s probably about the case. He sent you the report this morning,” she said. There was a time when she would have tried to hide her snooping but he was resigned to it these days.

“Did he?”

“It’s open on the laptop. You might not want to eat anything before you look at it though.”

Chris’s phone stopped ringing and he hit redial while Kalina retrieved her mug of tea and went in search of breakfast. She also set the coffee percolating, knowing Chris would need at least one cup before he left for the day.

“Sorry I missed you before. What’s... Jimmy, slow down and take a breath.” He switched the phone to his other ear. “It went to who? No, I’ll be there as soon as I can.”

He ended the call and pulled a travel mug from the cabinet beside the stove. “I’m going to need that to go. Another finger’s shown up.”

“Did it go to the precinct?”

“No. It was sent to a reporter named Beth Finnegan. Whoever this guy is, he’s getting bolder.”

Chapter 7

Kalina wanted to join Chris at the station to hear what the reporter had to say but she knew it would be better for the investigation if she wasn't present. There was still some digging she could do on her own. The name Margaret Fink was starting to ring a bell. So, as Chris hastily pulled on his coat and hat, she set about getting dressed so she could head to work. A plan was beginning to form in the back of her mind as she pulled in behind the shop a little before 8:30.

The interior was as she and AJ had left it the evening before: slightly messy but with a certain order to the chaos. She wasn't set to open for another half hour so she had time to search through the files for what she was looking for. Settling into one of the big chairs in the game room, she pulled up the roster of monthly orders. As she'd suspected, Margaret Fink had an outstanding order from a couple weeks earlier and she had listed Carter Whalen as an authorized person to pick up the orders. It wasn't as though comics were prescription drugs but many of her regulars took their collections seriously enough to only allow pick-up by certain people.

A quick bit of Facebook stalking revealed that Margaret and Carter had recently gotten engaged. She'd changed her profile picture to one of the two of them showing off the ring. Without being friends, Kalina couldn't enlarge the picture to get a good look at the ring but she had a hunch it resembled Gabriella's. She was about to dial Carter's phone number on the pretense of having him pick up her outstanding order when she realized she could at least confirm whether Carter had purchased the ring from Carmichael's.

"Damn." The curse escaped her lips before she could stop herself as the snapshot of the ledger confirmed that he was the other man on the list.

Overcome by sudden emotion, she had to sit in silence for a moment or two to collect herself. She wanted to believe it was the pregnancy hormones beginning to kick in but she was just lying to herself. Luring a man in to ask him questions about his dead fiancée was not what normal people did. Her hands shook as she entered his phone number and hit “Call”. As it rang, Kalina tried to prepare herself to leave as benign a message as possible.

“Hello?” A man’s baritone answered the call.

“Is this Carter Whalen?” Her voice hitched as she spoke his name.

“Yeah, who’s this?”

“My name is Kalina Greystone. I own Geeks and Things here in town. I’ve been trying to get in touch with Margaret Fink about an outstanding order that she has waiting for her. She has you listed as someone who can pick it up.”

“Oh. Sorry about that. Things have been kind of

crazy lately. I can come by and pick them up if you want."

"That'd be great. If you stop by now you can get them before we open."

"Great. I'll be there as soon as I can."

She ended the call and wiped at the corners of her eyes. She needed to look presentable and as though she didn't know his fiancée had been found murdered on the beach. The fact that she could have been dead for a few days by now made her curious. He didn't seem concerned about her whereabouts or wellbeing.

Ten minutes later, she heard a knock on the front door. She'd already pulled Margaret's order and packaged it up. Carter looked a little dazed as she pulled open the front door and flipped the front sign to "Open". He was shorter than she'd expected from the picture on Facebook.

"I'm glad you could come by," she said and darted behind the front counter.

"Sure. So how much do I owe you?"

"Fifteen dollars."

“Maggie loves these things. I’ve never seen someone get so into graphic novels before.”

She noted his use of the present tense. If he was lying, he was doing a very good job of it. She took his twenty dollar bill and handed a five back.

“So, do you know why she hasn’t been by to pick them up? Usually diehard fans are very prompt with their pick-up.”

Carter rubbed his neck and laughed. “That’s probably my fault. We got engaged a couple weeks ago and we’ve been diving head first into planning. We don’t want a long engagement.”

“Oh. That’s understandable. Congrats by the way.”

“Thanks.” He picked up the bag and tucked it carefully into his jacket. “She’s visiting some friends out of town for a few days right now. Sort of her last hurrah before we really get buried in the planning.”

He really didn’t know his fiancée was dead. No one could be that good at lying without having no emotions and this guy clearly cared a great deal about the woman he'd asked to marry him. Before she could say anything, her phone rang. The Caller ID indicated it was from the station.

"Excuse me," she said and turned her back to answer the call. "Hello?"

"Hey, hon. I have a weird question for you," Chris said on the other end.

"OK. What is it?"

"You don't happen to know a Carter Whalen? He's Margaret's fiancé."

"Yes, I know that. I can stop by if you want."

"He's there with you, isn't he?" Chris's tone carried an edge of worry.

"Yeah. So I'll see you soon."

She ended the call before Chris could say anything else and turned to face Carter. He was pulling on his gloves. "That was my fiancé. He's the new police captain."

"Oh. Well, I guess congratulations are in order for you too."

"He's looking for you. He needs to talk to you about Margaret."

"Why?"

"Because they found her on the beach last night."

Carter's stare turned blank and his body swayed side to side as he took in the information. Kalina wanted to offer a hand to steady him but she'd just delivered the worst news a person could get. He didn't want her comfort.

"I need to see her," he said barely above a whisper.

"I'll take you to the station. And I'm very sorry for your loss."

Chapter 8

Carter remained quiet during the short drive to the station. There were more cars in the lot than Kalina was expecting. A few more uniformed officers were heading into the building as she cut the engine and unbuckled her seatbelt. As soon as they pushed through the front doors she realized why the force was being called in. Not only did they have to speak with Carter and Gabriella's fiancé, but they were probably still questioning Beth about the finger she received in the mail. A female officer, who Kalina believed was named Vanessa, approached them as soon as the door swung shut.

"Mr. Whalen?" she said.

“Yes,” Kalina answered for him.

“Please come with me. We have a few questions for you.”

Carter nodded mutely and shuffled off after Vanessa. Kalina stayed rooted to the spot just taking in the hustle and bustle of the bull pen. She finally spotted Jimmy among the crowd, seated beside a young blonde woman. She had a tissue pressed to her cheek and Kalina guessed she was Beth, the reporter. Trying to be inconspicuous, Kalina picked her way through the throng of officers until she was within eavesdropping distance.

“So just to make sure I have everything clear, you found the package this morning on your front steps,” Jimmy said.

“Yes. I didn’t think anything of it at first. My mother orders stuff all the time and just puts my name on it. I figured that’s what she’d done but when I opened it...” Her cheeks paled and she visibly swallowed.

“Thank you.” Jimmy looked around until he spotted Kalina. “I’ll get someone to drive you home.”

"No. God, I can't go back there."

"Well, wherever you want then."

Jimmy left the desk and joined Kalina where she stood. "Could you do me a huge favor and take her wherever she wants to go? We're a little swamped here."

"Is that OK with Chris?" Kalina asked.

"Yeah, I'm sure it is."

"How is everything else going?" She gestured around her. "I thought it was just some interviews. It looks like the whole force is here."

"The captain set up a command post for everyone to check in. Forensics and the lab and everything. He wants information as soon as its available. He's worried we've got a serial on our hands."

"But it's just Margaret, right?"

"Not anymore. They found Gabriella Baez this morning."

"On the beach?"

"Yeah. Not too far from where we found Margaret."

"That's awful."

Beth rose from the seat where Jimmy had left her and shoved her used tissue in her oversized purse. Kalina sighed and took out her keys.

"I'll take her." She wanted to stay to hear what the fiancés of the respective victims had to say but getting Beth out of the cops' collective hair was probably a better use of her time.

"Thank you so much."

Kalina approached the reporter and held out her hand. "I'm Kalina."

"I know who you are."

"Oh. Well, Jimmy said you needed a ride. Where can I drop you?"

Beth shouldered a laptop bag that had been hidden behind her chair and gestured to the front of the building. "Anywhere but here."

"OK."

Once they were out in the crisp winter air, Beth exhaled a long breath. "You probably have work to do."

"Town isn't very big. I'm pretty sure my customers can wait a few minutes while I drop you somewhere."

"Actually, I can't really face work just yet. Would it be too much of an inconvenience if I hide out at your shop?"

"Well..."

"I swear I'll stay out of your way."

Kalina forced a smile. "Sure."

"It's unbelievable how much more exciting things have been in town the last few months," Beth remarked as they climbed into the car and hit the road.

"What do you mean?"

"The police captain is really a murderer. And then there was the real estate scam that shut down construction on the new condo development. Now someone is sending people fingers."

"I take it you're a crime reporter."

"Not really. But I think I might want to be now, if my editor will let me."

“Well maybe not this story.”

“Why not? It would make great headlines.”

“But you’re involved in the case now, since you were sent a finger. Chris—Captain Harper—wouldn’t appreciate you releasing details about the case.”

“You’re really close with him aren’t you?”

Kalina flashed her engagement ring. “Marrying the man in two weeks.”

“Oh. You’re right. I should just stay out of it.”

Kalina glanced at her passenger in the rearview mirror. She could see the same eagerness to solve the mystery in Beth that she saw in herself. It wasn’t a bad quality to have, especially for a reporter. But this case was escalating quickly. As she pulled into the back lot behind Geeks and Things a knot started to tighten in her gut. The small diamond on her left ring finger suddenly felt very heavy. Someone was targeting recently engaged couples. They’d sent the fingers to the police and the press respectively for a reason.

“You can hang out back here,” she told Beth

and gestured to the empty game room. It usually didn't fill up until the afternoon.

"Thanks." Beth settled into one of the chairs and pulled out her laptop.

Kalina paused, about to ask a question, but stopped herself. Whatever Beth was working on wasn't her business.

Chapter 9

Time passed quicker than Kalina expected that day. A steady stream of customers passed through the shop and she spotted Beth curled up in the back of the game room, unfazed by the small kids playing Zombie Dice at the table next to her. She seemed focused on what she was working on and Kalina supposed it was good for the woman to get buried in her work. A little after lunchtime Kalina's phone rang, displaying Chris's cell phone number on it.

"Hey, how are you holding up?" she asked as soon as she accepted the call.

"It's been crazy. How about you?"

“I’m fine. I’m babysitting the reporter. She didn’t want to go back to work.”

“It was nice of you to offer.”

Jimmy didn’t give me a choice. “I figured you were all so busy it was the least I could do. Dare I ask what happened with the other interviews?”

“I can’t really talk about it right now. I was just calling to see if you wanted to get lunch.”

On cue, Kalina’s stomach gurgled loudly. “Sure. Just give me like twenty minutes. I’ve got a few people coming in to pick up orders that I promised would be here during their lunch break.”

“I’ll come by and pick you up.” The line crackled as if he were putting his hand over the phone’s speaker. “And I promise I’ll share what I know.”

“I love you,” she said as the front door opened and couple of teenagers ambled in.

Before she could greet them or ask what she could help them with, Beth appeared, laptop bag swung over her shoulder. “Thanks again. I think I’m going to head out.”

“Are you sure? I’m not sure they want you going home yet.”

“I’ll be fine. I’m just going to get some fresh air and clear my head.”

With nothing else to say and no real authority to stop her, Kalina watched the blonde stride out of the shop. Kalina turned her attention back to the customers now leaning on the counter, studying the rows of freshly arrived comics on the wall behind her. In the end, they each walked away with a bag full of comics and significantly lighter allowances.

Chris arrived a little after 12:30 without food. Despite his attempt at looking cheerful, the lines around his eyes and the slightly pallid color of his cheeks told her otherwise. She wanted to just kiss him and make it all go away but that wasn’t possible.

“Where’s lunch?”

“I thought we could go home and I’d make you something from scratch.”

“I want quesadillas,” Kalina said and retrieved her coat from the back.

He offered her his arm and she took it. “Quesadillas it is.”

Half an hour later, they sat across from each other at the table, munching on their food. Kalina absently ran her right index finger along the band of her engagement ring. The weight of it had dissipated some but it was still more noticeable than it had been.

“So, what did Carter and Gabriella’s fiancés have to say?”

Chris blew out a breath and set his drink down. “They both claim they last saw their fiancées alive and they were very happy with their engagements. They both had alibis for the dates that Margaret and Gabriella went missing.”

“How long had Gabriella been dead?”

“A day, maybe two. Definitely less than Margaret.”

Kalina’s brow furrowed. “But we got Gabriella’s finger first.”

Chris cleared his throat. “It looks like hers was mailed before Margaret’s in an attempt to throw us off the trail.”

She nodded in understanding and took a big bite of lunch. Chewing contemplatively, a thought occurred to her. “This may sound crazy and stupid but did you ask about what each of them was doing when the other one’s fiancée went missing?”

He didn’t respond right away. She studied his face as he chose his words. “You think they each killed the other one’s fiancée in a *Strangers on a Train* type situation?”

“Like I said, it’s probably stupid but it could be a thing, right?”

“No, it’s possible. And I didn’t think to even ask about that. They both seemed so believable in their grief.”

“It’s probably nothing. Just forget I even brought it up. I don’t want to mess with your investigation.”

“It’s a good point and I’m going to check it out.”

“You know, I just thought of something else that might be useful,” she said after downing half her drink in one swallow.

“I’m listening.”

“When I was at the jewelers I noticed that there were three rings missing from the display case. There were only two entries on the ledger of people who bought rings there. It seems kind of odd now. You might want to talk to the guy who runs the place.”

“I’ll look into that too.” Chris cleared away his own plate and glass and glanced at her over his shoulder. “So, how are you really feeling?”

“I’m fine, I swear. I’m lucky that the morning sickness is really only in the morning.”

“Have you been to the doctor?”

“Not yet. I’m going to make an appointment. I’m guessing I’m close to the end of the first trimester right now. I was going to wait until after the wedding. Besides, I want you to be there for everything that you can be.”

“I’d love that.”

She smiled at him and tucked a stray curl of red hair behind her ear. In that moment she wondered what their baby was going to look like. Would he or she have her hair or Chris’s eyes or smile? There was so much to look forward to.

With a kiss to her forehead, he picked up her lunch dishes and set about washing them. She suspected he would be helping out a lot more around the house in the coming months. His phone buzzed with a text alert. With his hands busy, Kalina grabbed it and read the message aloud. “It’s from Jimmy. He says he sent you a link to the online edition of the afternoon paper. There’s an article you’re going to want to read.”

Chris shut off the water and dried his hands on the front of his pants. Kalina inwardly cringed at his lack of a dish towel but said nothing. She wasn’t going to change things this late in the game.

“What’s the article?” he asked.

“Why don’t you just open it on your laptop? Easier to read that way.”

He disappeared into the living room, returning a moment later with his laptop open and an internet browser waiting for the web address. She read it out to him and they both waited in silence as the page loaded. As soon as she saw the byline, Kalina let out an audible groan. She shouldn’t have been surprised.

Romance Kills Mood in Ellesworth

By: Beth Finnegan, Staff Writer

Police are investigating a series of grisly murders that have rocked the town in the last few days. The bodies of two young women were found on the beach in the early morning hours, each dead from apparent head trauma. Each was missing their ring finger on their left hand. According to sources inside the department, both had recently become engaged.

In a grim twist, the victims' fingers were sent to members of the public, including newly sworn-in Captain Christian Harper. This isn't the first time a crime has hit close to home for the captain. Last summer, a series of murders led to the arrest and confession of former Captain Daniel Cahill, Harper's mentor. A source within the department who wishes to remain anonymous, confirmed that the victims' fiancés are persons of interest. Stay tuned for more updates as the investigation unfolds.

The color drained from Chris's face and his shoulder muscles tightened. Kalina couldn't blame him for the anger he was clearly feeling. She felt a sense of betrayal. Beth had done exactly what Kalina had told her not to do. And now it appeared there was a leak within the department. Just what Chris needed on his first official day as the head of the department.

"I can't believe she did this." His voice came out in a low growl.

"I told her she shouldn't write anything about this. Especially since she got one of the fingers," Kalina said. She wanted to ease his anger even though she knew it wasn't directed at her.

"This is why I hate reporters. Hell, whoever killed Gabriella and Margaret probably wanted this to happen. See his deeds in print."

"I suppose she was decent enough to keep their names out of it."

"For now. I don't doubt in whatever piece she runs next she'll be dragging them and their fiancés through the mud. And now our witness interviews could be compromised."

"I can try to talk to her if you want," Kalina offered.

"No. I'll handle it. I need to know who is giving her this information. None of it should be available to the public. I don't even think we have a confirmed autopsy on either victim yet."

"Take a breath, honey. She's just one reporter who wrote one story."

He ran his hands through his hair and linked his fingers behind his head. "She had to bring up Cahill. It has nothing to do with this investigation but she's calling my ability to be objective into question. It's like I'm too stupid to see what's right in front of me."

"You can't let her get in your head. This case is barely a day or two old and you are doing everything right. You'll find who talked to her and you'll deal with it. Now, why don't I go with you to the jewelry store? I actually bought some earrings for the wedding that I want them to insure."

"I need to get someone to track down Beth Finnegan. You don't know where she went do you?"

"No. When she left Geeks and Things she was heading out to get some air. I feel horrible that I didn't pay more attention to what she was doing."

"You aren't her babysitter, Kal. You were doing the department a favor even driving her somewhere. This isn't on you. It's on us. And I swear we're going to make it right."

She stood up and planted a firm kiss on his lips. "You can make it right by catching whoever is doing this before they hurt anyone else."

Chapter 10

Kalina let Chris drive her back to the shop with the agreement that he'd meet her there at four and they could go to the jeweler's together. It would give her time to wrap up business for the day and hopefully Chris would be able to figure out who'd given confidential information to Beth. Her gut told her it wasn't Jimmy. He looked up to Chris too much to spill the beans, even to a pretty reporter. It had to be someone else in the department but she couldn't put her finger on anyone specific. Everyone seemed as though they walked the straight and narrow. Just as she flipped the front door sign to "Open" her cell phone buzzed in her pocket. Her mother.

"Hi Mom."

"Did your sister tell you about the earrings?"

"Yes. I got them this morning. Chris and I are going over later to make sure we get the paperwork for insurance purposes. Everything's going to be fine."

"I saw that article in the paper. How are you two holding up?"

Kalina let out a little sigh. "We're fine. Chris is just digging in to work. Not that I blame him."

"I just worry about you sometimes."

"And I know you'll never stop, no matter what I say. But I promise we're both safe. They're close to finding the person who did it." It was a lie but she knew it would assuage her mother's worry.

"As long as you're sure."

Kalina could see people approaching the front of the shop through the blinds on the front windows. "Mom, I've got to go. Customers await."

"OK. I love you."

Kalina ended the call and yanked the door open. Her nephew's rosy face greeted her. She quirked a brow at him but he said nothing, just stepped around her into the warmth of the shop. A few other people followed suit and, before she had closed the door, AJ jumped behind the counter and started taking orders. She settled in the corner and watched him dart around the shop like a pro. He kept a broad grin plastered to his face until the last customer had left the shop and the bell above the door quieted.

"You aren't supposed to be here," Kalina chided.

"I told Mom I left some stuff here yesterday."

"You shouldn't be lying to your mother."

"I know. But I saw that article on the news... Mom hasn't yet and I just wanted to see how you were holding up."

"I'm fine, kiddo. Chris is on the warpath but I don't blame him."

"It said there was a source in the police. Is that true?"

"I don't know. He's trying to find out."

On cue, her phone buzzed with a new text from Chris. “Leak in ME’s office. Ex-boyfriend of reporter.” “And it looks like they solved the leaky department problem.”

“Why do you think she brought up Captain Cahill?”

“To try to draw attention to what’s going on. It was a horrible thing for her to do. I should have realized she was going to write something even though I told her not to.”

“It isn’t your fault, Aunt K.”

Tears welled in her eyes. “I just feel like I could have done more to keep her quiet.”

AJ pulled her into a tight bear hug and she tightened her grip on him too. She wanted to tell him the truth about what was making her so emotional but she wanted to wait to share that news until everything was over, the wedding included.

“Do they have any leads?”

Kalina relinquished her grip on her nephew and wiped at her eyes. “I’m not sure. From what I know, the fiancés are clear.”

"So that reporter lied."

"Or she interpreted what she saw at the station when she was being interviewed."

"You and Chris will solve it. You always do."

She forced a watery smile. "Thanks for the vote of confidence." Kalina gave his arm an appreciative squeeze. "Now, you should get home before your mother has a heart attack because you aren't studying."

"Do I have to?"

"Yes. Move it, mister."

He pouted all the way to the front door but cracked a smile before wrapping his scarf over his mouth and heading out into the cold. As the door swung shut, she spotted Chris's car rolling up the block. He rolled down the passenger side window and leaned over. "You ready?"

"You're early."

"Didn't you see my text?"

"Yeah. But I thought you were going to try to talk to Beth again."

“I’ve got guys out looking for her. She’s not with the ex-boyfriend and there’s been no response at her house or office.”

“Let me grab my coat.”

The ride over to the jewelry store was short and quiet. Neither of them seemed to know what to say. Kalina still couldn’t shake the feeling that she should have done something more to stop Beth from posting the article. The anger that had made the lines of Chris’s face sharper a few hours ago had dulled a little. At least no one under his direct command had blabbed to the press.

“I’ve got the fiancés coming back in to be questioned about their whereabouts on the days the other women went missing,” Chris said as he pulled into a free spot in the parking lot. He chose the middle spot, equal distance from the door and the edge of the lot. She assumed it was to conceal his presence for as long as possible. There was only one other car in the lot.

“So how are we going to do this?” Kalina asked and unbuckled her seatbelt. She spotted a woman talking with Mr. Hempstead.

“I’ll go in first and see what I can find out. You should just stay here.”

She said nothing to his directive to stay in the car. They both knew it wasn’t going to happen. But she waited while he climbed out of the car and headed for the only entrance to the small shop. With his back turned to her, Kalina ducked out of the car and inched up the sidewalk so she could try to catch snippets of the conversation.

“I told you, I’m done having this conversation,” a woman’s voice said.

“Is everything all right?” Chris’s voice came through the partially opened front door.

“Fine. This is a private matter.” Mr. Hempstead’s tone was harsh.

“Are you sure you’re OK, miss?”

No response but Kalina caught the woman’s head bob up and down slightly.

“I was just going.” The woman’s voice filtered out into the open air. Kalina watched as Chris held the door open for her. She rushed out the front door and exhaled a long, clouded breath in the winter air. Kalina searched her coat pockets and found an unused tissue.

“Here.” She offered it to the woman.

“Thanks.”

Without a word, Kalina guided the woman out of view of the front door of the shop. The woman gave a hiccup and blew her nose loudly.

“I don’t mean to pry but that didn’t sound very good in there.”

“Oh, that. It’s nothing really. Just a little disagreement.”

“Mr. Hempstead seemed pretty upset.”

“He gets very passionate about things. Really, I’ll be fine. Just if you wouldn’t mind not telling him where I’m going. We both need some time to cool off.”

“Sure thing.” She fished for another tissue. “Just in case...”

“Fiona.”

“Well then, just in case, Fiona.”

After taking the proffered tissue, Fiona pulled out car keys, along with a hotel key card with a tree logo—which she promptly shoved back into her pocket—and the headlights flashed on the other car in the lot. Kalina waved her off before heading in to join Chris. She prayed he was having some luck questioning Mr. Hempstead.

The warmth of the shop greeted her as she walked in. Mr. Hempstead was nowhere to be seen but Chris waited at the counter, hands clasped in front of him.

“Hey. How’s it going in here?”

“I’m taking a look at his books.”

Kalina pointed to the display case of engagement rings, still with three empty spots. At least he hadn’t sold any more since she’d last been in. “That’s what I was talking about with the missing ring.”

“I see.” He glanced over his shoulder at the now empty parking lot. “Did you get anything out of the woman?”

“Her name is Fiona. I didn’t get a last name. I think she and the owner are a couple. She seemed upset. But I think she’s just going to cool off.”

“I get kind of an odd vibe from this guy,” Chris said in a whisper.

Mr. Hempstead appeared with the ledger in hand and stopped short when he spotted Kalina. “You’re back.”

She smiled at him. “Yeah, I realized I wanted to ask you for information on insurance for the purchase I made the other day. But I see you’re busy.”

Mr. Hempstead waved his hand dismissively in Chris’s direction. “It’s fine. I’m sure the officer can wait.”

“It’s Captain, actually. And, no, I can’t wait.”

Kalina stepped back with her hands held up in a gesture of surrender. She was a little curious to see how Chris handled the jeweler with an audience again. And not someone he could push around. Color flooded the man’s cheeks and he shoved the ledger across the counter to Chris. “Here’s what you asked for. I still don’t know what this has to do with that article in the paper.”

Chris flipped through the pages and slid his finger down the item line on one page in particular. “I see you’ve got two individuals who purchased diamond engagement rings but I notice that there’s a third one missing from the display.”

“Is there a question in there somewhere?”

Chris set the ledger down and crossed his arms over his chest. “Did you sell a third ring to someone?”

“I don’t remember.”

Kalina caught the tightening of her fiancé’s jaw as he fought to control his temper. Mr. Hempstead was clearly trying to exert dominance in the conversation and it wasn’t helping his case. After a tense moment, Chris said, “You keep meticulous records, Mr. Hempstead. I don’t believe for one second you sold something and didn’t record it. And you should know that, if you keep lying to me, I can have you arrested for obstructing a police investigation.”

“I only record items once they are picked up, paid for and a one week period passes for returns. That hasn’t happened for the third ring, yet.”

"I'm still going to need the name of the person who placed the order."

"I don't have it on hand."

Before Chris could call him on his bluff, his phone rang. "Captain Harper."

Kalina could make out Jimmy's voice, albeit tinny and distorted over the open phone line. "Both of the guys came back in. They have alibis for the other dates. Should we cut them loose?"

"You're absolutely sure?" A pause and a garbled response that Kalina couldn't hear. Then, "OK. Fine. Any luck locating our missing witness?" Another pause and, by the crestfallen look that came over his face, the answer wasn't what he'd wanted. "Keep looking. I'll see you back at the station."

He ended the call and looked at Mr. Hempstead. "I'm going to come back and I expect you to have that information. If you don't, I'm going to arrest you. Do you understand?"

"Yes. Fine. Can I help my other customer now?"

"You know what... I'll just come back another time. There's really no rush. You clearly have more important things to deal with. Thanks again for the earrings," Kalina said and backed out of the shop as quickly as possible.

Chris followed once he was sure Mr. Hempstead wouldn't see them get into the car together. He walked outside and exhaled a slow breath. "He's hiding something. I know it."

"You think he knows who the third person is?"

"I do. And if the fiancés have been cleared, we're back to no suspects."

"This might sound crazy but could Mr. Hempstead have been involved?"

"I don't see how. Sure, he sold the rings but what motive would he have to kill them and cut off their fingers? He'd just made a lot of money on those rings. It's not like he could resell them," she said once they were back in the car on their way back to the station.

"There's just something in my gut telling me that something is off about this guy. And why has Beth Finnegan all of a sudden fallen off the face of the planet?"

“I will admit that’s weird. Hey, do you think you could drop me off back at the shop?”

“Sure, but you should take it easy. I don’t want you overexerting yourself.”

She patted the hand that gripped the gear shift. “That’s sweet of you but the baby and I are perfectly fine.”

“And maybe I’m a little worried that whoever is going after people might go after you.”

“They are recently engaged couples, Chris. We’ve been engaged for a while. We’re getting married in two weeks. They aren’t going to target me. Besides, even if they did, I know you’d hunt them down.”

Chapter 11

The shop was quiet, almost eerily so, when she walked back through the front door. The mystery of who had hurt the women was gnawing at her thoughts and wouldn't let go. There was a piece they were all missing but she was going to find it. She flipped the front door sign to "Closed" and settled in the game room with her tablet propped on her knees. She started with searching for Mr. Hempstead on Facebook. There couldn't be many guys with that name. Her search returned only three results and the first was the subject for her investigation. His profile picture showed him and Fiona—albeit younger than they both were now—cozied up on a couch. She clicked over to his profile page and saw that his most recent update was a relationship status change to "Engaged". He'd also posted a short engagement notice.

Bruce Hempstead is pleased to announce his recent engagement to Fiona Hayes of Salem, Massachusetts. The couple has been together for ten years and are excited to forge their new path together as partners in marriage.

At least Kalina had a last name for Fiona now. She saw that Fiona was tagged in the post and so she clicked the link. Curiously, Fiona hadn't updated her status or shown any indication that she was now engaged. Come to think of it, Kalina hadn't seen any engagement ring on Fiona's hand. Did this mean that Fiona's ring was the third one missing? If that were the case, then Mr. Hempstead was unlikely to have filed it in his ledger. It made sense but in the age of Internet over-sharing, it was strange that Fiona hadn't followed suit and told the world she was now spoken for. Kalina hit the back button to check the dates on Bruce's page. It was almost a month ago. Fiona's latest posts were from a couple days ago so there was definitely time to update if she'd wanted to.

"The engagement must have been what they were arguing about earlier," she said aloud.

So that was one mystery solved. At least to a point. That still left the larger one of the missing reporter. Leaving Facebook for now, Kalina searched for the town's online edition of the paper. Luckily, the list of staff writers and reporters was easily accessible at the top of the home page. She found Beth's name and a list of articles she'd authored filled the screen with "Read More" links after the introductory sentence. The article she'd written about Margaret and Gabriella's deaths was the top story. It also had the most views of any of her articles. She'd mostly written fluff pieces about town history and small events going on. She really did want to be a crime reporter.

Setting the tablet aside for the moment, Kalina retrieved her phone and placed a call to Chris's cell. He answered on the first ring.

"Everything OK?" He couldn't mask his worry.

"I'm fine but I found something that might be helpful."

"What did you find, Kal?"

"So it looks like, at least according to Bruce Hempstead's Facebook page, he and Fiona are engaged. He posted about the engagement and changed his status about a month ago."

"That would explain the missing third ring."

"But here's the thing. When I was talking to Fiona earlier, I didn't see a ring on her finger. And she hasn't updated her status or even acknowledged the engagement. Speaking from experience, that's not the kind of thing you really ignore or forget to mention."

"Maybe she just hasn't gotten to it yet."

"She's posted other stuff since he posted the engagement notice. I don't think she's going to post about it. Chris, what if he proposed and she said no?"

"It would certainly piss him off."

"And if he gave her a similar ring to the ones that Margaret and Gabriella received, seeing them happily flaunting them around town might push him over the edge."

"But to kill them? Why would he do that?"

"I don't know. But I think talking to him again isn't a bad idea."

"Yeah, I think you're right," he said.

"Did you have any luck finding Beth?"

"None. She's disappeared and I still can't figure out how."

"One thing at a time. Go find out why Mr. Hempstead is flaunting an engagement that sounds like it hasn't happened."

"Thanks for the heads up."

"Go save the day," she said and smiled.

She heard him chuckle on the other end of the line before it went dead and the call ended. Time to dig a little deeper into their missing wannabe crime reporter. One of the more recent articles was a piece on some of the more established families in town. Kalina opened the article and skimmed it, stopping near the end at a particularly interesting passage.

Perhaps the most influential families in town were the Finnegans and the Hempsteads. Both families were among the first to settle in town after it was established and have been interconnected for several generations. The most recent generation is by far the closest in the town's history. Despite a large age gap, the Finnegan and Hempstead cousins share Sunday dinner every week. Their bond is deeper than any other family in town. There is nothing each family wouldn't do for the other in their hour of need.

Kalina's throat went dry. Everything was starting to make sense. She'd have to double check town records but she was almost certain Beth and Bruce were related. Attacking Gabriella and Margaret would serve each of them in different ways. Maybe, in some twisted way, it would make Fiona say yes to Bruce's proposal and Beth would get her shot at becoming a crime reporter. The realization turned her stomach and bile burned the back of her throat. She forced it back down and grabbed her phone and keys. She had an idea of where Beth might be hiding and, if that were the case, Fiona was in more trouble than they realized. She tried Chris's cell again but it went to voicemail.

"Chris, I think I know what's going on and where to find Beth. Call me back."

Chapter 12

Kalina's heart hammered against her rips as she yanked the driver side door open and tossed her phone onto the passenger seat. The car's engine fought her as she tried furiously to jam the keys into the ignition. "Come on!"

On the third try, the key slid into the slot and she was able to turn it, the engine rumbling to life. The tires squealed as she peeled out of the parking lot and turned onto Main Street. The tree symbol from the hotel key card danced in her vision. There was only one hotel in town. She didn't even need to look it up. The four-story building sat at the edge of town, leading toward the highway on and off ramps. It was a genius layout and the hotel's location also meant she saw it every time she came to town during college. She'd even stayed there a time or two when she stopped by and her parents were out of town.

Unfortunately, with all of the snow, the town maintenance hadn't gotten all of the roads cleared and her car swerved on unseen patches of black ice. Kalina's fingers gripped the steering wheel in a white-knuckled vice grip until the car righted itself and she slowed down. Beside her, the screen of her phone lit up with an incoming call. Chris's face flashed on the screen and she reached over and hit "Accept" and set the phone to speaker as she continued driving.

"Sorry I missed your call," her fiancé said over the phone line.

"Did you get to have your chat with Bruce Hempstead?"

"Nope. There was a sign on the front door saying he was going out of town for a few weeks and would be closed until then. He's in the wind."

"I know where Beth is hiding." The hotel's front

entrance loomed ahead of her on the right hand side of the road. "The Elm Tree Lodge."

"How do you figure?"

"I did some digging into Beth and the type of articles she'd written. When we were going back to the shop she mentioned wanting to be a crime reporter. The rest of her work was mostly boring town fluff pieces. But she'd also done a history of the town's most influential families. The Hempsteads and the Finnegans were on the list. I think she and Bruce are cousins."

"This seems like a long shot, Kal."

"Just hear me out, OK? If we're right, and Bruce proposed to Fiona and she turned him down, then maybe seeing Gabriella and Margaret happily wearing the ring he'd chosen set him off. I think dear Cousin Beth offered to help him find a way to convince Fiona to change her mind and in exchange he'd give her something to launch her career as a crime reporter."

"You think all of her emotion at getting the severed finger was just a ruse?"

"I've seen better actresses"—her sister's ex college roommate Savannah came to mind—"but she's definitely believable. It's not hard to conjure tears over someone losing a finger."

"Let's say you're right. Where does the hotel come into play?"

"When I was talking to Fiona earlier, she pulled out her car keys and I saw a key card with the hotel's logo on it. I didn't think much of it then but that has to be where she's staying to keep away from Bruce. I can't imagine Beth would let her out of her sight for long."

"OK. I'm going to get some officers to check it out."

"I'm already here," Kalina said and nearly strangled herself in her effort to get out of the car. "I'll see what I can find."

"Kalina, do not go in there. This situation just got a lot more dangerous." His tone took on a more emotional tone. "You aren't just thinking about yourself anymore. You have our child to consider. Please let me take it from here on out."

"OK." She wouldn't be interfering by just sitting in the lobby. If she was lucky she could find out what room Fiona was in. And Beth certainly couldn't be in the room with her, could she?

"I mean it, Kal. Stay out of it."

"I will."

She ended the call and stowed her phone in her coat pocket before heading through the revolving doors into the warm air of the lobby. It was just as she remembered with the warm, muted browns and reds in the carpet and furniture. Even the wood of the front desk had been stained a deep cherry color. A tired looking man stood in the reception area. Beth was nowhere in sight. That worried her a little. Kalina sidled up to the reception desk and leaned forward, chin propped in one hand.

"Checking in?" the desk clerk asked.

"No, I was actually looking for a friend of mine. Fiona Hayes. She mentioned she was staying here for a few days. She said I could stop by if I had time."

"I'm not supposed to give out guest information."

"Oh, I know. Guest privacy is very important. But she told me what the number was but I can't remember." She pulled out her phone and made a show of searching through her notes app. "I swear I put it in here but I think it got deleted. I had to do a restore on this stupid thing the other day. Such a pain."

The clerk gave a long sigh but turned to the computer and hit a few keys. "She's in room 117. Down the hall to the left."

"That's right. Thanks so much!" She kept her phone out and headed down the hallway he'd indicated.

The hall was pretty quiet except for the occasion blare of a TV. She reached a junction where rooms 113-121 branched. She approached slowly, staying to the far side of the hall, when a loud crash echoed ahead. She had a sinking feeling it had come from room 117.

Chapter 13

Kalina paused across the hall from room 117. Nothing came after the crash and she suddenly realized that she had no way of getting into the room. She had no key and if either Beth or Bruce was inside with Fiona, they wouldn't be letting her in willingly. Chewing her bottom lip, she glanced back down the hallway and back to the door. The silence was broken by a woman's scream coming from the room in front of her.

"That's it."

She barreled back down the hallway to the lobby. The clerk stared at her with only a mild interest. "I just heard a scream coming from Fiona's room."

“Probably the TV.”

“No. I don’t think so. Do you have a master key or something?”

“Look lady, I’m starting to think you don’t even know her.”

“OK, you’re right. I don’t really know her that well. But I know she’s in trouble. Her boyfriend has been violent before and she’s been staying here because they’ve been fighting. I think he’s found her.” She searched her phone for anything with a picture of Bruce. She finally settled on the “About Us” page from the jewelry store website. “This is what he looks like.”

The clerk took the phone and studied the picture. The color that had been in his cheeks a moment before drained in an instant. “He came here about a half hour ago. But he wasn’t meeting the woman in 117. He was here to see some reporter. She rented out 119.”

“Do they connect?”

“Yes, but they’re locked.”

“How hard is it to jimmy them open?”

"If you know what you're doing, probably not hard."

Kalina let out a groan at the revelation that, as long as Beth knew which room Fiona was in, all she'd need to do was get the adjoining room. "Get a key for 119 then. And whatever you need to unlock the door between the two rooms."

"Shouldn't we like call the police or something?"

"They're already on their way. Now come on. A woman's life depends on you moving your ass."

The clerk fumbled for a set of key cards and a regular metal key and followed after her down the hallway. The hall was silent again and that unnerved her. Kalina motioned for him to unlock 119. He dropped the key card three times before she yanked it from his fingers and slid it into the lock. The little light turned green and she eased it open as quietly as she could. It turned out they didn't need the metal key for the doors separating the rooms; the one leading from room 119 was already open. Kalina waved the clerk back. "Wait for the police," she whispered.

He backpedaled out of the room and she heard muffled footsteps going back down the hallway. She held her breath and pressed her ear to the door leading into room 117. She could hear shallow breathing and then a loud whimper.

“I did what you wanted.” Bruce’s voice was low and strained.

“Not enough.” Beth’s tone was far more authoritative than Kalina had heard her before.

“Says you. You have more than enough to take you as far as you want.”

“We shouldn’t be discussing this in here. In front of her.”

“She won’t say anything. Will you, sweetheart?”

A muffled whimper answered him. Did they have Fiona tied up and gagged? The image in her head was almost enough to give her away. Footsteps thudded toward the dividing door and Kalina pressed herself to the wall so that when the door swung inward it would hide her. She bit her tongue to keep from breathing too loudly as the door swung in and Beth pushed past. She didn’t seem to notice Kalina and neither did Bruce as he trudged after her, something shiny gripped in his hand. The door on the room 119 side closed and Kalina exhaled slowly. As quietly as she could, she slipped around the door and into the next room. Fiona sat on the bed, her left hand cradled to her chest. Her eyes shone with tears and her cheeks were pale. It became readily apparent what had happened as soon as Kalina held a finger to her lips for quiet and Fiona meekly raised her left arm a little. A hotel towel was wrapped around her hand.

“Let me see,” Kalina whispered.

“He ... they are insane,” Fiona moaned.

“Shh. I’m going to get you out of here but I need to see what happened.” As gently as possible, she unwrapped the towel and had to swallow back a new batch of bile. Fiona’s ring finger was missing just above the second knuckle. Just like Gabriella and Margaret.

“The police are on their way. As soon as we’re out of here, I’m going to call for an ambulance.”

“He still has it.”

Kalina's brow wrinkled in confusion. Then it hit her. The shiny item clutched in Bruce's hand had been her severed finger and the engagement ring. She prayed that Chris would arrive soon and apprehend Bruce before he did something even crazier.

Kalina helped Fiona scoot off the bed and wrapped the towel around her hand again to stem the bleeding. Together they eased their way out the front door of the hotel room and started toward the lobby. Fiona was uneasy on her feet due to the blood loss, which slowed them down. They were almost at the junction when a door slammed open behind them and Bruce appeared wielding a knife in one hand and Fiona's finger in the other. Without thinking, Kalina put herself in front of the injured woman.

His knife hand faltered an inch. "You?"

"It's over, Mr. Hempstead. The police are already on their way. You and Beth aren't going to get away with what you've done."

"And I thought I was the only one who had the chops to be an investigative reporter," Beth said from behind Bruce. She stepped up beside her cousin and brandished a gun.

Heavy footsteps thudded behind Kalina and she didn't have to turn to know that the police had arrived just in time to back her play.

"Put your weapons down and get on the floor," Jimmy ordered. His service weapon was held high, aimed right at Bruce's chest.

Bruce's lower lip trembled and he tossed the knife aside. As he got to his knees, he pressed Fiona's finger to his chest. "I love you."

Beth remained standing, weapon still pointing at the cluster of police. Jimmy's aim moved to her and after a moment she relented and tossed the weapon aside. Two uniformed officers approached and cuffed them.

Ambulance sirens wailed in the distance and Kalina turned to look at Jimmy. "Thank you." She flung her arms around his shoulders and held him close.

Chapter 14

Before long, paramedics huddled around Fiona, one of them packing her finger in ice for transport. Despite the amount of blood, they seemed confident it could be reattached without much issue. That was small consolation considering what the man who claimed to love her had put her through. Kalina wasn't certain but had an inkling that Beth had been the one to push him to such extremes. Of the two, she had the more dominant personality. Both of them had already been led away in handcuffs by the time Kalina trailed Fiona and the paramedics out to the parking lot. Just as the ambulance peeled away, lights flashing and sirens wailing anew, Chris's car came screaming into the lot. He pulled to a stop across several parking spaces and her cheeks burned with color.

“Please tell me you are OK,” he said and grabbed her by the wrists.

“I’m fine.”

He frantically checked her over for signs of injury. His hand stopped on a few splatters of blood on her jacket. She hadn’t even noticed it there.

“Chris, it’s not mine, I swear. Bruce Hempstead cut off Fiona’s finger. She had her hand wrapped in a towel. It must have gotten on me when I took a look.”

“I told you to stay put and let the police handle this, Kal.”

“If I hadn’t then maybe they would have done worse than they did.” She didn’t mean to start yelling at him.

Chris tightened his grip on her wrist and pulled out of view of the other officers still on scene. As soon as they were alone, he let go. “I know you like to help and I can’t say that it hasn’t been invaluable but this was really dangerous. They could have gone after you."

"But they didn't. They didn't even know I was there until the end. And by then Jimmy had already showed up. I helped that woman survive a trauma and I'm not going to apologize for it. Be angry at me if you have to. That's fine. But I'm not going to say I'm sorry when it would be a lie."

Chris exhaled a long, slow breath and scrubbed at his face with the heels of his hands. "The more you get involved the more I worry something is going to happen. And with the baby now... I can't do my job if I'm constantly worrying about you. Do you understand that?"

"I do. Of course I understand, Chris. And I never meant to make you worry or put me ahead of the needs of the job. Look, I'm going to go back to the shop and let you finish up here. We can talk about it when we get home."

She didn't give him time to respond before she dug the car keys out of her coat pocket and headed for her car. The streets were empty as she made the short journey back to Geeks and

Things. The shop felt almost lonely as she settled in behind the counter to do a cash count. She didn't regret taking action to save Fiona. There was no way she could have sat by and let them hurt her further. She tried to understand what would motivate someone to start cutting off body parts of the people they loved but let the train of thought derail quickly. It was too disturbing to consider. She also couldn't believe Beth was willing to throw away a career as a journalist just to get ahead in the business.

Chapter 15

The house had been tense for a few days after Fiona's rescue but Kalina and Chris managed to reconcile. They were both just relieved that they weren't receiving severed fingers in the mail any longer. It also didn't hurt that Fiona was going to make a full recovery with a little physical therapy. At present, Kalina stood off to the side as AJ manned the register. His imposed time away was now over and she was even happier to have him back for many reasons, not least of which was because she was under strict orders not to touch anything. Jillian had meticulously done Kalina's hair and nails for the wedding that afternoon and her sister would kill her if she messed them up.

“I think that’s the last one,” AJ said as he shut the cash register and leaned on his elbows.

Before Kalina could express her relief at the empty shop, the front door opened again and Fiona walked in. Her hand was bandaged but she looked better. A few days in the hospital had actually done her good.

“I can handle this, kiddo. Go get ready for this afternoon,” Kalina said and stepped behind the register.

AJ darted past her and out through the back of the shop. Kalina tried not to fuss with her hair and nails and Fiona rested her injured hand on the counter.

“I just wanted to come by and thank you properly,” Fiona said.

“You don’t have to do that. I’m just glad everything is going to be OK.”

“I should have known something was off when Bruce kept pushing for me to accept his proposal.”

“Not that it’s any of my business but can I ask why you didn’t?”

"Marriage isn't something I wanted. It's just not part of my life plan. I thought he understood that."

"I'm sorry this happened to you."

"I'm just sorry you had to get dragged into it."

Kalina bit her tongue to keep from retorting that she'd jumped in with both feet. Over Fiona's right shoulder, Kalina spotted a taxi cab. "So are you heading out of town?"

"Yeah. I'm going to stay with my parents for a while. I'm thinking of moving out of state too. I know Massachusetts is a big place but right now it feels like everywhere I turn he's there. I need a fresh start. I suppose it's small comfort that Bruce is taking a deal. He'll do some time and I don't have to testify."

"Well, I hope things work out for you."

Fiona dabbed at the corners of her eyes to ward off tears. "Thanks. I should let you go. It looks like you have somewhere to be."

"I'm actually getting married today." She couldn't hide the wide smile or her nerves.

"You're going to make a beautiful bride."

Kalina stepped out from behind the counter and gave Fiona a firm parting hug. They walked out to Main Street and Kalina waved Fiona off as she climbed into the back of the cab and headed in the direction of the highway. Blowing out a breath to settle her nerves, Kalina made the trek to her parents' house.

In her effort to keep her hair and nails intact, she'd worked up a bit of a sweat on the way over. Her mother fussed over her as she changed into her dress. It was a simple dress with cap sleeves and a modest neckline. She hadn't wanted to spend much on the dress even though her mother insisted she should get whatever dress she wanted. She fastened the emerald earrings into place and studied her reflection. Bruce Hempstead may have been delusional but he did have an eye for beautiful jewelry. She had to give him that.

"You look so beautiful," her mother said, wiping tears off her cheeks.

"Thanks."

"I can't believe this day is finally here. I didn't think it would come, Kal," Jillian said with a wry smile.

Kalina just rolled her eyes and laughed. Time to tie the knot and start her future with the man she loved. The church was only partly filled; they hadn't invited too many people. As the organist began the processional, everyone stood and turned their attention to her. She let out a breath and gripped her mother's arm. The only thing that could have made the day even better was if her father had been there to walk her down the aisle. But he was with them in spirit. Chris stood at the front of the church, Jimmy by his side. She couldn't help but beam up at both of them as she and her mother started down the aisle.

She studied the faces as she passed. Most were friends from college and business school and some of the other officers in town who had come up through the academy with Chris. Nadine stood near the very front row, smiling a big, toothy grin as Kalina passed. Letting go of her mother's arm, she leaned over and pulled her friend into a tight embrace. She was grateful that Nadine was back in her life, even if it had taken tragedy to reunite them.

Chris drummed his fingers against his wrist until Kalina let go and finished her procession up to the front of the church. As discreetly as possible, Kalina wiped the sweat from her palms on the front of her dress before taking Chris's hands in hers.

The officiant cleared his throat and began. "We are gathered here today to witness the union of Kalina and Christian. Is there anyone assembled here today who can show just cause why these two should not be joined in marriage?"

The church was silent. Kalina squeezed Chris's hands and he returned the gesture. The officiant nodded after another few seconds had passed. "Then Kalina and Christian have chosen to share brief vows with each other and exchange rings as a symbol of their devotion to each other."

Kalina turned to take the wedding band from Jillian and placed it on Chris' finger. "Christian Harper, I take you as my husband, with your faults and your strengths, as I offer myself to you with my faults and my strengths. I will help you when you need help, and turn to you when I need help. For richer or poorer, in sickness and in health, I choose you as the person with whom I will spend my life."

Chris took her wedding band from Jimmy and slid it onto her left ring finger. They both stared at it for a brief moment before he, too, recited his vows. “Kalina Greystone, I take you as my wife, with your faults and your strengths, as I offer myself to you with my faults and my strengths. I will help you when you need help, and turn to you when I need help. For richer or poorer, in sickness and in health, I choose you as the person with whom I will spend my life.”

“Having shared these vows and exchanged rings, by the power vested in me by the Commonwealth of Massachusetts, and in the sight of those assembled, I pronounce you husband and wife. You may kiss the bride.”

Chris pulled her tight to him and planted a kiss on her lips. It seemed to last forever, just the two of them, and then the recessional music blared from the organ at the back of the church and they paraded down the aisle, arm-in-arm, ready to begin their lives as a married couple and take on the next chapter of their lives. In no time at all they were going to be parents and Kalina couldn’t wait to see what that new journey brought.

Saints and Sinners

Geeks and Things Book 5

A GEEKS AND THINGS COZY MYSTERY

Saints and Sinners

S.E. BIGLOW

SAINTS AND SINNERS (A GEEKS AND THINGS MYSTERY)

If you enjoy this work, please consider leaving a review.

For information contact; www.sarah-biglow.com

Edited by Ken Marrow, M.A.

Cover Design by: Deranged Doctor Design

Published by Sarah Biglow: July 2016

10 9 8 7 6 5 4 3 2 1

 Created with Vellum

Chapter 1

The sun shone hot overhead as Kalina picked her way through the gravestones in the cemetery beside the church. Halfway to her destination she stopped and pressed a hand to her side, letting the muscle cramp work itself out. Her other hand supported her swollen belly. Pregnancy and summer heat were not a good combination but it would soon be over. With her due date fast approaching, she wouldn't have to worry about the swollen ankles much longer. Gaining her second wind, she trudged forward over damp grass—recently doused by the sprinklers—finally stopping at the grave in question: her father's. He'd been gone over a year but it still felt like she was saying her last goodbye at the funeral. Tears welled in her eyes and she let them fall. So much had happened in that year. She'd found her way back home to Ellesworth, MA and her family's comic book shop. It sated her need to be nerdy and gave her a purpose. And she'd found love again with her first love: Christian Harper. They'd been through betrayals and loss together but he'd also risen from detective to captain. And now they were married and about to become parents.

A few weeds poked up around the base of her father's headstone and she did her best to pluck them without being able to bend over properly. "Hi, Dad." She wiped at her cheeks with her free hand. "I know it's been a while since I visited and I'm sorry for that. I've just had a lot going on. Chris and I got married in January. You would have loved it. And you're about to be a grandfather again. It's a girl.

"I've kept the shop running just as you had it. Well, with a few technology upgrades. We're doing great business and it's reminded me how much I missed being there. It feels like home and when I'm there, I'm a little closer to you."

Fresh tears stained her cheeks and a breath caught in her throat. She hadn't expected this visit to be quite as emotional. But she was moving forward in her life without him and it hit her that there were so many things she'd longed to ask him that she'd never get answered. Sure, she had her mother and sister for support but sometimes a girl just needed her father.

Beads of sweat trickled down her neck in the summer warmth but she stayed where she was, hands resting at her sides, one still gripping the scraggly weeds. The silence of the cemetery pressed in around her and what should have been a comfort carried a sense of foreboding. The moisture on her next turned chilly in the summer air and butterflies danced in her stomach. Something had disturbed her peaceful, if teary, visit.

Casting the weeds aside, she made her way deeper into the cemetery. Simple headstone and ground-level plaques gave way to taller monuments to those who had passed on. Some had seen their fair share of rough weather. Engravings had worn down and were only partially legible. Some had seen their edges eroded over time. She stopped to study some of them, curious to see who lay beneath them. She recognized a few names from town history. There was an entire row of Finnegan family members, which only served to turn her stomach. Shortly before the wedding, Kalina and Chris had solved a series of deaths linked to a career-ladder climbing journalist and her love-struck cousin. Beth had been the latest generation of Finnegans in town. Kalina hurried past the rows and stopped when she spotted something sticking out between a couple of the tallest headstones. Shadows cast by the trees overhead obscured the area, forcing her to get closer to investigate.

She rubbed her belly as the baby kicked a time or two, landing solid shots to her ribs. The movement winded her temporarily and she had to stop and catch her breath again. “Thanks for that, baby girl.” She massaged the left side of her ribs until the pain lessened and she could continue forward.

The object that had caught her eye was a designer pump, dark brown and sharply pointed at the toe. Said shoe was still attached to a woman’s slender foot. Kalina moved between the two headstones to find a young woman, a few years younger than herself, laying between the graves with an angry red pool of blood congealing on her chest. Her eyes were still open, frozen in a look of what Kalina could only describe as curiosity. Whoever this woman had been, the fatal blow had not come as a shock. Beyond her designer footwear, she was dressed in an impeccable knee-length summer dress. It clung to her curves even as she lay sprawled on the ground in death. Her hair was still pinned up on the side of her head. Only a tiny trickle of blood marred her pale pink lips.

The shock of the discovery finally hit Kalina a minute later and she backpedaled as fast as possible. This wasn't the first dead body of unknown but definitely suspicious causes she'd seen in the last year. In fact, she'd seen more than she'd ever cared to in her thirty-four years of life. But that bug that bit her every time something like this happened in town took hold of her thoughts as she searched for her phone. This was going to be her last case. After the baby was born, she wouldn't have the time to go running off digging up clues. Her priorities needed to change and she'd accepted that. But this one intrigued her and she knew herself well enough to admit that she wasn't going to let this beautiful woman go. She finally found her phone and hit the first number on the speed dial: her husband.

"Hey honey. Is everything OK with the baby?"

"The baby's fine. But you need to get down to the cemetery and bring a coroner. I just found a body."

Chapter 2

Kalina kept a tight grip on her phone while she waited for Chris to arrive. The sun continued to beat down, making the scene even more unpleasant. She studied the woman's face in an effort to avoid looking at the bloody wound in her chest. Something about her eyes and the way her hair swooped down from her hairline made her look familiar. Sure, being the proprietor of the only shop that sold all things nerdy meant she came into contact with a large portion of the town, but that didn't mean she knew everyone. Still, something about this woman tickled a faint memory at the very edges of Kalina's memory.

She longed to check the woman for ID to sate her curiosity but she was a cop's wife and she knew better. Instead, she walked the perimeter around the gravestones, noting shoe depressions in the damp grass. Whoever had done this had been here recently, which likely meant she hadn't died long ago. It was bold, killing someone in broad daylight, even in a cemetery. As she rounded the second headstone, she noted a few flecks of red marring the pale granite stonework. She'd been killed here. Rubbing her lower back as she came to stand back where she'd started, she took note of whose graves bookended the dead woman's body.

Abigail and Harrison Fischer.

The names, much like the woman's face, rang a distant bell in her memory but it was so far buried she couldn't grab hold of it and bring it forward. A breeze picked up and tugged at the hem of her shirt and the stray hairs hanging out of the messy bun on top of her head.

"Kal!"

She turned toward the sound of her name and a broad grin broke out on her face. Chris trudged toward her, a few uniformed officers lagged behind him. She stayed put and waited for him. How had he known where to find her?

"How'd you find me?"

"GPS on your phone."

"You are tracking me now?"

"Only so I know where you are in case something happens with the baby."

She laughed. "You do realize that's kind of stalker behavior, right?"

"I was kidding. I called Clinton Mason to check the surveillance video to find where you were."

"There's surveillance cameras in the cemetery? Isn't that a little creepy? Watching people mourn their loved ones. It's supposed to be private."

"We had some vandalism a few months back," a deep bass voice said.

Clinton Mason was a thick-necked man with shaggy hair sticking up at odd angles along his head. He apparently didn't own a comb or, if he did, didn't know how to use it. His torso and upper body were beefy and muscled under his short-sleeved shirt.

“Who would vandalize a cemetery?’ she asked.

“Kids on dares mostly.”

“I didn’t see any signs warning about a security system when I came in.”

“You wouldn’t. We don’t advertise them. It gives those coming here to spend time with their loved ones the privacy they deserve,” Clinton said.

“So you caught whoever did this on cameras. That should make it an easy investigation.”

“Well, we hope we did. See”—Clinton pointed to the trees overhanging the Fischer graves—“the angle is a bit sharp on these so we may not get a clear picture.”

“But we’ll know for sure when it happened,” Chris said.

The uniformed officers finally caught up with the small group already gathered and Kalina realized one was carrying an evidence collection kit. She shifted her weight as the baby moved and the slight change in her stance caught Chris's attention.

"Clint, can we go see that video footage? I think my wife wouldn't mind sitting down in the air conditioning for a while."

"Oh, yeah. Sure thing, Captain."

Kalina took Chris's hand and they followed Clinton back to the single story building used for wakes. She hadn't been there since her father's service but it was exactly as she remembered. For a funeral parlor it was brightly lit and decorated. It gave off an almost cheery feel. The air conditioning was on high blast when they walked in and it sent shivers down her back and turned the sweat slicking her skin cold.

"The video monitors are right through here," Clint said and led them into a room she hadn't noticed before.

A computer with a single monitor sat on a squat mahogany desk. The screen flared to life when Clint jiggled the mouse, displaying four quadrants, each with a different angle. Without doing anything, the angles changed to display another four locations throughout the cemetery. Clint settled in front of the machine and after a few keystrokes brought up a single angle. Kalina saw the officers and the forensic technician bent over the body.

“Roll it back a couple hours,” Chris said.

“You got it.” Clint hit a button and the video began to rewind. Kalina watched as the last few minutes passed by in reverse. She tried not to feel embarrassed when Chris caught her circling the gravestones.

“I was just trying to see if there was anything else there,” she said, feeling the need to explain herself.

“I didn’t say anything,” Chris said and placed a hand on her shoulder.

The image on the screen continued to pass by in reverse. Kalina disappeared entirely but the body remained. No one approached or moved away for forty minutes according to the time stamp and then, finally, a hooded figure appeared, walking backwards until he bent over the woman’s body.

“Can you get a better look at his face?” Chris asked.

"Not from this angle."

The man stepped back and they could just make out a knife being pulled from her chest.

"At least it looks like we nailed down time of death for you," Clint said and pointed a meaty finger at the timestamp.

10:47 a.m.

They watched as the man backed up and the woman stood up, now alive. They appeared to be talking and then they disappeared off screen entirely.

"I'll see what I can do to clean up the footage. See what other angles I can find that they might have passed," Clint said.

"Good, thanks." Chris tugged on Kalina's arm. "I'm taking you back to the station. You need to give a statement."

Chapter 3

Kalina didn't want to leave the cool air of the office but she allowed Chris to lead her back outside into the heat and toward the parking lot abutting the church. She fanned herself as he unlocked the squad car he'd come over in. Her car sat a few spaces away.

"Can't we take mine? I'll probably just head over to the shop for a little while when I'm finished at the station."

"OK." He hit the button to lock the squad car again and followed her a few spaces over. "You want me to drive?"

She flashed him a smile. "I'm perfectly capable of driving, thank you. Besides, I've got the seat where I want it and I don't want you messing with it."

He held his hands up in surrender and rounded the front of the car to the passenger side. She settled in behind the wheel and started the engine. Chris buckled up beside her and studied something out the passenger side window. Kalina followed his gaze and spotted the uniformed officers loading the woman's body onto a stretcher.

Chris looked back at her. "How'd you find her?"

Kalina pulled out of the parking lot and headed toward the station. "It's hard to explain. I was visiting my dad's grave and then I just got this feeling like something was just ... off. I wandered a little and then I found her. I guess it was luck or something."

"Or a mother's intuition to protect her child," he said and she caught a small smile out of the corner of her eye.

"Maybe, but regardless of what it was, I'm glad she was found so quickly. It has to give you and your officers a better chance of finding the man who did this."

“Here’s hoping Clint can get a better angle on the man’s face.”

She eased to a stop at a crosswalk, allowing a gaggle of teenage girls to scurry past. “Speaking of faces, hers looked familiar somehow.”

“What do you mean?”

“Well, it was mostly her eyes that made me look twice. I swear I’ve seen her somewhere before, maybe a long time ago. It’s like there’s a memory buried in my brain but I just can’t reach it.”

Before Chris could answer, his phone buzzed and he answered the call. “Captain Harper.” A pause and he pinched the bridge of his nose. “OK. Well, take prints and we’ll run them and see what comes up.”

“What was that about?” she asked and made the final turn leading up to the police station parking lot.

“She didn’t have any photo ID on her so they’re going to run her prints and maybe we’ll get lucky.”

She pulled into a spot near the front door and killed the engine. Chris was out of the car and opening the driver side door before she'd had a chance to unbuckle her seatbelt and yank the keys from the ignition. She squeezed his hand as he helped her out of the car.

"Are you really doing OK with all of this?" he asked as they walked side by side into the station.

"Yes. She isn't the first dead body I've seen, Chris." *Even if it is the last*. She'd tell him about that promise she'd made to herself when this was over.

"I'm not trying to be overbearing. I just want you and the baby to be safe."

She leaned into his shoulder. "I know. And I appreciate that. More than you know."

"I also know you aren't going to let this drop. So just run whatever you find by me or Jimmy."

"Got it. And don't take any risks," she added.

"Exactly."

He held the door open for her and Jimmy greeted them before they'd made it past the reception desk. When all of her adventures in crime solving had begun a year ago, Jimmy had been a fresh-faced, newly minted officer. He'd grown a lot since then. She was pretty sure he'd actually added a few inches in height as well as the full beard he now sported. It made him look much older than his early twenties. He'd also grown as an officer. Only a few months ago he'd saved her from a knife wielding madman.

"They radioed from the scene. I'll take her statement," he said.

Kalina caught the look of pride on Chris's face as he headed for his office, leaving her and Jimmy alone. Silence fell between them for a moment and then Jimmy's business-like exterior melded a little.

"Come on, let's get you off your feet."

"You know, he may not say it but he's really proud of you," she said in a hushed tone.

"I try. I'm just glad he's been around. I have something to strive for, you know?"

"Well, he notices it. Keep it up and you'll make detective before you know it."

Jimmy gave a nervous laugh and led her over to a vacant desk in the bull pen. The computer was already displaying a blank witness statement form, ready for her words to fill it. Without having to ask, he put in her contact information and then turned to face her. “So, tell me everything you can remember.”

Kalina was about to fill him in on her graveyard visit when the forensic technician from the cemetery burst through the front doors and barreled past them to Chris’s office. He didn’t even bother knocking. She couldn’t hear what was being said but she didn’t have to wait long to find out what had the man so agitated.

“What’s wrong, boss?” Jimmy asked as Chris approached them.

“The fingerprints came back. They belong to a Verona Maxwell.”

“Why is he so upset then?” Kalina pointed toward the technician.

“Because they also belong to a dead girl.”

Chapter 4

Both Kalina and Jimmy stared in silence at Chris, letting the revelation sink in. It wasn't possible for two people to have the same fingerprints. Not even identical twins had the same prints. Kalina opened her mouth to ask the obvious question but Jimmy beat her to it.

"Who was the girl?"

"Paige Fischer."

"Wait, I know that name," Kalina said and looked between the two men. "She was a couple years younger than me. She died in an accident or something when she was ten or eleven if I remember right."

Chris nodded. “She and her brother, Patrick, both drowned.”

“But how does the department even have their prints? Did they take them when they found the bodies?” Kalina asked.

Chris shook his head and held up a pair of files with pictures of a young boy and girl. “Their parents had them printed in case something ever happened. Or so the files say.”

“What, did they expect someone to kidnap them?” Jimmy scoffed.

“They might have,” Kalina answered. “They were one of the richest families in town. I just remember other kids whispering about them when they started at public school.”

“You’ve got a better memory of them than I do.”

“You wouldn’t have interacted with them much. My mom insisted I do a youth mentorship program the school year before they died. It was to help younger kids improve their literacy.”

“No offense but if they were rich kids, couldn’t

their parents have afforded tutors or something?" Jimmy said.

Kalina's face fell at the thought of the pair of them. So young and inseparable. "Looking back, I don't think their parents really wanted to spend much time with them."

"Can't we just ask them if their daughter could still be alive?"

"No. Verona, if that's her real name, was found between the Fischers' graves. I didn't notice when they'd died but they're definitely both gone."

Chris set the files on the desk in front of Jimmy and massaged his temple. "I'm going to have the lab run the prints again."

"What about a DNA test?" Kalina suggested.

"If we can find something that belonged to Paige Fischer when she was ten then maybe."

Something about the girl's death was gnawing at Kalina's memory. She needed to get to the shop to do some digging. "I'm going to finish giving Jimmy my statement and then head to the shop to check on Jill and AJ."

“Good. I’m going to see what I can find about the deaths of Paige and Patrick Fischer,” Chris said and disappeared back to his office.

“This is going to be a weird one, isn’t it, Kal?” Jimmy said as soon as Chris was out of earshot.

“Yeah, I think it is.”

Twenty minutes later, she’d signed the statement and was back behind the wheel of her car. It was a short trip back to Main Street and the family-owned comic shop she’d inherited from her father. As she pulled up to the turn off for the lot behind the building, a sense of satisfaction warmed her. There was a steady stream of people coming and going. Business was booming. She made her way inside through the back door, which led into the game room. A group of teenagers sat huddled around one of the tables, snickering into whatever they’d drawn in Cards against Humanity. They didn’t react as she walked by and out to the front of the shop. Her sister, Jillian, stood behind the counter taking a five dollar bill from a boy who couldn’t have been older than seven or eight. Kalina watched as his eyes widened when Jillian handed over the package of comics safely sealed in protective covers.

“Hey,” Kalina said once the kid and his mother were gone.

Jillian jumped. “Kal, you scared me. What are you doing here?”

“I wanted to make sure everything was going OK.”

“Everything is fine. Although those kids back there have been very quiet.”

“Don’t worry about them. I actually needed to ask you something.”

Jillian pulled the stool over and Kalina settled atop it. “What’s on your mind, little sister?”

“Do you remember Paige and Patrick Fischer? They died in a drowning accident about fifteen years ago.”

Her sister rubbed at her chin in thought. “Sort of. I think Mom took us to a memorial service or a candlelight vigil.”

“What do you remember about what happened to them?”

“Just what the papers said. They were out at the beach and one of them got swept up in a wave and the other one went out to save them.”

“But they never found their bodies.”

“I don’t know, Kal. Why?”

“I was visiting Dad’s grave today and I found a dead woman.”

“It was a cemetery.”

“Not one who’d been buried. Chris ran her fingerprints and they matched Paige Fischer’s.”

“But that isn’t possible.”

“It wouldn’t be if she was actually dead. But what if she survived and someone found out?”

“Who would care all these years later?”

“I don’t know. But she was left between her parents’ graves. If this woman really is Paige, someone out there knew the truth and killed her for it.”

Jillian let out a groan. “You’re getting dragged into this. Don’t get dragged into this. Not now.”

“I can’t help it. And this is the last one, I swear. After this I’m out.”

“”You better be. Or else we’ll be going to your funeral because Chris will have killed you himself.”

Kalina laughed. “Thanks for the support. Why don’t you go grab some lunch? I can man the counter for a little while. Besides, I miss being here. Sitting at home was getting really boring.”

“Only you could think getting ready for a baby was boring.”

Before Kalina could get out a retort, Jillian headed out into the sunshine. Kalina retrieved her tablet from below the counter and pulled up the town’s newspaper archives. Because she couldn’t remember the exact date of the drowning, she input “Fischer twins death” into the search bar at the top of the page and waited for it to populate results.

The first result was their joint obituary from August of 1995. It was a brief paragraph with a photo of the twins side by side with the ocean as a backdrop. The next result, dated July 31, 1995, appeared to be the first article about the circumstances surrounding their mysterious drowning.

Fischer Children Lost At Sea

By: Andrew Fisk, Staff Reporter

It is a sad day for the people of Ellesworth as two of its youngest citizens were lost at sea. Ten-year-old Paige Fischer and her twin brother, Patrick, were presumed dead today after the family's boat, which went missing from the family's slip off the beach three days ago, was found abandoned near the shore near Marblehead, Massachusetts. Authorities say the children were believed to be aboard the ship when it went missing. No bodies have yet been recovered.

Mr. and Mrs. Fischer refused comment as they grieve the loss of their children. Some in town are suspicious of the way the children died. One neighbor, who wished to remain anonymous, noted that the parents didn't report the children missing until they received a call that the boat had been located. Others questioned how the children could have had access to the boat without adult supervision. It is unknown at this time whether the authorities will be investigating Abigail and Harrison Fischer for their role in the deaths.

Kalina's pulse quickened as she reread the second paragraph. The Fischers hadn't even reported their children missing. Her recollection that they hadn't been very involved parents came back to her with full force. Surely they couldn't have had anything to do with it. Even absent parents wouldn't purposely send their children to their deaths. There was one final result on the list. A follow-up article dated August 21, 1995.

Fischers Cleared of Wrongdoing in Tragic Death of Twins

By: Andrew Fisk, Staff Reporter

Less than a month after the family's boat was found off the shore of Marblehead, MA without the Fischer children aboard, the police have cleared Abigail and Harrison Fischer of any wrongdoing in the deaths of ten-year-old twins Patrick and Paige. A source close to the police shared that the

> parents were out of town on a business trip during the time the boat went missing.
>
> The children had been in the care of their nanny, Lois Hendrix. According to a statement from Mr. and Mrs. Fischer, Ms. Hendrix has been fired and charges have been filed. A source in the prosecutor's office declined to comment but it is expected Ms. Hendrix will take a plea deal if offered to avoid a trial.

Well, that was interesting. She didn't remember a nanny being around when she spent her summer reading to both children. Then again, she'd been wrapped up in her own life and her own friends as soon as the reading time was over. At least now she had something to follow up on while Chris and Jimmy determined whether Verona Maxwell really was Paige Fischer. Perhaps Lois Hendrix would know what happened to the Fischers too. But first she needed to find the woman. She didn't want to let Chris in on this lead until she had something concrete to tell him so she placed a call to the one person who might know the town's older, sordid secrets, Mrs. Margaret

Grant. She'd been one of former Captain Daniel Cahill's targets for lying on the stand at his father's murder trial. She and Kalina had kept in touch since the ordeal.

"Hello?" Margaret's voice was weak thanks to the partial paralysis she'd suffered at Cahill's hands.

"Hi Mrs. Grant, it's Kalina Greystone. How are you doing?"

"Fine. And I told you to call me Margaret."

"Right, sorry. I was hoping I could come by. I have something I need to ask you about."

"Yes, dear. Please do come by."

Chapter 5

After waiting for Jillian to get back to the shop, Kalina headed out to visit Mrs. Grant. She pulled up to the small front porch and found Mrs. Grant waiting outside. Kalina gave a wave as she climbed out of the car and made her way up to sit beside the older woman.

“My, look at you!” Margaret exclaimed.

“Due in a few weeks,” Kalina said and rubbed her belly as the baby kicked.

“I take it the little one isn’t what you wanted to talk about.”

“No. It’s not. Do you remember Patrick and Paige Fischer?”

Margaret nodded her head more vigorously than Kalina had seen her do in almost a year. “Such a tragedy. Poor dears, lost so young.”

“Do you remember what happened to their nanny, Lois Hendrix? She was charged with their deaths.”

“She did some time in prison but only a few years.”

“Do you know where she ended up when she got out?”

“Why the sudden interest?”

Kalina blew out a breath. “We found a body who we think might be Paige Fischer. But she wasn’t a child. She was an adult. I’m just trying to figure out if it’s possible she might have survived the boat accident. I thought Lois could tell me what she knew from when they went missing.”

“I heard she ended up settling down in Boston. Getting lost in the big city you know. No one there would know what she’d done.”

“Thank you,” Kalina said with a smile.

“Don’t give it up, dear.”

"Sorry?"

'This knack you've got for digging until you get the truth."

"My priorities are changing."

"Maybe but there will come a time when it will be right to pick it back up. Don't let it die completely. Promise me." The woman's tone was firm and her voice was as clear as the first time they'd talked.

"I promise." Kalina gripped the woman's partially paralyzed hand and gave a firm squeeze.

They sat in silence for a short time, both enjoying the sun on their faces. Inevitably the baby moved, landing a solid thump to her bladder and the spell broke. She knew she needed to talk to Lois Hendrix but she had no real reason to seek her out. Showing up on her doorstep unannounced asking about the Fischer children would likely close the woman off to answering questions. But she wasn't ready to share what she'd found with Chris yet.

"I should get going. Thanks again for letting me stop by," she said and bent as best she could to give the woman a hug. “Do you want me to help you back in?”

“Oh, no. I’ll be fine here a while.”

With a final wave, Kalina headed back to her car. As soon as she’d buckled up, she put her phone on speaker and placed a call to the station.

“Ellesworth PD,” Jimmy answered.

“Jimmy, it’s Kalina. I need you to do me a favor.”

“I’m listening.”

“I need you to find the last known address for Lois Hendrix. I think she lives in Boston. Would have moved there maybe fifteen years ago.”

“That name came up in some of the files I was reviewing.”

“I know. She was the Fischers’ nanny. She went to jail for a while over their deaths.”

“And you think I should talk to her.”

“I think I should go with you to talk to her.”

“I’m not sure the captain would like that.”

"I can make her feel at ease. Besides, you'd be surprised what a belly full of baby can get you," she said and patted just above her belly button.

"I'll see what I can find and text you."

"You're the best."

"Bye."

The connection died after Jimmy hung up and she focused on her short drive home. Even if she wasn't ready to tell Chris what she'd found, she did need to let him know where she was going and that it wouldn't be alone. She found him already at home on the couch staring at files. An untouched—and likely cold—cup of coffee sat on the side table next to him.

"Hi honey," she said.

He jumped at the sound of her voice, clearly oblivious to her presence. "Sorry. I thought you'd already be home."

"I stopped by the shop to check on Jill and then I paid Margaret Grant a visit. I hadn't seen her in a while."

"How is she doing?"

“Well, she’s not entering anything into the Solstice Fair this year but she is in pretty good spirits.”

He looked up from the folder in front of him and patted the vacant spot on the couch. “There’s something else. What is it?”

“I may have found someone who can help figure out if Paige survived that boat accident. I didn’t want to get your hopes up so I asked Jimmy to look into it.”

“Who’d you find?”

“Lois Hendrix.”

“Their nanny.”

“That’s part of the reason I went to go see Margaret. She told me that after Lois got out of prison, she moved away, to Boston. I want to talk to her. She must remember something. And maybe she knows what happened to Abigail and Harrison.”

“It’s worth a try. But don’t be surprised if she doesn’t want to talk to you.”

“I know. But we have to try.”

She looked at the myriad casefiles spread over the table. “What’s all this?”

“I pulled the files on the twins’ disappearance and supposed deaths. I also got the results back from the second fingerprint test.”

“Let me guess, they still say Verona Maxwell and Paige Fischer are the same person.”

“Yes. I’m even more convinced that she’s the same person because before 1996 Verona Maxwell didn’t exist. No birth certificate, no social security number. Nothing.”

Kalina cocked her head in thought. “And then all of a sudden she’s got all those things.”

“Yeah. I managed to reach out to her parents. They’re from out of town but I’m having them come in tomorrow. Either way, I need to notify them of their daughter’s murder.”

Kalina sighed and settled back on the couch. “Did Clint ever get you more useable footage of the killer?”

Chris let out a sigh of his own and shook his head. “He sent some more over but the techs are having a hell of a time cleaning it up. Whoever this guy is, he was careful not to let his face get caught on any of the cameras. He must have scoped out the cemetery before he took her there."

"He couldn't have been that smart. He left her somewhere that had a really good angle of her body. If I hadn't found her, someone else would have."

"I'm starting to think he wanted her to be found."

Kalina's phone beeped with a new text message, interrupting the conversation. She glanced at it. Jimmy had been successful in tracking down Lois Hendrix and he would pick her up the following morning at 7.

"That's early," Chris said and gave her a sympathetic smile.

"We need to beat the traffic. Besides, I'm guessing she has a job and us showing up unannounced is going to throw a big wrench in her day." She pushed herself to her feet and headed towards the kitchen. "Come on, let's eat. I'm starving."

"I'll be there in a minute."

She left him in the living room and listened as he made a call. She rummaged in the fridge, gathering ingredients to make chicken salad, suddenly craving a nice, thick sandwich.

“Jimmy, it’s Chris. Yes, I know about tomorrow. Call ahead and set up a time. Leave earlier if you have to.” A pause. “No I’ll make sure she’s ready. Thanks.”

She said nothing as he joined her by the sink and began pulling big leaves of lettuce off the head and running them under water. She was going to need to go to bed early if there was the possibility of Jimmy coming by earlier than expected.

Chapter 6

The sun was barely above the horizon line as Kalina packed a thermos full of decaf tea and some oatmeal into her bag. Chris stood bleary-eyed by her side at the front door, both waiting for Jimmy to arrive. He'd made arrangements to meet Lois Hendrix at 8:00 at a coffee shop before she went to work. According to him, Lois had been more than willing to talk about the Fischer children.

"Good luck today," Chris said, yawning.

"You, too," she answered and gave him a sideways hug. She hoped today would prove fruitful for both of them, getting the police that much closer to finding the killer.

Jimmy's hybrid pulled into the driveway and, after a quick kiss, Kalina headed out and crammed herself into the front seat. In the end, she had to push it almost all the way back to get comfortable. "So she sounded willing to talk?" she asked once they'd finally hit the highway.

"Yeah. I didn't give her much but she's willing to sit down with us so that's a start."

"I hope Chris can find something from Verona's parents."

Jimmy accelerated and shifted into the high occupancy lane. As the car settled into doing just over 60 MPH, he glanced across at her. "What do you think happened?"

Kalina shrugged. "I don't know. Maybe she survived the accident. She could have had some kind of head trauma that made her forget who she was and someone found her."

"But who would want her dead? I mean killing her at her parents' graves is pretty specific. Whoever it was knew she was really Paige Fischer."

"Until we talk to Lois Hendrix, I can't say with any certainty what could have happened."

The car fell silent as Jimmy focused on navigating the increased traffic on the roads. Kalina took the opportunity to doze, her head propped against the window of the passenger side door. The gentle, steady hum of the engine and the tires on the pavement lulled her into a peaceful unconsciousness until Jimmy slammed on the brakes.

"What happened?" She jolted upright.

"Sorry, the idiot in front of me didn't have his blinker on until the last second. I nearly hit him."

She waited for her heart rate to lower back to normal and managed to stay awake the rest of the trip. The edge of the city soon came into view and she dug her thermos and oatmeal from her bag, sipping the still warm tea.

"So where are we meeting her exactly?"

"Coffee shop in downtown."

"Good luck finding parking around there."

He quirked a brow at her but said nothing. She tried not to laugh at his frustration as half an hour later he drove down one-way streets looking for a place to park. The clock on the dash ticked away the minutes until their meeting with Lois.

"Just let me out by the coffee shop and I'll start without you," she said.

With a huff, he pulled up to the curb and she climbed out with some difficulty. She wouldn't have minded sticking with him until he found a spot except the baby was happily punting her bladder like a soccer ball and she was in desperate need of a bathroom.

Five minutes later, she scanned the small crowd in the coffee shop, hoping she would recognize Lois Hendrix. She pulled up her phone and tried to find the one photo she'd seen of the woman at the end of the article about her arrest. It was several decades out of date but it was enough for her to cautiously approach the woman with greying hair sitting by the window, a large coffee grasped between slender fingers.

"Ms. Hendrix?"

The woman looked over. “Yes.”

Kalina slid into the chair opposite her. “My name is Kalina Greystone.”

“You aren’t the officer I spoke with yesterday.”

“I’m with him. He’s parking.”

“Not from around here.”

“No, he’s definitely not a city boy.”

“What’s got the police in Ellesworth looking me up after all these years? I did my time but I never hurt those children.”

Kalina was torn. She wanted to dive in and get what she could but she knew Jimmy wouldn’t be happy with her.

“Maybe we should wait until Jim—Officer Griggs gets here.”

Lois drummed her fingers on the side of her cup. “Please, just tell me what this is about.”

“A woman was found yesterday and her fingerprints match Paige Fischer’s.”

If Lois hadn’t already been sitting down Kalina was sure she would have fallen at the news. “She was alive all this time?”

"It seems that way. We were just hoping you might be able to fill in some of the gaps about what really happened the day they went missing."

"I'll never forget that day."

The door to the shop opened and Jimmy stalked in, his neck and cheeks red. He was clearly not happy. Kalina pointed him to the counter and mimed drinking. He would be less irritable with some caffeine in his system.

"Ms. Hendrix, I presume," Jimmy said once he'd acquired an extra-large iced coffee and dragged a chair over to the table.

"Officer Griggs. Ms. Greystone was just telling me you found Paige."

"Yes, ma'am. She was going by the name Verona Maxwell."

"I don't know where the last name came from but she loved Shakespeare."

"She was adopted by a foster family," Jimmy answered.

"She was a little young for Shakespeare, wasn't she?" Kalina asked.

“She was a bright girl. She started reading before Patrick did and was on to novels by the time she’d hit second grade.”

“How were they together? I mean I know having an older sister can be a challenge. I can’t imagine having a sibling the same age as me, having to share everything.”

Lois looked around the shop as if someone might overhear. “They could be civil if they wanted but I won’t pretend things weren’t tense between them. Paige was a bit domineering—”

“So she was a bully,” Jimmy interrupted.

Lois shook her head. “Not to other children. It was strange if I’m being honest. She could be the sweetest thing you’d ever seen to other people and children her age. But when it was just her and Patrick, she could be quite nasty. I remember one time I found Patrick sitting at the bottom of the stairs with a bloody nose and a cut on his face. He said they’d been playing and Paige hit him. He begged me not to tell their parents.”

“Did that happen often?” Kalina pressed.

"It seemed to come in waves. There would be weeks, months even, when they got on really well and then other times when he was coming to me with bumps and bruises."

Jimmy pulled out a notepad from his shirt pocket and jotted some notes down, alternating that with taking large gulps of his coffee. Lois twisted her cup between her hands.

"It sounds horrible but I have to say that when you called I had a feeling it was something like they'd survived. But a part of me hoped it had been Patrick. That boy didn't deserve the way his sister treated him."

"And you never confronted her about it?"

"Oh, I tried a few times but she acted all innocent and their parents wouldn't believe me."

Jimmy nodded and took another swig from his coffee. "What can you tell us about the day they went missing?'

"I told the police all about this back then."

"We know but we're hoping we can figure out how Paige might have survived."

Lois sighed and rubbed at her eyes. Kalina could tell she was losing her patience. "Everything was fine until the afternoon. They both said they wanted to go out on the beach and look for shells. It was one of the times they were getting along so I let them. The fresh air could do them good anyway. I had a lot of other things to take care of. I was the cleaning lady as well as the nanny and so I didn't notice until after it got dark that they hadn't come back inside.

"I went looking for them as soon as I realized they were gone. I couldn't find them anywhere. I didn't notice until the next day that the boat was missing. It didn't even occur to me that they knew how to start the thing, let alone maneuver it in open water. Besides, I don't think Patrick would have gotten on the boat unless Paige goaded him into it."

"Could they both swim?" Jimmy asked.

"Of course. They were like fish when they got in the ocean. Both very strong and skilled."

"So if the boat went off course or got pulled into a current, they'd be able to swim to shore," Kalina said.

“I’d think so.” Tears glistened unshed in her eyes. “Do you think maybe Patrick is alive, too?”

“It’s possible. It would also shed some light on who might want her dead,” Jimmy answered.

Lois gave a soft hiccup and the tears began to fall. Kalina reached across the table and took the woman’s hand in comfort. Jimmy was on his feet retrieving napkins a moment later. Lois hiccupped again and sniffled a little more and then settled herself. Wiping at her eyes and cheeks, she said, “I’m so sorry. I just haven’t thought about those poor children in a long time. The idea that both of them survived is just overwhelming.”

“We understand. Ms. Hendrix, thank you for talking to us today. We should let you get back to your day,” Jimmy said with a smile.

“Please find out who killed Paige.”

“We’ll do our best,” Jimmy said and stood as she did.

Kalina reached out to stop her before she got too far. “One last thing, do you know how Mr. and Mrs. Fischer died?”

Lois shook her head. “I’m afraid not. I believe Abigail had a sister ... Bethany Fairfax. She might know.”

“Thank you.”

Lois shuffled out of the coffee shop. Jimmy settled back into his chair as soon as she was gone and exhaled. “I think the brother might be alive, too.”

“I got that feeling, too. I don’t know what happened that got them Marblehead but something did. And if she was abusive towards him, it would give him a very clear motive for wanting her dead,” Kalina agreed.

They stayed put until Jimmy finished his coffee. Kalina watched as people passed by the windows, oblivious to the world around them. A part of her missed the busy streets of Boston and the fast-paced lifestyle. But the part of her that returned to her roots and was content with her life as it was quickly shut down that longing. She had everything she’d always wanted back home in Ellesworth. Jimmy nudged her shoulder and brought her back to her surroundings.

“I just got a text from the captain. He wants me back at the station as soon as possible. He says he’s got something interesting to share from the Maxwells.”

Kalina heaved herself out of the chair and after a quick trip to the restroom she headed outside in the summer heat to wait for Jimmy to return with the car.

Chapter 7

Thanks to traffic headed out of the city to the beach, it took them longer than they'd hoped to get back to Ellesworth. It was almost noon by the time Jimmy pulled into the parking lot of the police station. Kalina made a beeline for the restroom while Jimmy headed into Chris's office. On her way back, she spotted a couple who were probably in their sixties sitting in the interview room. The door was open and no one seemed to be paying them any attention. She assumed they were the Maxwells. She heard Chris's voice in his office and she gravitated in that direction, eager to hear what had been interesting enough to make Jimmy race back to town.

"They got her a few months after the twins were presumed dead. She didn't speak for a while after that. Eventually, she told them her name was Verona," Chris said.

Kalina walked in and neither man reacted. She settled in one of the chairs across from her husband's desk and said, "I think she got the name Verona from Shakespeare. She was obsessed with his work according to Lois Hendrix."

"Interesting fact."

"Have you considered that maybe Patrick survived, too?" Jimmy asked.

Chris rubbed at his forehead. "I have but there's no evidence of that. At least not yet."

"Sir, did you bring us back here just to tell us she was mute for a while?" Jimmy asked.

"No. Mr. and Mrs. Maxwell shared with me that after she started talking again, they put her in therapy. They overheard her talking to herself, having whole conversations with herself, but when they asked her about it, it was like she didn't remember."

“Or she wouldn’t admit to them that she was talking to herself. I know I’m not a doctor or anything but what if she didn’t know Patrick survived? What if that was her way of coping with the loss of her brother?” Kalina said.

“It’s as reasonable a theory as anything else,” Chris agreed.

Before they could continue the conversation, the email inbox on Chris’s computer flashed with a new message. The subject line, “Maxwell autopsy results,” caught Kalina’s attention and she leaned forward to try to get a better look as Chris opened the email. He skimmed the report too quickly for her to read anything, which annoyed her a little. Her annoyance level increased when he grabbed a tablet and strode out of the room without a word. She and Jimmy exchanged confused looks and trailed after him. Chris appeared on the monitor connected to the interview room where Mr. and Mrs. Maxwell sat side by side.

“We’ve just received some medical information on your daughter,” Chris said and sat down opposite the couple. “She has old scars that are at least ten years old. Care to explain?”

Mrs. Maxwell pressed her fingers to her lips and glanced at her husband. She blinked rapidly several times before speaking. “We thought the therapy was working. She’d stopped talking to herself as much. But we didn’t realize she’d started hurting herself. It was never enough to have her hospitalized for injuries but it was worrying.”

“She got the treatment she needed and has been fine ever since,” Mr. Maxwell insisted. “She was running a small beauty boutique. She was happy and successful.”

Kalina bit her lip. They hadn’t been able to share the knowledge that Paige had abused her brother. Chris would no doubt find it useful.

“Did Verona ever talk about a boy named Patrick to you?”

“No.” Mr. Maxwell placed a hand on his wife’s forearm. “Who is that?”

Chris set the tablet down and tapped the screen a couple of times. Through the monitor, Kalina watched as he presented them with a photo of Paige and Patrick from the local paper. “This is Verona and her twin brother, Patrick, shortly before they were presumed dead in a boating accident. Her name back then was Paige. Paige Fischer."

"Presumed dead?"

Chris nodded. "We only found out that Paige survived the boat accident when we ran your daughter's fingerprints."

"What about DNA? Have you done a DNA test?" Mrs. Maxwell's voice barely carried over the monitor's audio.

"We're still trying to find a DNA sample from when Paige went missing to compare," Chris answered.

"Do you think someone found out she was Paige and came after her?" Mr. Maxwell asked.

Chris was quiet for a moment, likely contemplating his next words before he answered. "We're working every angle. Did your daughter have any enemies that you were aware of?"

"No. Everyone liked her. After she got over her trauma, she was lovely to everyone. No one had a bad word to say about her." Mrs. Maxwell lapsed into quiet weeping.

“She was seeing someone new. She seemed quite serious about him,” Mr. Maxwell added.

“Do you have his name?” Chris asked.

“No, I’m sorry.”

Kalina looked away from the monitor to wipe at her eyes. Maybe it was the fact that she was about to become a mother, but she could feel Mrs. Maxwell’s loss for her child. Jimmy pressed a tissue into her hand and smiled at him in thanks. She was vaguely aware of Chris telling the Maxwells that he would be in touch if he found anything else before they walked out, hand in hand. Neither of them gave Kalina or Jimmy a second glance as they moved past and to the front of the building.

“I need to call the techs and see if they’ve had any luck enhancing the surveillance footage,” Chris said.

“I think you should take a break and get something to eat first. Come on, I’m buying,” Kalina said. She wanted to fill him on what they’d learned from Lois Hendrix and maybe she could convince him to let her tag along when he interviewed Abigail Fischer’s sister.

Chris opened his mouth, likely to protest, but Jimmy stepped up and gave them both a smile. “You get something to eat, Captain. I can hold down the fort here. Besides, I think Kal’s got some really good information for you.”

Kalina barely hid the smile on her face as she headed for the front of the building. She waited for Chris to join her, ready to enjoy a nice, leisurely stroll through town in the warm summer air. As she shielded her eyes from the sun, taking in the tree line that bordered the far edge of the station’s parking lot, she could swear she saw someone watching her. That same sense that had settled over her in the cemetery hit her again. Was this Verona’s killer? Had he still been in the cemetery when Kalina had been drawn to the site of Verona’s murder? A shiver danced up her spine and she wrapped her arms around her torso to ward off the chill.

“You OK?” Chris asked as he finally joined her.

“Am I crazy or is there someone over there in the trees?” she asked in a whisper.

Chris followed her gaze but shook his head. “I don’t see anyone. Come on, let’s go find something to eat. I think maybe we're both just hungry."

Chapter 8

A half hour later, they sat across from each other at home. They hadn't intended to go all the way home for food but somehow they'd just wandered by the restaurants that peppered both sides of Main Street.

"I need to tell you what we found out from Lois Hendrix," Kalina said as she blew the steam off the spoonful of soup in front of her.

"OK."

"She said that Paige was kind of a bully toward Patrick. It got to the point that it could have been considered abuse. But Patrick wouldn't let her tell their parents about it. Lois was convinced that Paige talked Patrick into getting on the boat that day."

"Did they know how to operate it?"

"Apparently."

Chris took a sip of his drink and studied the sandwich crumbs on his plate. "That might explain some of the behavior the Maxwells observed. The talking to herself. The self-harm. In fact, they said it sounded sometimes like she was arguing with someone."

"That's what I thought, too. She was used to bossing Patrick around and hurting him. Without him there, maybe she just started hurting herself."

"But eventually it stopped. The talking and the cutting."

"Maybe she just blocked that part of her life out and accepted that she wasn't Paige Fischer anymore. She embraced being Verona Maxwell. I bet if you'd asked her anything about Paige, she wouldn't have a clue."

"You mean like multiple personalities?"

“Yeah. Something like that.” She let out a sigh. “I bet it would be really helpful to see what she talked about with her psychologist.”

“Those records would be difficult to get, especially with the patient dead.”

“You have to try.”

“I’ll see what I can do.”

“And you should talk to Abigail Fisher’s sister, Bethany. Something about the way the Fischers died doesn’t sit right with me. I tried to find their obituaries but there wasn’t much there.”

“It’s worth looking into. Besides, maybe she kept something from Paige’s childhood we could use for a DNA match. And I’m guessing you want to come along.”

“If that’s OK with you.” She batted her lashes at him and smiled.

“As long as you aren’t running off on your own, I’ll let you tag along. I need to keep an eye on you.”

They lapsed into silence for a while and Kalina focused on her soup. The baby gave a kick or jab to her bladder once or twice but she was much calmer than she'd been earlier in the day. She had enjoyed most of being pregnant but she was eager to meet her daughter and to hold her tiny fingers in her own hand. That thought sparked an idea. "You have Patrick's fingerprints, right?"

"Yes. Why?"

"Have you thought about running his prints to see if they match any adults around the same age he'd be now? To at least rule him out as a suspect. I mean if there's nothing then there's probably a good chance he isn't the killer."

"I'll get someone on it." He pushed his chair back and disappeared from the kitchen.

In his absence, Kalina pulled out her phone and Googled Bethany Fairfax. Lucky for her, there was only one in the entire state of Massachusetts and she lived not too far away in Marblehead. That couldn't be a coincidence. She copied the address she'd found online to the Notes app on her phone and grabbed her purse. She nearly collided with Chris as she tried to leave the kitchen.

"I found Bethany Fairfax," she announced. His furrowed brow told her he didn't know who she was talking about. "Abigail Fischer's sister. Fairfax was her maiden name."

"Oh, right. I've got the lab running Patrick's prints. Where does Ms. Fairfax live?"

"Marblehead."

"Is that so?"

"Yep. Want to go see if the aunt has any idea what might have happened to the rest of her family?"

"I'll drive."

Chapter 9

The trip out to Marblehead took about a half hour. The brief drive down the coast should have been pleasant, the weather had cooled off and a breeze blew through the open windows of the car, but Kalina couldn't shake the sense of dread squeezing her chest in a vice. All of the open water made her wonder what Patrick and Paige had endured on that fateful day twenty years ago. Had they been afraid of the open water? Had they lost control of the boat or were they out on the water with the intention of visiting their aunt?

"Kal, we're here." Chris's voice drew her back to the world.

“Did you call ahead?” she asked as he offered his hand to help her out of the car.

“No. I figured the element of surprise might be useful.”

“Anything yet on the prints?”

“Nothing yet, no. The lab will call if and when they have something. But there is some good news. We have an angle on one of the surveillance cameras from the cemetery that got a good shot of the guy’s face.”

“That’s great.”

“So we’ve got that running, too.”

They approached the single story, squat house that Google said belonged to Bethany Fairfax. Chris pulled out his badge and prepared to knock on the door. He didn’t get the chance because a woman bustled out in a floral-print sundress and enormous sunhat.

“Oh, excuse me,” she said.

“Are you Ms. Bethany Fairfax?” Chris asked.

“I am. Who are you?”

"My name is Captain Christian Harper. I'm with the Ellesworth police department. I was hoping I could speak with you for a few minutes about your niece and nephew."

Bethany took a step back into her front hall. "My niece and nephew died twenty years ago."

"I'm afraid that's not true. Your niece, Paige, was recently murdered. Please, it's just a few questions."

Bethany didn't look willing to give in until Kalina made a show of pressing a hand to her belly and grimacing. The older woman gave a sympathetic look and waved them inside.

"Thank you," Chris whispered just loud enough for Kalina to hear.

"Bet you're glad you brought me along," Kalina replied.

Bethany led them to a small living room cluttered with second-hand furniture and Tiffany lamps. It wasn't the set up Kalina had expected for a woman from a wealthy family. She eased herself onto the loveseat positioned beneath the mantle and Chris settled in a recliner next to her. Bethany paced back and forth in front of them for a few minutes before finally sitting on a wooden stool, setting her hat on the low coffee table between them.

“Thank you,” Kalina said, indicating the seat.

“Sure. When are you due?”

“A few weeks.” She looked around the room as best she could and caught a photo of Bethany and a young man who looked vaguely familiar. “Do you have children?”

“A son. Logan. He’s grown up now and moved out.”

“Ms. Fairfax, I know this news must be a shock for you but I really need your help,” Chris interrupted.

Bethany smoothed out the hem of her dress and twisted her fingers into the fabric. “I’m not sure how much help I’ll be, but OK.”

“What do you know about what happened to your niece and nephew?”

“They went out on the family boat and never came home.”

“Do you happen to have anything that belonged

to Paige as a child? A lock of hair or a toothbrush for when she stayed over?"

"Why? I thought you said she was dead."

"The fingerprints match but we want to be absolutely sure."

"I don't. I'm sorry. They never really stayed over here. Abigail, my sister, didn't like them being away from home."

That seemed odd to Kalina, given how much the Fischers seemed to travel and leave their children in Lois Hendrix's care. But she said nothing. She caught Bethany's gaze flit to a photo of Logan as a teenager. He was sandy-haired and suntanned with a broad grin. Still, she couldn't shake the familiar feeling. Much like she'd had when he found Paige in the cemetery. "How'd your son react to the news that his cousins had died? They look like they'd be about the same age," Kalina said.

"He was upset of course. We all were. It was such a shock."

"But Paige didn't die. She was taken into foster care and adopted. She ran a successful beauty shop until someone killed her," Chris said.

“I don’t know what I can tell you. Until you showed up at my door, I had no idea she was even alive.”

“This may seem like a strange question but do you know how your sister and brother-in-law died?”

“I think it was a faulty carbon monoxide detector in the house. That’s what the police said when they came to notify me.”

“When was that?”

“I don’t remember. A year ago maybe.”

“Did Logan get along with Paige?” Chris asked.

“Yes. Why are you asking about Logan? I thought this was about Paige.”

“Ma’am, is it possible that your nephew could have survived too?”

“I don’t know. I think I want you to leave. I’m sorry I can’t be more help.”

Kalina opened her mouth to press the issue but Chris shook his head and offered his hand to help her up. They started for the front of the house when Kalina stopped. “Could I use your bathroom?”

“Last door on the left down that hallway.”

Kalina took off down the hall at a brisk waddle. She really did need to use the bathroom but she figured she could also use the time to look around. The hallway was lined with more photos of Logan as a teenager. There was even one of him graduating from college. Oddly, there were no photos of him younger than eleven or twelve. The suspicious part of her mind tried to convince her that Logan was actually Patrick but it couldn’t rationalize why Bethany would have kept his survival a secret. Surely she would have returned him to his parents. She passed a room on the right with a partially closed door. She nudged it open with her foot and took in the room of a guy in his late twenties. The walls were bare except for a single photo of Logan and Bethany. There was a laptop sitting open on the desk. When she hit the Enter key to wake the machine up, it prompted her for a password.

“Damn.”

The desk had a center drawer that she eased open to find a print-out from a dating website. The figure in the profile picture was unmistakably Verona Maxwell. The baby chose that moment to press more insistently on her bladder and she had to retreat across the hall to the bathroom. She returned to the living room to find Chris, keys already in hand, and Bethany with her hat back on her head.

They left through the front door and said nothing until they were back in the car. Kalina watched as Bethany strode up the street at a brisk pace.

“Well that was a bust,” Chris muttered.

“Not entirely. I looked around a little bit while I was heading to the bathroom. There aren’t any pictures of Logan before the age of ten. And it looks like Bethany lied to us about Logan moving out. There’s a room that looks lived in. I saw a computer but it was locked. There’s definitely something off about all of this.”

“You think Logan is Patrick.”

“I got that same feeling looking at pictures of him that I did with Paige. And she was definitely avoiding talking about Logan as a young child. There has to be a reason.”

“It’s looking more like we have a suspect. We just have to find him.”

"I know it's not definitive but what if you used aging software on a picture of Patrick at ten and see if it looks like Logan now. And compare it to the surveillance photo."

Chris leaned over and kissed her cheek. "I knew I married you for a reason."

"There's something else. I found a print-out of a profile for Verona on a dating website in the top desk drawer. Even if Logan isn't Patrick, he still found Verona and it's worth talking to him."

Chris put the car into drive and did a quick U-turn so they could head out of town. "So let's see if we can find Logan Fairfax."

Chapter 10

Kalina expected Chris to be on the phone to the precinct giving orders but the hands free set remained unused. They spent the first ten minutes travelling in silence before Chris turned to look at her..

“How are you feeling?”

“I’m fine, Chris. I was only pretending earlier to get Bethany to talk to us.”

“All of this exertion just stresses me out. I don’t want anything to happen to you.”

“I’m fine. We’ve got a few weeks to go anyway.”

Just as Chris pulled onto the highway, his phone buzzed with an incoming call from the precinct. Kalina reached over and tapped the phone and set it to speaker.

“Hey Captain, is this a good time?” Jimmy’s voice filled the car through the speaker system.

“Yeah, it’s fine, Jimmy. What’s up?”

“I ran those prints like you asked and it came back with a match.”

Kalina and Chris shared an expectant glance before he said, “Go on.”

“The prints matched a guy with a criminal record named Logan Fairfax.”

Kalina bit down hard on her lip to keep from exclaiming that she’d been right. Chris nodded at her as he switched lanes.

“What’s the record for?”

“Misdemeanor possession. We’ve got an address in Marblehead.”

“His mother’s address. We were just there.”

“Sir? I thought you were going to interview their aunt.”

“I’ll explain when we get back. See if you can find any other address on Fairfax. We’ll be at the station in about fifteen minutes." He jabbed the screen to end the call.

"Shouldn't we go back and try to get more out of Bethany?" Kalina asked.

"Not yet. We need to see if we can get a location on Logan first."

"She could have tipped him off."

"At this point she only knows that her niece survived the accident too and someone's killed her."

"But wouldn't you think she'd put two and two together?"

"If we go back now, she'll shut down more."

Kalina ran a hand through her hair and stared out the passenger side window, trying to sort through the thoughts racing around her brain. How could Bethany not know the truth? And why hadn't she taken Patrick back to his parents when he showed up?

"Did you notice what dating website Verona had an account with?" Chris's voice interrupted her thoughts.

"It might have been OK Cupid. I didn't notice to be honest."

"That's all right. We'll get Verona's laptop and see who she was talking to."

"I can't imagine being separated for all those years and then they find each other on a dating website. Do you think they were actually attracted to each other?"

Chris shrugged his right shoulder. "Maybe. But if Logan knew she was Paige, he was probably using it to stalk her."

"I wonder if she realized who he was before she died."

"Something tells me he wouldn't let her go before she knew."

The conversation died down again as they got off the highway and pulled onto Main Street. "Can you drop me at the shop? I want to check in on things and I think I need to rest for a while," she said before he could make the turn toward the police station.

"Of course."

She pulled out her phone and sent a quick text to Jillian, letting her know she was on the way. There was no response before they pulled up in front of the shop's front door.

"Make sure you put your feet up and drink plenty of water," Chris called as she closed the passenger side door.

The bell above the front door 'dinged' as she entered and Jillian looked up from her phone.

"Just got your text. Shouldn't you be at home?"

"Why? I'd just be sitting around going crazy when I could be here obsessing over work."

"Or Paige Fischer?" Jillian slid the tablet they used for transactions across the counter.

Kalina picked it up and took it into the game room so she could put her feet up. Jillian followed after her, not saying a word. The tablet's screen displayed a news article from the town's online edition, published only a few hours ago.

Lost Twin Found … Murdered

By: Heather Casey, Staff Reporter

> In the late morning hours of June 10th, a twenty-year-old mystery unraveled. As many in town will remember, ten-year-old Paige Fischer and her brother perished at sea twenty years ago. But a woman with Paige's fingerprints was discovered in the cemetery by someone close to the local authorities.

"Damn, how did they find out?" Kalina groaned.

"People in town talk. I'm assuming once people found out this Verona woman was found at the Fischer family grave site, speculation began running wild," Jillian answered.

Kalina kept reading.

> The details are still unclear as to how Paige survived the boat accident that claimed her brother's life or who would want her dead all these years later. Some in town speculate that Paige returned home to mourn her parents who passed away last year under suspicious circumstances. Others question if Patrick may have survived as

well. And if that is true, why would they not have come home sooner?

A local school teacher recalled the twins as being quiet and reserved although there was always something about Paige that set the teacher on edge. "I remember she had this quiet intensity about her for such a young child. Like there was something deep down she was hiding." And of Patrick, the teacher noted, "He always looked scared to me. Afraid of his own shadow, especially when his sister was around. I should have done something back then. I knew something didn't seem right." Was it this inner secret that led to her death now? Could it be her brother came back for some twisted sort of revenge?

This story is developing. Please check back for updates.

"Chris is going to have a field day with this reporter. I can't imagine who talked to her. The guys on the force know better."

"What about you?" Jillian raised a brow at her sister.

"Me? I've been with Jimmy or Chris the whole day. And I am not going to talk to the press. Paige may have been a bully to her brother ... abusive even"—she tossed the tablet on a nearby table—"but she doesn't need to be dragged through the mud like this. No one, no matter how terrible, deserves to be murdered."

"Kal, I don't think that's what they were saying," Jillian said, her tone placating.

"I know you're right but it just makes me so angry. The way they just threw around all of these accusations like they're fact."

"But from what you said, it sounds like it isn't just speculation."

Kalina rubbed at the pressure building in her temples. She didn't want to argue with her sister over this. "Just forget it, OK?"

Jillian held up her hands in surrender. "Fine. I think all of this detective work is stressing you out. It's not good for you."

"These were kids we knew, Jill. Don't we owe it to them to find out what happened?"

"Yes. I guess they deserve to have their story told, even if it isn't a happy ending."

Jillian disappeared back to the front of the store just as Kalina's phone buzzed, displaying Chris's work number. She answered on the second ring. "Hi. Before you ask, yes, I've got my feet up." Breath caught in her throat as a sharp pain lanced across her belly. She grimaced and bit down on her lip to keep from groaning audibly through the pain.

"Good. I figured you'd like to know we got a hit on Verona's computer. We found a bunch of messages on OK Cupid between her and Logan. It doesn't seem like she knew who he was based on the messages but they were definitely in contact."

The pain subsided and she blew out a breath. "Have you had any luck tracking him down?"

"We're working on it. The last communication between them was from a day before the murder. They agreed to meet in town.'

"Did they say why here? Neither of them was living in town anymore."

"It sounded like Logan wanted to check out the beach. Or so he says." Muffled voices crackled over the phone connection. "I think we may have found something on his location."

"Keep me posted."

Chapter 11

Half an hour later, restless energy and a sense of anticipation compelled Kalina out of the shop and on a walk along Main Street. The pain had come and gone a time or two but she was doing her best to ignore it. She assumed Chris had found Logan by now. She was curious to know how it had happened. Had he known he'd found his sister when he and Verona first connected? And if he hadn't, when did it click for him? She strolled along the street with the fading sunlight falling in little patterns on the sidewalk for a while longer until she found herself standing at the front lawn of the Fischer estate. For a place that had been vacant for over a year, it looked oddly lived in. The front mat was askew and the curtains in the front room had been opened to allow the natural light in. She didn't get the feeling that Bethany Fairfax had been by to keep up appearances. Keeping Patrick a secret sent the very clear message that she didn't approve of her sister and her brother-in-law and their parenting style. Before she could even set foot on the front walk, wailing sirens erupted nearby and a squad car came screaming up the street. Jimmy jumped out of the passenger side before the car had come to a full stop. Chris followed suit moments later and Kalina stepped out of their way. From somewhere at the back of the house, a door slammed loud enough to echo throughout the yard.

"He's going around back," Chris called and Jimmy took off like a shot.

Chris moved methodically toward the front of the house and tried the front door. It swung inward on oiled hinges, barely betraying his entrance. His shout of "Police Department!" ruined any chance of stealth he had.

Kalina watched her husband disappear into the house and her heart beat faster in her chest. Until he came out, gun holstered, she couldn't breathe. Jimmy appeared moments later dragging along a man in his late 20s who looked like Logan Fairfax with his hands cuffed behind his back.

“I didn’t do anything!” Logan shouted.

Jimmy said nothing as he pushed him into the backseat of the cruiser. Chris stopped on his way to the car to place a hand on Kalina’s arm. “What are you doing here?’

“I don’t know. I was just out for a walk and ended up—” Breath caught in her chest as pain shot through her belly. She bent double until it passed.

“What’s wrong?”

“Nothing, I’m fine. It’s just a little pain.”

“You don’t look fine. Has this happened before?”

Kalina met Chris’s gaze and knew she couldn’t lie to him about this. “A few times. Maybe four times in the last hour. But, really, it passes and I’m OK.”

“Honey, it sounds like you’ve started to have

contractions. We need to get you to the hospital."

"No. It's too early. And my water hasn't broken."

Chris turned and waved at Jimmy. "Call for another car and get him back to the station."

"OK but why, sir?"

"We're going to the hospital."

Jimmy's face broke out in a broad grin and he pulled Logan from the backseat of the cruiser with one hand, the other already reaching for his radio. Kalina didn't protest as Chris ushered her into the passenger seat and they took off at what most would consider an unsafe speed. With the flip of a switch, the sirens blared to life, announcing their presence.

"The siren isn't necessary, Chris," Kalina said but Chris's attention was focused on the trip across town to the hospital.

He pulled the car to a screeching halt in front of the Emergency entrance. The siren still wailed and a nurse came running with a wheelchair. Taking a slow breath, Kalina unbuckled the seatbelt and calmly exited the car.

"I can walk, thank you," she said and stalked past the nurse.

Ten minutes later, they were escorted to a private room and Kalina settled on the bed to wait for the doctor to check in. Chris paced anxiously by the window.

"Sit down," she said and patted the bed next to her.

"Sorry. I'm just nervous," he said and settled next to her, wrapping his arm around her shoulders. "I don't think either of us expected this to happen quite so soon."

"I think Jill was right and this case is stressing me out," Kalina said and rubbed her belly.

Chris nodded but stayed silent. The way his gaze still drifted to the window told her he wasn't just anxious about the baby. He didn't like not being involved in the rest of the investigation.

"You're worried about how the interrogation is going, aren't you?"

"Jimmy's grown up a lot in the last year. He's capable of handling it."

“I know that. And I’m glad you see that too. Sometimes he doesn’t think you’ve paid attention to his progress. But even though you know he’s capable you don’t like to let cases go.”

“I guess we’ve both got a little control freak in us.”

Kalina snorted. “A little?”

He laughed and the little lines around his eyes crinkled. “OK, so a lot. But I have to realize that investigating the cases isn’t really my job anymore. I’m not a detective. I need to let them do the work.”

“Letting go of what you love is hard.” A lesson she was learning the hard way. Helping to solve these cases wasn’t a calling in the same way that Chris was called to police work, but it satisfied a passion in her. But as she’d told Mrs. Grant, she had no choice but to give it up ... at least for now.

A quick knock on the door brought the conversation to a halt. Kalina’s obstetrician appeared in the doorway, an ultrasound machine just in view. “How are we feeling?”

"OK right now."

"Any more pain since you came in?"

"No."

"Well, we're going to check you out anyway and figure out what's going on. I'm going to have you get undressed and we'll take a look."

Kalina stripped down, wrapping the hospital robe around her body before settling back on the bed. Chris stood by her side, his hand wrapped around hers. He squeezed it tight as the doctor strapped on a fetal heart monitor and began a physical exam.

"Well, you look to be a couple centimeters dilated but we're nowhere near delivering this baby."

"Is the baby all right?" Kalina asked.

The doctor pointed to the steady heartbeat on the monitor. "Everything looks good with the heartbeat. There's no sign of fetal distress."

Kalina breathed a sigh of relief. She didn't even react to the cool gel that the ultrasound technician squirted on her bare abdomen.

"Everything looks fine. I'm going to keep you here another couple of hours just to be sure but my guess is you had Braxton Hicks contractions."

"So it was a false alarm," Chris said.

The doctor nodded. "Most likely. But like I said, we'll keep her here for a few hours just to be sure."

"Thank you," Kalina said.

Chris sagged against the bed as soon as they were alone. "Thank God."

"Honey, they're going to let me leave in a couple hours. I can have my mom come by and give me a ride home. Go back to the station."

"No, I should be here with you."

Somewhere down the hall an alarm blared. Simultaneously, Chris's phone began to ring. He checked the display and stepped closer to the window for better reception. "Hello, this is Captain Harper."

Kalina strained to hear what was being said on the other end of the call but he had the volume turned down low and he was facing away from her, distorting her view of his facial expressions in the window. "No I'll meet you there. Text me when you've got a room number."

"What's going on?" she asked over the continued blare of the alarm.

"That was the officer on desk duty at the station. Jimmy had to call the paramedic to come sedate Logan."

"What? Why?"

"Apparently, when Jimmy started questioning him about Patrick Fischer, he lost it and attacked Jimmy."

"Oh God, is Jimmy OK?"

"I'm not sure. The officer said he had some lacerations. I told them to text me when they have more information."

"Did they bring Logan here?"

"Yeah, he's being admitted into the psych ward. Maybe with a doctor's help we can sort out what really happened and what prompted him to kill his sister after all these years."

Chapter 12

Fifteen minutes later, Chris had headed off in search of Jimmy. Kalina remained in hospital. The pain had returned and was coming in closer bouts. Her doctor had been nonplussed about the sudden change. At least she was allowed to walk around. In fact, her doctor had insisted that moving around would help things progress. So after sending a text to Chris, she wandered the halls until she found Jimmy sitting in a curtained off area in the very back of the Emergency Department with a couple of gauze bandages on his arm.

“How are you doing?” he asked when he spotted Kalina.

"OK. Apparently it wasn't as much of a false alarm as we thought. The doctor said walking is supposed to help labor progress." She pointed to his arm. "How about you? What happened?"

"It looks worse than it is. He got a hold of my keys. I shouldn't have kept a pocket knife on there." Jimmy looked at Chris but didn't meet his gaze. "He jabbed me a couple times as I was trying to calm him down. Started yelling about how I wasn't going to hurt Patrick. I think he's nuts."

"We'll let the professionals decide that," Chris said and clapped Jimmy on the shoulder. "You should take the rest of the day off. We'll talk about this when the case is wrapped up."

Kalina saw the hint of fear on Jimmy's face when Chris turned away and flagged down a nurse.

"Everything will be fine," she whispered and gave the hand of his injured arm a light squeeze that quickly turned into a vice grip as a contraction came on.

"Uh, boss, something's happening."

In a flash, Chris was at her side, rubbing her back as she breathed through the pain. It passed and she relinquished her grip on Jimmy's hand. He massaged the angry, red marks she'd left on his palm.

"Sorry about that," she said.

"Let's get you back to the maternity ward," Chris said and nudged her forward.

"Is it really not as bad as it looks?" she asked as they walked side by side through the pristine hospital halls.

"Yeah, it's minor."

"Has there been anything new on Logan? Has anyone talked to him?"

"The last I heard they were evaluating him. But you don't need to worry about that right now. I promise, Paige will get justice. Right now you need to focus on bringing our baby girl into this world, OK?"

"OK."

"Don't be too hard on Jimmy when you talk to him. He's a good officer and he just made a mistake."

"I'm not mad at him. He already knows what he should have done differently and I don't have any doubt that he will learn from the mistake. Just between you and me, I was planning on giving him his detective's shield in a few months."

"That's fast."

"He does good work. And I think the promotion will help propel his career forward. Sometimes you need someone to take a chance on you to show you just what you're capable of. And he kind of reminds me of myself when I was an officer. He's got that same drive."

"I'm glad." They arrived back at her room to find Jillian and AJ sitting by the window. "You guys didn't have to come."

"Mom insisted you not be alone. And I figured you could use your big sister here," Jillian answered and rushed over to give Kalina a tight embrace.

Her sister's mood had obviously improved since their squabble over the newspaper article. AJ stayed put and quiet, gazed focused on his phone, as Jillian let go and gave Chris a hug too.

“You doing all right, kiddo?” Kalina asked.

“Huh? I was just reading this article about the woman who was killed,” he said and offered his phone.

A pang of dread tightened Kalina’s chest as she looked at the screen but it disappeared immediately. It was the same article that had gotten her worked up before. Unfortunately, there were no edits or retractions noted. Whoever was handling the PR for the police hadn’t succeeded in getting the article removed. Her nephew kept glancing between the medical equipment and her stomach.

“Why don’t you go see if there’s a cafeteria or something and get your mom and Chris some coffee or something?” Kalina suggested.

Relief washed over his face and he darted out of the room. Jillian sat on the edge of the bed and motioned for Kalina to get under the covers.

“How far apart are your contractions?”

“About ten minutes. They’re more irritating than anything.”

“If you’re anything like me, they’ll speed up before you know it. I thought it was never going to end with AJ.”

“Let’s hope you’re right.”

Chris’s phone beeped with a new text message. “The attendant in the psych ward needs to talk to me about the case.”

“Go. I’ll be here when you get back.”

“Call me if anything ... big happens,” he said.

She nodded and he took off at a sprint. Jillian busied herself with plumping Kalina’s pillows and making sure the bed was at a comfortable angle.

“I was a little worried about you earlier. You just took off,” Jillian said.

“I’m sorry. I needed the air.”

“Where did you go?”

“It’s going to sound crazy but I ended up at the Fischer house. Logan ... Patrick ... whatever he’s going by was staying there. I didn’t mean to go there but I guess my subconscious had other ideas.”

"They found him though?"

"They did. He got violent when Jimmy tried to question him."

"I wonder what happened to him that made him snap like that."

"I don't know. Maybe he'd blocked out all the trauma and then seeing her again after all these years triggered those memories. I'm sure Chris will figure out what happened when he talks to the doctor."

"I still can't believe they both survived that boat accident. I'd really like to know how that happened."

"If the doctors can get him to talk I'm sure we'll find out." Kalina grit her teeth as another contraction hit her.

"Do you want me to call a nurse to see about getting an epidural?"

"Not yet. They said they'd do it the next time they checked me."

On cue, a nurse stuck her head through the door. "How're we doing in here?"

"I think I'd like that epidural now," Kalina answered.

"Let me grab the doctor and we'll take a peek."

By the time the doctor had checked her and the anesthesiologist had administered the drugs, her contractions were only four minutes apart. Chris was nowhere to be seen despite several texts from Kalina and Jillian. AJ hung back just outside the doorway, watching.

"You can come in, honey," Jillian said.

"No, that's OK. I'd just be in the way."

Kalina was aware of another contraction passing through her as she studied her nephew's face. "Kiddo, I need you to do me a huge favor and go find your uncle for me. The baby is going to be here soon and if he's not with me to witness it, we're going to have another homicide on our hands."

AJ's face brightened. "You got it!"

"Thanks," Jillian whispered as her son took off.

"Like I said before, teenage boys and birth don't usually mix."

Ten minutes later, AJ marched into the room with a triumphant grin on his face. “Got him!”

“Sorry! I’m here.” Chris rushed to her side and grabbed her left hand.

“We texted you. What’s going on?”

“I thought we were making progress with Logan but he’s shut down again. I didn’t hear my phone go off. It was on silent.”

Kalina gave him an annoyed sidelong glare as another contraction—this much closer together—faintly rippled through her belly. He’d been the one to tell them to call if anything big had changed. She bit her lower lip to keep from snapping at him. It wouldn’t do anything but frustrate him.

Her doctor reappeared with a new nurse, both in scrubs and face masks. “I’m just going to check to see how far you’ve progressed. It might be time to start pushing.”

“OK.”

Kalina blew out a slow breath as the doctor examined her. Chris’s grip was steady and present, making some of her irritation dissipate. He was here for the important part.

"Everything looks ready, so I'm going to need you to start pushing when you feel the urge, Kalina."

She had no idea how she was supposed to know but apparently the rest of her body was in tune with what was happening because a few minutes later her knees were raised and her chin was pressed to her chest.

"Nine. Ten. And relax," her doctor instructed.

Kalina lay back against the pillow, beads of sweat moistening her upper lip. "How much longer?"

"You're doing great." Chris brushed a strand of sweaty hair out of her face.

"Push again."

Kalina bore down and this time she could feel something change and move. She was so focused on the push she didn't register the sounds of encouragement around her.

"One more big push like that and I think we're going to have our baby," her doctor prompted.

She pushed one last time. The haze of the experience fell away as a wail filled the room.

"Our baby girl cried," Chris said.

Kalina turned to look at him and saw tears streaming down his cheeks. Her husband clearly didn't care that he was sobbing. He made no attempt to wipe them away. Instead, he released his grip on her hand and accepted the tiny, squirming baby wrapped in a hospital blanket. He settled their little girl on Kalina's chest.

"Welcome to the world, little lady," Chris whispered and stroked the baby's cheek.

"What are you going to call her?" Kalina jumped a little at the sound of her sister's voice.

"Nina Elise."

"That's a beautiful name."

Chris's attention diverted from the baby for a split second as his phone buzzed. "I'll get it later," he said.

"Take it. You're still working the case."

"He's not going anywhere."

"Chris, please just answer it."

He bent and kissed Nina's head before stepping out into the hallway. With his back to her, Kalina couldn't see his face. But his shoulders tensed and his back went rigid. Whatever was being communicated wasn't making him happy. The nurse took Nina from Kalina's arms.

"Where are you taking her?" Kalina's tone came out more desperate than she'd intended.

"To the nursery. Your husband is welcome to come with me."

"He's busy. AJ and I will go and keep an eye on her," Jillian offered.

The panic that had begun to tighten Kalina's chest subsided. At least someone would be watching over her daughter. Chris ended his call just as the nurse, Jillian and AJ walked by.

"What's wrong?" Kalina asked when she saw his face.

"Bethany Fairfax is here demanding to see her son."

"What are you going to do?"

He pinched the bridge of his nose and exhaled. “I don’t know.”

“Maybe you should talk to her.”

“I don’t know what good it will do. I mean I’m fairly certain she didn’t have anything to do with Paige’s death.”

“But she kept Patrick from his parents. Even if he wanted to stay that’s got to be illegal.”

“It will be a hard charge to prove. And the Fischers are dead now. They aren’t going to agree to file anything.”

“But you have to do something.”

He held up his hands. “I get it, Kal. Calm down. I’ll talk to her and see what happens. You rest.”

“I don’t want to rest. I want to know what happened.”

“I’ll make you a deal. I’ll talk to Bethany and let you know what happens if you promise to stay here and rest for a while. You just had a baby.”

“Fine.”

Chapter 13

Kalina fell into a light doze as soon as Chris left. She only awoke when she felt a hand on her arm. Blinking the sleep from her eyes, she saw Jimmy standing over her.

“What is it?” Her tongue felt thick.

“Ms. Fairfax wants to speak with you.”

Kalian dragged herself into a sitting position as Bethany Fairfax entered the room looking solemn. Her eyes were rimmed red from crying.

“Congratulations,” Bethany said.

“Thanks. What did you want to talk to me about?”

Bethany pulled a chair over to the edge of the bed and sat down. Her shoulders sagged and her mouth turned down at the edges. "I've spoken with Captain Harper. I realize now what I did was wrong and I'm going to take responsibility for it. I just wanted a child of my own so badly and when Patrick turned up on my doorstep, I took it as a sign. I loved him like my own but I see now he was broken."

"You knew how Paige treated him then?"

"He'd wake up from nightmares about her."

"Why didn't his parents do anything about it? I know Lois Hendrix kept the secret but surely they had to realize something was off."

"After they became parents they realized neither of them were very good at it. So they just got a nanny and said that was that. They played the grieving parents well enough but I don't doubt for a moment they were relieved when they were gone."

"I still don't understand why you needed to tell me all of this."

"Logan needs to admit to what he's done but he won't talk to the police and I made a decision a long time to ago not to force him to be Patrick anymore. But he liked you. Maybe you could reach him."

Kalina looked to Jimmy. "The captain's already approved it. He'll be there with you."

"I'll try."

Ten minutes later—after a quick wash in the bathroom and some fresh clothes—Kalina sat in another hospital room staring at Logan Fairfax handcuffed to a bedrail. He was still in the clothes he'd been wearing when Jimmy arrested him. He wouldn't meet her gaze and his face was set in a stony mask. So unlike the little boy she remembered.

"Logan, my name is Kalina. I knew you when you were younger. Do you remember me?"

"I've got no idea who you are, lady."

"No, I guess you wouldn't. But Patrick would, isn't that right?"

His face twitched, as if he wanted to acknowledge who she was but a part of him wouldn't let him. She supposed that was the truth; that he'd developed another personality to protect himself from his sister's abuse, even the memories.

"Patrick, I know you can hear me and I know you were a good kid. You just had a lot of bad things happen to you."

He turned and his face had relaxed. The ghost of a smile was on his lips and his eyes shone with unshed tears. "I remember you now. You read to me that summer." His voice had gone up several octaves. The little boy really had never grown up.

"Yes. I did." She reached out to take his hand gently in her own. "Do you mind if I just talk to you for a little while?"

"OK."

"I know it's scary to talk about but can you tell me what happened on the boat? A lot of people were really worried about you."

He chewed his lower lip. The inner war began again but, based on his expression, Patrick was still in the driver seat. "Paige wanted to go out on the boat. I told her it was a bad idea without Mom and Dad or Lois. But she didn't care. She wanted to go and she made me come too. She pinched me really hard"—he touched his upper arm—"until I said I'd go."

"I'm sorry she hurt you. Do you remember what happened once you were on the boat?"

"We took it out into the water but the current was too strong and it pushed us away from the beach. We got all turned around and then she started laughing. She thought it was a game. She dared me to jump off the side of the boat. I told her I wouldn't and then she pushed me. The next thing I know I'm on a beach."

"And that's when your Aunt Bethany found you?"

"Yeah."

"Thank you so much for telling me that." Kalina released her grip, anticipating a change in his demeanor when she asked her next question. "Do you remember meeting Paige again recently?"

Logan, the stony-faced protector, returned. "I knew it was her the moment I met her."

"Did you reach out to her on the dating site?"

“No, she found me. I let her think she was winning me over. Like we had a connection. Hell, I even let her kiss me on the first date. Had to drink a lot to get that image out of my head.”

“What made you decide to kill her?” She caught Chris out of the corner of her eye, watching the progress. Bethany had been right. She was able to get him to open up.

“She laughed and grabbed my arm. Stupid bitch. I knew then she hadn’t changed. She could put on nice clothes and call herself Verona but she would always still be Paige. I couldn’t let her hurt him again. And so I convinced her to go on a trip to the beach. I didn’t tell her where until we got there. She thought it was a joke until I showed her our graves. Right next to our parents. I made her admit she knew who I was right before I killed her.”

“They died last year.”

Logan grinned. “They never saw it coming. I had to work up to that one though, find the right way of doing it so they wouldn’t know who it was. After all, they never really saw him growing up."

Chris stepped into the room and motioned for Kalina to leave. "You did great. Thank you."

She expected Logan to protest as she left when Chris began reading him his rights but he looked resigned to his fate. Much like Bethany had. They'd been carrying the weight of the family's tragedies for too long and now it was being lifted. Kalina wound her way through the hospital to the nursery and found Jillian and AJ standing watch over Nina's bassinet through the window.

Jillian looked over and smiled. "What happened?"

"We solved the case. Paige lured Patrick out on the boat that day and pushed him overboard. He spent the last year planning his revenge on his parents and sister."

"That's messed up," AJ said.

"It is, but at least now we know the truth. And now Chris and I can focus on being parents." She waved to her daughter through the glass. "But I think we've solved our last case."

* * *

QUICK AUTHORS' NOTE

I learned a lot writing this series. As my first foray into cozy mysteries, I made some mistakes along the way. But thanks to readers like you, I was able to see where I'd gone awry and find myself in a place in my career where I could go back and make the necessary changes.

I had fun creating Kalina's world but in all truth, my heart has always lain with fantasy realms. So that's why when I realized paranormal cozies were a thing, I jumped for a joy! And you can now check out the first three books in my new paranormal cozy series!

Turn the page for a glimpse at *Brookhaven Paranormal Mysteries Volume 1...*

Brookhaven Paranormal Mysteries Volume 1

Starting over can be murder.

Darcy Ingram came to the small town of Brookhaven for a fresh start and a safe place to hone her hedge witch powers. She even landed a job at the local marijuana dispensary.

But before long, a series of supernatural mysteries ensnares her.

• • •

From murdered co-workers to infidelity and supernatural vendettas, Darcy faces an uphill battle against a Police Chief who doesn't trust her and townspeople who don't know her. Yet.

Aided by the snarky ghost who haunts the B&B where she lives and a telepathic chameleon, along with some trusted living allies, she might just be able to unravel these mysteries and get her blossoming magic under control.

* * *

Turn the page for a sneak peek from this collection...

I retreated back through the grow room to the employee break room. I found my phone and dialed Tania's number. It went to voicemail after four rings. I didn't bother leaving a message. Instead, I donned my jacket and made a quick trip to Ginny's. Thankfully, it wasn't crowded, and I could sit at the counter without getting stared at. To my surprise, Ginny wasn't around. Marco popped by to take my order and deposited it in front of me with a smile.

"Hey, can I ask you something?" I gripped the handle of my coffee mug.

"Sure," he answered.

"Ginny owns this place, right?"

"Her name's on the door," he replied.

"Yeah. But I've seen you give her lip and get away with it. How's that possible?"

"Pays to be the owner's cousin," he said with a one-shoulder shrug.

Well, that explained it. Tania had once told me the Hayes family was a big deal in Brookhaven. That seemed to still be true.

I checked the time and nearly choked on my sandwich. Lunch had again flown by. “Hey, Marco, can I get the coffee to go?” I called and gestured to my mug.

“Sure thing,” he answered, seeming to be in better spirits today.

After making a quick trip to the restroom, I found my coffee waiting at my chair. I left him a larger than normal tip and headed back toward the dispensary. I downed half of the To-Go cup on the short walk back. Almost out of nowhere, a thrumming started behind my eyes and my stomach sloshed with nausea. *Something’s off with the coffee.* I took a few deep breaths and made it back to the grow room before everything started to swim and went dark.

* * *

The halogen lights buzzed above me when I came to. My to-go cup lay on the floor beside me, spilled coffee reaching all the way to the wall. How long had I been passed out? My head throbbed now as I pushed myself to a seated position. The clock on the wall read

2:07. I'd been on my way back shortly before 1:00. No one had come to check on me. *Because they didn't have a reason*. They were probably busy doing their own jobs. And Sage was focused on manning the till out front.

My stomach still sloshed as I got to my feet. Hurrying into the kitchen I found a cloth to sop up the spilled mess before going to look for Sage. She was still out front. That's odd. Vera should have been back by now.

"You look terrible," Sage noted as the customer she'd been assisting turned her back and shoved a little green package into her purse.

"I'm not feeling great, if I'm honest. I think something from lunch didn't agree with me. I hate to do this, but I think I need to take the rest of the shift off."

"Go home and get some rest. And when you see Vera, tell her she better not skip out on me again without notice. I get needing air, but it's not okay to bail without letting me know."

Retracing my steps to the break room, I stopped long enough to pick up the umbrella we'd borrowed from the car that morning. The weather had cleared, but it was the courteous thing to return it to its rightful spot. I eased into the driver seat, but my stomach finally got the better of me. I barely managed to make it to a rubbish bin at the back of the building before getting sick.

I wiped my mouth with the sleeve of my jacket and then my hands on my pants to get rid of the sweat. My entire body felt clammy as I returned to the car. The umbrella sat across the front seats. I tugged it free and tried to set it along the small backseat when I noticed the hood of the boot blocking the view out the back window. If Vera hadn't shut it properly this morning, there could be water damage to the interior. A sense of foreboding washed over me like an unexpected wave as I rounded the car. My fingers trembled as I eased the lid open to reveal Vera's body crammed into the tight space, her unseeing gaze staring up at me.

* * *

Brookhaven Paranormal Mysteries Volume 1 *is available on all storefronts - find it on your favorite store today!*

About the Author

S.E. Biglow is the pen name of *USA Today* bestselling author Sarah Biglow. She lives in Massachusetts with her husband and son. She is a licensed attorney and spends her days combatting employment discrimination as an Investigator with the Massachusetts Commission Against Discrimination.

You can find an up-to-date list of all my books here

www.ingramcontent.com/pod-product-compliance
Lightning Source LLC
Chambersburg PA
CBHW020719310726
48979CB00004B/986

* 9 7 8 1 9 5 5 9 8 8 9 9 5 *